P9-CCW-066

MORE PRAISE FOR MARJORIE M. LIU!

TIGER EYE

"The romance between Delilah and Hari tantalizingly builds until it culminates in a sensual love scene.... [An appealing and] striking paranormal romance."

—*Publishers Weekly*

"The mystical meets the magical in *Tiger Eye*, and is sure to captivate lovers of paranormal romance."

—*Romance Reviews Today*

"I didn't just like this book, I LOVED this book. [Marjorie M. Liu] has a great new voice, a fresh premise, everything I love to read. Anyone who loves my work should love hers."

—*New York Times* Bestselling Author Christine Feehan

"A groundbreaking new paranormal novel. Author Marjorie M. Liu has crafted a stunning tour de force that combines raw action, unbelievable phenomena, and deep passion.... A definite keeper!"

—A Romance Review

"One of the coolest books you will read this year! It has everything an author can dish out, but it is unlike anything you have read before. It's full of mystery, murder, deception, greed, magic, romance, lust, and some sparkling humor."

—Romance Reader at Heart

"*Tiger Eye* reads like the offspring of a Feehan novel and an X-Men comic, and it is loads of fun...the most promising debut I've read in a long time...original, sensual, and action-packed."

—All About Romance

"Marjorie M. Liu writes an action-packed novel that will keep your attention from start to finish."

—Romance Junkies

FROM THE DARKNESS

It was a shock coming face to face with another prisoner. Not a ghost town any longer, running the edge of abandonment and solitude. It wasn't just her anymore, the lonely freak.

Elena wondered how long the Russian had been kept in the facility, if he was the man she had heard screaming. He certainly seemed unwell, though she could not say how except that it was instinct, her gift. He was a tall man, lean and well built with the pale skin of the sun-shy. Dark hair framed his face, the sparse angles of his cheeks and the hard line of his mouth, lovely and haunting.

Elena had difficulty looking at the Russian. His nudity was part of her discomfort, but there was also something fascinating about his face—so intense, so pained—that it instantly repelled her, as though her mind and heart simply could not take the force of his gaze. It was like looking into the sun.

Other *Love Spell* books by Marjorie M. Liu:

A TASTE OF CRIMSON (Crimson City Series)
TIGER EYE

MARJORIE M. LIU

SHADOW TOUCH

LOVE SPELL   NEW YORK CITY

*To my grandfathers, Harold F. Marlette
and Ku Pan Liu, who will always be sweethearts,
pioneers, and rascals in my heart.*

LOVE SPELL®

February 2006

Published by

Dorchester Publishing Co., Inc.
200 Madison Avenue
New York, NY 10016

ISBN 0-505-52630-1

The name "Love Spell" and its logo are trademarks of Dorchester
Publishing Co., Inc.

Printed in the United States of America.

Visit us on the web at www.dorchesterpub.com.

SHADOW TOUCH

Prologue

Shortly before being shot in the back with a tranquilizer dart and dumped half-dazed on a stretcher, right before being stolen from the hospital by silent men in white coats, Elena Baxter stood at the end of a dying child's bed, her hand on a small bare foot, and attempted to perform a miracle.

She was good at miracles. She had been practicing them for her entire life, and at twenty-eight years of age, had become quite proficient at the art of doing strange and wonderful things.

The child's name was Olivia McCoy. She was eight years old, with a large brain tumor swelling against her skull. Conventional treatments had only delayed the inevitable and likely worsened the quality of Olivia's end, and yet, unable to let go, Mr. and Mrs. McCoy had brought their daughter to the Milwaukee Children's Hospital for one last stand. The hospital had a good reputation for healing childhood cancer, and while the doctors frequently patted themselves on the back for their successes, each triumph was tainted by uneasiness.

They did not know why all the children in their ward inevitably recovered. The statistics simply did not allow for such a confluence of miracles.

Elena, a simple unpaid volunteer inside the hospital, was not so surprised.

Today she was delivering stool samples and plasma, running from one department to the next, taking the calls of the nurses who needed charts delivered, patients transferred, messes cleaned. Flowers had to be delivered from the gift shop, cards signed by forgetful and not-quite-so-loved ones. Kind words needed to be said to the dying, hands held for just a few moments to give comfort. The patients, young and old, liked Elena. She made people feel good, even if they did not know why.

The nurses and doctors knew this and, as Elena had anticipated, allowed her some freedom of movement. She could go into patient rooms and sit for a while, unattended. The children liked to be read to, especially when their parents had to leave for work or run errands or sleep. Olivia, for example, enjoyed hearing about the old woman who named things, or the story about a kitten with a big meow. Elena thought she was a very sweet girl.

Which was why, with the books piled on the bedstand and Olivia fast asleep, Elena decided it was time for a little miracle. It was clear to her—based on experience, careful eavesdropping, and sneakpeeks at Olivia's charts—that the treatments were not working and the girl would be dead in a week. With children—unlike adults—Elena could not bring herself to perform triage. Every life needed to be saved.

Olivia's foot was cold. Poor wasted body. She slept uncomfortably, with the pale exhaustion of the dying: a shallow rest, as though in her mind she knew the end was near, and was afraid of never waking up again.

Cancer always put a bad taste in Elena's mouth, like an unripe persimmon, shriveling the insides of her cheeks. No other disease caused quite the same reaction. Elena held on to the little girl's foot—and through that contact entered her dying body. Olivia's spirit felt older than her years: like a mummy, dry and brittle.

Elena, drifting like a ghost inside Olivia, played her game of possession. She breathed for the girl an image of health, coaxing and prodding, a gentle *heal yourself*, *bury it down*, because Olivia already had everything she needed: protective mechanisms that made it possible for any human to spontaneously regress even the most malignant of tumors. Natural human capabilities were a wondrous thing, but only if the body woke long enough to use them. Elena was very good at waking people up.

It took some time. Olivia's body was stubborn. Eventually, though, Elena felt the response: a subtle twist, a gathering of strength around the cancer in the child's brain. Little teeth gnawing away at the tumor. No more swelling after today. The girl would live longer than a week, longer than two, and in three—after exceeding everyone's expectations, after the deathwatch had grown tiresome—the doctors would perform another scan and discover the dying tumor, the healing brain, the happy child.

Elena fled back to her body. Sounds returned: the nurses, chattering softly in the hall outside Olivia's room, the click and beep of essential instruments, the squeal of stretcher wheels. She imagined the girl looked better already; there was pink in her cheeks.

Elena never heard the men enter the room. She felt pain between her shoulder blades, had a moment to think that was strange, because she was always careful on the farm and rarely pulled a muscle, and then she

3

started falling and it was impossible to stop, to hold on, to keep upright.

Hands caught her. Rough, strong hands. Lifting her off the ground. Her throat felt paralyzed. She saw white coats, hard eyes.

Oh, no, she thought, lucid enough to feel fear. *They finally found me.*

Elena was carried away.

Chapter One

The news media called the crimes a rampage of terror, but that was a cliché, an overused description that had long ago lost its power because there was already too much terror in the world, too much nightmare. Indeed, Artur Loginov felt quite certain the only words left to describe the violence before him would have to belong to the poetry of a madman—a literary undertaking he felt uniquely suited to contemplate when he finally lost his mind.

Which, hopefully, would not occur for another several years.

Still, Artur felt a moment of fear as he stood between mold-slick walls, a naked lightbulb swinging overhead. He imagined the first instance of his swift violation, a lingering degradation and pain. He forced himself to imagine the real terror written in the matted spatters of sticky blood cast on the concrete beneath him. He recalled what it felt like to die, alone with a murderer.

Those particular memories never changed, no matter

5

the circumstances, no matter the victim. His gift was a curse.

"You going to be okay?" Dean asked, standing near the stairs. He held a paper bag. The dim light hollowed out his face, stealing the sheen from his blond hair. He looked unwell, his mouth twisted in nausea and anger. Dean always had trouble staying detached from a case. Artur wondered what his own face looked like.

"How much time do we have?" he asked, ignoring Dean's question. Dean did not need an answer; it was the same question he always asked when they worked a case together. Ritual. Tradition. Dean never played by the rules, but in this he was predictable. Predictable like Artur, who did not want to be in this room that begged for his touch. Not so long ago he would have walked away from a scene like this, turned his back and fled, no matter if it meant leaving a killer free.

Those days were done, however, and though his desire to run was still present, it was tempered with purpose now, the moral fiber his employers had seen within him and encouraged.

Employers, friends, family . . . Is there a difference among any of those things now?

No, Artur answered himself. Not with Dirk & Steele, which was so much more than a detective agency, so much more than what it showed the public. The organization had to keep up the front, the lies; the truth was too fantastic, the idle dream of a sensationalist: that yes, a man *could* start a fire with his mind alone, or that another might read thoughts as easily as breathing; that animals could change into men and that men might alter reality with the snap of fingers—stop a bullet, levitate, shake the earth with nothing but a smile.

All these people like him and Dean—so few in number, working under the auspices of an internationally respected detective agency—were bound together by one mission, one promise: Help others, help those who need it. Do the right thing, no matter how difficult, and above all else, keep the secret safe. Keep *your* secret safe. Because Dirk & Steele was a means of helping more than one kind of people—the gifted, the unique—and without it, without that protection and purpose . . .

I would be alone. All of us, who are not family, would be alone. The world is too large, too full of fear for what we are capable of should the truth be discovered.

"Dean?" Artur asked again, when his friend remained silent. He wondered briefly if this would be the night that broke tradition, but Dean finally shook his head and tapped his forehead.

"Not much time. The Vetters are in their car. They'll be home soon."

Home. Artur recalled, for a moment, another basement—another lightbulb, swinging—and the cold taste of stone that was always pain, always something less than human. Bitter. He was always eating bitterness.

Artur stripped off his right glove, pushing away memory and replacing it with his earlier musings, the very worst of his considerable imagination, steeling himself with horror. Very few of his friends knew or approved of his coping mechanism, but Artur appreciated himself. As a child, in a place much like this, he had made his decision—a decision that meant postponing his inevitable insanity by means of another kind of madness: Assuming the worst of everyone. Preparing for nightmares by dreaming them first.

"Did you sense anything in the house while you attuned yourself to the Vetters?" Artur asked. He was aware his friend had spent a great deal of time in the living room and kitchen, soaking up the essence of the family who lived here, forming the requisite connection that allowed him to see objects and people across great distances. "Did the walls speak to you?"

"Glimpses," Dean replied, with a look in his eye that said he knew the question was a stall tactic. "But too many people have been through here since the murder. They got the scene screwed up for my head."

"Yes," Artur murmured. "'How simple it would all have been had I been here before they came like a herd of buffalo and wallowed all over it.'" His accent was thicker than usual; his English sounded almost unintelligible to his own ears. But too uneasy to feel embarrassed, he crouched with his hands hovering palms down over the red and sticky floor. His black leather coat felt hot, but he did not remove it. There were guns holstered in the lining, in addition to the .22 tucked in his shoulder rig. He never liked being far from his weapons.

"Didn't know you were a Sherlock Holmes fan," Dean said, recognizing the quote. He closed his eyes. "We've got two minutes, tops."

Artur admitted, "The original English is better than the Russian translation." He sensed Dean draw close, quiet. He sensed the walls and the floor and the old dark blood quivering with molecules of memory. He sensed the incredible fullness of consecutive moments caught in time, and he pressed the back of his pale hand against the floor, against blood, and . . .

It was like time travel, rewinding the actions of ghosts trapped in echoes, fast and faster, following the golden ball of memory to the center of a labyrinth, the emotional heart, the Minotaur on his bed of bones. Past police and crime-scene investigators, past screams of discovery, past—*I am dying, oh, God, please make it stop, please save me*—to darkness, a choking throat with fingers pressing hard, so hard, and—*stop, don't, please*—

Artur saw the murderer through the victim's eyes: brown hair, green eyes, a cold smile. So cold, so old with rage, a tethered death, caught on the end of a long black thread—

—and then he moved his hands and he was in the killer's head—*because it has been too long and please, scream a little when I touch you; just cry a little*—and he saw darkness, an empty street. He felt the calculation, the press of time and pattern, heard the quick tread of a running woman, like a heartbeat pounding on concrete—*so sweet, so pretty, just an appetizer until I have to go*—and the memories shifted and he was once again the woman, once again on the ground, sobbing and screaming, sharp shining metal poised above her throat, above her like the man, so silent, so quiet, as he . . . as he . . .

"No," gasped Artur, wrenching himself free, tearing his heart from the echo. The vision threw him back in a hard rush, a violent upheaval that was emotion translated into the physical. He felt lips on his body, pain and terror, as he . . . as he was . . .

Violated.

Artur vomited. He felt a paper bag around his mouth and Dean—Dean, who knew him so well—was holding it for him, careful not to touch any part of Artur's exposed skin, so careful not to abuse his spirit with more: more vision, more filth, more and more and more . . .

Artur could not stop heaving. Dean swore. He whispered, "We've run out of time, man. They're back." He pushed the soggy bag into Artur's hand and pulled the chain on the lightbulb. Darkness swallowed them. A soft dark fell, like a blindfold, the prelude to a caress.

Artur clenched his jaw tight, choking as his body continued to reject his mind's trauma. He hunched in on himself, aware of the floorboards creaking above his head. He heard a woman's muffled voice, querulously demanding, and the male response: short, clipped. Artur could not understand what they were saying, but Dean breathed, "Good," and for once—for the first time in years—Artur let someone else worry, and concentrated solely on regaining some semblance of precious self-control.

Long minutes passed. Artur's body settled slowly into itself, like his soul, drifting home. His heart rate slowed. He could breathe without gagging.

Above them came hard-soled footsteps, the click of high heels. A door slammed. There was just enough light from under the basement door to allow Artur to see, and he watched Dean close his eyes and shake his head.

"That was close," he said, still whispering. "Lucky for us, they didn't feel like spending the night above a crime scene."

"They are afraid the serial killer will come back."

"Yeah." Dean glanced at him. "Did you get what you needed?"

Too much. Too much of everything I did not need.

"No," he said, stuffing the bag full of vomit into his coat pocket. He had to stop eating on the days he worked. "A face, a mind. Emotion drowned the rest."

Dean opened his mouth. Hesitated. Artur said, "I know. We need to find another option."

Another option should have been unnecessary. Artur was the agency's trump card, the one who almost never failed, who could be counted on to provide a location, a name, something personal—a trail, most often of tears, leading to a resolution of the assigned case. But not this time.

"Come on," Dean said. "Let's get out of here."

They left the scene the way they came in, through the back door. Entering had been easy: old locks, simple to pick. It was, speculated some of their police sources, the same place where the murderer had entered the house with his victim. A serial killer, who had raped three women to death after taking them into the homes of strangers.

Marilyn Bennigton was the latest: a perky blond, twenty years old. A member of Kappa Kappa Gamma. She liked to run.

She had gone missing after one of those runs—disappeared for a full two days until the Vetters returned home from their vacation and found her body in the basement, naked and restrained. Internal injuries had killed her—that, and massive bleeding from certain orifices.

The police had no leads, no fingerprints or DNA. All they knew for certain was that the killer was incredibly strong and cunning, a classic sociopath, using death as a means of releasing a lifetime of repressed rage toward women. A typical profile, according to the police.

Except, Artur knew, there was nothing typical about the mind he had just listened to. Only an echo, a memory of a memory, but he had seen enough to know that the murderer was a man fueled by more than just rage and superiority. He took joy in his work. A hard, bitter joy that had less to do with women, and everything to do with pain.

It was only midnight. The crime scene had been released that afternoon, which usually meant news media clamoring at the front door and windows for an exclusive peek at death, but this time the police had done a good job preventing leaks. Maybe tomorrow the house would be swarmed, but not yet. Tonight it was perfect and quiet, the thick trees around the old Colonial a lovely cover for benign intruders. The Vetters lived in the countrified suburbs, with few neighbors and even fewer cars on the road.

Dean closed the back door. He pulled a handkerchief from his jeans pocket and began wiping down the brass knob. They'd worn no latex gloves to prevent fingerprints on this excursion. Dean did not normally take readings of objects, but in this case, Dirk & Steele had decided that four hands were better than two. Not that it had helped.

Artur heard a rustling sound: dry leaves, the movement of branches. Not the wind. He reached for his gun.

A small body sheathed in light glided from the trees. It landed on the grass with a hop, a flap of wings. The light dimmed; a crow peered up at Artur with sly golden eyes. Dean cursed. Artur understood his irritation.

"We are trying to be subtle," he said to the bird. The crow made a throaty noise that sounded suspiciously like laughter. Dean aimed a kick at its head and the crow jumped backward, easily, out of reach. Golden light rolled off its feathers, cold fire, and a moment later a naked man rose from the grass. Dark hair, golden eyes. The light went out.

"Got a cigarette?" he asked, rolling his shoulders. Tattoos spun down his long, lean arms. Artur smelled smoke, leather.

Dean shook his head. "I'm gonna kill you, Koni."

"Sure," said the shape-shifter. "That's what you always say."

Dean moved. Artur grabbed his shoulder.

Koni laughed softly. "Bastard. You think I would pull that trick if anyone was around? Give me credit."

"Did you learn anything while we were inside?" Artur squeezed Dean's shoulder: a warning. He did not have energy for an argument. Not now, with Marilyn still dying inside his head. And besides, he trusted Koni's instincts for subterfuge and concealment. One did not live in modern society as a creature beyond human ken without learning the trick of secrecy.

A year ago, Artur would have thought such tricks applied only to himself and his friends at the detective agency. Magic did not exist, except as a fallback to explanations science could not yet provide. Telepathy, telekinesis—these were infinitely rare abilities, but not beyond the realm of human possibility. At least, not to those who had reason to believe.

And then everything had changed. The world became stranger, inexplicable, mysterious. Legends walked; Artur could no longer think of myth as simple story, amusement for a child's bedtime. Myth breathed. It flew on black wings bathed in golden light, labored as immortal warriors cursed to enslavement, killed as madmen with fire for hands.

It will be aliens next. Little green men.

Or something even more bizarre. Artur, though he had never taken anything in his life for granted, had finally lost all expectations for what could be considered real and normal. Anything was possible now.

Anything.

"I didn't find any clues," Koni said, glancing around the darkened backyard. "I've been here all afternoon, searching. No hairs, no footprints or fibers in the grass. He didn't come back to gloat, either."

"More dead ends," Dean said. "No offense, man."

"None taken," Artur said, though his failure pained him.

"Is there any more for us to do?" Koni asked. "I need a drink."

So did Artur. His mouth tasted like vomit.

"Nothing," he said. "Go home."

"Wherever that is," Dean muttered.

Koni grinned. "I almost think you don't trust me." Black feathers sprouted through his skin, spreading across his shoulders and chest, liquid and rippling as golden light pierced the shadow. Dean averted his gaze, and Koni's sharp laughter turned raucous, cawing. Artur stepped backward to avoid being smacked in the face by a hard-beating wing.

"Smart-ass," Dean muttered, watching their colleague fly away. Artur watched as well. Koni had been a member of the agency for almost a year now, and Artur could say with absolute certainty he knew next to nothing about the shape-shifter. Koni had taken great pains to avoid his touch.

Artur respected that. It would have been easy for him to find some other way to learn about Koni, but knowing how the shape-shifter protected his privacy, Artur could not bring himself to do it. Perhaps he was going soft. Lazy. Or maybe he was just tired.

Dean and Artur walked to their car, parked down the road on a small turnoff meant for school buses. They kept close to shadow, the thick stand of trees. The world was quiet. Watchful. Artur imagined eyes upon eyes, tracking his every move, sensing the echo of his passing as he did with others.

When they were finally seated in the car, Dean glanced down at the bag of vomit in Artur's hand and said, "So. What really happened in there?"

Artur set the bag on the floor between his feet. He did not look at his friend. He knew what Dean was asking, but he did not feel like talking about it. Instead, he stared out the windshield, focusing on the Vetters' distant mailbox. A nice, clean object—it was better than suffering his thieved memories.

"Artur," Dean said. "Tell me something."

Artur sighed. "The murderer has brown hair. Green eyes. Sexuality is only one of his weapons, but he has used rape in his recent killings because it has . . . been a while."

"Okay, that's good to know. Just not what I was asking for."

"I know," Artur said, but added nothing more because knowledge had begun to unfold, new tendrils of stolen thoughts surfacing from his vision. Common, for memories to reveal additional secrets after a viewing—but Artur had not expected any this time. He had felt almost completely shut out from the most private part of the murderer's mind, without even a name or history to draw upon.

"He has one more task," Artur said softly. "Something important he needs to do. After that, he plans on disappearing. He believes no one will ever catch him."

"Cocky."

"No," Artur said, the words flowing through him as though he were another person—the killer, perhaps, reciting facts. "He has protection. Someone is protecting him." Unbidden, honest: the serial killer believed this, knew this to be the truth.

"Who would protect that sicko?"

"I do not know. Someone with power," Artur murmured, touching his nose. His fingers came away red.

"Shit," Dean said, fumbling for the box of tissues in the backseat. He threw a handful at Artur. "This has to stop."

"Yes," he agreed, distant, still trying to puzzle out that incongruous, chilling memory. He shoved the tissue against his nose. The blood did not bother him. His nose had been bleeding quite frequently for the past several months. "We will find him."

"I wasn't talking about that," Dean said. "Not really."

He did not go on. Artur waited. It was clear he could no longer run from this conversation, change the subject as he had managed to do for the past month. So he listened to the engine hum, the low-volume beat of some radio rock song. He listened to Marilyn scream. He tasted blood.

Dean squirmed, his hands playing with the steering wheel, knuckles popping. Artur had never seen him quite so uncomfortable.

"Okay," Dean finally said, hard, fast. "I should have told you this a long time ago, but it's difficult. You understand, Artur? This isn't easy for me to say. I'm not good with this kind of thing. You know . . . emotional stuff."

"Dean, stop." Artur tried not to smile. "You know we cannot be together. Ours is a forbidden love."

"Fuck you," Dean said. "This is serious."

Artur leaned back in his seat. "Fine. Serious. Tell me what is bothering you."

Dean gave him a hard look. "Don't try to pretend with me. Your shit is fucked the hell up. This is getting to be too much for you. Hell, tonight was almost too much for me, and all I picked up were some bad vibes. You got the entire show."

"Yes? What is your point?" Artur felt too weary to be having this conversation. He always got the whole show—always would, until the day he died. Talking about it did not do anything but point out the obvious.

Dean glared at him. "My point is that the last six months have scared me shitless. When we first met, you could've laid your hand on Charles freakin' Manson and eaten pizza at the same time. Now—I swear to God—you're going to have an aneurysm so big it'll blow your head off."

"Heartwarming, I am sure."

"Don't make jokes about this. Your reactions are getting worse. You need a break. A vacation. No more bad touching."

"All the touching I do is bad, Dean. I am, as they tell me in this country, a bad boy."

It was the wrong thing to say. Real anger hardened Dean's face. He gunned the engine and steered the car into the street. "Fine. I'll go to Roland."

Artur stared, startled. Dean *was* serious. A first.

"No," he said, concerned. "No, you *cannot* tell Roland."

Dean's gaze flickered from the dark road. "It's not like he'll fire you."

"He will make me stop. He will assign me to other cases."

"And that's bad? You like this shit? You like being inside the heads of murderers and victims, getting your craw busted open every time you have a vision? You like it that much?"

"No," Artur said, "but I need it. I need it like you need it. Like Koni and the others need this work."

Because even though it was ugly—horrifying—the work gave his abilities purpose, a reason for being. If he did not have that—if he could not make a difference—all those sacrifices, the ugliness of his life, would mean nothing. Nothing, if he did not fight with his last dying breath to make them worth something more than pain.

There are worse ways to live, he reminded himself. Yes. Worse. At least now he had friends. At least now he did not have to stand alone. At least now he was not forced to kill for a living. Not always, anyway.

Dean, still watching the road, said, "You're staring at me."

"Yes." Artur noted the hard lines of his friend's mouth with a feeling of dread.

Dean tore his gaze from the road and looked Artur

17

straight in the eyes. "You are such a pain in the ass. The Russian people probably made it an official holiday when you left the country."

"Probably," Artur said, wondering if it was too early to feel relieved.

"Probably? Shit. You're going to go insane, die, or lose permanent control over your bladder—probably in that order—and chances are I'll be there when it happens."

"You want me dying last, Dean, not second. Think of the fun you will have if I begin pissing my pants while we are in public."

"I'm going to shoot you before that happens."

"You should begin carrying adult diapers. I promise to put them on all by myself."

Dean gave him the finger. Artur smiled and settled back in his seat.

"Why are you smiling? You think you won?"

"I think you are my friend. I think you understand my predicament."

"I think I understand you need serious help, and I'm not the one who can give it to you."

"I prefer to handle my own problems," Artur said more firmly. "Besides, you and I both know there is no solution. I see, Dean. That is all. It cannot be stopped."

"It can," Dean argued. "You just won't make that choice."

"What choice? To never take my gloves off again? To never leave my home? What kind of choice is that?"

"It's better than dying."

"*Dean.*"

For once, Dean took the hint. He shut his mouth and drove. Artur got out his cell phone and reluctantly dialed their boss, Roland Dirk. He did not want to speak to Roland—not now, with Dean sitting beside him, so unpredictable—but time was of the essence.

Roland answered the phone with his customary charm. "Jesus Christ. You look like shit, Artie."

Artur tried not to frown. He did not like speaking to Roland on the phone. The man was one of the most psychically powerful individuals he had ever met: a clairvoyant, a telepath. All Roland needed was a connection—and in the case of his far-seeing abilities, a telephone was enough. Artur did not understand how or why. Only that it made him uncomfortable knowing his boss could see him.

"We just left the house," Artur said, and then hit the speaker button so that Dean could participate in the conversation. "We were not able to glean much from the crime scene except for a description of the killer and his emotional state."

"He has issues," Dean said. "Big ones."

"Really. How very fucking nice for him. I've got issues, too. Agent Braun from the FBI called today. She got wind of our investigation and said she doesn't give a rat's ass if we were hired by one of the victims' parents. If she catches any of us on her turf, she's handcuffing our balls to a cell."

"Nice imagery. I'm so turned-on."

"We need access to more of the evidence," Artur said, ignoring Dean. "Restraints, clothing from the victims, anything the murderer might have touched. Perhaps that will provide a clearer vision."

"Sorry. This case is too high-profile. The best we can do is slink around released crime scenes and hack into the medical examiner's reports along with the major news channels. Strictly undercover. If we invite too much attention, people like Braun will start asking harder questions, and I don't want to explain why I lied about us being hired on to this case."

"Still no explanation why this one is so important?

Besides the obvious reasons, like saving lives and stuff."
Dean's gaze lingered on the rearview mirror. Artur
glanced over his shoulder. No headlights or signs of
pursuit. It was good to be careful, though. Like many of
his colleagues at the agency, Artur did not take anything
for granted when it came to personal safety.

Roland made a rumbling sound; Artur thought he
heard pencils breaking. "When Nancy doesn't want to
answer questions, you don't keep asking them. She's the
precog. When she says we have to be involved with
something, we damn well get involved."

"A couple hints would be nice," Dean muttered. Artur agreed, but he stayed silent. Nancy was the true
power behind the agency, and one of its founders. Long
ago, she and her husband had transformed a small secret
society of psychics into something much larger and
more proactive. The reverberations and influence of
that one decision had crossed the world.

Which meant that no one argued with Nancy, ever.
Not even her own family, of which Roland was a distant member. An old woman approaching her eighties,
and still she inspired fear. Fear, respect, and a good deal
of awe.

Something on Roland's end beeped. He said, "I need
to go. Where are you guys headed now?"

"Home," Dean said, before Artur could answer. His
expression was relaxed, easygoing—but Artur did not
miss the hard glint in Dean's eyes as they flickered in his
direction. Artur did not dare argue with him, not in
front of Roland.

"Fine," Roland said. "This was supposed to be your
night off anyway. Get some sleep. Especially you, Artie.
You look like—"

"Shit. Yes, I know." Artur frowned, glaring at his
phone. Roland chuckled.

"Strength, boys. You'd better rest up, 'cause tomorrow's gonna be hell."

He hung up. Artur looked at Dean. "Home?"

"You can't shoot me," Dean said. "I'm driving."

"I am not sure I care. I think the satisfaction alone might keep me alive."

"Ungrateful . . . Besides, what else do you think you could get done tonight? Game's up, man."

"We could go back to the place where Marilyn disappeared and try to take another impression."

"We already did that. We got nothing, remember?"

Artur frowned. "I do not understand why this murderer is so difficult to track. Usually there is *something*."

"Hey, it's not like you went blind or anything. We know more now than we did before. Got a description and everything. One anonymous tip to the police via our contacts, and we'll get the ball rolling."

Artur supposed Dean was right. It took an hour to drive back into the city. After Dean pulled off the freeway, he headed into the quiet outskirts of downtown: the upscale residential neighborhoods filled with old town houses and lovely Victorians. A nice place to live, but tonight it felt decadent, the privilege of a man who did not deserve luxury—not when there was still so much left undone.

"I do not like this," Artur said. "Turn around. I want to go to the office."

Dean shook his head. "There has to be a line drawn somewhere. You've got so many memories swimming inside your head, I don't know how you function sometimes. Just take a rest. One night won't kill you."

"You did not see what that man did to Marilyn. You did not feel his enjoyment. There is no time for just 'one night,' Dean. Later, maybe. Not now."

"Listen. I won't pretend to understand what you felt

inside that murderer's head, but I know you. There's never going to be a later. Every case is the most important, and you are constitutionally incapable of irresponsibility. If someone doesn't make you take a break, you'll go until you drop. I'm not going to let that happen."

"I am so grateful you care."

Dean shot him a dirty look. Artur glanced away, out the window. In truth, he did need the rest, a slice of home where he could shut out the world and all its waiting misery. Just a little peace, a little silence for his aching brain.

But not now. Not with Marilyn still weeping inside his tired head.

They pulled up to Artur's home, an old brick town house set off the road by a winding stone path. Dean tapped the steering wheel. Artur sat there, waiting.

"You can get the hell out of the car now," Dean finally said. "Don't make you push you."

"Why not? You enjoy it so much."

Dean opened his mouth; Artur cut him off with a wave of his gloved hands. "Fine, fine. I am getting out of the car. I will go into my home like a good little boy and take a sleep. Happy?"

"You'd better stay there," Dean warned.

"Yes, my *matushka*."

"Right. Thank God I'm not really your mother."

Artur did not bother telling Dean that he would probably make a better mother than his own. There was already enough pity in the air tonight.

Artur got out of the car. Maybe he would take a nap—just an hour or two—and then head back to the office. Dean would probably be there too, along with the others from their particular branch. No one slept when there was a case to solve, and there were always cases of varying complexity and urgency. Artur stood in the street until Dean pulled away. He watched the tail-lights disappear at the intersection.

Uneasiness spread through his heart; even though he planned on returning to work, it felt like a mistake letting Dean leave without him. Irresponsible. Marilyn still sobbed.

His discomfort grew more intense as he walked up the narrow path to his home. The air smelled like his neighbor's petunias, fresh and slightly bitter.

Artur took off his gloves and touched the front door. He traced the wood around the keyhole, the brass knob. Nothing. Just the lingering echo of his soul. Slightly comforted, he entered his home. Shut the door on petunias and night shadows. Kicked off his shoes.

The town house was large, because Artur had never owned anything large that was all his own, and he had promised himself at a young age that if he ever had the opportunity to have a place of his own, it would be spacious and comfortable and clean. His home also had windows, many windows of many different sizes, because he had spent much of his life trapped in dark rooms, and now to be without light, some vision of the world beyond four walls, felt like punishment, a sin. It did not matter that windows were inherently dangerous. He did not care.

The shades were open. Artur left them that way. He did not turn on any of the stained-glass lamps scattered delicately about the room like cold flowers. He walked through his home in near darkness: ritual, an old habit dying hard. At night, light within meant pulling down the shades to make himself less a target. He was too tired for that now. Too weary to indulge his paranoia.

You should not be too tired. A little safety is worth more than weariness.

Artur dropped his gloves on the dining table, its sur-

23

face reflecting the gleam of a streetlight outside his home. He ran his fingers against the glossy surface, savoring the smooth, cool wood, the slight oil of polish. Like a blind man, seeing precious details with his hands—except here, now, nothing stirred in him but the familiarity of his own mind. Artur took off his jacket and hung it from the back of his chair. He pulled off his socks. The hardwood floor felt good beneath his feet. Good and safe and familiar.

Home was the only reliable place in his life. Everything around him had been in his possession long enough to have lost the taint of strangers. Every piece of furniture, every article of clothing, every spoon and fork and plate had been handled for long hours before he could touch them and feel only himself. Even his walls were tuned only to his presence.

Artur never allowed guests. He did not like surprises in his home. Surprises were kept for work, the world beyond his windows and doors. Home was supposed to be predictable. Sweetly, wonderfully predictable.

He went into the kitchen to get a drink. The answering machine blinked at him. One message.

That was very odd. Artur did not usually get messages. His number was unlisted, and all his friends at the agency knew he preferred calls to his cell phone. No one ever called his home. In six years he could count the times on one hand. He could not imagine who this might be.

Still, he had an answering machine for a reason. He hit the button. Took a step back and opened the dishwasher for a clean glass. The machine whirred, spit out a time, and then—

A woman's voice prattled into the quiet air of his home. Soft and Russian and oh, so familiar. Artur almost dropped his glass.

Tatyana. Tatyana Dmitriyevna. Calling *him*.

He was so bewildered by the sound of her voice, so entirely stunned, he completely missed the message. He listened to it a second time, and still could not comprehend what she was saying to him. All he could think of was the impossibility of her call. Hearing her voice was almost as ridiculous as hearing his mother's.

Artur replayed the message a third time. He listened hard, gripping the edge of the counter and closing his eyes. The connection she had called on was bad; the clarity of her words wavered.

"Hello, Artur. Yes, this is me. Do not get your hopes up. I am not calling for pleasantries. I have come into money now, so you can stop sending your checks. I do not need you anymore. No more charity. You wonder why, yes? Maybe I marry rich old bastard? Ha! What a joke. No, some men came asking questions about you. They wanted to know everything. *Everything*, Artur. They paid me very well for the information. I am sure you understand. I did not call to warn you about these men. I just do not want your money anymore. Do not call me back."

Do not call me back. As if he would dare. He listened to the message again, concentrating on the part where she talked about men coming to speak with her. Men who had asked specifically about him. Men who had enough wealth to allow Tatyana a comfortable, independent life.

That would require a lot of money. Artur knew Tatyana very well; she had expensive tastes. She might hate him—and rightly so—but she still loved his cash. For her to tell him to stop sending any, after more than six years of monthly payments . . .

This is not good.

Not good, because Tatyana was one of the few people

outside the agency who knew about his gift. She was his first love, his first angel; he had given her everything, trusting her with his most precious secrets. Long before Dirk & Steele had approached him, Artur had relied on Tatyana as his shining anchor, his little star.

Yes, well. Great love could turn into an even greater hate. He knew that now. Had learned his lesson very well.

Of course she betrayed you. How could you expect anything less? You did, after all, ruin her life.

But who had done the asking? Who would want to know about him? He could not imagine any of his old Russian bosses still holding an interest—not after all this time. Nor did he believe that anyone from the Mafia in Moscow would pay for information they could simply take. Money saved was money earned. A large stick and steel knuckles were the same as cash in the bank.

I must speak with Roland. If I have been compromised, then the agency is not far behind.

A nightmare possibility. Artur had been given so little in his life—so very little. He knew the price of not protecting those he cared about. Friends were all he had. The men and women of Dirk & Steele were his family. Artur picked up his phone and began dialing Roland.

He had no warning—no memories in his floor, no strangers' fierce echoes. He heard a puff of air, and something sharp pierced his back.

Artur whirled. He glimpsed a slim figure in the shadows of the hall: a man with dark hair and a familiar face. Too familiar. In Artur's head, Marilyn began screaming again.

Artur's legs gave out. Simple and dead, as though his limbs were no longer connected to his brain. He crashed to the floor, thinking, *No, this is impossible; the others are in danger . . .*

He watched the serial killer move close, a dart gun in his hands. He said, "Go to sleep, Mr. Loginov."

Artur tried not to. He tried to fight.

Darkness found him.

Chapter Two

It is the endless sleep. Endless and undying, the perfect noth-ing. Torture, is it not? I could trap you here. I could keep you here, if you do not obey . . .

Artur opened his eyes. The voice lingered, fading slowly like the last tendril of a hard dream. He did not know how long those words had filled his head, but it felt like a lifetime. Endless and undying.

Warm shadows surrounded Artur, holding him softly beneath a gold-embroidered crimson coverlet. A small lamp burned on the bedside table, real flame flickering inside shimmering antique glass. A gentle light, easy on his eyes. Artur lay very still, his gaze wandering over the large room. He studied the red cloth–paneled walls, which displayed a gilt-edged diamond-and-floral pattern. Drapes of a similar design hung from the tall bedposts. He smelled wood polish and old cigarettes, the scent made strong by the stuffy air.

He had no idea where he was, except that the room looked like it had been decorated with the malignant focus of an elderly woman with absolutely no taste.

The room did not look like a prison. Despite—or because of—the overdone decoration, it reminded Artur of the old salons his Russian bosses had frequented; antique styles of wealth that appealed to Mafia lords seeking illusions of class and dignity for their business dealings. Artur had never liked those places, although the hypocrisy associated with their use bothered him more than the strain on his eyes.

You were just muscle, a gun for hire. What did you know about hypocrisy? You were pretending, just like them. Pretending to be something more important than a runaway, an orphan, a freak. You lived your life as an illusion.

Artur tilted his head so that his cheek touched the satin pillow. The image of a woman came to him, but the echo of her thoughts was dull, so thick and slow he could not read anything useful. Her name was Greta. She was young, and had been trained for a long time in simple menial tasks. She never left the building Artur was in. She did not know where she was. She spoke English, but sometimes she heard words around her that were different. Incomprehensible. She was not abused, though. That was all that mattered to her.

His gloves were on. *His* gloves, and not some new pair. He could tell by the feel and stretch of the leather, the familiar comfort of his own echo. That he wore his gloves did not seem right, and Artur remembered he had removed them inside his home, laid them down on the table.

Artur took off a glove and held it. He felt nothing. Not a trace of the man who had attacked him in his home, and then dressed his hands.

Brown hair, green eyes. There was no mistaking the man's identity. This was the same man who had murdered Marilyn and others—perhaps many others—and had incapacitated Artur in a move as simple as breathing. The serial killer had come looking for him with a purpose. With knowledge. Someone had sent him to do a job, and that job was Artur.

He had one more task to complete. One more task before disappearing. All that death, leading up to . . . me.

"*Bozhe moy*," Artur murmured, stunned. Horrified. *My God. It makes no sense. Who would do this? Who would hire a serial killer to kidnap a man? And why kidnap me? Why go to such lengths?*

Marilyn's weeping turned accusatory; Artur wondered with dull shock if she and the two other women had been some kind of payment. If they had died for a man they did not know. The thought alone was almost enough to make *him* want to die. Artur knew he had enemies, but none of them were so subtle, so motivated. A bullet would be good enough. A bullet would be just fine. But not this. No one went to so much trouble for a man whose only fate was a quick grave. Not for any man, ever.

So. Someone wanted him alive. Someone wanted to use him. Someone who had gone through the difficulty of hunting down his past, of researching his movements, his habits, his home. Someone who had large sums of money and almost no ethics. Someone powerful enough to rein in a serial killer.

Right. He was in a lot of trouble.

Artur carefully pushed away the covers. His head hurt—a dull throb that radiated from the base of his skull into his eyes. He tried ignoring the pain, the weakness in his limbs. He gazed down at his body. The rest of his clothing seemed intact. No visible injuries. No guns, either. He had been plucked from his home like a doll. He removed his other glove and placed both in his pockets.

He slid off the bed. His shoes—someone had thought of that, too—sank into the thick red shag carpet. There was a door in front of him, richly carved in the same diamond pattern of the wall. Artur began walking toward it, struggling to stay upright. The ache in his head was excruciating. He wondered what kind of sedative had been used. He wondered, too, what kind of man could sneak up on him in his own home, with his feet naked and so sensitive to the lingering echo of others.

"The door is locked," said a low voice.

Artur spun—too fast, too hard; he was too used to being graceful on his feet. Pain flared. His knees buckled. He staggered, clutching the bedpost for support. Humiliating weakness.

At first he did not see anyone. Silence, the quiet dark. And then he caught movement on the other side of the large room, deep within an alcove made of drapes and woodwork. Shadows shifted, like a ghost unfolding its limbs. A thin, pale face floated free. Artur saw a skullcap of blond hair, an impossibly slender body clad in a fitted gray suit.

"Greetings," said the woman. Her voice was melodically quiet. She looked unarmed.

Artur straightened slowly, gathering enough strength to step away from the bed. A stupid mistake to have assumed he was alone. He wondered what else he had missed about his room, which was filled with many hiding places: voluminous drapes, a large wardrobe, even the space beneath the bed.

The woman in front of him stood quite still, cold and gray as a spindly statue. Artur had trouble focusing on her face; his headache seemed to radiate into his eyes, blinding him with quick, short bursts.

"Who are you?" he asked, struggling to speak clearly.

A thin smile touched the woman's pale lips. "That is always the first question. I can think of so many others that would be more useful. More intelligent."

Artur briefly closed his eyes. "If you are looking for intelligence, you chose the wrong man to take from his home."

The smile widened. "Very nice. A Russian smart-ass. I like that."

"Surely I am not such a novelty." Artur ran his hands over the end of the bed. The woman shook her head.

"You are the perfect novelty. And really, don't bother. You won't discover anything about me or my associates in this room. Even my shoes are new. Quite impersonal. The only people who have been allowed here are those without any real connection to my life or organization. Your gift is useless."

"I could touch *you*," Artur said, disturbed by the woman's knowledge. Tatyana's fault, probably. He had no doubt this woman was responsible for the men who had approached his former lover. He did not believe in coincidence. Nor did it matter that he already knew of Tatyana's betrayal; to be faced with his secrets and have them used against him by clear enemies was profoundly unsettling.

"Touch me?" She looked amused. "Oh, I'm *sure*. That, however, would be cheating. Some things must be earned the hard way, Mr. Loginov. Like the truth. Like certain . . . rewards."

"Rewards." Artur narrowed his eyes. "Who *are* you? Who do you work for?"

The woman tilted her head: a sharp motion, precise and measured. She reminded him of the serial killer—that cold assessment, ruthless calculation hidden by the facade of human expression.

"You may call me Ms. Graves," she finally said. "I represent the Consortium."

"I have never heard of your organization," Artur said, because there was something in her voice that suggested he should be familiar with the name. Unfortunately, she looked pleased with his response, which made Artur uneasy—and rather nauseous. He wanted to lie down. He felt as if someone were hammering a nail into the base of his skull.

Graves said, "I've brought you here for a job. The Consortium hires men like you."

Artur said, "No."

"Really. That was a speedy decision. You've heard so little. I had no idea curiosity was such a rare commodity in the criminally reformed. Not to mention all the work that has gone into acquiring your services or making you comfortable in a familiar setting. Surely you can suffer us a moment."

No, he could not. Artur did not have time for patience, especially not for a woman who used serial killers to kidnap him from his home. He lunged toward her, hands outstretched for the truth. He took one step—

—and found a gun pointed at his face. A fast draw; Artur never saw her move.

She looked very calm. "I was told you are a patient man. Unemotional and calculating. I believe my source was wrong."

Tatyana. Artur struggled not to vomit. Moving so quickly had almost incapacitated him. "I am an opportunist. A survivor. Whoever you spoke with forgot to mention that, as well."

"No. I simply expected more self-control." The woman gestured for Artur to sit on the bed. "Please, make yourself comfortable. You look ready to faint."

Artur remained standing. Graves sighed and sidled several steps left. She sat gracefully on the deep seat of a rich red velvet armchair. The entire room was beginning to remind Artur of a bleeding heart. Perhaps his own, if he was not careful.

Graves propped her gun hand on her knee. Her aim never wavered.

"Normally I take the time for pleasantries and explanations—time enough to ease a man into his required role—but you are different. You, Mr. Loginov, do not require ease or sweet words. You already know the truth, that you are not alone in this world. You are accustomed to using your gift in return for money. I like this about you. It makes my task easier."

"I question your taste."

She laughed: a sharp, brittle sound. "My taste is perfect."

"So perfect, you assume I will take your mysterious offer, even though I know nothing about your organization, except that it must be despicable? How charmingly naive."

"Sticks and stones, Mr. Loginov. Besides, I call your presence here an invitation to a leap of faith. A faith born of clear advantage, power, and financial gain. You really cannot go wrong when you have all three of those in your pocket."

"And what of ethics? Can you defend an organization that hires a serial killer to kidnap a man from his own home?"

"A moot point. The Consortium does what it has to. We believe in guarantees, which our select employees provide with their natural abilities. Our methods have worked very nicely for some time. Your profile provided no reason to diverge from that pattern."

"What kind of organization considers violence to be a 'certain guarantee'?"

"The kind you used to work for. The kind you *still* work for."

"I do not think you know what you are talking about," Artur said.

"Oh, I think I do. I think I have a very good understanding of your particular situation. I can assure you, Mr. Loginov, the Consortium is not all that different from your current employers. We simply don't *pretend* the way your esteemed Dirk and Steele does. We don't hide behind acceptable social constructs as a means of using our powers. We don't justify the use of our gifts with Pollyanna hypocrisy." Graves spit those last words, her voice hard and long and sharp. "Oh, your shock. Really. Did you truly believe yours was the only organization of its kind?"

It took him a moment to make his voice work. It was difficult to speak in the face of his worst nightmare, the pitiless coil of a stranger's gaze bearing down upon all his most precious secrets. "How did you find us?" he finally managed, and his voice sounded old and worn and tired.

Graves leaned back in her chair. Her gaze was steady, unafraid. Softly she said, "It was inevitable. The world is too small for what we do, who we are. Only we found you first." She shook her head, tapping her jaw with one pale bony finger. "It was Chinatown that did it, Mr. Loginov. Wen Zhang's murder. Dirk and Steele should have minded its own business. You cost us a great deal of money."

It was Chinatown that did it. Wen Zhang's murder. My God. It all makes sense now. Memory rolled over him; those horrible days when so many at the agency had come close to losing one of their dearest friends. Wen Zhang had been the leader of a major crime group in New York City's Chinatown, who a year ago had attempted to murder Nancy Dirk's granddaughter, Dela Reese. He'd come close; the young woman had almost lost her life.

The grand matriarch of the shape-shifters—the dragon woman, Long Nü—had put the final stop to Wen's actions, but not before he discovered Dela's telekinetic abilities. Artur still remembered Wen's voice, accusing Dela of belonging to a new crime syndicate encroaching on his territory, a syndicate whose members also exhibited strange powers.

An unsettling idea. Roland had conducted an in-depth investigation into the matter, but found nothing. Like ghosts, the story remained unsubstantiated.

But they were real. They paid attention. They found us. We are not alone.

Artur found himself wishing they were.

"You are so stubborn," Graves said, studying his face. "So delightfully obtuse. You are an interesting man, Mr. Loginov. So much potential wasted. An entire lifetime of misdirection and failed ambition. I wonder if you ever feel sorry for yourself?"

"Not particularly," he replied. "But thank you for the compliments."

Her smile was cold. "I need an answer, Mr. Loginov."

"You have given me nothing to answer with. Do you think I should run into the arms of your Consortium simply because it exists, because you have brought me here under duress?" His head pounded; something was digging, still digging at the back of his skull. A dart, with teeth. "Show me something, Ms. Graves. Give me a real reason." *Give me something I can use against you.*

"How about your life?" she said quietly. "You can join

us or die. It's simple, really. I don't need to give you anything, because here I hold all the leverage. Make your leap or don't. The choice is yours."

"You did not go to all this trouble just to kill me."

"No, we went to all this trouble for a resource that would pay itself out in spades. You have a lucrative gift, Mr. Loginov. Not only that, but you know much about Dirk and Steele, our surprise rival. That is worth something all by itself. But you are worthless if you will not cooperate. A liability. Do you want to be a liability, Mr. Loginov?"

For a moment he considered playing her game, saying yes and offering himself up like a lamb. Making the sacrifice of his dignity so that he could learn something—learn something and then take the chance to escape. Patience, perseverance, survival.

"All I need is a word," Graves whispered. "A verbal signed-on-the-dotted-line. We will do the rest, Mr. Loginov. Never you fear. We will do the rest."

The pain intensified, cracking through his head with such intensity he almost imagined voices—one voice, a woman whispering. All the ghosts of his past rose up to drown him in one last shout of agony. *Endless. I can make this endless.*

"No," Artur said, forcing that word past his closing throat. "My answer is no."

No more games, no more pretending. He had left that world—left behind the man who put on a mask before his superiors, who said what they wanted to hear or said nothing at all when silence meant the difference between life and a very painful death. He had lived for years as a coward pretending to be a strong man, hating every moment of that existence but powerless to change his circumstances. Drawn in slowly, bit by bit, caught in the sticky web until there was no room to run, no way to leave the violence and death without suffering the same fate.

No more. Artur had finally found a way to live as an honorable man. He would not give that up again, not even as a lie to save his life. One crack, one sign of weakness—sometimes that was all it took to slide down that slippery path to hell. He could not believe he had contemplated a return to that existence for even one moment.

Graves sat back. Shadows hid her eyes, but not her mouth: hard, narrow, her lips suddenly gray. Artur stared at that strange mouth, at the sharp lines of her slender body.

His old bosses and the men they dealt with had always been of two kinds: blustering men, the kind for big gestures—big gifts, big cars, big violence—and the quiet kind, watchful and intelligent, men for whom gestures meant nothing, who could wait and wait, patient in the knowledge that everything they did would tick-tock its way like clockwork into success.

Quiet now, he remembered Nikolai Petrovona whispering, when one of his brothers grew angry at not being allowed a cut of a new arms shipment. *Hush now. Gentle.*

This Graves was the same. A "hush" woman, a "gentle" woman, with just enough edge to distract from that cold, calm core. Very dangerous. Very difficult to predict. He watched her gun, and wondered if he had time to touch her—one touch before he died. One last vision of the truth.

"What a pity," Graves said, and shot Artur in the chest.

Chapter Three

As far as kidnappings went, Elena thought hers had played out rather smoothly for the bad guys. Not that she had much experience with that sort of thing. She watched movies, though. The sci-fi-thriller kind, where nefarious men in dark suits targeted some poor, lonely freak and unleashed two hours of street chases, near misses, and loud explosions. Boom, boom. Yee-haw. Let's all live happily ever after.

Except this was not a movie, and Elena had nowhere to run. She was also having trouble breathing and her heart refused to slow down. Bad signs. She leaned over and vomited on her kidnapper's shoes.

"Shit," he said, shaking his foot. Elena thought he was rather lucky it was not really shit; she was contemplating flinging some at the next available opportunity.

Elena had no idea how long she had been unconscious, but now she was being pushed in a wheelchair down a long concrete corridor. Her head felt too fuzzy to make out details, only that the air was cold, the lights quite bright, and her flimsy hospital gown offered absolutely no protection from either one. She could practically see her cellulite through that sheer cloth. Or maybe those were goose pimples. Her mind always focused on the most inane things when she was stressed.

She thought the men were different from the two who had kidnapped her, but it was hard to tell. They looked big and tough. The only way Elena would be able to beat them up would be to transform herself into a true badass: a *Kill Bill* Bride, a Buffy, a Xena. Maybe Red Sonja, just for good measure. Scream a battle cry, wave a sword, go a little crazy. Kill, pussycat, kill.

They stopped her wheelchair in front of a green door. Elena did not bother stifling her nausea. Feeling as if there were pinwheels spinning in her eyes, she aimed for the nearest body and once again spewed. A perfect projectile spray. She loved herself sometimes. The man's deep-throated curses sounded like music.

The door opened. They pushed her through. For a moment all she saw was white—white everywhere— surrounding a long stainless-steel table armed with leather restraints and stirrups.

Oh. Bad.

An old man stood by the table. A stethoscope hung around his neck. He had clinical eyes, that impatient, critical gaze that medical professionals attained only after years of hard work and self-important analysis. The word *doctor* might as well have been stamped on his forehead.

The men hauled Elena off the wheelchair and began removing the hospital gown. She tried to fight them. The doctor said, "Don't be afraid, my dear. This is a medical facility. Nurses and doctors, just like you're used to."

Elena was too upset to laugh. The doctor peered into her face.

"Fascinating," he said, in a voice that was almost reverent. "Truly. I am quite pleased to meet you, Ms. Baxter. I do hope you feel the same about me, seeing as how I am such an admirer of your work."

"Go to hell," Elena said. At least, she tried to. The moment she opened her mouth, the doctor slipped in a gag. His movements were quick, precise. Practiced. He dodged her teeth with easy grace, pushing hard inside her mouth until she choked on the thick cotton.

The male nurses, who had more business being called thugs than medical assistants, wrapped their hands around her body. They did not hit her, simply grabbed her wrists and ankles, held tight with smiles haunting their lips. Elena, watching their eyes, stopped struggling; the men enjoyed it too much.

In one smooth motion they hefted her onto the steel examining table, slamming her down with enough force to smash the breath from her lungs. Her skin burned—from the frigid metal, their hands. She wore only a bra and panties.

"Hush now," soothed the gray-haired doctor, gently patting her shoulder as the men bound her wrists and ankles to the table. Her skin felt cold—as cold as the doctor's eyes and the narrow thrust of his tiny chin and sharp cheeks. "This will only hurt a little."

The doctor settled down on a small stool and reached for a syringe: one of many, placed side by side on a metal tray like a row of empty soldiers. The room was large, nondescript in a lab or hospital sort of way, the walls lined with an array of medical equipment illuminated by harsh fluorescence. Elena smelled antiseptic, and underneath, another scent. Faintly bitter. Urine, maybe. Blood.

"Prepare her," said the doctor, still occupied. One of the men, his pants stained yellow with Elena's vomit, rummaged through a drawer and found a long rubber tube. He bound her arm so tightly her hand tingled— sharp like needle pricks—sharp like the fingernail he dragged down to her bound wrist, measuring her reaction with predatory indifference. Sharp, sharp, sharp.

Blood tests followed, a series of invasions into her pale flesh. The nurses stared at her breasts and thighs while the doctor puttered over her body, humming as he filled each syringe, full and red. Elena did not fight him. She wanted to *take the syringe and pop an eye, stick it right through to his brain*, but she could not move. She lay still, burning with shame, rage.

Superpowers, Elena thought bitterly. *If only*.

The doctor finished taking blood. He removed her gag. "There, now. I like to reward good behavior. You seem like a good girl."

Elena's tongue felt thick, dry. It stuck to the roof of her mouth. She tried to swallow. "Why are you doing this? Where am I?"

The doctor tilted his head. A smile played on his lips. It was a distraction, perhaps; his hand curled into a fist and slammed into her face, rocking Elena's head back against the steel table.

"No questions," he said, and then, after a moment, added, "Interesting. It appears you cannot heal yourself."

Elena barely heard him through the ringing in her ears. Her head felt like a hammered thumb, swollen and miserable with pain. She tasted blood on her lips and licked at it, moistening her tongue. The doctor leaned close. He brushed her mouth with his fingers, which came away red. "Still no reaction. How very curious. You, my dear, are a true evolutionary dupe."

He turned to pack up the vials of her blood. The men began untying her. "Back to bed. We'll save the more interesting tests for later."

"Just how interesting?" Elena ignored his ban on questions, too angry and horrified for fear. Her heart refused to slow. She thought it would pound right through the bones of her chest.

This time the doctor did not seem to mind. His smile widened.

"Oh," he said. "They'll be thrilling."

The men put her back in the wheelchair and rolled her away.

She passed out in the hall, or perhaps the men gave her another tranquilizer. Elena remembered feeling woozy; her heart, thudding like a hammer in her chest, making it hard to get air into her lungs. She felt as though she were dying, and suspected it was just panic. Either way, going unconscious was probably a good thing.

When she woke, she found herself resting flat and nearly naked on a bare foam mattress. Her body was slick with sweat and her heart still swung a tango with her ribs. Her cheek hurt.

She did not want to move, so she let her eyes do the work and examined her room from the corner where she lay. There was not much to see. Her cell was white, white and clean, with slick floors and walls that looked softly padded like a gym mat. It was like being inside a synthetic igloo or the inside of an egg. A toilet, a sink, and some tissue paper sat in the corner. Set in the wall across from her was a wide mirror. Two-way, she thought. How nifty that someone could be watching her even now, checking out her limp body, or soon, watching her use the toilet and wipe off crap. Sheer titillation.

Psychological warfare, too. No privacy, no safety, no power. Whoever had kidnapped Elena was stripping her down to the very basics, taking away her identity, her independence. *We can do anything to you*, this room was supposed to say. *Don't cross us or we'll hurt you.*

Which, really, was an overdone show of force for just one little individual like herself, even if she could do some fairly remarkable things. A room like this—as well as the treatment she had thus far received—meant her kidnappers wanted to cow her into submission, make her meek and pliable for whatever they next threw at her. That or they were paranoid and afraid, and everything she had experienced up until this point was a symptom of that unease.

Remembering the doctor, Elena felt quite confident it was the former.

She tried to sit up, but could not do much more than lean against the soft wall. It was horribly uncomfortable, but she refused to lie down. She might never move again if she did that. The way she felt, it would be far too easy to curl into a tiny ball and just surrender. Temporarily, at least. Elena did not want to give anyone that satisfaction.

Still, she rested for a time. Closed her eyes and tried imagining herself back on the farm in Wisconsin, with the wall behind her a pear tree, the padded foam mattress a blanket spread on roots and grass. These were visualization techniques used with desperation. It helped that there was still dirt under her nails—dirt from home, the garden and the orchard. The apples would be ready for harvest soon, as would the plums. She had already reserved her spot at the Madison farmers market. Saturday mornings at the capital, with her cardboard boxes full of organic specialties. This would be her third year as a seller—her third year alone, without her grandfather.

You are going to get home. You are going to get the hell out of this place.

And then what? It was obvious these people knew where she lived and what her habits were. She was just surprised they'd had the balls to steal her directly from the hospital. If they had waited only three more hours, she would have been home on the farm, nicely secluded in the middle of more than one hundred acres of fruit trees, rivers, and rolling hills. Easy pickings. Not that she had given them any trouble in the first place. Whoever *they* were. Elena favored some secret government agency, a cabal of old fat men who thought she would be the perfect experiment.

Elena closed her eyes and curled her hands together, palm to warm palm. She had always known exposure was a possibility. Just . . . nothing like this. Some tabloid, where she would be on the front cover of a grocery-store rag, sharing billing with the werewolf love child of a U.S. president and Marilyn Monroe. Because who else would take her seriously? Who in their wildest dreams would believe a human capable of miracles?

Someone believed. Someone with the resources to truck the statistics and then narrow the common denominator down to you. One woman in billions, and only because you got sloppy.

Too many children, too many recoveries. Milwaukee and Madison were too small for what she had been doing, but they were close to home, and Elena did not have enough money to expand her range, not even to Chicago. The tolls alone would kill her. She barely had enough to keep herself fed. Every penny she had went to the farm and staying mobile enough to use her gift. Not that she was mobile now.

Elena looked at the mirror. There was a bruise on her face the size of an apple. Her long brown hair resembled a rat's nest. Her body was pasty with a dash of flab. She wasn't even wearing her good underwear. *Oh, tragedy.*

Her heart agreed. She fought for calm, for control, trying to think of other, more pleasant things. She knew what this was—had read about panic attacks in the hospital magazines—but even with the knowing, there were moments when it got so bad she wanted to wail and gnash her teeth, cry out for help because it wasn't just her heart, but it was her closing throat, the chills, the nausea riding high in her mouth. She felt as if she were having a heart attack, and the idea—even though it was just in her head—scared her more than captivity. She wanted to live more than she wanted to die, even if it was in a prison as some little human experiment. She wanted to live.

She also wanted to heal herself, but that just wasn't possible. So ironic. So devastatingly typical. She wanted to hate herself for that, but she was too practical. There were so many other people in the world to hate—like the doctor, like those thugs pretending to be nurses, like whoever had decided to bring her here. So easy.

Breathe, she told herself. She wished someone would lower the temperature. Cold air was easier on the lungs—cold, bracing air, like in Wisconsin, where the winters froze the snot in your nose, turned flesh to ice in minutes. Good snow, clear skies, crisp and lovely.

Her heart pounded. Pounded. *Don't panic, don't panic, you have to focus now, quiet, now isn't the time to go nuts or hysterical because there's no one here but yourself so you have to be strong, you have to be an army of one, you have to be well so your mind can plan and you can get out of here, you have to get out of here—*

It got better. She got well enough to sleep and lie down in a ball. Sleep helped. She did not dream. When she opened her eyes it was still a nightmare, but her heart no longer raced and she could breathe. That was a start. All she could ask for, really. Little miracles, bit by bit. Tiny triumphs. *All you can ask for is your health*, her grandfather had liked to say.

Elena lay on the mattress and listened to her heartbeat mark the passing of her life. She listened for a very long while.

The doctor lied. A long period passed without tests. Or maybe he watched her from the other side of the glass, and her reaction to this place was a test all by itself—to see if she cracked, if she inflicted wounds, if she began frothing at the mouth and speaking in tongues. She thought the old man might like that. She almost tried it, just to see what would happen, but eventually decided it was a bad idea; a part of her feared that any attempts to pretend madness might just invite the real thing.

Elena paid attention to when she was fed—food on a tray, shoved through a slot in the base of her door. Clothes accompanied her first dinner in the facility: soft green scrubs and thick white socks. She was happy for them.

After her second meal—a small ham sandwich and an apple—she settled down on her mattress, closed her eyes, and began counting. Every time she got to sixty she tore off a scrap of toilet paper. One minute, one mark. She did this until she accumulated more than two hundred forty marks of toilet paper, and then the door made a noise and a tray slid through the slot. It was not an exact science, but Elena did not care. Four hours between meals. Three meals a day. After the last meal, nothing. Not for double those hours.

By the seventh meal, she reckoned she had been captive for more than two days—probably more, depending on where she was being held and how long she had been kept unconscious. Elena used that time to explore every inch of her cell, looking for anything that could be used as a weapon. The tank behind the toilet did not have a removable lid. The seat could not be taken off. There was nothing to hit with, except for some rolls of toilet paper. Elena could imagine all kinds of Monty Python–esque hilarity with that choice of weapon. Unfortunately, she was probably the only person in this place who would find it funny.

Elena eventually resorted to using her teeth to roughen her nails. Made them jagged, sharp. Good for scratching. Fighting. It wasn't a sword or a stake or even a butter knife, but at least it was something. Illusion was nine-tenths of staying happy, after all.

And she was calm. Her heart beat slow and sure. She could breathe. That was good. She wondered how Olivia was doing, if she was feeling better. By now she should be up and walking. Elena was happy she had managed to do at least that much before the kidnapping. This situation—while horrible, awful, insane—would be so much worse if she had been stolen away, knowing Olivia was dying, dead, already gone.

Have a good life, she thought at the girl. *Do something nice with the time you've got.*

Because it would not last. It never did, not for anyone. Death was the end for all, whether you found it in ten years or one hundred. All Elena did was postpone the inevitable, give that second chance nature had denied. Cancer was an easy reverse; the human body was already inclined to help her. Heart disease, paralysis, internal wounds—harder, but not impossible. Genetic problems, which required complex manipulation and specific knowledge, were beyond her power.

Not that she ever complained. What she could already do was miracle enough.

A miracle with your freedom as its price.

Maybe so, but she had no regrets. Doing nothing at

all was unacceptable. She had a gift that could help people in profound ways; not to use it would be a crime.

Her stomach rumbled; she thought it must be getting close to mealtime. Sure enough, she soon heard footsteps in the corridor outside her room.

This time, however, the door clicked. The lock. Not the food slot.

Elena jumped to her feet, digging jagged nails into her palm. The door opened. It was the doctor. Behind him stood a dark-skinned man with brilliant green eyes. He wore a tight black shirt and loose cargo pants.

The two men stepped inside the cell. The doctor studied Elena, a clinical analysis.

"You've settled in," he said. "I hope you haven't been too lonely. I apologize for the wait, but something more important took precedence. I'm sure you understand."

Elena said nothing. She was quite certain the doctor would not want to hear her colorful opinion on everything she did and did not understand about this place.

He peered hard at her cheek. "Still no healing. I simply cannot understand that. Surely you have tried to do for yourself what comes so easily for others?"

Elena continued to remain silent, trying to summon up the deadest, dullest valley-girl expression she could possibly muster. No brains, not a chance. No need to ask questions of the dumbest girl alive. Just a dope with power, that was her. A moron, a fool.

Go ahead. Underestimate my ass.

The doctor frowned. "Come, my dear. There are no secrets. I know what you are capable of. If I chose to, I could produce a list of names dating back ten years. Miraculous recoveries from terminal illnesses, most of them in children, almost all in Wisconsin. Tell me you had nothing to do with them. Tell me there is not a miracle in your touch."

"There's no miracle in my touch," Elena deadpanned.

The old man sighed. "My dear, that was rhetorical. As you barely finished high school, however, I will assume you don't know what that means."

Ouch. Acting stupid was working just a little too well.

The doctor gestured to the man beside him. "This is Rictor. He will be your liaison during your stay with us."

"My stay. You make it sound like this place is a resort."

"It is a house of learning," he said, "and you and I are both students of each other."

"I don't find that particularly comforting."

"My heart weeps to hear that," he said. Elena was almost positive he was being sarcastic.

She glanced at Rictor. He looked bored. She suspected it was an act. She could not imagine anyone feeling safe enough to be bored in this place.

"Why are you doing this?" Elena asked the doctor, repeating the same question that had gotten her hit in the face. It must have been a trigger, one of those things that pinched his buttons; a hint of displeasure appeared around the old man's wrinkled mouth. He looked at Rictor.

"Take her. I'll join you shortly."

Rictor grabbed Elena's upper arm. He did not squeeze, but his grasp was firm, warm. He tugged her to the open door. Elena fought to stand her ground.

"My dear," said the doctor, "unless you want him to do more than simply pull, I suggest you start walking."

Elena gritted her teeth. "Why are you doing this? Who do you work for?"

The doctor raised his hand. Rictor yanked Elena out the door. No time to protest, and after a moment she lost all desire to complain. Up and down the long concrete corridor, wide black curtains hung against the wall in set intervals that seemed calculated by the placement of narrow metal doors. Elena turned around; there was a curtain in front of her own cell, pulled slightly back to reveal the stark white interior, littered with old meal trays and dirty dishes.

"Oh, my God," Elena murmured. "There are more."

Many more, if every cell was filled. Even if they were not, the fact that they existed, that this facility had multiple rooms built specifically for the observation of its inhabitants, was astonishing and disturbing. Impossible, even—but only because it still seemed too surreal, her kidnapping like something out of a movie. Because people did not really do these things to one another, right?

Right.

Rictor tugged her into motion. Elena had no choice but to follow him, but it was like walking as a zombie, shuffling along with only one focus: those black curtains, those doors. Walking past them gave Elena the sense of treading the razor's edge of something vast and mysterious, the heavy weight of potential riding her shoulders. Beyond every door, a story. Beyond the curtains, views of another world.

Views, perhaps, of people like her. Which was almost too incredible to accept. The odds could not possibly allow it. Elena had always thought she was alone—and perhaps she was. Perhaps she was the first, some odd rarity her mysterious kidnappers had stumbled upon. Or not.

She glanced up at the man beside her. He looked tough. Not scary like the pseudonurses, but still, with an edge of iron in his face.

"Will you tell me where I am?" she asked.

"No," he said, and there was a tone of finality there, a warning against being a pest. Elena was not usually very good at taking warnings, but this time she kept her mouth shut. Rictor was an unknown; some people were natural-born bullies, while others were not. Until she had that much figured out about him, she was not going to push her luck.

He kept a firm hand on her arm until they passed through a large green door separating the holding cells from the rest of the facility. On the other side, in the main corridor, he turned her loose.

Rictor pointed. "Go."

"I'm not a dog," Elena said, but she started walking. Her arm felt sore from his grip, but she did not rub it.

They were the only people in the hall, which resembled every underground military base Elena had ever seen on television: dark, shiny concrete with white piping running parallel along the walls, a curved ceiling where caged lightbulbs dangled. The air smelled coarse, dusty. Elena tried memorizing their path, watching for special marks in the floors and walls. Anything to orient herself if she tried to escape. It was difficult. Everything looked the same.

The facility also felt huge, the product of a long-term plan and a lot of money. A lot of money and not many employees. Only once did she hear other people, and they were far away. Voices, too muffled to understand with any clarity, though Elena thought she heard a woman say, ". . . shift mechanism unknown . . . tank isn't big enough . . ."

"Tough shit," said a man, in a much louder voice. And then the conversation faded into something truly incomprehensible. Elena mulled over those few words, trying to make sense of them. She almost laughed. Making sense of anything in this place was a joke. A killing kind of joke.

Rictor slowed down. Elena saw a green metal door. On it was the stick figure of a woman.

"A public bathroom?" She could not hide her surprise.

"Locker rooms," he said. "Our facilities are limited to the basics. Everyone has to share."

Elena tried to imagine Rictor taking a shower in the same room as the doctor. The image hurt her head. Rictor gave her an odd look, and then pushed open the door, gesturing for Elena to precede him. She did, taking in the surreal normality of white tile and shiny fixtures. Open shower stalls were on her right. Toilets on the left. The air smelled damp, and the floor and walls were slick with moisture. Someone had just been here. She had never been so glad to see a regular bathroom.

"You don't have to take a full shower, but we will need to do something about your hair." Rictor leaned against the wall. It was strange hearing so many words come out of his mouth; he did not strike her as a big talker. Of course, what he was saying also made no sense whatsoever.

Elena touched her hair. It was so tangled, her hand bounced. Reaching through to her actual scalp might require a diamond-bit drill. "You a hairdresser? Because hey, if this place is really a salon or beauty school, I think you all kidnapped the wrong chick."

"You're funny," Rictor said, looking about as amused as an overmilked goat. "I haven't seen funny in a long time."

"Yeah," Elena said. "I can tell."

He ignored that. "Your hair is a mess. The doctor considers it a liability. He wants me to cut it."

"Your doctor is a crack-ass nutcase. What does he think my hair can do? Reach out and slug someone?"

Rictor held out his hand and showed her a pair of gleaming scissors—a startling reveal, like dealing with a magician. Elena wondered where he had gotten them, and whether she could bring herself to stab him if she got the chance to wrap her fingers around that shiny metal.

Through the eyes and throat. Soft places.

"It might be safer if I do it," he said, as though reading her mind.

Elena scowled. "Leave me the hell alone. Haven't you guys already done enough? Besides, that cell is cold. If you take my hair, I'll die of exposure."

His jaw tightened. There was no pity in his eyes. "I can make you."

"You can make me do a lot of things. Everyone in this place can. What's stopping you?"

"Fine," he muttered. Before Elena could stop him, he grabbed a handful of her hair and began cutting through it. She cried out, twisting away, but he pinned her hard against a locker and kept cutting. Clumps of hair fell around their feet—ten years of her grandfather smiling over those long brown strands. Elena hooked her sharp nails into Rictor's neck, raking down. He grunted, but kept on working.

When he finally released her, it was sudden, a shock. Elena stumbled, catching herself against the locker. She touched her scalp. Found that she had nothing left but a short stubble. Her head felt light and cold.

"Better," Rictor said without emotion. Long red welts covered his neck. The floor looked like the back of a Wookiee. "Go to the sink and wash your head. We don't have much time."

When Elena did not immediately move, he grabbed her arm and hauled her over to a deep white sink. He grabbed a bottle of shampoo from the open shower stall and handed it to her.

"I do not want to do this for you," he said. Elena believed him. She took the shampoo and washed the remains of her hair. It took less than a minute; there was hardly anything left.

When she was done, he handed her a towel. She

scrubbed her head—furious, frustrated—and then pointed at it with a shaking hand. "Clean enough?"

"Dry it some more," he suggested. "There can't be any moisture." A specific detail that provided Elena with some idea of why the doctor might believe her ratty hair had to go—though his actions seemed more inclined to sadism and control, rather than the pursuit of exact medical science.

Elena dried her hair until Rictor told her to stop. They left the locker room.

He walked faster this time. Elena struggled to keep up. She examined as much of the halls as she could, memorizing every twist and turn and landmark. She thought she might be able to find her way back here if the opportunity arose. She might even be able to do more than that, especially if this place was as empty as it seemed.

Or not, she thought, as a man suddenly screamed. Distant, faint; the echo of his heartrending voice twisted down the corridor until he sounded more animal than human. Or perhaps there never was a man, and she had only imagined the brief baritone that now raked the air like a wildcat's cry: high, ripping. Elena missed a step.

Rictor said, "Keep walking."

"What's being done to him?" The screaming continued; a spit and howl that broke her heart—and scared the shit out of her.

"It's nothing you need to worry about," he said. The screaming stopped abruptly. The silence was almost as horrible, heavy with exhaustion, as though the air itself were glad of the man's quieted cries. For a moment Elena felt the strain of guilty comfort. She was not alone in this place. Someone else was here, suffering. Someone else had been targeted, their comfortable world ravaged.

I'm sorry, she thought, remembering the anguish in that one long note of pain. *I'm so sorry for my selfishness.*

Just not sorry enough to take it back.

Again she studied Rictor. She wondered why he ranked more important than the men in white, what he had done to earn a place inside this facility, why he would even want to work for people who kidnapped women and then treated them like lab experiments. Must be tough to get a girlfriend, with a background like that.

Rictor's pace faltered and he gave her an odd look— something almost like confusion. It was the most human expression she had seen on him so far. He tore his gaze away. Quiet, he said: "Do what the doctor tells you. Don't push him too far. He needs you, but he'll take only so much defiance."

Hearing him give advice—after everything he had just done to her—stunned Elena. She could not tell if he was trying to trick her, or whether he was serious. If he was serious, then he was definitely in the wrong line of work—and his motivations were totally suspicious.

Rictor glanced at her. "Are you going to listen to me?"

"Why should I?"

He remained silent. Elena said, "Hey."

"We're here," he said. She shut her mouth.

It was a different room than she expected. No cabinets full of medicines and equipment. No tables with restraints or bloody hooks or ropes or dirty scalpels. Nothing very maniacal at all. Just white walls, a white tile floor with a drain in the center, and a small table with some familiar electrical equipment perched on top: a black flat-screen monitor and a plastic box full of wires. The table had a chair beside it. Rictor gestured for Elena to sit.

He pulled a small tube of gel from a drawer in the table. "This is why we had to wash and cut your hair."

"I figured it out," she said, still trying understand his sudden surge of helpfulness. "EEGs can't handle scalp oil or moisture." *Although I could have kept my hair, you son of a bitch.*

"No," he said, "you couldn't have."

Elena blinked, startled. Rictor spread glue on the end of an electrode and stuck it on her head. She watched his face, but he was as impassive as ever. A bored man, doing a boring job. He totally deserved an Oscar.

"Rictor."

"Hold still."

Elena thought about bouncing up and down just to aggravate him, but killed that idea when his hands tightened on her head. She felt like a fool, but had to ask. "Can you read my thoughts?"

He put another electrode on her head.

"How about the doctor?"

"What about him?" Another electrode.

"You know."

She thought he would say, *Oh, what folly! What an imagination! Such things certainly do not exist!* Instead Rictor said, "No. He is not like us."

"Oh, God." Elena stared at him. "And there are more? Are there more prisoners in this place? And why the hell aren't *you* locked up?"

He did not answer. Out of all the things that had happened to her—the kidnapping, waking up in a strange place only to be manhandled like a lab rat—*this* rattled her the most. It shook up her mind, her heart, her entire view of the world, because she had wondered, she had hoped, and now, finally, here was confirmation. She was not alone. There were others like her.

Once upon a time, dreaming as a child dreams, she had wished for such a thing. Oh, how lovely it would be. Not a freak, not some lightning that struck only once and never again.

But she would rather be alone than find out like this.

Elena tried to speak, found her voice too weak. Tried again, whispering, "How? It doesn't make sense. There can't be so many. Regular people would notice, wouldn't they? It would be in the news."

"You managed to stay out of the news," Rictor said. "Or so I hear."

"That doesn't mean—"

"There are six billion people in the world," Rictor said, interrupting her. He still looked bored, still continued to glue electrodes to her head, but he was talking, and Elena was desperate for words. "If even half of one percent of the population exhibited some kind of unique wiring, that would be thirty million. Cut the percentages even steeper, and you're still talking about a lot of people. Now *be quiet.*"

Elena did not want to shut up, but she heard someone at the door. It was the doctor. He held a cardboard box in his hands.

"Ah," he said, when he saw Rictor gluing electrodes to Elena's scalp. "I thought you would be done by now." He studied the scratches on his neck. "Problems?"

"No," Rictor said. He kept working.

The doctor studied Elena's head. "A very nice look on you, my dear."

She resisted the desire to tell him just how quickly he could go to hell. From the way Rictor's hands tensed on her head, she thought that was a good idea.

The box rattled. Elena heard a whimper.

"I'm done." Rictor stepped away from Elena and flipped a switch on the machine. After several seconds the monitor flickered to life, revealing a set of numbers, prompts.

"Hold out your hands," said the doctor. Elena hesitated. She thought about what Rictor had told her. *Do what the doctor tells you. Don't push him too far.*

She remembered the screaming man, the pure animal sound of his voice.

Elena held out her hands. The doctor looked at Rictor, who reached past her to take the box. The old man flipped open its flimsy lid. Elena smelled blood.

"No," she breathed when he pulled out the body. She thought it might be a puppy, a little beagle, but it was difficult to tell because of its injuries, the blood covering its broken body. A small paw moved; closed eyes twitched beneath the lids.

"I like to start small," the doctor said. "To set certain parameters. Think of this as a flashlight blinking in your eyes."

He placed the dying animal in her hands. Horrified, Elena grappled with the puppy, trying to hold it in a way that would not cause more pain. Blood smeared against her legs, dripping on the white floor. Now she knew why there was a drain. The doctor smiled. Rictor looked bored.

"I can't," she whispered. "I—"

"The injuries are very recent and quite severe," interrupted the doctor. "He is going into shock. If you wait much longer he will die, and then I will be forced to do this experiment again, on a different animal. Are you really that heartless, my dear?"

Yes, I really am that heartless. Because if she saved this puppy, she had no doubts as to the doctor's willingness to harm it again for another kind of test. That was a torture no living creature should endure.

But then the puppy opened its eyes and looked at her,

looked at her in the way only a small helpless animal could, and she remembered a little rabbit, torn, her mother saying, "God, you are such a freak," and her grandfather, running, running to hold back the ax. She laid the puppy flat on her lap. She did not look at the doctor or Rictor as she pressed her hands to the animal's jutting ribs. She tried not to think of them at all as she sank deep within her heart, summoning up the strength that was hers, the essence of beautiful pain that she grappled with every time she used herself for others. Her skin prickled as the power rose—higher, stronger—until her body felt encased by lightning. Cancer was different. Cancer was easy. This required more, more and ever more. She lost her vision, but her hands were still on the puppy and she could feel—could feel that little heart, that broken, twisted body, and she pressed her will upon its spirit and goaded it to heal.

Just take a little of me, she told it. *Just take a little of what I have to give.*

It did, and through the roaring in her ears, through the pain, she heard the doctor whisper, "Thrilling."

Chapter Four

In his last moment of consciousness, Artur felt certain he was dying. The explosive pain in his head and chest felt immense as a thundercrash—lethal, final—so that when he fell into the nightmare it was the same as hell, that ready inferno waiting sharp as a kiss of hot iron, burning his mind blind with the furious tide of his sins. It was a nightmare symphony, screaming cries of myriad lives—his own and other's—sucked back into the past where the world was full of concrete and windowless rooms, dozens of starved, filthy boys crammed together to live and grow and die like animals, unwanted because they were broken, defective, lost beyond help, beyond love . . .

Endless and undying. I could trap you in a memory, you know. Choose one, Artur. Choose your perfect horror. Your mother, perhaps? When she left you at the orphanage and you watched her sign the papers, watched her scrawl that lovely name while you screamed and beat your fists against the floor as the men took you away and she never turned around to say good-bye, never turned to say, "I love you," or,

"Sorry," or, "I'll be back," because no—no—it was forever, and she left you to die, you unnatural son, you burden, you pariah—

No. Artur pulled himself free of that sinuous voice, so dark and persuasive. He fought for true consciousness. *No. You are wrong.*

I am never wrong, Artur. Never. You should have come to me while you had the chance, while you still had a choice, while you still had—

Artur felt pain. He clung to that discomfort and it led him away from the voice. He savored the rawness of his throat, the spinning of his head, the ache in his chest. He rolled his mind through agony and was happy for it. Happy for the torture of the physical, which anchored him safely away from that voice with its horribly patient certainty.

He was alive. That was good, too.

Artur moved his arms, his hands, sliding his fingers over the surface beneath him, which was cool and slick, carrying echoes of another kind of pain. Confusion—*where am I, oh, God, oh—damn it, I hurt; I—please don't touch me please I was just going in for a medical study; please—*

Artur froze. Lifted up his hands and opened his eyes.

He was not wearing gloves. He was not, in fact, wearing much of anything. Except for underwear he was completely naked. Naked to the world.

Artur shot to his feet, stumbling as dizziness racked his tall frame. He doubled over, gagging, but his throat was so dry that all he felt was pain. Pain, pain . . . his own and others'—and he could not stop the onslaught, could not control the rush inside his head as his bare feet danced over the cold floor, trying to find safety, a virgin tile, something yet untouched.

Nothing. Everywhere he stepped, the memory of

souls—so much was swimming through his head, it was difficult to tell where he stopped and strangers began. A scream bubbled up in his throat but he swallowed it down, forced it away and quiet. If he began screaming he would not stop, would not stop; he could not stop screaming when he was a boy, and his mother, his poor mother—

Do not lose yourself. Be in the now, this moment. Nothing else matters. Nothing else.

Artur forced himself to stop moving. He planted his feet firmly on the ground, forced his chest to expand for air. Every breath invited a vision, a piece of another soul. He felt the taste of a stranger's fear inside his head—endless, undying in its certainty of doom: *I am never going to leave here alive.*

It was an emotion Artur recognized. He had felt it before, more than twenty years ago—been swamped in a similar manner, cast out to lose his mind among strangers squatting in darkness. He'd been twelve years of age and untested in his gift. Exposed. Helpless.

I thought I had grown stronger. He was older now, more practiced. Had become, over the years, slightly desensitized to the shocking flood of memory and emotion, the schizophrenic invasion of minds so different from his own.

None of that mattered now. Not in the slightest.

It was difficult to breathe. His chest hurt. Artur looked down. A large purple bruise covered his skin. He saw a puncture wound above his heart. A tranquilizer dart, not a bullet after all.

It was all a lie. She still wants you. Still needs you.

Artur gazed around the cold room. White tile everywhere. No furniture or restraints. One door. Artur did not want to go to the door. Walking meant more, new—everything that might conspire to strike the final blow against his weakening brain. He touched his nose. No blood yet.

Stand here and die, or do something and die. It is your choice.

Artur walked to the door. It took every ounce of his strength not to run on his toes like some overgrown cartoon character. He was certain there were cameras, that someone was observing him. He kept his pace dignified, as though he did not care that his brain was on fire or that at any moment it might burst.

Memories not his own flashed by: rough men, strong men, grappling with the half-dazed, the stripped and feebly fighting. The men thinking, *Why the bloody fuck go to all this trouble*, and *Jesus Christ, she tried to bite me*, and *Fuck this all, fuck this freak, fuck you*—

Artur stopped in front of the door and pulled off his underwear. He tore it down the seam and wrapped his feet, trying desperately to knot the edges around his ankles. His hands shook; his fingers felt stiff, clumsy. The cloth kept slipping. Artur finally gave up; standing on his underwear would have to be enough.

It was. Relief sang through his head, the cool emptiness of perfect silence. Artur pressed his palms against his eyes. His skull hurt, still felt nails bursting from its base, but the quiet was a balm. He was perched on two islands of cloth, naked as the day he was born.

Artur opened his eyes. The door waited for him like a monster. He touched the knob . . .

New memories surged: the same people—captor and captive—from different angles, different moments, imprinting themselves until his mind cried out with the echoes of their souls, the echoes of hard fear and confusion. His scalp felt as if it were peeling back from his skull. Too full, too much fire, and—

—it is time for me to lose my mind—

A sound filtered through the chaos. Real sound, not from his head. Artur's hand flew off the knob. Blessed silence returned, but only for a moment; he heard the shuffle of feet, the low rasp of voices. A loud click. The knob turned.

Artur stumbled sideways, leaving the protection of his cloth shields. Chaos returned, but the visions were familiar; Artur could partition them, summon up strength to focus. The door opened just a fraction, not enough to see into or out of the room. A hard voice said, "Step away so that I can see you. Do it now."

Artur did not move. He heard low words behind the door, familiar as the images in his mind, and knew like a memory that this was routine, that these men had practice dealing with recalcitrance. Ruthless, they were allowed to be ruthless . . . but only up to a point.

Artur would have smiled had the pain in his head been less severe. These men could not kill him: he felt the truth of that in the layers of vision beneath his skull. They might be permitted to beat him, abuse him, but in the end, life would still be his. Death was a decision left to other people. Other, more frightening individuals.

Like Ms. Graves.

The door slammed open, the edge of it a blur, a bare miss as Artur jumped backward and—*focus, here and now*—pushed off the balls of his feet, launching himself into the three white-coated men who entered the room. The first got slammed in the face with a hard right hook, a—*jail time has to be better than this*—kick to his kneecap, taking the man down to the floor, howling. The second, thick around the neck and waist, shouted and came at Artur with his fists raised. Artur drove a palm into his nose, savoring the crack, the cries, the *fuck, this ain't worth the money*, and the man doubled over, cradling his nose, leaving Artur wide-open to knock him unconscious with a massive blow to the back of his head. Unskilled fighters. Thugs. Not used to resistance. Perfect.

One man remained. Small and lean, dressed all in black. Brown hair, green eyes. "Hello again," he said, smiling. "Do you recognize me?"

"I do," said Artur, and beneath the shouting in his head, the chaos, he heard a low familiar sob.

Artur went for the throat and groin. The man blocked his blows—quick, strong. Artur fought for openings, grappling with wiry muscles that refused to yield, refused to be held. His hands slid off air again and again and he was blocked. Denied. In more ways than one.

"You are a psychometrist," said the man calmly. "You learn secrets through touch. Have you learned anything from me yet?"

"No," Artur said, wondering why that was.

"Interesting," said the man. "Let's try this again."

He hit Artur—moved so fast there was no time to dodge. Pain sparked light in Artur's vision, filling it up with images of darkness, something solitary and quiet and—*I am very good at waiting*—

Artur struck back. Landed blows, but they were light, glancing—as though his opponent wanted to be hit, touched. And every time Artur laid his hands on the man it was like watching a nuclear explosion inside his head: a mushroom cloud of singular images riddled together in themes. A boy playing God with a trapped squirrel, peeling it open like a banana; the same boy, older, doing the same to a girl, and then—*because it is his turn now*—a man.

Artur's body rebelled. Just as in the cellar, he doubled over, vomiting: dry heaves, bile. Pinpricks of throbbing light broke up his vision. The man beside him smiled.

"So, you like that." He placed his cold hand on the back of Artur's neck. "Try *this*."

It was like having a nail gun drive iron into his brain: a precise agony, concentrated in one spot. Images flashed—controlled, sharp snapshots of deliberate cruelty that went beyond anything Artur had ever experienced. The cold human power of a strong mind, bearing down upon his soul, stripping him like that squirrel: inside to out.

It did not matter how. It did not matter why. Anger sidled hard against pain, and Artur held tight to his fury. *No more*, he thought, gathering his strength. *This is just a picture show, a movie. It is not real.*

Not real. Only the past, only real for another—a man whose hand pressed tight against Artur's body, still linked, ripe for opportunity. That cold flesh, that cold heart, with secrets still to tell.

You are mine now, Artur told him, and his mind focused to a needle point and shoved hard, up through memory, up through the channel of his assailant's thoughts. A cold place, an oubliette rich with dark layers, and Artur saw a boy, the same boy, beaten bloody by a man—*father, my father*—scrabbling to pull up his pants, to think past the pain, the shame—*why, why*—and then the boy running away, running to the woods, beyond woods to the town, to the city, surviving by theft, by murder, by whoring, by—

"Get out of my head," snarled the man. He released Artur, tried to step back, but Artur spun and grabbed his ankle, holding him still. Whatever shields the man had were now gone. New, fresh images filled Artur's head: a small woman with inhuman eyes, black eyes, alien, framed by tangled blond curls tumbling to her pale shoulders. Confined to a wheelchair, smiling and smiling—

The man kicked Artur away, but not before he shared his bitter, quiet rage at being bound to such a woman, tied to her body and soul—*the black thread of the spider*—holding him like a dog, like a—*soldier, her first guard*—with her voice in his dreams—*endless and undying.*

The man touched his head, a slow, deliberate gesture. "You should not have done that."

Artur struggled to stand, to focus past the fire in his head. "You are a pitiful man. Not even your own man, are you? A joke. You showed me your worst because you thought it would be more than I could endure, but your worst is nothing. You are nothing, Charles Darling."

The name slipped off his tongue, a gift from his unconscious. Artur knew instantly it was not a true birth name, but a name this man had used for so long it had become part of his identity. The only identity that mattered to him.

Charles went very still. Quietly, in a voice scaled with venom, he said, "How unfortunate. There are not many people who know that name." He looked at his two companions, only one of whom was still conscious. It was the man with the broken kneecap. He had stopped howling, but sweat rolled down his white face. He rocked back and forth. Artur did not think he had heard anything of their conversation; he seemed completely absorbed by his own pain.

Charles took two quick steps and grabbed the man's head. He twisted hard to the right. Artur heard a crack. The man slumped, dead. Fast, merciless, breathtakingly efficient.

Charles gazed down at the second man, who still lay unconscious. He said, "What do you think?"

Artur thought he was in a lot of trouble. "That man is already dead to the world. No need to make it permanent."

The corner of Charles's mouth tugged upward. "Permanent is my specialty. But you know that."

"Yes," Artur said, but memory filled him and he remembered rules—rules and something else. Some*one* else. A dark face, green eyes. And that other, the woman. *Sweet Beatrix. L'araignée.* The spider.

"Interesting," Charles said. He backed away from the unconscious man like a snake with a mouse in its belly, full on death. Maybe later Charles would kill this colleague—when he got the itch, when he got hungry—but he was satisfied for now. Good enough to move on. The rules that bound Charles did not protect the people he worked with, which was significant and familiar. As with the mob, certain people were expendable: disposable resources, thrown away when broken or inconvenient. It did not speak very highly of the Consortium.

That, and they employed serial killers. Serial killers, leashed. If the Consortium could do such a thing with this man, they could do it with others.

It is what they plan to do with me.

"Come on," Charles said to Artur, and it was unsettling being spoken to by this man, this murderer, remembering him through Marilyn's eyes, the eyes of a dying woman.

Charles pointed to the open door. Artur's gaze flickered to the remains of his underwear. Impossible. He would have to cope. Take advantage of the situation no matter how much it pained his mind. Hold out as long as he could until Dean and the others from the agency found him. Or until he found a way to escape on his own.

Artur walked from the room into a stark corridor lined with white pipes. His feet touched the concrete floor, and . . . a bombardment, a fresh stream of new impressions: excitement, concern, fear. The orderly intentions of men and women who moved with clinical detachment and purpose.

Not so many people, though; Artur encountered the same minds again and again, filling up on white coats, black monitors, glass windows . . . the sensation of a great expanse. Soft rooms, steel tables. A dark hallway filled with curtains. Every step opened a door into a separate world of memory, spreading warm like the pain radiating from the base of his skull into his eyes and ears. Artur swallowed every vision, pushing it back, away, deep into his unconscious where later it might prove useful, where until that moment of recollection he could try to forget all those lives stolen from the echoes of his passing.

The halls began to look familiar, seen again and again through other eyes. He knew that fifty yards to his left would be the mess hall, that down another nearby corridor were men's locker rooms. And down lower, lower . . . images rolled: a dolphin in a large tank, slick gray flesh covered with sensors, men and women staring, waiting, staring—*oh, my God, oh, my God*—a cheetah, circling, golden eyes bright with intelligence—*so fucking stubborn we'll use the electric prods next*—and a room where no one was ever allowed, no one ever, a chamber—*the Black Hole*—of secrets known only to a handful, the bosses, the—*women in suits, with hands like guns 'cause when they point at you it's like* bang-bang, *you're dead*—

One level down. All of those things he had seen were one level down. Artur knew it as well as the individuals who walked these floors, stepping where Artur now stepped. A code filtered into his mind. Access to that level. Access to even more than that.

Surely there had to be a trick. Ms. Graves was not so stupid.

But she is arrogant. Sometimes that is one and the same.

The base of his skull pulsed, like fingers digging into his brain stem, tearing the fibers of his mind bit by bit. The embarrassment of being naked faded in comparison to Artur's struggle to stay upright. He glanced at Charles, who walked beside him, relaxed, quiet. Marilyn still begged for her life. Artur wanted to kill the man.

"Most guards bind their prisoners. You are not concerned I will try to escape?"

Charles did not look at him. "You are too weak to fight. Too weak to run. And even if you were not weak, no one escapes this place. Not ever."

"You were able to leave."

Charles smiled. "I'm not a prisoner."

Not true, Artur thought, recalling his vision. *You are even more a prisoner than I am.*

He heard footsteps: the heavy tread of boots, accompanied by something light, the brush of cloth. The corridor forked; from the left passage appeared two figures: a tall, muscular man with dark brown skin, and a small, pale woman dressed in blood-soaked scrubs. Her hands were red, glistening and wet. A bruise masked one cheek.

Charles missed a step. The man and woman stopped.

The man, whose face held a familiar place in Artur's new memories, wore an intense expression of displeasure that seemed solely directed at Charles. Artur did not miss the way he touched the woman's elbow, slowing her. Perhaps even cautioning her.

"Rictor," Charles said, though he looked at the woman when he spoke. She met his gaze, unblinking.

Rictor said nothing. His fingers still grazed the woman's elbow. He stared at Charles, slow, steady, and unafraid. It was not an act; Artur sensed no fear from the man, not a trace of unease. Whoever Rictor was, he knew Charles Darling well enough to be wary—but wary only for the woman.

Just as Charles was wary of Rictor.

Rictor looked at Artur. He had far-seeing eyes, too old for his face. Artur felt something tickle his brain, soft, a whisper beneath the swarm of memories filling his head. Rictor's frown deepened.

"The Russian should be wearing something," he said, still studying Artur. "A straitjacket, maybe. Socks and gloves at the very least. For fuck's sake, you brought him in. You were briefed on his abilities."

"Those were not my orders," Charles replied.

"Convenient," Rictor said. "Where are the others?"

Charles smiled. Rictor's jaw tightened. He looked at Artur again, and then turned to the woman.

"Give me your socks," he said.

"Or what?" she asked. Her voice was different than Artur expected: deeper, richer. It struck his heart—that wry strength, effortless as breathing.

"Give me the socks," Rictor said again. The woman bent, slow, unbalanced. She seemed exhausted. Artur watched her—all the men watched her—and he found himself wishing that were not the case, that she not be the focus of such predatory scrutiny. Artur glanced at Charles, found the man wholly absorbed, staring with the fascination of a scientist, a cold, analytical scrutiny that missed nothing, that tallied and calculated and planned, moments to be played like music in his head—

Artur could not take it, could not allow it. He turned and stepped in front of Charles, blocking his view of the blood-covered woman. Charles's head snapped up, like an animal: quick, nostrils flaring.

"What are you doing?" he asked quietly.

Artur felt the woman watching. There was nothing he could say that would not alarm her, so he remained silent, unmoving. Charles narrowed his eyes. Artur prepared himself.

"Don't." Rictor appeared beside them—fast, silent. He and Artur were the same height, but up close Rictor felt like the bigger man. "Don't even think about it."

Will you know if we do? Artur asked silently, gambling on instinct, that odd, feathering sensation in his aching brain. Rictor's gaze flickered in his direction. He took that as a yes.

"Step back," Rictor said to Charles. Charles did not move. His defiance did not surprise Artur, though he sensed it was unusual. The hint of a memory—something about Rictor, a particular power Charles was wary of, that kept him playing by the rules. Those singular rules . . .

Artur blinked. It was getting harder to think, to focus.

Rictor edged sideways, close. Artur gave him room, slipping backward toward the woman. It surprised him: Rictor, exposing himself, allowing Artur an opportunity to strike from behind. Even if he was a telepath, able to sense Artur's intentions, it was a risky move.

But what surprised Artur more—what stole his breath—was that he did not *want* to take the opportunity. There were some things worse than death, worse than postponing a dash to freedom. Charles Darling was one of them.

Artur stood close to the woman. He felt the heat of her body on his skin, and it shamed him to be so exposed to her. She did not deserve the indignity. She held a pair of large white socks; her small, pale toes wriggled against the concrete. Her touch stained the cotton red, though he no longer believed the blood was hers. She refused to look at him, and so he openly studied the bruise on her cheek. Artur wondered if Rictor had hit her.

"Are you deaf?" Rictor said to Charles—so deadly, so quiet. "I said to get the fuck back."

"I heard you," Charles said. "I'm just very slow."

The woman moved. Artur turned, and for a moment—the first, it seemed—their gazes met. It was different, looking into her eyes—as though the distance between them were nothing, less than a thought, and it stunned him to feel the intensity of her dark gaze, which was everything he had imagined and more—sharp, inquisitive, defiant. It was so defiant that Artur felt himself begin to smile, because here was another fighter, another captive, and he was not alone.

She has a clean spirit. Clean and bright and strong.

Overwhelmed as he was, Artur still wanted to touch her—the first time he had ever felt that way about anyone, including Tatyana. He had to touch her, to be sure, to be proven right or wrong, but even as his fingers flexed she tore her gaze from his face and looked past him at Charles. The fierce light in her eyes faltered, but she collected herself enough to lift her chin and stare unblinking into his cold green eyes.

Artur wanted to say, *No, do not, have a care with your life*, but he said nothing, because it would have been an insult, and he could see the pride that kept her straight, her gaze keen. He wondered if she did not realize how dangerous Charles Darling was to her—how lethal his touch would be.

But then Artur looked deeper, noted the white knuckles and utter stillness of her body. Tension, singing.

She knows. My God, she knows.

Charles smiled: slow, chilling. "You must be new. I don't know your face."

The woman's eyes darkened. Rictor shoved Charles back.

"You overstep your bounds," Rictor murmured, though there was nothing soft about his voice. "You forget your place."

"No," Charles said. "*You* forget my place. Or don't you recall why I am here, the things I am supposed to do?"

"Supposed to do, or *want* to do?" Rictor raised an eyebrow, his lips twisted with contempt. "You're in love with your monster."

"It takes a monster to train a monster." Charles glanced over Rictor's shoulder at Artur, past him to the woman. "Or have *you* forgotten *that*? Have *l'araignée's* lessons faded so quickly?"

No one trained you, Artur thought, shifting sideways so that Charles could not look at the woman. A moment later he felt her move so that once again she stood in plain sight. Artur did not understand her quiet insistence; it troubled him.

Troubles you because it is familiar. You would do the same. Too much pride.

The woman locked gazes with Charles: a staring contest with a serial killer. Artur could not imagine anything more horrible—or admirable. He felt Rictor watching him. Artur met his gaze. Staring contests all around. Captor, captive—the lines were blurring inside his head, warping around pain.

"I like the blood," Charles said to the woman.

"Funny," she said.

Charles's expression did not change, but Rictor gave him a sharp look, began to step in front—

Charles struck at his throat. Rictor twisted sideways so that the man's hooked fingers slid harmlessly through the air. Rictor grabbed his wrist, twisting down hard. Artur heard a joint pop; Charles's shoulder suddenly protruded at an unnatural angle from the rest of his body. Fast, fast, fast.

"I thought you were a patient man," Rictor said softly, as though they were alone, holding a gentle conversation.

"But I am a man," Charles replied, not a hint of strain in his voice. "Temptation, you know."

The woman made a sound, low in her throat. "Who *are* you people?"

"They call themselves the Consortium," Artur answered. He turned to face the woman. Urgency moved him, the need to give her something to protect herself with—fast now, quick, before anyone could stop him. "They are nothing more than criminals."

"They're doing experiments on people like us," she whispered. "But you're the first—"

She stopped. Artur wondered why she stared at him with such rapt concern.

Something dribbled from his nose. Artur touched his face. His fingertips came away red. He felt warmth in his ears, liquid pushing through the soft canal, rolling down his neck. He smelled blood, and this time it was not from the woman.

The pain had become so much a part of him he had forgotten it, partitioned it like he partitioned memory so that he could focus on the present, on what needed to be done. Too long, too much—the breaking point had come and gone and now . . . *I am going to pay*—

An ax lodged in his head would have been kinder. Artur felt as though giants were cracking the shell of his skull for meat, chewing on his brain. He staggered. The woman reached out to touch him even as Rictor said, "No."

Her hands were soft. He noticed that first, even as her shadow rolled through him, settling light within his aching mind. Her skin felt good, sweet.

Images flickered, but they were warped, impossible to

sort through his dying brain. All he could make sense of was her voice, whispering—*I can fix him, oh, God, what have they done to this man, why are we here, why are they so cruel, please hang on, please don't die, listen to me, listen—*

He listened, falling to the ground. The woman—*Elena*—moved with him, her hands sliding from his shoulders to his chest. He tried to look at her face but all he saw was the man looming behind her. Rictor, a dark blur, who began to pull Elena away, but stopped at the last moment. Stopped and stepped back. Artur imagined his eyes glowed.

And then the woman filled his vision, her lips moving, and in his head—his breaking, shattering head—he heard her say, *Rest a little, sleep a little, just take a little of my heart.*

He did, and for the first time in his life, it was good.

Chapter Five

It was good that Elena had some practice maintaining her composure under stressful circumstances. Trying to heal lethal diseases in the middle of crowded hospitals had taught her a certain level of self-possession, the desperate I-have-a-secret-identity kind that now served her well. Sort of, if she did not count her sole panic attack. Which she did not.

Still, it was a shock coming face-to-face with another prisoner. Not a ghost town any longer, running the edge of abandonment and solitude. It wasn't just her, the lonely freak—accompanied by another freak who seemed to be acting as both jailer and adviser.

Elena wondered how long the Russian had been kept in the facility, if he was the man she had heard screaming. He certainly seemed unwell, though she could not say how except that it was instinct, her gift. He was a tall man, lean and well built with the pale skin of the sun-shy. Dark hair framed his face, the sparse angles of his cheeks, and the hard line of his mouth, lovely and haunting.

Elena had difficulty looking at the Russian. His nudity was part of her discomfort, but there was also something fascinating about his face—so intense, so pained that it instantly repelled her, as though her mind and heart simply could not take the force of his gaze. Stupid, stupid; it was the most inappropriate case of shyness she had ever felt. Ill-timed, as well; Elena knew she was missing the perfect opportunity to make contact—contact of any kind—with a fellow captive.

But the Russian was not alone, and inside her head Elena heard a voice whispering, *Quiet, it is always the quiet ones that kill you,* and she had no idea why she felt such visceral revulsion to the man with brown hair and green eyes, the quiet man with that cold, detached gaze that seemed to swallow down her spirit into a dark place, empty and frightening. The Quiet Man raised within her the same phobia one might hold for a snake or spider. Inexplicable, mysterious fear.

And his voice—that voice—did not match his appearance in the slightest. When he spoke—*You must be new . . . I like the blood*—it was like hearing an orator, an educated storyteller, an expert of rolling vowels.

Dangerous. This is the most dangerous man you have ever met in your life. She felt like the gazelle to the lion. What a cracktastic way to live.

Elena was thankful she was not the only person who felt the threat; the Russian's playing hero only confirmed it. Understated, simple: a step and turn. What relief—what painful, wonderful relief, to be freed for even one moment from the Quiet Man's cold gaze. She could not pray enough thanks.

But it was wrong. She could not accept it. She had to fight her own battles, because depending on anyone in this place invited punishment, failure, and there was too much at stake. She needed to start out strong. No weakness. Be an army of one.

Still, the Russian's gesture made her feel good. It gave her hope. More than hope, even, when she finally chanced a look and found him staring at her.

Old-soul eyes, she thought, captured by the suffering in his face, the edge of bitter sweetness. *What gives a man those eyes?*

There was no escaping his nudity. Elena did not let her gaze falter from his eyes. He held himself with too much dignity to give him such rough insult. Her own embarrassment still burned—her introduction to forced nudity ranking high with the blackmail of her gift. Violation after violation. Elena could not accept it, that theft of her most personal privacy and control. She did not think this man would accept it, either. She did not know him, but she sensed his stubborn pride, the hard edge of resolve. A fighter.

Fighting right up until the very end.

What have they done to you? Oh, God. What have they done? Blood trickled from his nose and ears. Realization poured through his haunted gaze, the certain knowledge of death knocking at his heart. The Russian collapsed. Elena fell with him, sending her strength into his body, following the course of his suffering with the inner knowledge that directed her gift. *It is his brain. His brain is dying.*

"Hold on," Elena whispered, kneeling over the Russian's pale, prone body, which was fast becoming a corpse, that great vitality slipping away. His dark eyes with their old-soul gaze fluttered shut. Elena hoped she could make them open again.

Her body prickled. She heard a song in her fingertips as she traveled from her body into his, seeking the flow of his spirit. Instinct guided her; the vigor of her will, forcing him to listen as she delivered a simple plea to do what should come so naturally. The Russian did not resist her. She felt embraced by warmth.

The metaphysical representation of the Russian's brain was a curious thing; it filled her vision like a white ghost bleeding shadow, losing form in darkness. Elena trapped the lost light, holding it against her as she pressed close, gathering the Russian's mind into her heart. She fed him pieces of herself—her compassion, her will—goading him to knit, to heal, to dream again without pain. Blind, unable to sit straight, she leaned down to rest her head on the Russian's warm chest.

Heal, she begged, peering into the white light of his mind. She saw cracks, hairline fissures, tiny earthquakes in his brain. She could not imagine what had caused such injuries, which looked old, ingrained. Tentative, running on instinct, Elena reached into the light, touching wounds, stroking them, knitting—

—filth, he hates the filth of that room, how they must shit in the bowl and how the bowl is too full and that corner of the room reeks of piss and worse, worse, because the little ones are starving and they think it might taste good—

No. Elena retreated from the memory, seeking another fissure—*a sunny room with blue walls, a soft bed, a soft body cradled around pale flesh, whispering, "I love you, Tatyana, I love"*—and she healed the breach, folding it off.

Beside it, another—*a wet alley with a body on the ground and a gun pressed to his temple, the nozzle cold and hard with a price for disloyalty and bodies on top, fighting, a lightbulb swinging, swinging like a pendulum, and somewhere someone whispering, "It is time, I am going to kill you—"*

Elena felt someone touch her physical body, her cheek. At first she thought it was Rictor, but a deep voice whispered, "No, do not. Please."

The Russian. His accent was thicker than she remembered. Elena could not respond to him; she hurt too much. If she opened her mouth it would be to cry out, and she would not give the Quiet Man—or even Rictor—that satisfaction.

"You are hurting yourself," said the man. "Stop. I am better now."

No, he was not better. He was conscious, he could speak, but only because the swelling had gone down, the bleeding stopped. What Elena could do defied science—she accepted this, had long ago given up trying to find an explanation—but it also meant she was keenly aware of every physical flaw, every weakness. His brain still suffered. Until she encouraged the healing of every fissure, anything she did for him now would only be temporary. He might die in his sleep tonight. He might live another twenty years and collapse from a stroke.

I can't stop, she told him, pretending he could hear. *If I do you'll die.*

The white light within his mind flickered. *You are in such discomfort. I can feel it. Do not hurt yourself for me.*

The sound of his voice in her thoughts was so startling she almost broke the connection. *You heard me. I . . . Is this for real? How?*

I do not know. He sounded weary. *Please, stop.*

I won't let you die. Elena reached for another fissure, shadows spilling out from the wound.

There is too much. No one should see this. I do not know you.

Strangers in paradise, she whispered. *Please, we have to hurry.*

He said nothing, but she felt his assent like a sigh in her heart, and she touched the fissure. Images flickered through her mind, a picture show of pain split with brief happiness—an older woman, arms extended for a hug; a cheerfully battered kitchen filled with the scent of hot bread, sweets—and then all of it swept away into a grim institution where the only colors were brown and gray and the white, sun-starved faces of gaunt boys huddled in cold rooms, living on nothing but emptiness.

What is this place? Elena tried not to look too deep into his memories as she worked.

An orphanage outside Moscow. I was sent there when I was twelve.

Sent there to die. The thought came to her, unbidden. Shame filled her heart.

No, he said quietly. *There is no shame in the truth. My mother left me.*

How could she? Elena thought of her own mother, that last conversation, the ax, and her grandfather running, running. . . .

I was a burden and she was alone with no money. His voice was flat, without emotion. Elena did not press him for more. It was none of her business.

She closed the fissure, and after that three more. Old wounds, places where his mind had been weakened by stress. It occurred to her as she worked that these places, while linked to his physical illness, were metaphysical in nature, and that now she was doing more than just healing his body. This was new, strange territory. She hoped she did not change his personality.

Low laughter filled her mind. *No. But I do feel different.*

Different good or different bad?

I do not know. Good, I think. The pain is not gone, but I . . . feel stronger inside my head.

I'm almost done. Hold on.

She closed the last fissure—caught the image of men sitting around a table, laughing and joking, a feeling of deep comfort and camaraderie—and then began to pull away. At the last moment, though, she felt something tickle her senses. A deep chill. Unnatural. She cast herself wide, searching for the source. When she found it, wiggling and black like a worm, she swore.

What is wrong?

You have something sticking out of your brain. And it's alive. Kind of.

Silence, and then, *That is unusual, yes?*

I've never performed psychic surgery before, but . . . yes, this doesn't look normal.

Can you remove it?

Elena did not answer. She was too busy examining its root. She touched it.

Pain exploded through her body, a fine, hard rain of nails, tearing her like she was cloth. Elena cried out, dimly aware of the Russian arching his back, echoing her. She heard Rictor say her name but she could not respond, could only cling to the man beneath her, shuddering from that terrible agony. The Russian touched her back, holding her against him. It was difficult to tell if his touch was real or illusion, so entrenched was she becoming in the world of his mind.

No, she said, answering his unspoken question. *I have to get rid of it.*

It will kill you.

No, she said again, and wrapped herself around the worm. Again, pain, but Elena refused to let go, refused to succumb to the awful darkness bucking within her grasp. She heard a woman's voice whisper—*stop, let go*—

Elena refused. She yanked hard, ripping . . . tearing . . .

It was almost enough. Almost. Elena was not strong enough to pull the worm completely free. A tendril remained, stuck fast within the Russian's memories. The pain intensified; her heart felt like it was on fire. She could not breathe.

And then the Russian was there, a large, warm presence, wrapping himself around her spirit, gathering up his strength with her own. The pain diminished, and she realized he was stealing the burden from her, draining all that agony into himself.

Try it again, he said, his voice tight with strain.

They pulled together and the worm stretched like a scream, long and wicked. Elena thought her spirit would tear, but the Russian refused to release her. He held her so tight she felt their spirits merge.

An odd emerald light flickered on the edge of her spiritual vision. With it came strength. The worm snapped free. Elena tried to capture it, but the creature dissolved into shadow the moment it lost its hold on the Russian's mind. The pain vanished. Elena felt a momentary disconnect, as though she no longer had anything left to measure her existence by. The pain had been everything, all-consuming. Without it, her reality felt lessened, depleted, and for the first time in her life she found her spirit adrift within another body, too exhausted to pull herself fully home. She could feel her physical self resting heavily on the Russian, but it was a distant sensation. The Russian's mind felt more real than flesh, more comfortable than skin.

You must go, he said. *Your body cannot live without you.*

Just give me a minute. I'm tired.

No. She felt him nudge her, but they were so tightly bound, a nudge was not enough. He tugged again, harder this time.

Slowly, she told him, and then, with weary humor, *Be gentle.*

Always. And he was gentle, and he was slow, and still it hurt. Not the same kind of pain they had just suffered, but a pain nonetheless. Heartache, perhaps; as they untangled themselves, Elena felt as though a piece of her soul were being left behind. She wondered if the Russian felt the same.

Your name, she asked him. *What is it?*

Artur. Artur Loginov.

Artur. She liked that. *My name is Elena Baxter.*

Greetings, he whispered. An odd light flickered through his mind, tinted green as emerald. Elena recognized it. Before she could say anything, she felt herself pulled away from Artur's grasp, weightless as air, insubstantial as a lost dream. She reached out to him—instinctively—but he could not hold her.

She landed back in her body with a rude thud, but darkness—always darkness—crept close against her vision and she could not lift her head from the Russian's chest.

She lost herself again.

When Elena healed people, the journey back into her body was almost always instantaneous, never accompanied by unconsciousness or periods of confusion. Which was why, when Elena next opened her eyes and found herself back in the locker room—the Russian nowhere in sight—she knew something bad had happened.

Namely, Rictor.

"What did you do?" Elena asked, trying to stand. Her body would not obey; she felt weak, dehydrated. Rictor, impassive, stood less than a yard away. It took her a moment to realize she sat inside one of the shower stalls. Her clothes were still on, her body dry.

Rictor ignored the question. "You need to shower before I return you to the cell. Doctor's orders."

"What did you do to me?" Elena asked again, furious. "Where is Artur?"

Rictor crouched. He looked bored. Gently he said, "You should not have interfered."

Elena stared at him, trying to read his face. It was impossible. "He would have died, Rictor. I had to do something."

"You complicated matters."

"How could I possibly have complicated anything around here? You guys are so in control you might as well brand your names on our asses and make us moo."

Rictor briefly closed his eyes. "If you really felt that way, you wouldn't be thinking so hard about all the ways you can escape. Now stand up. You need to shower."

"Where's Artur?" she asked again, unmoving. Her heart ached—a physical pain, as though a piece of her were missing.

"The Russian is where he should be. Alive, thanks to you." Rictor did not sound terribly happy about that. His green eyes flickered to a deep emerald, catching light, an impossible amount of light—

Elena's breath caught, remembering that same light inside Artur's head. "You were there with us. You . . . helped." *You helped pull out the worm. You stole me away from Artur.*

"I would be a fool to do that," he said.

"Bullshit."

Rictor grabbed Elena's arm and hauled her up. She barely had strength to stand on her own, so he had to hold her. She hated that, pushed feebly at his chest until he let her lean against the tile wall.

"Swearing doesn't become you," he said quietly. "You don't do it naturally."

"I don't think you're in any position to lecture me about good language. Or did I imagine all those times you said 'fuck'?"

Rictor's mouth tightened. He reached out and turned the shower knob. Cold water blasted over Elena's body. She gasped, trying to jerk away. Rictor held her still, getting sloshed with the same cold water. After a minute—the longest of her life—the water turned warm. Her scrubs hung heavy against her body.

"What's the point of this?" she spluttered, feebly wiping water from her eyes. "Or is this just another kind of torture?"

"Cleanliness promotes health," Rictor said, in a dry monotone that sounded as if he were reciting from a manual. "And the doctor wants you in *perfect* health."

"Your doctor is crazy," she said, and then, quieter, "Why did you do it, Rictor? Why did you get involved? If I wasn't supposed to help Artur, you could have stopped me. It wouldn't have been hard for you to do."

Rictor said nothing. He did not look at her. Elena wondered if there were cameras watching them, but Rictor had started this, hadn't he? Surely it was safe.

"Is he still alive?" she asked, insistent. "At least you can tell me that. Did I heal him just so he could just get shot in the head?" The possibility made her sick.

More silence. Maddening, horrible—

"*Rictor.*"

"No. Like I said, you complicated matters. Maybe we both did." He stepped away before she could respond, peering at her body with a clinical detachment that rivaled that of most doctors. "Can you undress yourself?"

Elena stared at him. "I sincerely hope you don't expect me to take a shower—a real shower—right in front of you."

His silence was answer enough. Elena felt pure heat spread across her face. Her fingers curled against the slick tile.

"No," she said, low. "No. I don't care what kind of

sick place this is, I'm not taking any more. You turn around, Rictor. You turn around or leave this bathroom or do something the hell different, but I am not stripping naked in front of you."

"It's the rules," he said. "I have to follow them."

"Why? Is there someone watching us to make sure you do?"

"No," Rictor said. "It's just something I have to do."

He bit out the words, and Elena could not tell what made him angrier: her resistance, or his own inability to bend the rules for her benefit. She did not care, either way.

"I won't do it," she said.

"I can make you," he replied.

"Then you deserve to be here. You deserve this life, and worse."

Rictor's expression darkened. "You should not talk to me like that."

"Why not? You already know what I'm thinking. Why shouldn't I speak my mind?"

He went very still. Stared at her, thoughtful. It made Elena uneasy when he looked at her like that.

"I made a mistake," he finally said, slowly. "I should have made you afraid of me."

"You call that a mistake? Holy crap." Elena briefly closed her eyes, weary. She needed to lie down. "You're no better than the rest of them . . . whoever they are."

Elena felt a large, warm hand on her neck. It was not a friendly touch. Rictor stood so close she could see herself in his eyes. "You'd better hope that's not the case," he whispered. "You'd better pray I'm better than that."

Elena said nothing. Her voice would not work. His terrible anger shot into her spine like a thunderbolt, jarring her security, her tentative trust. There was power inside him, immense and tightly reined. Like Niagara, dammed.

Elena swallowed hard. "You've proven your point. Now let me go."

Rictor's hand dropped away. He stepped back and turned sideways so that he faced the locker room door. "This is the best I can do, Elena. Take your shower."

He stared at the wall. If he wanted to, he could watch her from the corner of his eye—but Elena had lost all desire to argue. Her heart pounded so hard she felt dizzy.

Why, Rictor? Why should I be afraid of you?

He said nothing. Of course.

Face hot, pride taking a nosedive into the drain beneath her feet, Elena shucked off her filthy clothes and kicked them away from her. There was soap in the stall. She scrubbed her skin raw, turning so she did not have to look at Rictor. Despite her humiliation, it felt good to be clean again.

"You have five minutes," he finally said.

Elena turned off the water. She glanced around for a towel and found one folded on the floor by the shower. Next to it were some fresh scrubs and a pair of white socks. Rictor waited until she was dressed before tilting his head to look her over.

"Clean enough?" she asked, bracing herself against the shower wall. The hot water had restored her calm; she felt angry, though too weak to do much about it. Healing Artur had completely wrecked her endurance.

"You'll do." Rictor did not move. He watched her, thoughtful. Elena waited, happy to play the silence game.

"Are you ready?" he finally asked, and his voice was so quiet she had to lean forward to hear him. Even then, it took a moment to register his words. The question felt heavy, loaded.

She said, "Does it matter?"

He said, "It always matters."

"And if my answer is no?"

She felt the great weight of his gaze upon her, measuring and judging, and he said, "Then you won't survive. You need to be strong in the head, Elena. You need to be ready."

"Ready for what? How can I trust you? You tell me these things, but then you say I should be afraid. I am not like you, Rictor—I can't read minds. Why are you doing this?"

He moved close, the warm, rich brown of his skin holding the light, just as his eyes seemed to reflect it, flashing green and bright. Again she felt his power, power edged with some careful, timeless grace, and she remembered that brief presence inside Artur's mind, surrounding them, sharing strength to fight the worm.

Rictor grabbed her arm and yanked her from the shower stall. She stumbled and caught her balance against him. He did not hurt her, but his strength was inexorable; he dragged her like a doll to the door.

"This is all I *can* do, Elena." His voice was hard, quiet. "And when they kill me, you won't even have that."

"Rictor," she breathed. He did not look at her. He refused to say anything more.

Chapter Six

Artur came to consciousness with the sense of cold plastic beneath his back. He did not open his eyes. He felt a low vibration, heard the click and whir of instruments. Typing. He smelled antiseptic.

He listened to the echo of the table he lay on. He sensed the faint presence of another man. Dying—that man had been dying when he lay here, not so long ago. Bleeding internally from some terrible impact. Another victim of some third-world promise: *A day of easy work for a lot of money. Just get in the car. We'll do all the rest.*

The pain was gone. Still naked, still unprotected—but that soul-splitting headache had finally disappeared. Even the influx of vision in his head felt improved, as though the memories pouring through him were clean and cold, distant and not a part of him. Artur had not felt that way in a very long time. It was like having his youth restored, the youth he had never been able to have.

Elena gave me this gift. She did more than simply heal me. Which was utterly remarkable. He had never

92

imagined—even as strange as his life could be—that a person could do such things. Part of him still reached out for her, which disturbed him. It made no sense to feel such aching loss for a stranger.

Not a stranger. Not when he could clearly recall the touch of Elena's spirit against his own, how it felt to have her so tightly bound against him they risked becoming one creature. It frightened him to be so exposed.

And yet . . . he could not deny it felt safe and right. To hold and be held—for once, to let the visions in his head sweep into darkness without being carried with them. Elena had anchored him, protected him, and though he looked down into the heart of her soul—looked deep, because he had no choice, never any choice—he was not repulsed by what he found. Elena's skeletons were clean like her spirit, untainted by the tragedies in her life. She walked tall and lovely inside her heart, a heart that had embraced a stranger, a heart that had almost killed itself to help him.

And it pained him that he was unable to do more for her. Even in the end she had been pulled away from his embrace, stolen from his mind. Yes, she'd had to return to her body, but her disappearance felt like theft. He could not hold her—was too weak from the psychic battle with the strange creature inhabiting his thoughts.

A worm, a shadow, a vein into his head. Any description was meaningless, insofar as its purpose was concerned. Something had been done to him. His mind had been invaded, set upon by a leech.

Such a thing was not unheard of. Roland was an expert at psychic manipulation, as was Max Reese, another of Artur's friends. According to them, it was close to impossible for a true telepath to hear anything beyond a person's surface thoughts. It had to do with the low level of electricity every human generated—the kind of thing that allowed brain waves to be measured, or a slight charge registered by touching a field-strength meter. The only way to discover secrets that lay below the surface of a person's consciousness was to lay down a thread of some kind—build a link between minds—and wait for the underground to surface.

Only, the secrets inside Artur's head were the kind that should never be shared.

Perhaps the fail-safe was triggered. If so, then Roland will know something is wrong. He will be able to warn the others—perhaps even find me, if Dean has not already.

The fail-safe was Roland's own creation, his version of a black worm. Years ago he had created a telepathic alarm system, a trick to keep the agency's true purpose safe from betrayal. When someone was ready to be brought into the fold, Roland—with the individual's permission—created a mental link, a connection between all the agency's secret information and the emotional center of the brain. It did not take much to trigger the link. A single discussion with the wrong person—just one word, even—and Roland would know. All threads led back to him.

The black thread of the spider. Charles's memory drifted cold through his mind. The black thread, holding him like a dog, with a voice in his dreams. Artur remembered his own dreams, his nightmares. A woman whispering, *endless and undying.*

She was trying to control me. I would have been another killer, leashed. A pet, like Charles Darling. And when she had me, she would have also had my secrets.

He recalled Ms. Graves pressing him for his assent, for just one word: yes. Chills shuddered up Artur's spine. He had come so close to saying that word, and it would not have mattered if it was a lie in his heart; like Roland, whoever had set the worm upon him—be it

94

Graves or someone else—needed his permission. Some agreement, which would have translated into the spiritual, opening a crack in his mind for the worm to slip through and take control. Of course, it did not matter to Graves if she truly convinced him to join—all she needed was to wear him down until he said something to appease her. The mind was a tricky thing, with natural barriers and natural weaknesses, but the old adage played true: Give an inch and someone would take a mile. Might take your whole life, too.

"You're awake," said a smooth voice, startling Artur. "Don't try to pretend otherwise. Your brain activity has increased significantly since your last scan."

Artur opened his eyes. Directly above him was the inner wall of a creamy plastic dome—a ring—curving down around him like the center of a smooth doughnut. He tried sitting up and found himself bound to the table, tight bands holding his ankles, wrists, and chest. There was a restraint around his forehead. He tried to look down his body at the man addressing him and heard a low laugh.

"No, dear boy. I am not in the room. I am speaking to you via an intercom."

"Who are you?" Artur tested his bonds. Waking up completely helpless was growing tiresome.

Another low laugh. "A doctor, of course. *Your* doctor. And you, Mr. Loginov, are fast becoming one of my favorite patients."

That was not a comforting thought, considering that Artur had some notion of what this man did to his patients. Still, he was not above taking advantage of a good opening. "Might I ask what is so fascinating?"

"Your brain," said the doctor, a smile in his voice. "I have never seen anything quite like it. The activity in your anterior cingulate cortex is incredibly intense. You are, to put it mildly, lit up like a Christmas tree. Which is remarkable, considering *that* is the area of the brain most closely associated with a great number of mental illnesses, including schizophrenia. Your extraordinary ability to process complex information must be the only reason you're not yet insane."

"How interesting," Artur said. "I always wondered."

"Delightful. I like it when my patients appreciate the process."

Yes. Not very comforting at all.

Artur gazed down his body again. Outside the machine, past his feet, he saw a blank flatscreen monitor hanging from the ceiling; just below sat another monitor, this one blinking numbers. Artur heard more typing, which he realized was coming through the intercom. "How many patients do you have?" he asked, attempting a subtle examination of his restraints.

"Not so many," said the doctor. "Although there has been a recent surge in some truly fascinating conditions. None that will surprise *you* all that much." His emphasis was disturbing. But before Artur could respond, the doctor said, "Tell me how you feel."

"How I feel?"

"Yes, dear boy. You suffered a collapse after your arrival. Or don't you remember?"

"I remember," Artur said, careful.

"And how do you feel now? Are you in pain?"

"No," he said. "I feel fine."

The doctor made a humming sound. "Interesting. What an unexpected reversal."

Yes, but only if he expected Artur to be dead or incapacitated. Which meant that Elena's intervention—healing his brain, removing the worm—had completely upset someone's plans.

A scream cut the air. Artur jumped against his bonds.

The cry was sharp, an animal howl, wicked with teeth and fury. It took him a moment to realize it was not originating inside the room with him. Close, though— perhaps just outside the door to where he was being kept. He heard men shout—muffled words over a song of snarls—and then something large slammed once, twice, against a wall.

Silence. Artur remembered his vision: a cheetah, circling. The animal he had just heard certainly sounded like a cat, though he had no idea why the Consortium would be concerning themselves with animals, unless it was for some kind of biological experiment.

Artur forced himself to remember, pushing, prodding, dredging up more of the cheetah—someone's recollection of the animal—and then, again, a strong memory that had made an impression on more than one individual.

The dolphin. A living dolphin, held within a small tank that was only as wide and long as its body. The water looked dirty. The animal seemed tired, exhausted, it did not struggle in the harness that ran beneath its belly, holding it just above the water's surface.

Artur peered close. *How curious.* Why would such a creature be here, in a place that seemed to have nothing at all to do with marine life—

He saw gold. Gold in the dolphin's eyes. Dolphins did not have golden eyes.

No. Only shape-shifters do.

"*Bozhe moy,*" Artur murmured, too shocked to be mindful of anyone who might hear him. *My God. How did they know? How did they find one? How, when we have searched for months without any luck?*

Searching—it was part of Dirk & Steele's bargain with the dragon woman, Long Nü. So few shape-shifters were left in the world, and they were in danger of dying, of fading into legend. If Dirk & Steele could offer the remaining shape-shifters a resource, a way of reconnecting with others of their kind . . .

A dolphin. Remarkable. Koni and Hari told me shape-shifters inhabited the oceans, that they flourished there while their landlocked brothers and sisters languished. Yet, to find one here . . . It is like discovering a unicorn.

And who was to say *those* did not exist as well? The world was full of vast possibility. Magic, science—all of it working together to create an extraordinary riddle without an answer, where the only response was acceptance. Accept, because the alternative was a small life, a small mind.

It was not so difficult for Artur to imagine the possibilities. Not when his life had been gifted with such highs and lows of pain and miracle. He had learned to accept a great deal from a very young age, and a little magic seemed easier and lovelier than the other truths he had swallowed.

So. A shape-shifter, here.

He thought of the cheetah. The big cat also had golden eyes, but that was typical of its kind. Artur could not say for certain the animal was anything more than what it appeared to be.

But what if? They already have one shape-shifter. Two, though remarkable, is not impossible.

But it was humbling.

I need to help them, Artur decided. He thought of Elena—felt his heart ache, like a little death. *And you. I am coming for you, Elena. You are not alone. I am still with you.*

Still with her, and tied naked to a table.

Well. He never had expected an easy life.

Muted voices outside the room broke Artur's concentration. He listened, and a moment later heard the doctor's high, loud voice over the garbled mess of words and accents.

"Inexcusable," Artur heard him say. "You should have been more careful."

More talking, again interrupted by the doctor. "No, I told you his metabolism works faster than a normal animal's. You simply did not listen. Now take him back and clean up this mess. Fast."

His metabolism works faster than a normal animal's.

That clarified things, and considering what Artur remembered from his visions, he had a fairly good idea of who was screaming out in the hall. The Consortium really did have two shape-shifters in its custody—one of whom still had enough strength to fight. Good. That was very good.

Artur heard a loud click. Muffled voices, scuffing noises, followed by a single pair of footsteps. Definitely in the room this time.

An elderly man in a white lab coat appeared beside Artur's feet. He held a black plastic bag. His smile was faintly unpleasant, his face too narrow and his eyes too sharp to allow the baring of teeth. Artur watched him as best he could. The old man tapped a button on the side of the machine. The table Artur lay upon slid out. Artur blinked as the bright ceiling lights blinded him.

"I apologize," said the doctor. "I hate interruptions."

"And yet you manage them so well. That was an animal I heard, yes?"

"Very much so." The doctor smiled. "Quite difficult to train."

"Cats usually are. They are so *much* like people. Minds of their own, as you know."

The doctor's smile faltered. Yes. It was quite clear he did know. The hand holding the black plastic bag clenched tighter, knuckles rolling white.

"What a skill you have," said the doctor softly. "What a knack for learning. Fascinating. They say you are a dangerous man. I quite believe it. And yet, I find myself wondering how it is that a man such as yourself, a man who can see the most hidden secrets of anyone in the world, does not run his own empire, his own kingdom to rival the one you are about to join."

"I am sorry," Artur said, "but I have no idea what you are talking about."

The doctor raised an eyebrow. "I suppose that answers it, then. You really are no better than a thug."

Which, Artur reasoned, was the same as being called stupid. He could live with that, considering the source.

The doctor said, "I wish I could dissect you."

Artur fought the urge to laugh. "Forgive me if I do not share that wish."

"Of course. I'm a patient man."

"You must be, faced as you are with so much disappointment."

"I seem to be encountering an overabundance of bad humor."

"Then you should stop inviting jokes."

The doctor wanted to hit him: Artur could see that in his eyes, the quick flex of his fingers. He recognized that expression, that—*sharp pain, shocking, so unexpected, and why . . . why*—

Elena. Her memories, dredged from his unconscious. He remembered. The doctor had hit her, given her that bruise on her face. He had made her taste blood—blood and pain—and it was terrible. Artur's anger was terrible, so shocking and unexpected, because he did not know this woman—not truly, not with his heart, and . . .

Artur wanted to kill him. Perhaps the doctor saw it in his eyes; he swayed backward. Just a fraction, a sliver of weakness. Artur smiled.

"Do it," he said. "Touch me."

The doctor's jaw tightened. "I am afraid you have misjudged my enthusiasm."

"I think you like giving pain. So I have misjudged *nothing*."

"Really." The doctor drew out the word, low and hard. "You are lucky I am a man of control, Mr. Loginov."

Artur thought of Elena. "You overestimate yourself."

"And *you* are under the mistaken impression that you are entitled to an opinion."

He could not help himself; Artur laughed. Cold, slipping into the mask of his youth, the hard way of the gun and fist, he said, "If I killed you, it would be a favor."

The doctor raised his hand.

"Stop." One word, a familiar voice. The doctor froze. Artur rolled his gaze, trying to find the camera. He did not see it, but over the intercom Graves said, "You should leave the room, Doctor."

The doctor lowered his hand. Calm entered his gaze, but Artur did not miss the hard set of his mouth, the tension in his slim shoulders. He dropped the black bag on the floor and left. Just outside the door stood Ms. Graves. Artur thought he saw blood on the wall behind her. Clumps of golden hair.

Graves laid her hand on the doctor's shoulder as he passed. She whispered into his ear. His expression brightened. He left her with a light step, which was no comfort to Artur.

Graves entered the room and closed the door behind her. She looked different than Artur remembered. Without shadows to hide within, to add ghost flesh, her appearance was truly skeletal. She stood straight, but with a hint of concavity to her chest, a hollowness that seemed deeper than flesh.

"You called my bluff," she said.

"No," he said. "I thought I was choosing death."

If that surprised her, she did not show it. She swayed close, studying his face with cold detachment.

"Really," she said, quiet. "Was my offer really so horrible?"

Artur smiled. "I preferred the alternative."

Her expression darkened. She picked up the black bag and dumped its contents on top of Artur's body. A one-piece jumpsuit tumbled out, as did a pair of leather gloves and socks. Artur listened for a story. He heard nothing but the gentle thoughts of the woman who had prepared the ornate red room—and beyond her, the manufacturer, an Asian woman in a sweatshop, back aching, stomach growling for the promised bowl of *mi fan* . . .

Nothing about where Artur was being held captive. Not anything he had touched so far contained that one piece of crucial information, something to place the facility within the real world. His stolen memories contained no windows, phones, or connections. Everyone brought here was kept hooded and sedated, tethered and misdirected. The money was good and the employees had nothing to lose: reason enough to give up freedom. Even the scientists did not care. The work they were doing was too compelling. If the corporation wanted to play the top-secret spy game, let them.

Corporation. Now that was interesting.

Graves frowned. "Something surprised you. Strange. You could not have found anything useful from those clothes. They were screened just for your benefit."

How one could screen clothes for him was a mystery, but Artur did not remark upon it. Too much was already a mystery; dwelling on the small details would make him insane. Again.

"I was momentarily overcome by my appreciation of

bondage," he told her, tugging on his restraints. "I am sure you have experienced the same feeling."

Her mouth twisted. "I should never have complimented your sense of humor."

"You should never have kidnapped me. Alas, hindsight." Artur glanced down at the clothes. "Am I to dress myself while restrained?"

"What a trick *that* would be. But no, someone will be in to undo your restraints. Eventually. I simply wanted to speak with you first. Hear your impressions of the place."

"I think it is a madhouse," Artur said. "I see no direction or purpose, save to harm others."

"Harsh words."

"Honest words."

"Oh, God save us from honest men." Graves paced to the end of the table, standing so close to Artur's feet he could almost touch her with his toes. Artur strained, and—

"Nice try," she said, swaying just out of reach. "Seriously, though. Tell me your thoughts."

"I prefer questions," Artur said. "Such as why you allowed me to wake up, naked, in a room that required I walk through your base, soaking up your secrets? It does not seem like good planning. I am already a liability, as you say."

"Call it an experiment. I wanted to see if all that stimuli would short-circuit your brain. Weaken it."

"Weaken it for what?" He waited, but the answer already burned inside that empty place in the back of his head that had radiated a digging, prying pain.

Graves gave him a disdainful look. "Do not pretend with me, Mr. Loginov. You know very well *for what*. You must, since you removed it."

No, I did not. Artur wondered if Graves knew of

Elena's role in destroying the worm, saving his life. He said, "You underestimated me."

"Yes," Graves agreed. "And you are the first to ever have the privilege of saying so." She crouched beside the table so that she sat just below Artur's eye level, like a skeleton, tapping her long white nails on the floor. "The Consortium still wants you, Mr. Loginov. Not just for your power, but for your knowledge."

"You want Dirk and Steele. You thought I would be an easy way of learning its secrets."

"Secrets are power. You know that. And how could we resist, especially when we learned of your background? Former Russian Mafia, a man who has killed for his supper. It was as though you were made ready-to-order, just for us. A perfect candidate for temptation."

"On the surface, perhaps."

"No. Every man can be tempted. Every man has his price. I simply made the mistake of believing yours was just money."

Once upon a time, money would have been enough. No questions asked. Artur said, "You cannot buy me."

"And what of your so-called friends? Perhaps they will have a different opinion."

"I doubt that."

"Such a pessimist. So very contrary. You are an unnatural man, Mr. Loginov. Disturbingly so."

"Please, no more compliments."

Graves did not smile. "Something went wrong with you. All our plans, awry. Until we know why, we will simply have to go about this the old-fashioned way. Methods, I'm sure, you are well acquainted with. Mother Russia trains her wayward children well." She leaned close. Her breath smelled like mints, her body like lilies. "It isn't too late, Mr. Loginov. I will give you another chance."

So many chances, so many unrealized threats. Artur did not understand why she had not killed him already and moved on to another of his colleagues. He did not understand why she continued talking, when the doctor was probably frothing at the mouth for a chance to stick him with sharp objects.

"You are desperate and afraid. You kidnapped me because you thought I was your best choice, but you do not dare take another of my friends until you know more. Until you are sure you will not be caught. You know nothing about us, do you? Absolutely nothing."

"We know enough to be dangerous."

"Dangerous, but not lethal. You cannot destroy us. You cannot even make some juvenile attempt to expose us. Our reputations would not allow it. The preconceived notions of the public would not allow it. Psychics—true psychics—working in tandem toward a common goal? Who would accept that, ever?"

"We could kill you. Bullets are cheap. Easy."

"Again?" Artur smiled. "No, Ms. Graves. I do not think you want to kill me. I do not think you want to kill any of us. You are not that wasteful."

Graves stared at him. "You're wrong about one thing, Mr. Loginov. I *do* want to kill you. Either that or fuck you. I can't decide."

"I prefer the killing."

"I'll try not to be insulted."

"No," Artur said. "Feel free to be insulted."

Diamond-hard, her eyes glittered with a cutting light. "Be careful what you say to me, Mr. Loginov. I could have the doctor turn you into a woman."

"What a waste that would be," he replied.

Her gaze wandered down Artur's body to the area between his legs, hidden by the clothing. "Yes," she said. "A waste."

Artur smiled. "It must be difficult, not being able to touch something you want."

"You would like that, wouldn't you? To have me touch you. To have me soak my secrets into your skin."

"The thought holds some attraction for me," Artur said, though truly the idea made him want to cringe. Information, however, was key in this place: the motives and dreams of the captors. So much unknown, beyond imagining . . .

But imagination is one step removed from reality. And every little fact about this place will lead me closer to the truth.

The truth was the only thing that would give him enough power to fight. This was a place steeped in lies—lies for the sake of lying—lies to break the mind and heart. Artur would not suffer any more of it.

Graves said, "Perhaps I can arrange another kind of touching, Mr. Loginov. Since you seem so . . . eager."

She walked to the door and opened it. The doctor stood just outside, holding a stainless steel pan with a pair of tongs hanging off the edge. Artur wondered how long he had been waiting there. He wore an expression that reminded Artur of a little boy afraid of causing trouble with his mother. It was amusing to see: the pitiless old man, trying to stifle his unease. A Mengele, chained.

There were two other men behind him; one had blood spatters on his white pant leg. They entered the room with the doctor. No one spoke; the men began pulling electrodes and wires from a small panel set in the MRI machine. They applied the sensors to Artur's chest. The glue felt cold. They wore latex gloves, which kept him from absorbing anything beyond shallow surface memories—fleeting, available only because they had touched the gloves to put them on. They still had cheetahs on their minds.

"Your heart rate is going to be important," said the doctor. "We don't want you to have an attack and die."

"Not yet, anyway," said Ms. Graves.

Not until you get what you want. Not until you discover everything I know. Not until you make me say yes.

"Are you ready?" Graves asked the doctor.

"Quite." He still held the metal tray. Artur could not see what lay inside it. The doctor gestured for the men to leave the room. When they were gone, the door shut behind them, the old man picked up the tongs.

He pulled out a rag. A red rag, stiff with old blood. He moved close to Artur, peered down into his eyes, and said, "Watch your tongue, dear boy. Be careful not to bite it off."

The doctor dropped the rag on Artur's chest—on his chest—on—

Water. Calm blue water, floating like a ghost in the sea.

And then a brush against his leg, like a feather. Another, another, and below him the sight of something large and dark and—*oh, my God*—a fin, striking sun, striking—pain—hot, a cloud of red streaming like wet smoke in the water, and oh, the fear, that stinking, shit-loosening fear, as—*Ken*—lost control of his bowels as he lost his legs, the—*crunch, snap, dangle of bone reverberating*—as he got dragged like a doll, pulled below a cold ocean wave, swallowing water as he screamed—*endless*—

Artur died for a very long time.

Chapter Seven

After Rictor returned Elena to her cell, she sat down on the foam mattress, leaned against the wall with her legs outstretched before her, and thought about death. Her own possible death. Artur's near death. Rictor's promised death. She thought about the Quiet Man, who reminded her of death. Death walking, with a smile.

She thought about her mother. Her mother's face: a specific face, at a specific moment, wearing an expression that still pained Elena. A pale face, drawn and hard, with years of rough living carving the youth from Ronnie Baxter's hollow cheeks.

"Bad girl," she had said, all those years ago. "God, you are such a freak. Put the rabbit down."

A tiny rabbit, just a baby, a sweet little thing. The orange tabby had torn its stomach into ribbons. Dying, bleeding, going into shock—and Elena did not care if it was against the rules, that her mother thought it dirty and wrong. She had to help. She had to do *something*.

And her mother had watched. Looking at her face was like seeing death in motion, as though Elena were the embodiment of a zombie's kiss: horrific, strange—*I knew you were a freak even in my womb*—and Elena would never forget how her mother's gaze darted to the ax leaning against the woodpile—*it is in her hands*—how her grandfather came running out of the house to stand between Elena and her mother—and her mother, turning away, turning, sunlight glinting off steel. . . .

I still love you, Elena thought. Or at least, she thought it was love. It had been a long time since she had contemplated the emotions attached to the memories of her mother, whom she had not seen in almost two decades. Perhaps the current circumstances made Elena more sympathetic. Willing to forgive. Maybe desperate. It was easy to come to terms with the bad times when she might be close to losing her life.

Elena fell asleep thinking of her mother. She did not want to sleep, but her body was exhausted. She could not keep her eyes open. Fighting for consciousness, jerking awake after scant seconds, made her sick.

Mommy, she thought. *Lay me down. Take me someplace safe.*

Elena dreamed. She dreamed she was back on the farm in her sunny kitchen with its bright blue cabinets and cracked green walls, old linoleum peeling up at the corners. The radio played a fast song from the eighties, and she smelled lasagna in the oven. Warm, sweet, homey goodness.

Artur sat at the table. He was still naked. He did not look well.

It did not matter that it was only a dream. Elena sat across from him. Reached out and touched his hand. "What's wrong?"

He stared at their joined hands. A fine tremor ran through his body. "They are torturing me. I must have fallen unconscious."

Elena said nothing. She knew it could not be real, but his voice was so solemn and quiet, the shadows gathered thick beneath his dark eyes. Her dream Artur looked like a hurting man, and she could not imagine why her mind would be so cruel to someone she barely knew.

"This does not feel like a dream," Artur said, as though he could read her thoughts. He turned his hand so that their palms nested together, holding warmth. "I can sense you, Elena."

"Cool," she said, without having any idea what he was talking about. "Don't get too excited. This is *my* dream."

"Of course." He did not look terribly convinced. "And why do you suppose *I* am in *your* dream?"

"Because I think you're hot."

"Really." He looked amused. "Hot?"

Elena pushed her finger against the table and made a hissing sound. "Sizzling. Smokin'. Top dog of the pile."

"Thank you," he said. "I feel better already."

Elena laughed. She liked this dream. She pulled her hand away—surprisingly difficult, as though their palms were glued together—and stood. Walked to the oven. Got some hot pads and took the lasagna out. She needed a decent meal, even if it were all in her head. Good dreams meant simple pleasures.

"You hungry?" she asked Artur. When he did not say anything, she turned around. Stifled a gasp. He was already beside her, quick as thought, a shocking presence. He felt very tall and very warm and he smelled very good. The red-checked tablecloth looked nice around his lean waist. Little white ducks appeared from the air and waddled around their feet, singing backup to a radio version of "Ain't No Mountain High Enough." Elena found herself humming along with them. For once she was not tone-deaf.

Artur said, "I am worried about you, Elena."

Elena said, "You should be more concerned about yourself."

He shook his head. "They know the worm is gone. So far they seem to be blaming only me, but that could be a trick. If they find out you saved my life, that you destroyed their trap, they might come for you next."

"They already have me," Elena said. "They can't do much more than that."

He touched her shoulders; she felt the heat of his hands sink through her clothing into skin; hot like his urgency, the insistence of his dark gaze. "They can *hurt* you, Elena. They can hurt you like they are hurting me. Please, you must listen."

"This is just a dream," she said, but she touched his chest and felt her spirit sink through his imaginary flesh, deep and . . .

She felt pain.

"Artur," she said, struggling to breathe.

"Do not," he said. "No, Elena. It is hurting you."

But she could not stop. She flowed into the lee of his body, maximizing the contact, pushing hard until she found his shining mind. No fissures, but parts of it burned red: hateful, angry. Not his emotions, but from some exterior source. She could not block it. Could not ease the suffering.

"Your head." Her hands slid up his chest to his face and neck. "What are they doing to you?"

"I am not in pain. I am unconscious. Dreaming. Remember?"

"No," she breathed. "This is *not* just a dream."

Artur gathered her tight against him. Flesh was not as close as the spirit; Elena felt herself slide sweetly into his soul, perfect, like coming home. Her heart stopped hurting. That ache, which had so quickly become a part of her soul, dissipated like the worm, the edge of a bad dream.

"I wish it were a dream," Artur murmured. "Oh, Elena."

"I'm so sorry," she whispered, caressing his mind with her spirit. "I can't fix this. Nothing is broken. Nothing . . . permanent."

"It is all right, Elena."

"No, it's *not*. How are they doing this to you?"

"I am unable to touch anything or anyone without hearing its story. Some are . . . worse than others."

Elena pulled back just far enough to look into his eyes. A little distance meant nothing; a part of her still rested inside his body, and unlike their first meeting—that first healing—there was still enough of Elena rooted inside her own flesh to avoid losing herself. Like a rope around her waist, strong and singing with tension.

I am safe, she thought.

Yes, Artur said a moment later. *For now, with me. You are safe. I will not allow you to lose yourself.*

"And what about you?" she asked, disturbed by the intimacy of speaking mind-to-mind. "How do you keep from losing yourself? Because that's what happened, isn't it? You almost lost yourself. Your brain almost died because they took all your protection—your clothes. Made you feel too much."

"I have endured more than I was given," Artur said. "But I was weak. The worm. My age. I do not believe men like me are meant to live a long time."

"But I fixed it. I healed the cracks in your head."

"You did. You saved my life." Artur reached out to touch her cheek. His hand felt good. She leaned into his palm, and after a moment he drew her back into the circle of his arms. Elena pressed against his body and looked down. The ducks were still grooving. Jackie Wilson, this time. Love was lifting them higher. Literally.

"Are these ducks yours?" Elena asked Artur. She watched them swim through the air of her kitchen, bobbing their heads in unison, singing high.

"Ah, no." Artur stared at them. "At least, I do not think so."

"Oh. I guess part of this really is a dream." A thought came to her, a realization. She stepped out of his embrace. "When you touched my hand—here, now, in this dream—you said you could sense me. Earlier, when I healed you, I was all over your body. Did you . . ." Elena had to stop, swallow hard. "What did you see?"

His gaze became so very solemn that at first she felt afraid. But then he reached out and cupped her face in his large warm hands, and said, "I saw a good woman. A good heart. Which is rarer than you know. You have nothing to hide from me, Elena Baxter."

"I'm not sure there's anything I *can* hide from you," she said, but did not pull away from him again. The idea of this man being able to see into her life was unsettling, but no more so than anything else she had encountered in the past few days. At the very least, Artur did not want to kill her.

"I would never hurt you," he said.

Elena briefly shut her eyes. "I would really appreciate it if people stopped reading my mind."

"I am sorry. We are still . . . touching."

Elena frowned. "We're not really touching. I mean, I can accept that the two of us are communicating via our unconscious minds—however impossible that feels—but that's *not* the same as being physical." Even if it felt like it.

Artur shrugged. "I also do not understand it, but I

think the link must begin in our spirits. We connected on a very . . . deep level when you healed me. Very deep."

"Groovy." Elena glanced around the kitchen. The ducks had moved on to Huey Lewis and were flashing their feathers at each other. "We need to escape this place, Artur. And I'm not talking about the dream."

"It will not be easy. I have learned some things about the facility, but not enough."

"Well, when you figure it out, let me know."

"Of course." Artur wrapped both arms around Elena, his touch sliding up, up, past her waist, over her shoulder blades, until again he cradled her face in his hands. Elena's breath caught. Really, she should tell him to stop touching her. Really, there was no reason in the world he should think to get away with that kind of behavior, but . . .

"Are you sure this is not real?" he murmured, close. "Truly? Maybe our bodies are together. Maybe we slipped away."

"The mind plays tricks," she whispered, and touched his mouth lightly, with her fingertips. Artur closed his eyes. The ducks stopped singing. The radio switched off. Perfect silence.

He kissed her fingers. Elena swallowed hard. This was a *really* good dream. Or not-dream. Whatever. It was good.

The ducks suddenly quacked—an ugly, flat sound that was definitely not eighties rock—and then scattered in a feathered flurry. The sunlight pouring through the kitchen window faded to gray. Elena heard footsteps, echoing hard and ominous.

"Elena," said Artur. He looked concerned.

"Someone's coming," she whispered. "Don't let go."

He tried. Even though it was just a dream, a shared

fantasy between two minds, she felt his strong, hard arms press around her body, holding her close. It was not enough. Elena woke up, breathing hard, terrified. She lay still for one long moment, trying to calm herself. White walls, cold and sterile, glared at her. Elena tried to remember sunlight and color and music. She tried to hold on to Artur, to find him again. Her heart did not ache, which meant something to her, though she did not know exactly what.

The door to Elena's cell opened. The Quiet Man entered.

Holy shit. I am in deep trouble.

The Quiet Man appeared normal enough; he was a standard white male, with an easygoing face. His cold green eyes marked him as something else: a nut, a dangerous man. It did not matter to Elena either way. Her soul screamed when she looked at him. He could resemble Gandhi and she would still feel the same.

"Hello," said the Quiet Man. He shut the door. Never took his gaze from her.

"Hello." Elena stood up. "This is a surprise."

"I had some time to spare. I've been thinking of you."

"Oh?" Her heart slammed against her ribs; she felt breathless.

Calm down. If he lays one hand on you, kill him. Eat his face off. Flush his balls.

The Quiet Man said, "You remind me of someone."

"Who would that be?" *No panic. Fight mode. Fight.*

"A woman, of course." So still, so quiet, his gaze so disturbing. "Until I saw you in the hall, I had not thought of her in a very long time. I needed the reminder. Better days, you know. Free days." He tilted his head. "I bet you're hungry for some freedom right about now. Some word of the outside. I could sit here for a while and keep you company. You must be very lonely."

"No." Sweat trickled down her ribs. "I am quite fine, thank you."

"Such manners. Remarkable. I noticed your beauty first, that singular resemblance, but I must admit that it is your composure I am most impressed with. Truly. You do not know how rare it is for me to encounter someone in this place who behaves so well."

"Do you encounter many?" Elena asked, forcing herself to engage him. It was difficult to think straight with the Quiet Man standing so near, in such a confined space; she had not realized how the presence of Rictor and the Russian had softened her terrible fear of him. What an inexcusable time to discover weakness.

"No one like you." The Quiet Man did not move; his perfect stillness was eerie, unnatural. Much like the silence that followed. Elena expected him to talk, but instead he stared—stared with the same intensity that had marked their previous, albeit short-lived encounter. Elena refused to turn from his gaze, swallowing down her discomfort, the horrible sense of oppression that accompanied his quiet eyes.

"Taken your fill yet?" Elena asked, when still he did not speak. She could not stand much more of his inaction, his deadly silence.

He smiled. "Not yet, Elena. It will take some time to understand you. To learn what makes you tick. But time, thankfully, is something we both have."

"I'm really not that complicated."

"Oh, no. You are so strong, Elena. You know what I am. I can see it in your face. *You know what I am*, and yet you do not look away."

Elena did not know how to respond. He said, "Good. That is good, Elena. Strength is its own currency in this place. Power, too. You have both. The only thing left to measure is your resolve."

"My resolve is fine," she said.

"We'll see," said the Quiet Man. He moved.

It was not a surprise—Elena had some warning—but he was fast and strong and he grabbed her by the ear, wrenching it so hard she lost her balance. Even as Elena fell, she lashed out with her hands. A blind strike, but true: She caught an eye, his bottom lip. Dug her jagged nails into wet flesh and yanked hard. The Quiet Man grunted; he slammed his fist into her shoulder. Elena refused to let go. He put his hands around her neck. She saw her reflection in his eyes, her face so bright and pale she could not see the color of his gaze, and then she could not breathe—could not draw air to live—and there was nothing in his face but calculation, measurement, and she knew he could choke her until the brink of death and then bring her back, again and again, like a necromancer playing a game of life—so sure, so confident, looking at her as though he had already won and that the strength he bragged upon for her sake was nothing, just a toy with words, just another weak woman—pliant in his deadly hands—and she refused to be that woman. She refused to die.

She entered his body. It was not difficult. He had barriers, but she had strength and anger and desperate desire, and his resistance lasted only seconds. She entered his body and it was like breathing to her, like the breathing she was not capable of, and she thought, *I could heal you; I could kill you—the two are so very much alike*, and she went looking for his heart, for that precious muscle. She found it. Wrapped her spirit tight around the pulse, the beat, and squeezed.

The Quiet Man's eyes widened. He gasped. Let go of Elena's neck and kicked her away. The link between them died. Elena hit the floor hard, gasping for breath, gagging on air. The Quiet Man clutched his chest.

"You tried to kill me," he whispered. "I felt you try to kill me."

"All's fair," Elena spit, still on her hands and knees. "Touch me again and I'll finish the job."

She heard something outside the hall: the hard pounding of feet. The door slammed open. Rictor. A sheen of sweat covered his dark forehead.

"Boo," said the Quiet Man, still holding his chest. His face was pale, his lips almost ashen. Elena wanted to laugh, but felt too sick. She could not sit up. Her throat ached.

Rictor stepped into the room. There was nothing different about his appearance, but Elena sensed a change, some subtle charge within his eyes, the slant of his hard mouth. He glanced at Elena. His jaw flexed.

"This is the second time you've broken the rules, Charles." Rictor's eyes glinted bright. "You did not fucking learn your lesson."

The Quiet Man straightened, his hand falling to rest against his side. His body quaked. Elena would bet he needed to lie down, too. "I'm not myself, Rictor. She does things to me."

"I can see that," Rictor said. "She almost killed you. Maybe you should have let her. When *l'araignée* finds out"

"*L'araignée* will do nothing, Rictor. She needs me."

"She does not need you more than Elena." Rictor bared his teeth. "Temptation. I always knew you wouldn't stay leashed. The black thread grows tiresome, doesn't it?"

The Quiet Man looked at Elena. Rictor stepped in front of him.

"Don't look at her," he said, low. "Don't think of her."

The Quiet Man bared his teeth. "You cannot control a man's thoughts, Rictor. That is the last realm of his dignity, his sole and most perfect possession. Even you cannot touch that."

"Are you sure?" Rictor whispered. Elena thought his eyes glowed. "Be careful, Charles. You don't know all my tricks."

The Quiet Man hesitated. "You are still caught in the same web. *L'araignée's* black thread may not hold you, but it is the same for us both. She has our souls."

Rictor said nothing. A moment later the Quiet Man winced. He touched his temple.

"Get out of here," Rictor said. "Stay out."

The Quiet Man said nothing. Elena did not think he looked especially cowed, but he did avert his eyes as he stood. Elena watched his face, the terrible nature of its ordinariness, and felt more afraid than she had before.

I'll be a challenge to him now. This isn't a man who gives up.

The Quiet Man left. When the door closed behind him, Elena waited a moment and said, "Is he really gone?" She glanced at the two-way mirror. Rictor nodded. Elena lay down on the floor and sprawled out on her back. She stared at the ceiling. Weakness be damned. It did not mean jack shit to pretend courage, not after that. Her heart pounded; her head and throat hurt. She felt sick to her stomach. It was the end of the adrenaline rush.

Rictor crouched beside her. "Maybe you should put your head between your knees."

Elena squeezed her eyes shut. She was going to vomit, she was going vomit, she was—

Rictor dragged her to the toilet just in time. She hurled. Nothing but bile came up, but that was ugly enough. Face red, eyes watery, Elena slumped back down on the floor.

"I hate this," she said. *"I hate this."*

"Tell me what happened."

Elena tapped her head. "Don't you already know?"

His mouth tightened. "This is for your benefit, Elena. It will help you."

"What would really help me is getting out of here, Rictor. Think you can do something about that?"

He said nothing. Elena sighed. "I almost killed him. Committed murder. I never, ever thought about using my gift in that way, but for just one moment—one—it seemed like the most natural thing in the world."

"Of course it did." His voice was quiet, calm. "You can't get much more natural than the desire to live."

"It shouldn't have happened," Elena said. "What kind of zoo are you running here?"

"The kind that keeps men like Charles Darling as pets." Rictor stood. He held out his hand to Elena, but she did not take it. She stood on her own. It was not easy or pretty. She gingerly touched her neck.

"Who is he? And how could anyone keep that man as a pet?"

"Charles is a serial killer," Rictor said—simple, easy, like the name of a recipe for fancy breads: homicide wheat supreme or psycho banana walnut. Nice and warm. "He likes women, but he'll do either gender if the timing and circumstances are right. You look exactly like his first kill."

Elena stared at him. "And you're telling me this *now?*"

"I didn't want to alarm you. I knew Charles was interested, but I thought he would have enough sense to stay away."

"Because of that . . . that *l'ara*-what's-her-name?"

"Yes." One word, tense. Elena waited. He said nothing more. Stood there as though silence were the only friend he had.

Unacceptable. Elena was through with the scraps, riddles. She wanted answers. After what she had just experienced—the line she had almost crossed—she wanted them so badly she was ready to get down and fight all over again.

She stepped near. "Rictor. Who is she?"

He moved away, but Elena stayed close, pushing him with nothing more than her gaze. "No," she said. "You tell me. Who is this woman, and why am I more important to her than the Quiet Man?"

"She is coming here today to meet you," he said. "Soon, in fact. You'll see for yourself why she wants you."

He sounded like a man proclaiming a death sentence. Elena could not read his expression; he was trying to pull off "bored," but he was not quite detached enough to do it. She saw the fear in his gaze, the sliver of anger—at her or this *l'araignée*, she could not tell.

"Wait," she said. "*L'araignée* . . . what does that mean?"

"Spider," Rictor said, and his voice was dull. "It means spider. The spider with her black thread. Her black *worm*."

Elena stared at him. "The woman who put that *thing* into Artur's psyche is coming here to see me?"

Rictor's jaw flexed. "Do you remember what I said about being strong in the head, Elena? Do you remember what I told you?"

She nodded, unable to speak. The expression on his face terrified her.

"Good," he said. "Because she is almost ready for you."

Artur opened his eyes in the real world, the hard white world of the facility. Graves was the first person he saw.

The rag was gone. Sweat rolled off his scalp, his body, soaking his clothing. His throat ached. Screaming—he had been screaming.

And not just because of the rag and the death it held. *Elena*, he thought, reaching out to her. He could still feel her presence inside his heart—not just the thought of her, but an actual presence. It did not matter; he could not find her. He could not see the outcome of her terrible battle with Charles Darling.

The connection between them had been so strong that when Elena was pulled away, a piece of Artur went with her: the seeing part of his mind, a sliver of consciousness. A vision without the physical, which should have been impossible, but his powers were of the mind, were they not? And there were so many different kinds of touch. Touch of skin, touch of thought, touch of spirit.

He saw. He saw Charles enter her room. Saw and heard and could do nothing to help her. Screaming as if it were the end of his life, raging, fighting in his ghost prison as Charles wrapped his hands around her throat and squeezed.

And then . . . nothing. Here, now, Graves gazing down at his face with a puzzled frown.

"Your mind went somewhere," she said.

Artur could not speak. He fought to control his breathing. Graves traced the air just above the crown of his sweat-plastered hair.

"What secrets sleep?" she murmured. "Such complex emotions, Mr. Loginov. Your heart just spins on a dime, from calm to anxiety to fear to courage. It is all I can do just to keep up with the emotions you throw at me."

"It is his brain," said the doctor, who stood on the far side of the room with a clipboard and pen in his hands.

"Every time Mr. Loginov has a vision, he toes the line of madness. It's no wonder he has mood swings."

Graves quirked her lips. "I think you're falling into oversimplification, Doctor, but that's all right. Sometimes complex men need a little simplicity in their lives." She leaned close to Artur, her gray eyes as cold as her name. "But you and I need to talk now."

Artur ignored her. Marilyn sobbed. Poor dead Marilyn. If the same happened to Elena . . .

"Mr. Loginov."

"No," he spit. He remembered the mold-slick basement that smelled of blood; the woman who had died there still lived with him, begging for peace. And now her killer had his hands wrapped around another woman's throat and he could do nothing. Nothing but hope and pray. "No, Ms. Graves. I will not divulge the secrets of my agency. Keep hurting me if you like, but *you have lost me.*"

Her mouth turned down; an ugly mouth, gray and hard. "There goes that mood swing. You certainly are fickle." She glanced over her shoulder at the doctor, who watched them both with undisguised interest. "I think you have another appointment to go to, Doctor. You don't want to be late."

Disappointment flickered over the old man's face, but he nodded and left the room. When he was gone, Graves found a chair and pulled it close to the table, sat down, and crossed her legs. Artur did not see a gun, but he was sure she was armed.

Graves said, "I should have killed you."

"You still could."

"No," she said. "It's too late. You're a challenge now. I don't need a challenge, but with you, I cannot seem to help myself."

"You must live a very sad life if torturing me is the only thing that brings you excitement."

She laughed. "Oh, Mr. Loginov. The things we have in store for you. You are telling yourself it cannot get worse. You are thinking there is nothing more terrible than what I just made you endure. You are thinking you can buy enough time, learn enough secrets, to help you escape. Poor man. You are so very wrong."

"Why are you doing this?" he asked. "It will not make me join your Consortium or betray my friends. You will not learn anything of great scientific value from these . . . tests. You are merely acting as a sadist."

"Of course," said Graves, as though it were the most natural thing in the world. "It is a question of power, Mr. Loginov. Mine, at the moment, is greater than yours."

"Power," Artur scoffed. "Your power is an illusion. You crave it like a drug, but it is meaningless. You do these things because you need to be perceived as something more than what you are. A fatal weakness in your ego. It is very . . . sad."

She almost killed him. He saw it in her eyes, that lethal sweep of gray. "I think you want to die. I think you want a clean, quick end, something sweet and merciless. That is the only reason anyone would act so stupid." She leaned close. "I am not going to give it to you."

Which was what Artur had counted on. It was nice knowing he could insult someone without repercussion. Or at least, a repercussion he did not already expect.

Someone knocked on the door. The man with the bloodstained pants peered into the room. His face was very pale.

"She's in the facility," he said.

Graves's demeanor completely changed. Her shoulders relaxed; a deep breath escaped her body. She looked down at Artur, and her smile, loose and genuine, made his skin crawl.

"Lovely," Graves said. "Is she coming here now, or going to her other project?"

"Here," he said, and looked ready to run. The man glanced down the hall behind him. Artur heard wheels.

Graves walked to the door and pulled it all the way open. The man stumbled back from her; she gave him a hard look and he turned and walked quickly away. Escape, escape—Artur did not blame him.

She walked into the hall. Artur listened to the wheels, and as he did a memory from Charles Darling surfaced—a face framed by blond curls—and he knew, he knew what was coming, the spider creeping down her black thread web. . . .

Graves stepped aside as a diminutive figure in a wheelchair rolled into the doorway. Artur did not need to touch her. He knew the truth when she entered the room and stopped, staring at him with black, pitiless eyes that were unnatural, strange—full obsidian bleeding into white, until all Artur saw when he looked into her face was a deep, abiding darkness that sucked at the edges of his mind.

He barely noticed the rest of her: the thin body set in a gleaming wheelchair, the black suit with diamond glinting in the buttons. She was not young, but she was not old, either. She was timeless.

"Mr. Loginov," Graves said softly. "Please meet my associate, Ms. Beatrix Weave."

"I believe we have already met," Artur said.

Ms. Weave smiled.

Chapter Eight

Endless and undying.

"Leave us," said Ms. Weave. Graves said nothing; she backed away like the perfect sycophant, and it was clear to Artur that despite Graves's appearance of power, she was just another tool, a means to an end. Ultimately inconsequential to the woman in the wheelchair.

As Graves shut the door, she met Artur's gaze. There was no triumph in her eyes—just calm certainty, as though the end had already come, the outcome of his life decided. Artur felt as though it was Graves who should be careful. In organizations like this, outliving usefulness was one of the highest causes of mortality among otherwise fine, upstanding individuals. Artur had no such illusions about himself.

Silence rested heavy. Artur, strapped naked to the table with those dark clothes still jumbled in his lap, listened to Ms. Weave breathe. Listened, too, for Elena. Marilyn wept.

Ms. Weave studied him. Artur could not look away from her inhuman eyes. When she smiled it was ghastly because it was beautiful, breathtaking, the most perfect horror, and when she spoke her voice rasped like a dozen dull chimes. "I thought I would make the first foray with you. I can see now that was a mistake. Your mind is too strong, the safeguards around your secrets built too well. I commend its maker, whoever he is." Her accent was faint, but distinctly French.

Artur breathed deep; he smelled lilacs. His throat still hurt. "You are the boss, the leader of this Consortium, yes?"

"I am."

"Then I ask you, why? Why go to all this trouble? If you wanted to know us, you could simply have knocked on our doors. Talked. Asked questions. We might have answered them all."

"And received the same information we already have. Names, addresses, histories, public records documenting the cases your agency has solved—the ones people actually know about. No. That would be a waste of time, and besides, there are barriers to that, as well. The situation is complex, Mr. Loginov. Far more complex than anyone knows, including Ms. Graves."

"Our different philosophies, perhaps." Artur felt chilled. "We help others. It is clear you help only yourselves."

Her teeth flashed—bright like the gems in her buttons, cold and hard and sharp. "Aren't those two the same? Help one, help the other, help goes all around? Good tidings into good karma? I do not think you know me well enough to condemn what I do with my energies, Mr. Loginov."

"I know you keep a serial killer as a pet. I know you let him loose to play. I know you are not above a little pain and torture. Tell me, Ms. Weave, if that is not an excellent indicator of one's . . . energy."

She shrugged, graceful. "My focus is different, as are my goals. Each of us must accomplish our tasks in different ways. Mine, I suppose, are unique—but not terribly so. In fact, I would guess that our two organizations have quite a lot in common."

"No," Artur said. "That is—"

"Impossible?" She smiled. "Did Nancy Dirk ever explain why she and her husband created their agency?"

Her interruption, her question, left him silent, stunned. He said nothing, and she nodded. "Of course she never explained. No one on our side ever explained either. It was just the way. Old history. I don't know why I expected anything different. You're not even family. Perhaps I should have been bolder. Risked it all and gone for her grandchildren, Max and Dela."

Artur swallowed hard. "You talk as though you have known of us for much longer than just a year."

"Oh," she said. "A lifetime at the very least."

Ms. Weave pushed a switch on the armrest of her wheelchair and rolled so close that her arm rubbed up against the table. Artur struggled for calm, strength, as her hand slowly flexed toward his exposed wrist. She had only enough movement left in her body for that one motion.

"I am going to touch you," she said. "Are you ready, Mr. Loginov? I am going to try something a little different, but it will not be gentle."

"I know that," Artur said. "I do not believe you are a woman who cares for gentle touches."

"Too true," she whispered, and her pinkie grazed his skin.

It was like drowning in hot tar. All he saw inside his head was a thick darkness that glistened wet, coating his brain, latching onto his surface thoughts with greasy abandon. He could not think. He could not fight. His lungs worked, but that did not matter; she stole the oxygen from his brain, snuffing him out, thought by thought. He felt a sharp pain at the base of his skull, digging, and he tried to scream—

You must breathe, she said as she suffocated his mind. *If you want to breathe, you will let me in.*

Artur glimpsed a vision of himself, resting on the bed of the red room, with this woman's hand on his temple, birthing a worm to steal the secrets from his head. The house was distant; it was her home, it was her—

Stop, she said.

No, he said. *Get out.*

She tightened her hold upon his mind, plunging deeper, and for the first time since joining the agency, Artur felt keenly aware of Roland's barrier, the fail-safe, the black wall he had put inside Artur's head, which kept secret every memory pertaining to Dirk & Steele. He could not imagine what Ms. Weave wanted; it seemed to him she already had everything she needed, and more—more than even Artur knew.

But if she could not get Artur's permission to enter, it appeared she was going to take him by force—drown him, weaken him, kill him—thread him into her web, the spider with her hands in his head. He tried to fight, to break through the darkness tarring his mind, but she was too strong. She fought him down, and all he could do was struggle, crying out—crying with his heart. . . .

A heart that held a presence, burning bright and clean. Elena. Sweet Elena.

The darkness coating his mind shattered. Ms. Weave cried out, and visions flooded him: three old women sitting around a long conference table in a high-rise, saying—*No, no, it is wrong, you cannot*—and—*There is a covenant, my dear, a trust we cannot break*—*Sisters, blood, you must understand what we have promised*—and then a dark room with snow falling beyond a tall window, and Ms. Weave, Beatrix, staring at her hands, her naked legs, at the naked man tied to the floor at her feet, a young man with brown hair and cold green eyes—*Charles Darling, I think I want you for my own*—and then another man, dark-skinned, kneeling in a circle of sand, green eyes glowing—*another prize, another*—darkness, absolute, words said wrong, and—*I am just like my great-grandfather*—just like—*magic*—him—*the stories are true*—immortal—*daughters, so many daughters, so much power lost*—so much power to gain, so much—*the Russians will help us; we almost have the syndicates now, and after them the Japanese, the Yakuza, and after that*—

Ms. Weave gasped, her hand flexing away from him. Her eyes were large, black all the way through, like those of an animal.

"Impossible," she murmured. "You had help."

Artur said nothing. He stamped down all his thoughts of Elena, all his joy that she was alive and still with him, still fighting—

"No," said Ms. Weave. "I thought I felt someone the first time you broke the link, but it did not make sense. The girl does not have that kind of gift."

Ms. Weave stopped rubbing her hand. She leaned close—so close Artur saw his face mirrored in the dark cradle of her impossible eyes. "I do not make the same mistakes twice, Mr. Loginov." She paused, studying his face. "My sources were told you shake the hand of every person you are about to do business with. Skin-to-skin. You do it to keep yourself safe. Tell me, Mr. Loginov, did you ever shake Nancy Dirk's hand?"

"No," he lied. "She would not let me."

Her expression never changed; Artur could not tell if she recognized his deceit. Her wheelchair whirred backward. "I will make you mine," she said quietly. "No one has ever escaped me."

"The black thread," he said.

"My precious thread," she said. "My special weave. My little web." She shook her head. "I enjoyed my brief time inside you. Your nightmares are so very sweet. Better, almost, than Mr. Darling's. I am quite sorry for the loss."

He could not help himself. "You cannot possibly be human."

"Oh." She smiled, her teeth glittering. Some of them looked sharper than he remembered. "I was human once. But that was a long time ago."

Artur's breath caught. Ms. Weave tilted her head.

"I will have some men come and dress you, take you to a room so you can rest. We will be speaking again very soon, Mr. Loginov. But first, I think, I need to have a conversation with the girl who is living inside your heart."

Rictor escorted Elena to her next appointment with the doctor. He looked tired. Elena tried not to feel overly concerned for him. She had given him some trust—which was crazy enough, considering the situation—but anything else would just be stupid. He was the enemy. Sort of.

"Yes," Rictor said. "You shouldn't trust me. I'm not safe."

"I believe you," Elena said. "That doesn't mean you're a bad person."

He stopped walking and stared at her.

"Okay," she said. "You're bad."

He started walking again. He looked troubled. "I should never have let it go this far."

"We already had this conversation. If you think I should be afraid—"

"No. I was referring to something different."

"Like what?"

When he remained silent—uncomfortably so—Elena said, "Does this have anything to do with Stockholm syndrome? Because that is *so* not happening. I'm just not into that whole captive-woman, strong-virile-captor, power-imbalanced love thing."

"Excuse me? Elena, I . . ." He seemed genuinely startled. "Did you just call me virile?"

"Never mind," she snapped, flushing red. "What were you trying to say?"

He still stared. "Nothing. Forget it."

Of course. She wanted to hit him.

"You're not strong enough to hurt me," he said.

"You want me to give it a shot?" After dealing with Charles Darling, she could handle anything. Red Sonja could kiss her ass.

Rictor ignored her. They arrived at the lab—the same room that Elena had been wheeled into that first day. The doctor was there, and on the table behind him she saw part of a man. For a moment she thought it was Artur and she almost made a sound—a gasp, a sigh—but she swallowed it down and tried to calm her racing heart.

Artur. She called out to him, remembering those dark eyes, his gentle touch. *Artur, please be all right.*

"Don't worry," Rictor murmured. "It's not him."

"Thank you," she breathed.

"No," he said, just as quiet. "Don't."

Closer, she saw the figure was elderly, a wrinkled, white-haired gentleman with skinny legs and a slack, bristled face. He was not tied down. His body was more machine than flesh: wires poked from his pale, blue-veined arms. Electrodes covered his chest. His breathing was shallow. Elena did not have to touch him to know he was not long for the world.

"You're a psychopath," she told the doctor. She was appalled, and yet grateful—horribly thankful—that the person resting before her was not a child. She suspected the doctor was that cold. He had studied her, knew her history, her weaknesses.

"No, my dear," he said. "The psychopath would be Mr. Darling." He gestured at the unconscious man. "What is your diagnosis?"

"Well, he's old."

The doctor frowned. "I was looking for something more . . . in-depth."

Right. Heal first; be a smart-ass later. Her compassion had to be stronger than pride or fear. She could not allow this . . . this Consortium . . . to take that from her. She refused to let them harden her heart. Innocence lost could never be regained.

That's inevitable. If you ever want to escape these people, you're going to have to do some nasty things. Maybe something truly irrevocable.

She had already taken one long step down the hard slope. Murder was a cruel line to cross. A tough line to live with. Even if it was committed against someone like the Quiet Man. Charles Darling.

I could have lived with myself if I had killed him. I wouldn't have lost any sleep. And if he comes at me again, I'll do the same. Feel the same.

Which disturbed her. Not that she should defend herself, but that she could feel so cold about it.

Then again, desperate times meant desperate measures. A little craziness was necessary to survive—and she did mean to come out of this alive and intact. No matter what.

Elena touched the sleeping man's shoulder. His skin was cold. "What's his name?"

The doctor glanced down at his clipboard. "John Burkles."

John. She wondered what in his life had brought him here. Rictor could probably tell her, magical mind-reader that he was. He stood by the door, his body half cast in shadow. She wondered what he would do if she tried to bash the doctor's brains down to his toes. She wondered what he would do if she made the old man cry for his mommy. God. She would make road-kill look pretty in comparison. So much for compassion.

Talk is cheap.

Maybe, but Elena was feeling pretty cheap. Going from talk to action did not seem much of a stretch.

Elena sank deep into the old man's spirit, searching out the root of the decay she sensed within his body. She found it almost immediately. Cancer. A lump within his colon.

More, too . . . there was something wrong with his spine. Her own back hurt when she found it. Sympathy pains for paralysis. The break was recent—his legs had not yet atrophied—but Elena was unsure how to handle his disability. She knew how to fix it, but this was one area she had always stayed away from. The effects of such a healing were so extraordinarily noticeable. Not that it mattered now.

She treated the cancer first. Held herself still and breathed in the image of health, coaxing and cajoling. He responded, as she thought he would. It was a rare man who did not fight for life when given the opportunity to do so.

She moved on to his spine. Nerve regeneration was more difficult, but not impossible; scientists were doing it in rats, restoring spinal cords through a variety of treatments, some of which were electrical in nature. When nerves in the central nervous system were cut, they usually just stopped. Never grew back, like nerves did in other parts of the body. They switched off. At least, that was what all the science magazines and documentaries said. Self-education had its limits.

Elena could turn them back on again. She did not know how; just that she wanted it, visualized it, and the body responded. It was not easy; the task required a soft touch, instinct, but she could do it. She could do it.

And she did. John Burkles's body listened, nerves itching free of their frozen bonds. Elena could make no guarantees, but over time—a long time, perhaps—he would find increased mobility in his legs. If old age did not kill him, he might find himself walking in those last days before the grave.

"It's done," Elena said. It was a struggle to keep her words from slurring. She felt exhausted. She leaned on the table, her knees buckling.

"The cancer is gone?" The doctor's eyes were bright. "He'll be able to walk again?"

"No and maybe. You need to give it time. He's heading into regression as we speak, and I stimulated his nerve fibers to grow. The cancer will disappear in a week or so. Regaining use of his legs will take much longer."

"I was under the impression that your results were more . . . immediate." He sounded put out. Elena glared at him.

"Who do I look like? If you want the tumor to disappear, take it out yourself. If you want him to walk, put strings on his heels and dance him around like a puppet. What I do is a natural process, Doctor. It takes time. He's not dying anymore, though. That should be all that matters."

"We are all dying," said the doctor, making notes on his clipboard. "Unless you know a way of postponing that as well."

"I'm not God," Elena said.

"A gift from, perhaps." The doctor gazed down upon John Burkles's prone body. "When did you first manifest?"

"Manifest?"

"Your gift. Surely you haven't always been able to do this."

"If you say so."

The doctor looked startled—a first. "Are you telling me you've had access to your abilities for your entire life?"

"Well, sure. How could I *not* have access to them?"

"For most individuals it takes a precise amount of biological stress to manifest their latent gifts. Puberty, usually. The same can be said of certain mental illnesses, which are mere genetic predispositions until certain factors combine to create the perfect circumstances for emergence. How remarkable you were not so handicapped."

Yes, very. "You must have studied a lot of people to figure out that much."

"Not nearly enough. That is why you are so important. Telekinesis and telepathy are so mundane, you know. So . . . passé."

"Of course," Elena said. "Because just *everyone* can do them."

"You would be surprised," said the doctor, this time with some sternness. He put down the clipboard. "I have conducted extensive trials all over the world, utilizing a diversity of test subjects. The most common psi-trait is some form of telepathy. A sixth sense. Knowing when a friend or relative is in trouble, prophetic dreams, déjà vu. All quite common." The doctor moved close, studying Elena. "You, on the other hand, defy logic. My first assumption was that you used some kind of combined telepathy and telekinesis, but that, I fear, may be an oversimplification."

"I always knew I was special," Elena said, batting her eyelashes at him. The doctor frowned. So did Rictor.

"Your sense of humor is becoming an annoyance. I do not believe you truly understand the precariousness of your situation."

Elena was too tired to care about tact. "I understand that you kidnapped and imprisoned me. I understand that you're conducting human experiments on myself and others. I understand that you employ deeply disturbed individuals who are just itching to commit murder. Precarious, Doctor? I'm up Shit Creek without a paddle."

For once, the doctor was not offended. He leaned against the examining table, brushing up against John Burkles's body. "Why aren't you a doctor? Why didn't you ever train your gift, turn yourself into something more than just a . . . a faith healer?"

His voice was gentle, almost kind. Elena did not trust it, although his question took her off guard. Being a doctor was an old dream, one that had been impossible to fulfill—which was her fault and no other's. At eighteen she had been unable to cope with the idea of going away to school—was too afraid, too uncertain of her ability to hide her gifts. Excuse after excuse, always postponing, always promising her grandfather.

And then he died. And school, suddenly, did not seem all that important anymore. She was smart. She could educate herself. Who needed a piece of paper to say otherwise? A degree certainly could not keep her from healing.

Her silence dragged on too long. The doctor said, "The Consortium could give you that education, my dear. The finest schools and teachers. Anything and everything, right at your fingertips. You could help so many."

Temptation, the first hook. It was perfect, and the doctor knew it.

"I *was* helping people," Elena said, angry for feeling even a little enticed. "Right up until the moment your Consortium kidnapped me."

The doctor waved his hand; a shooing motion. "You were nothing but a child healing children. Earnest, but utterly misguided. You should not be ashamed of that. You do, however, have a responsibility to improve yourself and not waste this great blessing you have been given. Really, my dear. Who do you think you are?"

The hypocrisy was too much. Elena laughed out loud. "You are so full of it."

Rictor briefly closed his eyes. The doctor did not notice. He was too busy staring at Elena. She held her ground, unrepentant and defiant. It was difficult; the old man's expression flickered to pity. Brief, no more than a ghost. Impossible, a figment of her imagination. This man was not capable of compassion.

"I was offering you a way out of this place," said the doctor. "Isn't your freedom worth a little compromise?"

"Not when the deal is with the devil," she said, refusing to go along with him, to pretend acceptance. That would be the smart thing to do. Strategic. Earn their trust, and then get the hell out.

A nice concept in theory, but Elena sensed the execution would be quite different. No matter what they promised, nothing could be trusted here. Even if the Consortium did follow through, the doctor and the people he worked for would find some other way of imprisoning her, of keeping her bound to them for the remainder of her life.

No, thanks. Elena knew what slippery slopes looked like, and this one was the holy Montezuma of them all. She wondered if that was how Rictor had lost his soul to the Consortium. Just a little promise, a little carrot on the stick. One step after another, until he had fallen all the way down into hell.

You are the keeper of monsters, Elena thought at him. *What do you think that makes you?*

Rictor ignored her. Elena did not expect anything different. One day of playing captive to his captor had been enough to show her that Rictor had his own game to play. She simply did not understand his motivations. Either way, he was certainly big enough and scary enough to change his circumstances if he really wanted to.

Elena gestured at John. "What's going to happen to him?"

"Why, he'll be released back into the wild." The doctor's smile was bitter, sharp.

"I suppose the 'wild' is where you found him."

"You could say that. The desperate are quite willing to subject themselves to anything, for a price. John and his family believe he is the recipient of a new experimental cancer treatment, courtesy of a particular organization which shall yet go unnamed."

"You have your fingers dipped in everything," she said, gazing down into John's slack face. Cancer, eating him alive. She thought of Olivia. "Just what is it you have planned for me, Doctor? Am I going to be your resource? The experimental therapy of the rich and famous? Elena Baxter, miracle maker?"

"Questions," said the doctor.

"You have a selective distaste for them. All you need

to do is not answer. Unless you have a thing for dishing out really good *spankings*."

Again Rictor closed his eyes. The doctor frowned. "You should contemplate better word choices, my dear. That was not ladylike."

Elena opened her mouth to tell him just how ladylike she really was, but he said, "We have a great deal planned. You have the potential to make huge contributions to the organization—to the world, even. It is very likely that everything we learn from your abilities will completely revolutionize medical science. You are a walking cure for cancer, after all. And imagine, that is just the beginning of what you can do. The possibilities are endless."

"I know my limits," she said, unnerved by the blistering light in his eyes.

"Yes," he said. "But I do not. So we will see just how far beyond those limits a little patience can take us. Time, fortunately, is on my side."

Which was about the same as writing I OWN YOU on her face with a big red marker. Yeah. Life did not get much better than this.

Rictor twitched. The doctor did not seem to notice, but Elena did. Rictor was not the kind of man who made unnecessary movements.

A moment later a sharp pain in Elena's heart doubled her over. She clutched her chest, gasping. The doctor touched her shoulder. Elena did not try to push him away. The pain dragged her deep; she felt as if she were suffocating, dying—except that was not right, her heart had to be fine, she was too young, too healthy, too full of life, and this was not panic . . . this was not . . .

Artur.

She felt him—his spirit stretching out across the same line that had bound their dreams—and she reached back, holding tight, sharing the agony as someone killed him, a slow murder, strangling his mind in the same way the Quiet Man had tried to strangle her body: by sheer unrelenting force, by darkness and a cold, hard will.

Elena plunged through the link, grappling with Artur's spirit, pulling herself across the distance separating them. She left her body completely, breaking the tether—breaking—and it did not matter because he was dying, suffering, and she could not allow that, not even if it meant her life.

Darkness—she entered darkness—wriggling across the surface of Artur's mind like the worm, a glistening sea of shadow, oily and slick. She felt the presence of another, the alien focus of someone strange and horrible, but it was nothing to her fury, and she raised her fists, raised them burning bright, and brought them down hard against the shadow strangling Artur's mind. The darkness broke. Elena heard a woman cry out.

And then she was back in her own body, stretched on the floor with Rictor cradling her head and the doctor standing above them both, ashen-faced.

"Elena," Rictor said. His eyes glowed. "Elena, talk to me. I need to know if you're all there."

"I'm there," she breathed, exhausted. "Or here. Whatever you want me to say."

Rictor briefly closed his eyes. "You did it again, Elena. You complicated matters."

"Story of my life."

The doctor crouched beside them. "What is going on here?"

"A panic attack," Rictor said calmly. "You remember, she had one when she first arrived."

"I've never seen symptoms come on quite this suddenly, though." He frowned, peering into Elena's eyes.

A strange ringing tone suddenly filled the room. Like

a phone, but different. The doctor stood and walked over to a plastic case set in the wall. He flipped it open, revealing an intercom. Pushed down a red button.

"I'm here," he said. He sounded uneasy, and continued to glance over his shoulder at Elena.

"We have a problem down in the tank room," said a woman, breathless. "We did like you asked and brought the African down to see him, but it was too much. The subject went crazy, broke the glass. He refuses to shift, and the weight of his body is crushing him. He's going to die."

"What about the other tank?"

"It hasn't arrived yet. We're pouring water on him manually, but it's not enough." Elena heard glass shatter; something hard crashed down to the ground. A man cried out. "He's fighting us! God . . . he . . . he just managed to impale himself—"

Rictor gazed down into Elena's eyes, and she saw something in his face—something that looked like hope—and he grabbed her arms and hauled her up. It was hard to stand—she felt dizzy, hot—but Rictor's hands tightened on her arms, and he looked at the doctor. "We need her down there. She can save his life."

"It's too early," protested the doctor, his concern striking Elena as unnatural. "She's not ready."

"What is more important?" Rictor tugged on Elena; she staggered against him, but he kept pulling and she got her balance back. The bewildered doctor tried to stop them, but Rictor marched her past and hit the corridor at a run.

"What is going on?" Elena tried to ask, but she was running so hard the words came out in a garbled mush. She grappled with his hand, trying to keep up. Her legs felt weak; she was certain that at any moment she would fall flat on her face.

"I just decided to die a little earlier," he said. "But at this point, one week or two will make no difference at all."

"Rictor."

"I am forbidden to break the rules," he said. *"Forbidden.* But I can bend them. I should have started doing it a long time ago, but I didn't see a reason or an opportunity. I let her make me weak. I let things go too far."

Which made no sense at all, but Elena was willing to roll with whatever he had in mind. She was running too fast to do anything else. Fast, fast—she had never been forced to run so fast in her life—and when Rictor suddenly dug in his heels and staggered to a stop, she ran hard into his shoulder, bounced several steps, and almost fell to her knees. She began to protest—her gut ached; her lungs burned like a dry furnace—but Rictor pulled her backward, silent and quick. Elena did not hear anything behind them, but he whispered, *"L'araignée* is coming for you."

"You told me that would happen."

"But now she's angry."

"Can she sense us?" Elena had no idea what the woman was capable of, but if she could rein in someone like the Quiet Man, anything was possible.

"Only me, but she won't think of tracking my movements. *L'araignée* has perfect faith in my obedience. She hasn't bound you to her yet, so she'll look for you the old-fashioned way. The lab, first. The doctor will tell her there was an accident, but she won't go down to level one herself. She'll send a nurse to find you. That will buy us time."

"Can't she read your mind? With that . . . that worm?"

He gave her a hard look. "She's not controlling me like that. Which is why I am less free than Charles Darling, but have more loopholes than he'll ever dream of seeing."

"Nothing you're saying makes sense, Rictor. Why are you different?"

"Blood," he said, and then made her run. They pounded down the twisting corridors with terrifying abandon. Elena did not know how they could travel so fast without being detected, but Rictor moved with utter confidence. Elena did not share his bravado, but then again, she was no mind reader.

He slowed, finally; Elena heard male voices.

"Pretend," he whispered, and then they turned a corner and came face-to-face with two large men in white. Between them walked Artur.

Tricky bastard, she thought at Rictor. *You planned this.*

Artur was no longer naked. He wore a black jumpsuit that was partially unzipped down his chest. Black gloves covered his hands, which were bound together by plastic restraints. He wore socks. He looked tired, but healthy. Alive. Elena met his gaze and it was like coming home.

"Come on," Rictor said, pulling her slowly past the men. Too slowly. She did not miss the way he tilted his chin at Artur, or how the Russian stared back with narrowed, knowing eyes.

The hall was not that wide. The nurses stepped sideways to accommodate Rictor's passage. For one brief instant Elena felt the men watch her instead of Artur. A stupid mistake.

Elena turned her back; she heard the hard thump of flesh, a startled grunt. She whirled and saw one nurse slumped against the wall, unconscious. The other doubled over as Artur slammed a knee into his groin and then delivered one last kick into his face. The man stopped whimpering. Artur's hands were still bound.

"What took you so long to make your break?" Rictor

moved quickly to the fallen men. Calm, quiet. There was no fear in his voice or face. He had known this would happen—Elena was certain of it. She watched him sling a man over his shoulder. Artur grabbed the other nurse's ankles. Elena helped him.

"I was waiting for her," Artur said, looking at Elena with such intensity her breath caught. "It is good to see you, Elena. I cannot tell you how good."

"Ditto," she said.

"Hurry." Rictor led them a short distance to a green unmarked door. It was unlocked; the inside looked remarkably like a broom closet.

"Yes, Elena. Even evil keeps itself clean." Rictor dumped his man in the corner; Artur and Elena did the same. "There's nothing to tie them up with, but I think they'll stay out for a while. You hit them good." He grabbed Elena's hand, said, "Pretend you're my prisoners if we see anyone," and pulled her back out into the corridor. She dug in her heels, but Rictor was inexorable. Nothing made him lose his stride, until Artur slipped in front of him. His gloves were off and stuffed in his jumper pocket. He extended his bound hands and Rictor hesitated.

"Don't," he said. "Don't touch me."

"Let her go," Artur said. "Let her go and you can keep your secrets."

"I would kill you first."

"All it takes is one touch. Just one. I am a man of my word, Rictor. You know this." Artur touched his own forehead. "How much are your secrets worth?"

"How much are your shape-shifters worth?" Rictor's voice was hard. "Because the longer we stand here talking, the sooner one of them will die. And when that happens, I won't be able to help you. You'll have lost your only ticket out of this shithole."

"I do not trust you," Artur said.

"Talk to *her* about it." Rictor gestured at Elena. "She doesn't stop thinking about that, ever."

"You can't possibly be surprised by that," she said. "And besides, mind . . . -dropping . . . is totally rude."

"Totally," he drawled, sarcastic. "Now get the fuck moving."

Artur, for whatever reason, let that slide. He stepped aside. As Rictor passed him, hauling Elena, Artur reached out and grabbed her other wrist. His hands were warm. Something coiled around her heart, gentle and strong, and she heard, *I am here, Elena. I am here.*

Rictor released her. He did not look at them. "Someone's coming," he said, and they began moving again, fast. Artur ran easily, with a loose-limbed grace that was utterly natural and effortless. Elena felt him glance at her throat. She wondered what it looked like.

"Where is Charles Darling?" Artur asked. His voice was low, furious.

"You don't have time," Rictor said. "He's in another part of the facility. Forget about him."

"She will send him after us."

"For fuck's sake. Can't you just handle one problem at a time? Elena's alive. She almost killed him. Just leave it at that until you get the hell out of here."

Artur did not want to leave it, but Elena shook her head. Now was not the time. She wondered, though, if there were any other prisoners they could help. It did not seem right to leave anyone down here.

"There are only four, including yourselves," Rictor said, still apparently unconcerned by his rampant mental invasions. "The doctor dispatched his low-level subjects a week ago in preparation for your arrivals. He did not want any more people here than were necessary. He doesn't believe in diverting resources."

"Dispatched them?" she echoed. "You mean he killed them?"

"Put them down like dogs," he agreed. "Their lives were worthless compared to yours. Why study the stars on paper when you can hold one in your hand?"

"Because then you get burned," Artur said. Rictor smiled, grim. They ran down an adjoining corridor. At the end of it was an elevator. Rictor put his hand on a wide plastic panel and the doors slid open. As Elena ran on, she thought of Charles Darling, the doctor, the mysterious *l'araignée*, and incredulity swept through her.

I think we are escaping. Maybe, with a little luck. With a miracle.

The doors closed. Elena's stomach lurched.

"Down to level one?" Artur asked. Rictor nodded. He stared at Elena. His eyes glowed.

"Why are you here?" she asked him, unable to look away from that unnatural, inhuman gaze. *What are you, Rictor? Why the hell are you looking at me like that?*

"Stupidity," he said, which was impossibly vague. "I said yes to something when I should have said no."

"The worm?" Artur asked.

Rictor shook his head. "Worse. Something that binds me to this place. At least for a while longer. My time is running out. A man like me can take chains for only so long."

"A man like you?" Elena said, and then, "Wait. You're coming with us, aren't you? Aren't you helping us escape so you can leave, too?"

"I would have left a long time ago if I could," he said, and looked away at the digital panel above the elevator doors.

"You can't stay here," she argued. Rictor might confuse the hell out of her—had proven to be an asshole of gargantuan proportions—but he did not deserve to die or spend his last days in this facility. No one deserved that.

"Elena," he began, but then stopped, giving Artur such a sharp look, she was afraid they would come to blows.

"You know," he said, and in his voice was surprise, horror.

"Just a glimpse. I was inside her head."

Rictor's jaw tightened. "Then you also know it's hopeless. I have no way of entering that room, and even if I could, I'm not allowed to break the circle."

"One of *us* could do that," Artur said quietly. The elevator lurched to a stop. The doors opened. There was no one in the hall, but Rictor did not move. He stared at Artur, still and unblinking. Elena caught the doors as they began to close again.

"Guys," she said. "Are we coming or going?"

"I do not trust you. I do not even like you. But I do owe you the same effort you are showing us," Artur said.

"No," Rictor said. "You don't know what I am. She caught me because of my stupidity, but she found me because of my nature."

"Right now, I concern myself only with debts," Artur said, and Elena knew she had never been in the presence of two men more suited for a game of poker. Their faces gave nothing away. Which might be fun to watch, another time, but not now.

"Hey!" she snapped. "We're trying to escape here, right? I don't see your asses moving."

Silence. Rictor said, somewhat mildly: "Are you sure you really want to keep her? Her temper is only going to get worse. She nearly killed a man today."

"My kind of woman," Artur said. "I like them dangerous."

"Oh, for Christ's sake." Elena stopped holding the el-

evator doors and stepped out into the corridor. She felt
Artur and Rictor follow her.

"The shape-shifters first," Rictor said. Elena had no
idea what he meant by that term. "One of them is hurt.
If you have time, then me."

They ran. This time they passed people in the hall,
but Rictor did not seem to care if they were seen. The
people down here looked pale and anemic. Scientists,
Elena thought. The men and women gave them a wide
berth as they came pounding down the hall; Elena wondered if they were expected. She also wondered if Rictor trotted around with all his prisoners.

She heard the screaming before they reached the
room—human screams, the screams of an animal. Rictor slowed, turning to look at Artur and Elena.

"If there's trouble, I won't be able to help you. I am
forbidden to strike anyone in this facility, unless it is for
the purpose of protecting Elena. Those were my commands. I can't disobey."

"I have heard of something similar," Artur said.

"Think some more," Rictor said. "The similarities
run deeper than you can imagine."

Elena did not wait for them to finish their conversation; people sounded like they were dying. She pulled
her hand away from Artur and ran past Rictor—slipped
through his fingertips as he reached for her—and
headed through the open doorway just ahead on her
left. Stopped in her tracks.

It was like looking at the lab of some freakish animal-
fetished Dr. Frankenstein. The first thing she saw was
the remains of a shattered tank—huge, at least eight
feet long, glass and wires and thick black straps scattered in a bowel-like tangle across the floor. A dolphin
lay unmoving in the midst of that mess. A true, honest-
to-God dolphin. It was covered in blood. On the other

side of the room was a cage on a wheeled platform. A cheetah screamed from within, battering itself against the bars. Several men surrounded the platform, trying to keep it from turning over. The room was filled with men and women in lab coats, all of whom were in various states of injury, complete meltdown, and utter helpless indecision.

"*Shit*," Elena said. "Oh, shit. Where do I start?"

Rictor stood beside her in the doorway. "The dolphin. Heal the dolphin."

"What the fuck do you mean, heal the dolphin?"

"The dolphin is one of the prisoners," Rictor said.

"You're insane."

Artur edged close, pushing Rictor aside. He placed his bare bound hands on one shoulder and leaned down to look into her eyes. His was an old-souled gaze, dark and strong.

"Elena," he said quietly. "Do you trust me?"

She swallowed hard. "Yes."

"Then heal the dolphin. Rictor is right. It is not just an animal."

"Oh, God. You're both on crack."

"Elena," both men said.

"Fine, yes. Get out of my way."

Socks were not the best footwear for this room; she had to tiptoe around broken glass, and the thick cotton was quickly soaked through with water. She squelched her way to the dolphin, which was surrounded by a loose circle of men and women in lab coats. Some of them held buckets, but none moved to pour water. They stared at the thick piece of glass jutting from the animal's side.

When they noticed Elena, who was so obviously not one of them, they snapped back into themselves.

"Is this the healer?" asked a blond woman. She had

blood smeared all over her white pants. When Rictor nodded, she gave Elena a sharp look and said, "You need to make him shift. It doesn't matter if you heal his wounds; his body is too heavy to stay out of the water. We don't have anything to put him in."

"Shift?" Elena crouched close to the dolphin. "I have no clue what—"

Rictor yanked hard on Elena's shoulder just as the animal lunged at her. She fell hard on her ass, scrabbling backward as the dolphin snapped its long jaws at her feet. She got a good look at its eyes: shocking burnished gold, like precious metal made of soft tissue.

"He won't let us get close anymore," said one man. Elena wished someone had told her that beforehand.

"Anything else?" she asked, not sure she wanted to hear the answer.

"He wants to die," said the blond woman with complete seriousness. "That's the only way I can explain his resistance."

A suicidal dolphin. That was a new one.

Artur got down on the ground beside Elena. He slid sideways toward the dolphin in an impossibly graceful movement that looked more like a dance than a shuffle. "Look at me," he whispered, as though there were no one else in the room but the two of them, and all that mattered was words, a voice. "Look at me."

Rictor began pushing the scientists back, even the injured, herding them toward the door. He gestured at the men holding the cheetah's cage. "Out," he said, over their protests. "You want him to live, don't you? Get out. We need some quiet in here."

"The girl is not trained—," said the woman, but Rictor shoved her out the door and slammed it shut. Turned the lock. Elena heard fists pound against the heavy metal.

"We don't have much time," he said. "Do what you have to, but make it quick."

"Artur," Elena said, concerned for his safety. He ignored her, still sliding close to the prone dolphin. The creature lay very still, but its eyes were bright, uncanny with intelligence. Elena felt uneasy looking into those eyes.

Artur held up his bound hands. "Do you see this? I am also a prisoner here. All of us, prisoners. But we do not have to stay that way. We have an opportunity to escape, but we must do it now. Please. I cannot leave you here." He looked over his shoulder at the cheetah, which had stopped howling the moment Artur began speaking. Its eyes were also golden, bright, and Elena had the very uncomfortable feeling it understood every word Artur said.

"Rictor," Artur said. "Open his cage."

"He doesn't trust us."

"I know," he whispered, staring at the cheetah. "But I also know he can save his brother's life. That is worth a little risk, yes?"

Rictor said, "I am forbidden, Artur. Opening the cage is the same as allowing him to escape."

"And yet we are here."

"Loopholes," Rictor said. "I am here because Elena can be here."

"I'll do it," she said, and before they could argue she was beside the cage, gazing at a wild furred face with eyes that seemed to see straight into her soul. Her heart pounded. From the corner of her eye she saw Artur stand. Rictor moved close.

"Don't bite me," she said to the cat, and removed the triple layer of pins holding the door in place. She swung it open. The cheetah jumped out. Elena held her breath. This was craziness—*she* was crazy, listening to these men who talked to wild animals like they were people, like they could make bargains not to kill, and why, why, *why* was she so stupid . . .

The cheetah's eyes began to glow. Light spilled forth. Golden eyes, golden fire—a golden body embraced by the halo of the sun. Elena forgot how to breathe. She staggered backward into Rictor's arms.

And then the cheetah rose up on its back legs—stretching, growing—and Elena blinked just once, and in that moment fur smoothed to skin, claw to nail and finger, and Elena found herself looking at a man. A golden-eyed man with black skin and fine chiseled features. He held himself tall and straight, like nobility: a prince.

"Greetings," he said, and his voice was rich, rolling with a buttery accent.

"Hi," she breathed, and looked at Artur. She let out a silent scream of awe.

"No," he said. "You are not imagining it."

"But even if you are, you don't have time to indulge the fantasy." Rictor tapped Elena's shoulder. "Come on."

Dazed, in shock, Elena stumbled back to the dolphin, whose gaze rested solely on the former cheetah moving gracefully across the floor to stand beside Elena. His close-cropped hair contained a wiry patchwork of blond to black. He was naked, whip-thin, with a sinewy strength that reminded her of a cat.

"Brother," said the man urgently. "Brother, you must change."

The dolphin closed its eyes; opened them again, slow.

"He's been done over so much he isn't sure he wants to live," Rictor said.

"No," soothed the man, crouching. He reached out with one long arm and touched the dolphin's head. "No, you still have some fight left in you. You fought when

153

you saw me, did you not? You answered the call of our kind? Come now. Just one shift. I will do the rest."

"We all will," Artur said.

The man gave him a hard look, appraising and cold. "I do not know you."

Artur glanced at Elena. "Strangers in paradise, then."

She would have smiled, but there was a man beside her who had just changed his shape, another whose eyes glowed green, and a dolphin who was dying in glass, bleeding and miserable. It was all too much. She wanted out of there. She wanted to run. She wanted to get the hell away from all this craziness.

So be crazy, she told herself, and sidled close to peer down into a golden eye. The dolphin gazed back at her with something akin to suspicion.

"All right," Elena said. "I guess I can take a leap of faith and assume you're not just an animal. That's good. It means you understand me. *So you listen up.* These men, apparently, are not going to leave without you. I will not leave without them. So unless you are one heartless, selfish son of a bitch, you will do *exactly* what these fine gentlemen ask of you, or else die knowing you brought four other people to the grave. You got that?"

The dolphin gave Elena no indication he was willing to help, but she took a deep breath and rested her hands upon his body. He did not attack her. She looked at the others. "Get that glass shard out of him now."

"Hurry," Rictor said. "More than scientists are coming."

The other shape-shifter did not wait; he reached out and pulled the glass from the dolphin's side. The creature let out a high-pitched squeal; blood gushed from the wound and Rictor pulled off his shirt to wad against it.

Elena worked fast. She had no time to be gentle. The dolphin cried out again but did not move. Elena compelled his body's cooperation—platelets swarmed the wound, clotting—but it was too slow, the cut too large. She needed results now.

"Artur," she said. He did not hesitate; he placed his bound hands against her neck. Elena felt the link between them come instantly alive, a white-hot thread, clean and pure.

What do you need?

More power. I've slowed the bleeding, but the wound is too big. I need to force his body to knit most of it shut.

Take what you need, he said, and she felt him wrap his spirit tight around her own—so natural, so easy—his strength adding to her own, and she was a giant in her own body, like a superhero full of cosmic abilities, and she used that power to slam the dolphin's sluggish tissues into overdrive, shoving energy down the reproducing cells, electrifying them into hyperactivity.

It's working, Artur said, and his voice was full of wonder. *His wound is closing. I can see it.*

The only thing Elena could see was energy; the only thing she could feel, Artur. She pulled her spirit out of the dolphin, Artur flowing with her . . . and then he was gone, back into his own body. Elena swayed, clutching her head. What a rush. She did not feel diminished by his absence; in fact, she still sensed some presence, a lingering afterglow. She looked at the wound, and it was raw, pink—but healed enough for him to begin moving. Though how they were going to haul ass with a dolphin in tow . . .

"I've done my part," Elena said to the dolphin, abandoning sanity for the fantasy of the inexplicable. "What's your excuse?"

The dolphin's eyes glowed—its entire body burning

golden—flippers stretching, the long, flat tail splitting . . . and Elena found it beautiful and eerie and utterly terrifying. Seconds, stretching to a lifetime, and she did not blink. She watched a dolphin flow into a man, and when the light died all she could see was a strong young face framed by coarse hair streaked with the colors of the sea and clouds: variations of blue, green, thunderstorm gray. Golden, tired eyes.

"Satisfied?" he asked. His voice was hoarse, as if it had not been used in a very long time.

"Very," Rictor answered for her. "Can you stand?"

"I recognize your face. You're one of them."

"Technicalities. Now stand the fuck up so we can get out of here."

Elena turned around. Artur stood at a long counter, rummaging through drawers. He pulled out a scalpel and turned it around in his hands. He began slicing awkwardly through the plastic binding his wrists. She went to him and wordlessly took the scalpel. Within seconds she freed him.

"Thank you," he said. "I did not think to ask for help."

"Tough guy," she said, holding on to the scalpel. She gazed around the room for another weapon. Artur glanced past her at the naked man who had been a dolphin. He stood now, but just barely. "What is your name?"

The man swayed. Rictor reached out a hand to steady him, but he jerked away from the touch.

"Rik," he said. He gazed at his palms and then rubbed his face, slow and careful. The other shape-shifter drew close. He rested his hand on Rik's shoulder, and Elena sensed the world slide away from the two men as they gazed at each other.

"I am Amiri," said the dark man. "You know what I run as."

"Yes," Rik whispered.

"Greetings later," Rictor snapped. He stared at the lab door. Metal pounded, accompanied by shouts. "Time's up."

Amiri's body glowed, golden fire rippling across his skin. He bent down; a moment later a cheetah shook free of light and stalked to the door.

"The scientists are there," Rictor said, eyes distant. "Some of the men from upstairs. They don't know what we're planning, but they are concerned our ineptitude is hurting their experiment."

"Weapons?" Artur asked, unscrewing a long metal bar from an odd structure built into the broken tank. He tossed the bar to Rik, and then set about removing another.

"No-kill. Pepper spray and retractable batons, but they're not planning on using them. I'm in here, so they think everything must be under control."

"Of course," Artur said dryly. "Since you are so very biddable to your mistress's wishes."

"So very," he agreed. "But then, the same could be said of everyone inside this facility—except for you four. Which is a very big problem. Once *l'araignée* realizes you are trying to escape, she can force everyone in this building to kamikaze you. Most of them don't even realize she's fucked their heads. They still think they own themselves. They have no idea."

"How is this a problem?" Rik swung the bar, his expression cool. He looked tired, but dangerous. Pent-up. Explosive. A young man ready for trouble. "They are just scientists. They have no training as fighters."

"That's just it. They are noncombatants."

"No," Rik said, hard. "They are just bodies."

Artur moved. Shoved his weapon hard up under the shape-shifter's chin and leaned close. Softly he said, "We have risked our lives for you. An act of faith, because *I* believed you worthy of that risk." His voice dropped even lower, into a hush. "Do not make me regret that act."

"You do not understand what they did to me," Rik whispered. "What they are."

Artur touched the shape-shifter's shoulder; tension rippled through them both. "I understand. Right now, I simply do not care. Kill if you must protect yourself, but do not seek death out for pleasure."

Rik's expression darkened. Elena said, "Rictor, how are we going to get out of here?"

"Move fast," he said, also watching the shape-shifter. "*L'araignée* is arrogant. She doesn't believe anyone can escape her."

Artur stepped away from Rik. "Charles Darling told me the only way to escape is if they let you go."

Rictor smiled, humorless. "Charles Darling has a thread in his head. Wearing a leash will do that to a man."

"And what is to keep her from turning *you* against *us*?"

"The nature of her hold on me. I have to be within hearing range for her commands to take effect." He glanced at Elena. "Look meek, will you?"

"Excuse me?"

"And you." He pointed at Rik. "Get over there, behind the door."

Rik did not argue, though Elena suspected it was a struggle. Amiri joined him, crouching low to the ground. Artur stood directly behind Elena. The metal bar in his hands pressed against her back.

"Using me as a shield?" she murmured. He touched

her neck, a brief grazing of fingertips against flesh, and she shivered.

"Camouflage," he said. "Besides, I do not want you standing here alone when they enter the room."

Elena's palm felt sweaty around the scalpel; she pressed it tight against her thigh. "I'll be fine."

"I know," he said, gentle. "Humor me."

Rictor looked at all of them, his gaze resting finally on Elena. "Remember," he said, and it seemed he was speaking only to her, "I can act only if Elena is threatened."

Small comfort. Rictor opened the door.

There was no mad rush, as Elena expected. She had underestimated what Rictor's presence meant to these people. They both feared and trusted him, searching his hard face for some tentative assurance that everything was okay.

Elena almost felt sorry for them. Almost, but not quite.

Several men in white nurse uniforms pushed their way to the front of the gathered scientists. Elena recognized them from her first encounter with the doctor. She wondered how long it had taken to get rid of the vomit smell.

"Ms. Weave sent us down for the girl," said the tallest, thick around the neck and shoulders. He spoke with a Russian accent. He glanced past Rictor at Elena and Artur. A deep furrow formed in his forehead. "What is *he* doing here?"

Rictor stepped aside to let the man pass; his companions followed close behind. The scientists tried to enter, but he held them back with nothing more than a hard look and an outstretched arm.

It happened fast. The moment the nurses entered the room, Amiri lunged. Quiet, deadly, a golden blur; Elena heard a tearing sound and then Artur yanked her backward, lifting her off the ground and setting her down a safe distance from the fight. Screaming—the man beneath Amiri screamed—and Elena watched as the cheetah clamped down around the man's leg, ripping—ripping—and then Rik was there, leaping over Amiri at the other two men, swinging the metal bar with a fury. Bone cracked; the second nurse fell. Artur spun back into the fight; the last nurse standing saw him come. He shouted something in Russian, but Artur did not respond. His face was hard, his movement inexorable. Two sharp blows and the man collapsed.

Elena did not have time to react to the violence. Artur stepped back, grabbed her hand, and pulled her to the door. Rictor was already there, plowing through the scientists, who scattered back with their mouths hanging open, expressions of utter shock and disbelief in their eyes. And then Amiri unlocked his jaws from the bleeding leg, stepped off the writhing body, and faced the door.

Screams. Chaos. The scientists ran.

"This won't last!" Rictor shouted at the others. "Come on!"

They took off down the hall, Rictor at the lead. They were racing hard, feet and paws pounding the concrete floor, and at any moment Elena expected to come face-to-face with zombies, an army of the living, the mind-controlled dead, which was ridiculous—but after seeing animals turn into men, utterly believable. Anything was possible in this place. Terrifying.

A siren blasted the air. Amiri's ears flattened.

"Step one," Rictor said, running straight through a three-way intersection of halls.

"We're going in the wrong direction," Artur said. "We haven't freed you yet."

"No time." Rictor glanced over his shoulder at Elena.

"All for one and one for all," she said, and looked at Artur. "Where is it?"

"Back and to the left."

"No," Rictor said, but Elena was already turning with Artur. Rik stared, confused. She heard him swear, and then follow. Amiri stayed by their sides, alert.

The door looked like any other. A keypad jutted from the wall.

"Forget this," Rictor hissed. "It's a waste of time. There's no way in there without the code. *L'araignée* is the only one who knows it, and I can't read her mind."

Artur raised one dark brow. He touched the keypad. His gaze went distant. His fingers danced, punching numbers. A green light blinked. They all heard a click. Rictor stared.

"I am very talented," Artur said, a cold smile haunting his lips. "You may thank me now."

Elena opened the door. It was heavy. She looked inside and all she saw was blackness. No floor, no walls, just a sheet of dark that seemed to swallow light.

"That's unnatural," she said.

"Yes," Rictor said. Sweat rolled down his face. He appeared unwell. Artur looked at the shape-shifters.

"Stand guard, please."

Rik began to argue, but Amiri slapped a hard paw on his leg. He looked at the cheetah, startled.

Artur grabbed Rictor's arm and hauled him into the room. They disappeared behind the veil—swallowed, hidden behind a tongue of darkness. Taking a deep breath, Elena followed.

The moment she stepped into the room, the wail of the siren stopped. Pure silence hit her, and it was not enough to call it quiet—even her raging heartbeat felt dulled, sluggish. The ground beneath her soggy-socked feet yielded softly, like sand.

The darkness was not absolute. A ring of white light cut it, a halo set in black that streamed upward, pure and still. Elena's heart faltered. She had never seen anything so terrible or beautiful. Never an eerier sight.

"Cut the sand," Rictor said, desperate. Elena could not see him or Artur. "Cut the light, the lines, drive them flat. Hurry. *Hurry*."

Silence, and then Artur said, "I cannot. My foot bounces off the light."

More silence. Rictor said, "That's it, then. Damn it. I should have known she—"

Elena stopped listening. She took two fast steps and drove her foot through the circle of light. Nothing bounced. She cut the circle with just one step, freeing the emptiness gathered inside that large, dark space. She felt movement against her face, like the wind, but richer—deeper—filled with the scent of spring rain, new sweetgrass, the bud of a first bloom. Like youth, bottled into one glorious breath, the exhalation of wonder. The light went out.

"Oh, my God," she breathed. "Oh, God. What was that?"

She heard weeping and turned. She could see; the room was still dark, but light streamed in from the open doorway, hitting sand, the outline of bodies. Just a room now. No halos or impenetrable, bottled night.

Rictor was on his knees beside Artur, his fists bunched up against his eyes. His shoulders shook; he was crying. Crying. Racked with sobs.

"Rictor," Elena said. "Oh, Rictor. What did she do to you?"

Rictor made no effort to wipe his face. He stood, and there was something new in his movement: an ageless quality, full of a timeless grace powerful in its beauty. He set his tearstained gaze upon Artur and Elena. His eyes glowed green.

"Let's get out of here," he said.

Chapter Nine

They ran from the room and down the hall. As they ran, Artur thought of magic, the inexplicable quality of altering reality to suit one's desires. He knew it existed—had seen the product of its use in more than one form—but still, always, it was a shock. It seemed more unnatural than shape-shifters, more unpredictable than anger. The metaphysical could be so startling.

The same could be said of your life.

True. Because how could he have predicted this moment, running for his life and freedom in the company of shape-shifters and psychics, and a man who most certainly might not be human?

Never. But then again, he preferred an extraordinary life.

Men and women whose faces he had seen only as echoes passed before him in reality, pressed up against the corridor walls, watching their quick passage with expressions of true terror. Artur's heart hurt to look at their faces; he was nothing but a monster to them. All of them, monsters.

"No one is attacking us yet," Elena said, falling back to run at his side. She had to shout to be heard over the alarm. Her face was flushed, her throat and cheek mottled with bruises, but her eyes—those dark eyes—were filled with perfect stubborn hope. Looking at her gave *him* hope, though for what, he could not say. Moment by moment—that was all he could live for until they escaped this place.

"Just wait," Rictor said. His eyes still glowed, which was somewhat disturbing. Artur still did not entirely trust the man—and the way he behaved toward Elena had not gone unnoticed. It bothered Artur. Ridiculous, of course. He had no claim on Elena, no matter what had passed between them. Which was not all that much, unless one counted the astonishing existence of their spirit link, or the merging of their souls.

Well, yes. Perhaps that did count for quite a lot. As long as she felt the same way about the experience.

Now is not the time, he told himself, resisting the urge to catch her hand. He needed to be free to move, to fight—his head clear of vision. He glanced down; sometime during the run she had lost her weapon, that tiny scalpel.

Artur succumbed to weakness. He grabbed her hand. The visions he saw did not affect him as they had earlier; instead they felt comfortable, like a warm blanket. He was growing accustomed to her touch. Elena smiled.

"We've got company coming," Rictor said.

"I don't suppose this would include people I am morally permitted to hit?" Rik asked. Artur thought he must feeling better. It took energy to be that sarcastic.

"Maybe a couple." Rictor glanced at him. "But they're mine."

Artur did not bother suggesting they hide. This part of the facility lacked any doors; it was just a network of tunnels, like a warren for those who feared the sun. The layout and design felt so very military, Artur wondered if the Consortium did not have ties to some government agency.

Rictor held out his hand; everyone slowed, including Amiri. His tail wound briefly around Rik's deeply tanned legs. Artur heard boots pound concrete, hard, and he tugged Elena behind him. She resisted—of course—but Artur refused to leave her exposed.

Men appeared. Artur thought he would never look at white uniforms in the same way.

Though admit it: they remind you of childhood, the doctors and their so-called nurses. You have always hated the color white.

Five big men. Two of them carried guns. Artur was almost certain they were loaded with tranquilizers.

"Rictor," said one of them. "What you doin', man?"

"Being myself," he said, and threw out his hands. The nurses flew back with such force they had no time to cry out. Like dolls they slammed against the concrete walls, crushing bones. The guns clattered to the ground alongside their bodies.

Silence. Rictor still had his hands outstretched. He stared at the men, his hands, and Artur remembered what it felt like to watch him break down and cry. He had met Rictor only once before—had never taken the measure of the man—but his instincts rarely lied. Tears were as surreal on him as magic, rings of light, seeing a shape-shifter for the first time. Unnatural and strange.

He waited a moment, but when Rictor gave no sign of madness, or that he would continue punishing the fallen, Artur let go of Elena's hand and ran forward to collect the guns. He checked them. As he thought, both had tranquilizers loaded. It felt good to hold the guns in his hands. Knowledge seeped like water, trickling through his brain. He heard more movement from down the corridor.

"Run or fight?" Rik asked, twirling his metal bar with agile fingers.

"Run," Artur said, without giving anyone else a chance to respond. He knew this game—had lived it on the streets and in the orphanage. Running was not always the coward's route; it was a matter of survival. The fewer violent encounters one invited, the longer the life. And right now Artur wanted to live a very long time. He wanted Elena to live, too—and to do so without another nightmare. He had spent most of his adult life in violence; he did not wish the same for her. Not for that bright, clean spirit.

He found Rictor staring at him. It was a measuring gaze—there was no doubt he had heard every single one of Artur's thoughts. He looked at Elena, who stood watching the corridor, listening to the sounds of approach with stubborn, frightened defiance. Rictor's outstretched hands dropped to his sides, clenched tight into fists. He wanted to fight; Artur could see it in his eyes. But for Elena . . . for her . . .

She is mine, Artur thought at him, and was shocked at how freely and vehemently those words came to him. *She is mine* felt like a war cry, the declaration of some mighty prayer: a promise and a threat.

Rictor's eyes flashed bright and hot. Elena said, "The two of you, get a room. I want out of here."

She backed down the hall, staring at them expectantly. Amiri moved with her; Rik did the same.

"Go," said Rictor. "You know the way. I'll catch up with you."

He turned around to face the sounds of approach. Lifted his arms. Artur glimpsed a parade of bodies. The scientists now. They no longer looked afraid. They had very little expression on their faces at all.

Artur turned and ran. He held a tranquilizer gun in each hand. Elena kept close to his side, Rik bringing up the rear. Amiri sprang ahead, loping with easy grace over the dull concrete.

From behind, Artur heard screams. Elena missed a step. He said, "No. Keep going."

Try not to think about it. Try not to imagine.

Artur remembered the way; all those echoes and stolen visions made him as much an expert of these halls as Rictor. There were two elevators on this level, but neither of them was safe. Stairs, then. Also unsafe, but at least they would not be trapped in a box.

The first stairwell they found was locked by a digital keypad. Artur touched the pad, soaking in the memory of the last man who had used the stairs—with a woman—one of the scientists—for sex, because it was private and little-used—and found the code. He punched it in and the door unlocked.

"You don't have a plan, do you?" Rik said, as he filed past Artur. Amiri was already halfway up the stairs, slinking low, careful.

"The will to survive," Artur said, giving him a hard look. "That is the only plan I need."

Up the stairs, up and up and up, pausing only on the second level—their home for such a short time—before following the stairs past that floor, higher and higher. Such strange design. Artur's subconscious recalled these stairs as he traversed them, but they seemed an odd choice to include in this place. Easy access to the surface?

Easy, if you are like us, and uncontrolled. The others, even the employees, might never make it this far. And maybe this facility was not always used for this purpose. It could have been converted from something else.

Amiri growled, fur rising high on his back. Artur pushed Elena against the wall as Graves appeared on the landing above. She held a tranquilizer gun, as did the two men in white who appeared behind her. The doctor stood with them, unarmed. He was the only person who looked upset. Graves might have been manicuring her nails, for all the emotion she showed.

"I thought so," she said, though it was difficult to hear her over the continued wail of the alarms. "I have no idea how you made it this far, but I suspected you might know how to access the stairs. Remarkable, Mr. Loginov. I am so impressed by you. Here for less than a day and you've already defied my employer, broken your bonds, and made a very good attempt at freeing the rest of our guests. That, I can assure you, is a record."

"You will always underestimate me," he said. "Poor woman."

Her mouth thinned. "Never fear. More are coming to help return you to your proper place. Which, I can assure you, will soon be a very deep grave."

Again Amiri growled. Artur said, "The interesting thing about those guns, Ms. Graves, is that they have only one shot in them."

"Yes," Graves said, and aimed it right at him. "I also know this circus won't last long without your participation."

Amiri moved fast. He blew past Graves before she could react, knocking her off balance. She squeezed the trigger, but her shot went high. Artur's did not. He caught her in the chest and she went down hard.

Amiri clamped his jaws around the doctor's throat. The old man screamed—*screamed*—and then could scream no longer, and the nurses forgot all about Artur and the other captives because they kept trying to find that perfect shot to stop Amiri, and the cheetah would not stand still long enough to give it to them. A shot went off, driving into the wall. A near miss.

Artur fired at the man closest to him, and as the other turned to unload a tranquilizer, Amiri released the doctor and fixed his teeth on the nurse's crotch, biting hard, pushing and pulling the man to the ground as his screams grew high and strangled.

"Whoa," Rik murmured.

Artur discarded his guns. He did not touch Amiri, who had now traveled up the body to the neck and was biting the nurse to death, but he did say, "We need to go," and then gestured for Rik and Elena to follow. Elena reached out to touch Amiri's back, and Artur grabbed her hand. Rik shook his head as well.

"Never come between a shape-shifter and his prey in the middle of a blood-rage," he whispered, as though to speak louder would attract Amiri's attention for the worse. "They'll turn on you."

Elena's face paled even more. Artur tugged on her arm. They moved on, leaving Amiri behind. He had to trust that the shape-shifter would catch up. Elena tried not to look at the doctor as they stepped over his sprawled body. Amiri had nearly decapitated him. The old man appeared far more pleasant in death than he had in life.

The stairs ran out. In front of them was a solid iron door. Artur touched it, but felt nothing but the old echo of a large, dark space. This was not an exit used very often. He had no idea what would greet them on the other side, but if Graves had found them . . .

He pushed Elena and Rik up against the wall, took a deep breath, and opened the door.

Rictor stood on the other side. There were many

bodies scattered around him. "What took you so long?" he asked.

Artur almost shot him as a matter of principle. Rictor smiled, a clear invitation to do his worst.

Elena pushed past and stood between the two men. If she noticed the tension, she made no comment, merely stared up and out at the poorly lit room, which resembled nothing more than a very large—and very empty—garage. Artur felt something brush his legs. Amiri. The cheetah's muzzle was bright red.

"They don't keep vehicles here," Rictor said, leading them down a side corridor. "That would mean drivers who actually live here, who know what the hell is going on, and who go out into the real world. The Consortium likes to keep people in the dark. You'll have to make your break on foot."

"Wonderful," Rik muttered.

At the end of the hall was another door with another keypad. It was more difficult learning the combination on this lock—it had not been used in years—but he found it, and the door clicked open. Sunlight blinded him, a wild rush of crisp air filling his lungs. Artur had almost forgotten the sun. As they all filed out, Artur turned. The door was set into a hill, and had been painted a mottled camouflage. It was impossible to imagine that below them lay a sprawling complex, a prison, a place of nightmares.

"No one is out here yet," Rictor said, his eyes going distant. "Let's go."

Rik had trouble keeping up. He was naked, had no shoes, and it was quite clear he was unused to continued strenuous exertion on land. Rictor stayed close, occasionally grabbing the young man's arm and hauling him forward, driving him with insults and anger. There was no time for kindness, though Artur wondered if Rictor did not enjoy the abuse, just a little.

He kept expecting to be recaptured—knew from the occasional brief contact that Elena felt the same—and Rictor said, "They were completely unprepared for anyone to ever escape. The only people who have been here before were easy, weak. Kidnapped college students who thought they were going in for paid medical studies. Poor uneducated men and women from third-world countries. Beatrix's mind control did the rest."

"I still don't get you," Elena said, gasping for breath. She was not a very good runner, either.

"Does it matter?" Rictor looked completely unbothered by the run. He wasn't even sweating. The branches and vines that snagged his body did not leave marks.

Elena gave him a hard look. Artur knew what she was thinking. It mattered a great deal.

They finally stopped, pressed close inside a hollow place in the forest where the trees did not touch and the vines did not cut. After a minute of rest, Amiri pushed ahead. Despite his obvious exhaustion, Rik joined him.

"I can't stay," Rictor said when the others were gone. "*L'araignée* found me once and she can do it again. Doesn't mean she can recapture me, but if I travel with you, I might as well put a neon sign over your heads that says, 'Shoot me.'"

"Where will you go?" Elena asked.

"I'll play decoy," Rictor said. "Follow the kind of path you might take. Which, of course, will be the opposite direction of your actual route."

"Beatrix Weave is not a foolish woman," Artur said. "Why might she think you would stay with us?"

Rictor smiled. "I tasted Graves's thoughts before you shot her. She had just been in contact with *l'araignée*, who most certainly felt her spell decay. Graves told her

I'm in love with Elena. Or at least, that's what the doctor suggested before Amiri killed him. It was the only explanation any of them could understand that would explain my radical behavior."

Elena stared. Artur carefully brushed up against her.

"Is it true?" Elena asked. He felt her think, *Impossible*.

"Nothing is impossible," Rictor said. "But in this case, highly improbable."

"Oh." Artur shared her confusion, her *I don't know whether to be insulted or relieved.*

"Neither." Rictor touched her chin. "I owe you one, Elena Baxter. You, too, Artur Loginov. I owe you both a debt of life, and I am a man who repays."

"So we will be seeing you again." Artur was not happy about that.

Rictor smiled. He moved backward, spreading out his hands as though to embrace the wind. His eyes glowed.

"What are you?" Artur asked. "Another kind of shape-shifter?"

"No," Rictor said. "I'm something older."

And he vanished.

Despite his recent feelings that nothing in the world would ever, *ever* surprise him again, Artur was rather taken aback by Rictor's abrupt disappearance.

Elena, apparently, was a little more so.

"Holy shit," she said, swaying. Hands pressed over her mouth, she walked to the spot where Rictor had just stood and stared at the ground. "Oh, shit. Am I losing my mind?"

"No," he said. "But if we don't leave this place, you might just lose your life."

"Drama queen," she said, but without much heat. She looked dazed. Artur grabbed her hand and pulled her deeper into the woods. He found Rik and Amiri waiting for them beside a fallen tree.

"Where's the turncoat?" Rik asked. He was still breathing hard. Living in a tank the size of a large aquarium apparently hadn't given him much exercise.

"He's leading the bad guys away from us." Elena gave the shape-shifter a sharp look. Her composure seemed to be returning. Artur was glad, though a part of him hoped it was not due solely to her desire to defend Rictor.

And when did you become a petty, jealous man? Even with Tatyana you were not so bold.

But Tatyana was not Elena.

Artur led them east, keeping the glimmer of sunlight in his face. He hoped Rictor did his part, that the wild-goose chase he promised would keep Beatrix Weave and her people off their somewhat literal tails. Though, based on the power he had just seen, Artur felt rather confused as to why Rictor could not simply make a stand and fight for all their lives. Fight—and win.

Another mystery. Nothing ever is as it seems.

As the day wore on, they all began stumbling more, dragging their feet against the ground. Stomachs rumbled. Only Amiri retained his grace and power; he slid through the forest like a spotted ghost, silent and deadly. Artur wondered if the cheetah would be able to hunt for them, should the need arise. He hoped it did not.

Their strength was not the only thing that ebbed. The weather changed as well. Dark clouds pushed in, crowding out the taste of blue sky. Sunlight died. Artur heard thunder.

"Oh, no," Elena said. She looked at her hands, and a big fat raindrop splattered on her palm. Another followed, and more . . . more . . .

The sky opened. The forest gave little protection against the wind and rain, which conspired to blind. It was sharp, biting into his unprotected face and body. Mixed with hail, perhaps. Either way, this was no time to be without proper clothing and shelter. Artur hugged Elena close against his side, trying to protect her. A fruitless gesture, but her arm snaked warm around his waist, holding him just as tight.

Fur brushed his legs. Amiri pushed past, quickly disappearing into the torrential gloom. Rik was a shadow on Artur's left, hunched over, fighting to keep his footing.

Artur listened hard, but the pounding rain—its strike on leaves, ground, flesh—drowned out the rest of the world. Just water, just breath, the thrum of his heart. That was all he could hear. If they were being pursued, it was likely they would not have any warning until the last instant.

Speed, he thought, quickening his pace. Elena struggled for a moment, but he continued to hold her close, and she managed to keep up. Not that he would leave her behind. If the moment came when she could no longer travel with him, he would carry her or stop. Make his final stand. He would not leave her behind, not for anything.

No one talked. It was difficult enough just walking, standing upright against the sheet of water and hail striking them. Artur glanced down at Elena. Her skin was white, the bruises on her neck and cheek purple, almost glowing. After this night she would probably have more injuries.

"I am sorry," he murmured. Elena brushed water out of her face—a useless effort; she looked soaked through to the bone. She scowled, but he did not think it was meant for him.

"What are you sorry for?" she asked.

"All of this," Artur said. "I do not know. Just that I am."

"It's not your fault," she said.

He did not disagree with her even though he wanted to. If he spoke he would say something idiotic, like, *I wish I could protect you. I wish I could take you in my arms and cover you with my body so that the sharp wind might not cut yours. I wish I could take you from this place, Elena. I wish I could make you safe.*

In the distance, wolves howled.

"Is that what I think it is?" Elena asked.

"Yes," he said, still listening. Elena stared into the trees. The wolves howled again, closer this time. Very close, if Artur could hear them so clearly over the storm.

"Where are we, Artur? Can't you . . . I don't know . . . touch one of these trees and find out?"

Artur shook his head. "There would be no point. Trees know nothing of geography, and I doubt anyone human has been through here recently. Searching for the echo of a person in this forest would be impossible. Walking will probably find us answers faster."

"Right," Rik said, drawing near. "We could be doing that for a very long time."

"Don't worry," Elena said, pushing forward. "If it rains much longer, you can swim your way out of here."

"Very funny," he muttered.

The rain finally stopped, but they were still wet, and Elena began to shiver. Rik, despite his nudity, did not seem affected by the cold, and Artur wondered if his in-human abilities contributed to his ability to cope with the falling temperature.

The sky darkened without a hint of stars, still hidden by low-lying clouds. Artur contemplated stopping for the night when Amiri appeared among them. The shape-shifter had been gone scouting for quite some time. Slowly, without the ease of his earlier transformations, he became a man. He looked haggard.

"There is a house up ahead," he said. "I did not move close enough to examine it, but if it is empty . . ." He held out his hands, shrugging.

Food, shelter, rest. At least for a short time. Perhaps they could finally discover where in the world they had been taken.

They hurried, and minutes later peered into a small clearing. A small cabin rested at its center. There were no electrical lines. An old truck was parked nearby, but it looked as though it had not been used in quite some time.

"Is anyone there?" Elena asked.

"Wait," Amiri said, golden light spinning in his eyes. It flowed downward, enveloping his body in a golden caress, until nothing was left but a cheetah. Artur found himself watching Elena instead. He studied her wonder-struck eyes, listened to her sudden intake of breath as she remembered to use her lungs again. The miracle had not gone dull for her.

Amiri slid through the underbrush, clinging to shadow. Within moments he reached the cabin. He disappeared out of sight; Artur waited, hopeful.

Amiri was gone for a long time, but when he finally reappeared he walked as a man and waved his arms in their direction. Everyone stumbled out of the underbrush. The hairs on the back of Artur's neck tingled immediately; he hated exposure. No matter how careful they tried to be, there was always the chance of being found.

"I scented humans," Amiri said, when they drew close, "but the trace is old. No one has been here in at least a week."

"Which does not mean the owners will fail to return, but we should be safe for at least several hours." Artur went to the front door and examined the lock. It was very old. Feeling a twinge of guilt, he stepped back and kicked. It took several tries, but he finally broke the lock. The sound of his foot connecting with the wood echoed loudly; he did not miss how everyone winced. He hoped no one else was close enough to hear.

Inside the air smelled musty. Artur fumbled against the wall. He felt Amiri slide past him like a warm ghost. "There are shutters," Amiri whispered. "I believe they are thick enough to keep in any light, should there be searchers in the woods."

Rik and Elena pushed into the cabin behind Artur and he quietly shut the door after them. Waiting in the darkness, Artur listened to Amiri prowl around the cabin's small interior. Less than a minute later he heard something rattle and then hiss into bright flame. Matches.

"There are candles," Amiri said, and then lit one. The light felt like a balm to Artur's tired eyes.

The cabin had only one room. A large bed sat close up against the farthest wall, a narrow wardrobe beside it. In the opposite corner stood a small stove and some cabinets. Their feet made squelching sounds on the wood floor.

"Check the closet," Artur told Elena. "See if you can find some dry clothes."

Rik and Amiri were already in the cabinets, rummaging for food. Their hands emerged full with tinned meat and fruit, as well as several bottles of water.

"Hey," Rik said, holding one up to Artur. "This is foreign."

Artur took the bottle. Foreign to Rik, perhaps, but to Artur the writing was pure home. Cyrillic. Russian.

They were in Russia. Stunned, Artur spun on his heels, looking for more. There was a bookshelf by the front door, and Artur rummaged through its contents. He found old magazines, most of them national publications. Several, though, were distinctly nautical in content, and the mailing addresses were in Vladivostok, a large port city that rested on the edge of the Pacific.

"*Bozhe moy*," Artur said.

"What was that?" Elena said, still rummaging through the wardrobe, pulling out clothes and tossing them on the bed.

"We are in Russia," he told them, still trying to cope with his shock. "I believe we are close to the coast, the Pacific."

Rik dropped a can. "Are you serious?"

"It is an educated guess," Artur said, and there was no mistaking the hunger that swept through the young man's face: a desperate longing mixed with heartbreak. It was horrible to gaze upon. Horrible, because one brief touch had shown Artur all that Rik had endured. Locked in a tank for three months, restrained and unable to move, experimented upon, tortured in attempts to force a shift. Rik was no older than eighteen. He had stayed strong for a very long time, but in recent weeks had succumbed to despair. No one was coming for him. He would die in that tank, sitting in his own waste. He would die.

"Rik. Amiri." Elena's voice was quiet. "You must both be cold. Check out these clothes."

Artur doubted the cold affected them as it did Elena and himself, but the shape-shifters nonetheless grabbed up the pants and sweaters. Rik said, "This is stealing," but Artur was too weary to care about morality.

Everyone changed. The men turned their backs while Elena stripped off her wet scrubs. Artur tried not to think about Elena's body, the feel of it against him in her dream, or against his side in the forest. It was difficult. For every rustle of cloth he imagined skin, soft and warm and pale, and he wanted so badly to turn and stare like an adolescent. He could not believe himself. Since leaving Russia, he thought—foolishly now, it seemed— that he had somehow trained himself out of wanting women, forced desire out of his body.

Those days were done. If he and Elena had been alone, he might have gathered enough courage to test their bond—with a touch; perhaps the brush of hands, lips. Simple and exquisite. But maybe it was better they were not alone; Artur suspected that one taste of Elena would end his life as he knew it, transform him into something new and unfamiliar. He did not know if he was ready for that.

When Artur did finally turn, Elena was swaddled in a heavy gray sweater and a long green skirt that hung down to her ankles. She had traded her socks for sandals. The outfit was far too large on her; with her dark eyes and shorn hair she looked more waif than woman.

And yet lovely.

Do not be a fool, he told himself, meeting her shy gaze with his heart in his throat. *You are more than ready.*

They ate quickly from the meager stores in the cabin, and it went unspoken that they could not stay, that as soon as they were finished it would be time to travel. They could not stop for anything until they reached some semblance of safety, security, which might be a long time coming. Artur had some idea of where they could go for help, but it would be a long shot. Of course, in their situation, a long shot was better than nothing.

He drank down a can of mixed fruit, the taste of which had disappeared with the preparation, and then went outside to check the truck. He felt someone leave the cabin with him; it was Amiri, eyes glowing golden, twin fires in the night shadows.

The truck door was unlocked. Amiri watched him climb inside, and Artur said, "You want to ask me something, yes?"

Silence: a contemplative quiet. "We are all strangers here. Our only connection to each other is our circumstances—this kidnapping and imprisonment. I am not comfortable with only that as a bond between men."

"You do not know me, so you do not trust me. That is fine."

Amiri shrugged. "It is not an insult, simply the truth. I have stayed with you this long only because my brother is weak and I will not abandon him." He hesitated. "That, and because you said you know of us. The shifting kind. You were not surprised in the slightest by our existence. I would like to know why."

Ah, his strange life. "I know several shape-shifters. A good friend married one. His name is Hari. He runs as a tiger."

Artur might have named something truly fantastic: a pegasus, a Medusa. Amiri looked stunned. "A tiger? I did not know there were any tigers left in the world."

"He and his wife just had a son. So no, not the last. But close."

Amiri closed his eyes. "What about the others?"

"Koni, who works with me. He flies as crow. There is a dragon, too, who calls herself Long Nü. She has asked my employers to help find your kind. She fears for your survival as a race."

"She has good reason to fear." Amiri opened his eyes. His gaze was different—not exactly trusting, but filled with grudging acceptance. Perhaps respect. "There are so few of us left. Just pockets here and there, telling tales of all the others who used to roam. There were many of us once." His voice dropped to a whisper. "When I saw Rik for the first time, when I felt the call between us, it was a revelation. A miracle. I was not alone. And now, to hear you say there are even more, and that they are searching for us all . . ." He stopped, swallowing hard.

Artur said, "How were you captured?"

"Bad luck." Amiri's hands balled into fists; his skin shimmered golden, fur rippling against his arms before subsiding into flesh. "I am a teacher back in Kenya. I live in the capital city. It is a good job, and I like helping my students. But sometimes I need to run. Sometimes I need to hunt. And so on my day off I took my car and went to a place where I thought no one would see me, and I shifted."

"But someone did see you."

His smile was bitter. "I was stupid. A naturalist was nearby in a blind, and the wind favored her. As did technology. She had a long-range scope on her camera, and I am sure she captured the entire thing on film. When I realized what had happened, I fled."

"She did not publish the photographs," Artur said, quite certain a woman claiming to have proof of shapeshifters would have attracted the attention of Dirk and Steele's agents.

Amiri shrugged. "I never saw the pictures, never heard anything about them. I admit, I thought I was safe. And then one night, several weeks ago, I was taken from my home. Drugged and shackled. The rest, you know."

"I, too, was taken from my home." Artur thought of Charles Darling, alive and free, and probably still obsessed with Elena. He climbed into the truck. He searched for its keys but found nothing. "I am able to read the histories of people and objects by touching them. The Consortium thought that would be useful. They are no better than a criminal organization. They want to use us as experiments or slaves, all in the name of furthering their agenda."

"Which is?"

Artur pried off the panel beneath the steering wheel. "It is more than just wealth and power, though I cannot say what, exactly. Only that their leader, Beatrix Weave, has plans. Large, long-ranging plans."

"And you?" Amiri stepped close. "What is your plan for escaping this nightmare?"

Artur stopped working. He looked Amiri in the eye and said, "If you like, my plan can be our plan. We will find a way to contact my friends and then stay hidden until they can come for us. And if they cannot come for us, then we will find a way to go to them. Either way, we will *not* return to the Consortium."

"I would rather die first," Amiri said, and there was something in his voice that felt quite literal, and very serious. Artur was not the kind of man who often preferred death over hardship, but even he agreed. Losing control over his mind to Beatrix Weave was a far worse punishment than the endless sleep.

"I will remember that," Artur told him, and then, quieter: "Perhaps you could do the same for me."

Because there was no greater act of trust than to give your life into another's keeping, and Artur knew that would mean something to the shape-shifter.

"Of course," Amiri said softly, after a moment's hesitation. He bowed his head and said nothing else as Artur hot-wired the truck. The engine roared to life, a loud rumble that sounded more animal than mechanical. Elena and Rik appeared in the cabin's doorway.

"Are you ready?" Artur called out to them.

Elena did not hesitate. She ran to the passenger side and climbed in. Rik tried his best to close the cabin's broken door, and then joined Amiri as he leaped into the bed.

"Will we ever be able to pay them back?" Elena frowned at the little cabin. Her fingers plucked at the gray wool.

"We will try," Artur promised, though he was not optimistic. He did not like stealing, but it was a necessity—and in this situation, worrying about the loss of clothing and some food was not his priority.

He turned on the headlights and they drove away. The gravel track leading from the cabin was rough, and the main road—once they hit it after a long, bone-jarring, nausea-inducing drive—was little better. Potholes were everywhere, one minute the road was reasonably smooth, and in the next, nothing more than an irregular track.

After driving for more than an hour, Artur saw signs pointing the way to Vladivostok. The sky brightened.

"That was a short night," Elena commented.

"We are very far north and it is summer. The days are long." Artur would have preferred more darkness. Anyone driving past them would be able to see quite clearly into their vehicle.

The road improved. Alongside it in regular intervals were small rest stops crowded with tiny restaurants the size of closets. Artur tried to remember if there were any police checkpoints outside the city. If they were stopped, there would be no hiding the fact that some them were foreigners. Foreigners without passports, money, or hotel registration stamps, driving a stolen car. Lovely.

Elena leaned close and peered at the dials beneath the wheel. "We don't need gas, do we?"

Artur looked down at the gauge and swore. Stupid. He was losing his mind, his touch. Common sense flying out the window. He had forgotten to check the gas before leaving, and the arrow was aimed at a dishearteningly low part of the gauge.

"Are there any stations around here?" Rik asked.

"Better you ask how we will pay for it," Artur said. There was a full gallon left in the tank, but that was not nearly enough to get them to Vladivostok.

"I don't suppose people here barter?" Elena turned to peer at the back of the truck. "Is there anything in there we could trade?"

"It is empty," Amiri said.

"We will manage." Artur was already working on a story, on anything that would get them the fuel. Fuel was the same as food, as shelter, and he had talked and thieved his way into those necessities more times than he could count. He could do it again. He was simply out of practice.

Your mistakes might get you or the others killed. You cannot afford to make a wrong move now—even driving on this road is a risk.

But he was banking on Rictor leading the Consortium away from them—depending, too, on Beatrix Weave underestimating his boldness. After all, Artur was nothing more than a thug to them, a former criminal. Ultimately a survivor and a coward. She and Graves no doubt expected him to hole up in a cave along with his fellow escapees, or travel on alone while everyone else scattered to fend for themselves.

At least, he hoped that was what she thought. It was a risk—but then, risk had always kept him alive while the meek died behind him, starved and abused.

Artur drove until he saw a familiar shape jutting from the side of the road. "There is our benzene station." He felt Elena's questioning glance and said, "Gas."

They were the only customers there, which was good. In the center of the fueling station, between the pumps, stood a very tiny building with metal bars over the window. Artur glimpsed big hair.

"Everyone out," he said. "Look upset."

"Oh, that's going to be difficult," Rik muttered. They clambered from the truck: ill-dressed refugees, exhausted and afraid. Artur was very proud of them. He drew Elena close as he inserted the pump nozzle into the tank and whispered, "You have been brutally attacked, you understand?"

"Yes," she said without hesitation, and he took her with him to the little window where a middle-aged woman sat, long nails clicking the plastic counter, a cigarette hanging from her mouth. She looked at Elena's face and neck, and in Russian said, "You beat her like that?"

"No," said Artur, noting with some admiration Elena's too-bright eyes, the fine edge of a sob working at her throat. "She and her friends were visiting our country when they were attacked by thieves. Juveniles, to hear her talk about it. They did their business with her, then took everything. Passport, money, clothes. I happened upon them. We are going to Vladivostok. The city has a U.S. consulate."

"Bah," spit the woman, gazing with sympathy at Elena. "These young people nowadays have no respect. Most of them are from the orphanages, you know. Little abandoned nothings, being raised like animals in there. No wonder they are becoming a social crisis."

"Yes," Artur said, "I understand what you mean."

The woman peered out her window at Rik and Amiri, who were doing an admirable job of looking like shattered men. "God, more foreigners. So sad what happened to them." She sniffed. "How much benzene?"

Artur hesitated, affecting an air of deep consternation. "It is embarrassing to say this, but . . . well, you can see I am not a rich man. I used all the money in my pockets just to clothe and feed these people. Americans, you know . . . they require so much more than we do. And the woman . . . I wanted to make sure she was well taken care of, especially after what happened. She was in such a state."

The attendant scowled; her cigarette drooped. "You have no money?"

Artur held out his hands. Elena shivered and hugged herself. She was so convincing he wanted to hug her, too.

"Bah," said the woman again, shaking her head. "You are such a fuckup."

"I know," Artur said, meek. "But what can a man do?"

Her long fingernails tapped furiously on the plastic counter. Smoke curled around her big red hair. "Fine. I cannot punish a fuckup who does good. But I am only giving you enough gas to reach Vladivostock. You will have to purchase your own when you get there, and then"—she leaned forward, pursing her red lips— "you can come back here and repay me."

There was little doubt as to what she expected that repayment to be.

"Ah," Artur said. "Of course."

The woman sat back with an even deeper scowl. "I hope you are better in bed than you are at giving out lines. Now go! Fill up your tank." She looked at Elena, and in rough English said, "I am sorry you see country in bad way. I wish you good."

Elena, swallowing down a sob, gave the woman a weak smile.

"Heartbreaking," said the attendant, and waved Artur

and Elena away from the window. Artur pumped the gas, while everyone else climbed quietly into the truck. He waved to the woman one last time.

And then they left, fast.

Artur said, "Thank you. You were all very convincing." Especially Elena, though he did not know how to tell her that. Was it polite to tell a good woman that she had the potential to become a master con artist? Or had that really been all an act?

"You were very convincing, too," Amiri said. "So convincing, I would say you have had considerable practice."

Artur had no response. He glanced at Elena, and found her watching him with a sad, knowing smile.

"Maybe just a little," he confessed, unable to stop himself. Her gaze, so compassionate and sweet, compelled the truth.

And it was not such a bad thing, telling the truth to Elena. He liked it.

Chapter Ten

Elena's first impression of Vladivostok was one of beauty. The city lay sprinkled over a series of peaks, peninsulas, and islands, with the sea glittering serenely just beyond the shore.

"Does it look that good close-up?" Elena asked, as Artur drove down the winding mountain path.

"Distance is fine on the eyes," Artur said, "but yes, parts of the city are quite beautiful. Odd, considering that it has always been used as nothing more than a glorified naval base." He gestured toward the bay. "Do you see all the shipyards? The Russian Pacific fleet is stationed in those waters. Very strategic. It has been only ten years since foreigners were allowed in this city."

Elena smiled. "You've got a secret crush on boats and submarines, don't you?"

Artur glanced at her, surprised. A smile crept onto his face. He looked almost boyish. "I like them, yes. When I was very young I think I wanted to be a pirate. With a parrot, yes? And the sword and pistol."

"Peg leg, too?"

"No, no." He shook his head, laughing quietly. "No, I wanted to climb the rigging. I wanted to run. I wanted the freedom. The open sea, with nothing between me and the sun and the wind." He hesitated. "You have seen pictures of old Soviet apartment blocks? Big and gray? They are monstrous buildings, very poorly constructed. My *matushka*—mother—did her best to make our home happy, but in a place like that it was difficult. So much controls you. In Moscow, especially. Money, your neighbors, politics."

"And pirates don't care about any of those things, do they?"

"Maybe the money," Artur said, still smiling. "A little gold never hurt."

Elena grinned. She glanced over her shoulder to see if the others were listening, but Rik looked fast asleep. He lay on the floor of the covered truck bed, curled into a ball. Amiri lay beside him. He was not asleep, but he made no move to acknowledge Elena. She did not take offense. She thought it quite possible that both men did not trust her or Artur—and to be honest, she had similar feelings toward them as well. Thrown together like beads in a bag, clanking up against one another. Who could say if they were showing their true selves?

Rictor could.

Well, yes, but Rictor was not here. And that, probably, was a good thing. She had mixed feelings about him, as well.

"Speaking of money—" Elena said, and then stopped because it was quite clear Artur was thinking about the same thing. A slight furrow appeared in his brow; his jaw tightened.

"I know someone in this city. He owes me, but he will not be happy to pay off his debt."

"Typical," Elena said. "What did you do for him?"

"Oh . . ." He hesitated. "Well, I suppose I saved his life. Perhaps the lives of his family, too. I was never quite sure about that."

Elena stared. "You saved his life? And you don't think he'll be happy to repay you for that?"

Artur looked extremely uncomfortable, which was odd. He had acted so cool under pressure, Elena had suspected he lacked some crucial wires in his brain.

"Hey," she said.

"The way in which I saved him was not . . . ideal," Artur said, and he refused to tell her anything more.

They entered the city. Elena rolled down her mud-stained window, savoring the breeze. Raised anchors covered the iron railings that lined the streets, and on almost every rooftop Elena saw statues of men gazing out at the sea. Small carved waves lapped across building facades, and in the middle of several intersections sat the hulking, rusting remains of ship cannons, which no doubt had some historical significance, and which were decorated by pots of small flowers. Everywhere was a nautical decor—though some touches were more kitschy than others.

The cool air felt good on Elena's face. She smelled the ocean and the docks, mingling with the exhaust of the Japanese sedans zipping past their monstrous truck.

"I think I like this place," Elena said, as they passed a giant cardboard Poseidon, its trident flapping in the breeze.

"It is more pleasant than most cities in Russia," Artur said. "Vladivostok is poor, but thanks to the sea the people here never go hungry. There is always some work to be found because of the tourists and shipyards."

"Did you ever live here?"

"No. Just . . . a trip. Every now and then."

Elena thought of her brief foray into his mind, the

violence she had seen. It was not a good time to ask, but she wanted to know. Artur was a fighter. To say he was not would be foolish. But he was not *just* a fighter. She wanted more. Everything.

"What did you do in Moscow?" she asked quietly. She hesitated, and then reached out to touch his hand. His gloves were back on. She slid her fingers beneath the leather. His skin was warm. She felt bone, sinew. She watched him swallow hard and fought not to do the same. Her heart beat faster.

I was not a good man. Artur watched the road, but Elena felt his focus inside her head, strong like his spirit as it wrapped around her own. The idea of sharing her mind and body with another, a stranger, should have been torture, and if Elena had been told that such a thing was possible—had it proven to her—she would have feared it. Privacy was critical.

And yet, with Artur, sharing the innermost part of her felt natural as breathing. Good, sweet. Safe as home. They had known each other only a day, but in that day—a lifetime.

You know I don't believe that. Elena studied the line of his throat, the angular bones of his pale face. His dark hair looked rough. He needed to shave.

I know, he said quietly. *But you feel that way because you do not know everything I have done.*

Tell me.

I cannot.

You're afraid.

Yes. He looked at her. *I worked for the Russian Mafia. I was a hired gun. I killed people for money. You see? Pleasant, yes?*

No, it was not pleasant. But it was also not a complete surprise. *Do you still kill for money?*

His expression never changed, but she felt his confusion. *Did you hear what I said, Elena? I have killed for money.*

Yes, I heard. I'm asking if you still do.

No. His mind felt quiet. *Not for a long time, and only in self-defense.*

Elena closed her eyes. She savored the cool salty air rushing in through the open window. She wondered what Amiri made of all this peculiar silence, or her fingers resting inside his glove. Did the man even know what Artur was capable of?

I told him. He probably showed more surprise than you just did.

What? You expected screams? Accusations? Revulsion?

Yes. At the very least, shock.

I've seen some things, Artur. I already knew you had a violent past. The Mafia makes sense.

But still—

No. If I had never been inside you, if we had met like two normal human beings, I would find your past highly disturbing. I would not trust you. I would be afraid. But we did not meet like that, and I have been inside your mind. You can't lie to a person when they're sitting in your brain. You can't pretend to be anything but what you are. And you're a good guy, Artur Loginov. Really. I like you.

Silence followed, though it was not a true quiet: Artur's emotions made their own music, conflicted and lovely.

You are remarkable, he finally said, so faintly she could barely hear him. *Truly, Elena. I never imagined I would meet anyone like you.*

You're making me blush. Truth. Her face felt hot. Speaking mind-to-mind was also making her hot in other ways. Oh, that was embarrassing. She hoped he did not notice; she hoped—

I did not notice.

She almost said something out loud, but remembered at the last moment that they were not alone. *Please forget you heard all that.*

I would rather not. His mental voice was soft, teasing.

Elena stopped touching him. He caught her gently, caressing her palm with his thumb. Brought her hand to his lips and kissed the back of it.

I like you, too, he said, his mouth still touching her skin. Her breath caught and she snatched her hand away to clutch it in her lap. She continued to feel the weight of his fingers, his lips, the memory as real as flesh. *God.* He was good.

Touching him was too dangerous. She said, "So. How did you get out?"

He gave her an amused look. "I was recruited by an American detective agency called Dirk and Steele."

"Sounds like the name of a seventies cop show."

Artur shrugged. "They gave me new purpose, a place to go. It was probably one of the best things that ever happened in my life."

Elena thought of the woman in Artur's memories, his soft voice saying, *I love you.* She wondered where that woman was now, and what had happened between her and Artur. She wondered if Artur still loved her. Had she been one of his best things?

Elena could not ask. Never ever would she be able to bring herself to ask that question.

"Tell me about Dirk and Steele," she said instead.

"As I said, it is a detective agency. Or at least, that is the face it shows the world. In truth, it is an organization whose purpose is to seek out people like you and me—or like Rik and Amiri—and give us a place where we do not have to be alone, where we can use our gifts to help others and receive support while doing so."

"A movie would be easier to believe."

"Yes, but this is much better because it is real."

Elena shook her head. "I'm having enough trouble wrapping my brain around everything else I've seen and experienced. Even before my kidnapping I could barely come to terms with my own abilities. And now—" She stopped, staring out the window at the passing antique facades of Russian buildings, soaking in the air of a foreign land, which suddenly did not feel so foreign— merely different, in the same way an apple was different from tree to tree. Because difference was relative, and when compared to a girl who could heal, or shape- shifters who could turn into animals, the rest of the world felt like fruit, and she was the psychedelically charged mushroom. Like, radical, dude.

"Elena?" Artur asked, clearly waiting for her to finish.

"My life is changed," Elena said simply, and hearing herself say those words made her want to cry. "I can never go home again. I can never be the same person. Not just because the Consortium could find me again, but because . . . my eyes are bigger now. I know things."

"Do you regret that knowledge?"

"No," she said, and then hesitated. "Maybe. Some- times ignorance is bliss."

Artur smiled grimly. "I have always wished for some kind of ignorance, but I suppose I should be thankful I was never given any. I would be dead by now, otherwise."

Elena did not know how to respond to that, so she said nothing at all. Minutes later Artur parked the truck in front of a seedy little building. A large sign hung over the chipped, gilt-encrusted door. Above a long line of Cyrillic, Elena read: HOTEL EKVATOR: RUSSIAN COMFORT.

"My old contact owns this place," Artur said. "The rooms are not so bad, but Mikhail does not like using money for renovation. He thinks it is a waste."

"Sure," Elena said, hearing an ominous cracking sound far above her head from one of the hotel windows. She began to get out of the car, but Artur laid a hand on her arm.

"No, Elena. You should stay here with the others. I am not certain what kind of reception I will receive."

"I'm not staying here," she said. She glanced back at the shape-shifters; Amiri looked ready to leap out of the truck, and Rik was awake and alert. She wondered how much of their conversation had sunk in. "How about you guys?"

"No way in hell I'm letting you out of my sight," Rik said. "You might sell me down the river."

"I'm sure they're big on seafood here," Elena said, noting the brief—and quickly hidden—smile that passed over Amiri's face. Rik scowled. So did Artur.

"It is dangerous," he said.

"I thought you liked dangerous women," Elena replied, and jumped from the truck before he could say another word.

Amiri and Rik clambered out of the back, and oh, what a sight all four of them made on the city street. Elena could only imagine what she looked like—brutalized hair and face, wearing a sweater and skirt three sizes too big. The men, while all stunningly handsome, carried themselves like soldiers of a long war, and it was strange to see the three of them standing together in broad daylight on a crowded thoroughfare. Elena had grown accustomed to her companions, but in public, among regular people, they looked so different as to be alien. Even Artur, with his normal hair and eyes, still seemed . . . other. More than human. More than ordinary.

Magic. I am surrounded by magic.

"Are you sure about this?" Artur asked them.

"We are here," Amiri said. "I believe that is as strong an answer as you will receive."

They entered the hotel, Artur taking the lead. Elena wished she were more of a fighter. Those action movies always made it look easy. A good kick, a hard punch, a little guts and glory.

Reality meant a lot of running, a good dose of exhaustion accompanied by danger and pure gut-wrenching fear—and no way at all to complain, because that would just be childish, and no one liked a whiner. Which sucked. Elena made no claims to an easy life, but this was ridiculous.

A young woman sat at the hotel's front desk. She looked like something out of a fifties beach movie: perky, blond, with a cute button nose and bright red lipstick. She stopped filing her nails when they entered the lobby, her mouth forming a perfect crimson O.

"We are here to see Mikhail Petrovich," Artur said. "Please tell him an old friend has come to town."

The girl hesitated, her gaze flickering sideways, past Artur. Past all of them.

Stricken by premonition, Elena turned. A portly man with a bald, pasty head descended a narrow staircase off the lobby. He held a gun in his hand. He aimed it at Artur's back. The safety clicked off. Elena watched, horrified.

"Artur Loginov," he said, in badly accented English. "What an unpleasant surprise."

Artur knew who was behind him even before he heard the safety click. The girl's eyes gave it away. The gun did not surprise him, either. He expected the threat of bullets. It was why he had wanted so badly to come into this place alone. Mikhail might not actually shoot him, but where there was a gun, there was the possibility—and Mikhail was a very good shot.

What Artur was *not* prepared for, however, was Elena's voice whispering, "No," and the feel of her body sliding against his own, standing in front of him, shielding him, protecting him with her arms outstretched, like she could catch a bullet, deflect that charm of death.

"Elena!" he snapped, so full of shock—fear—that he forgot to be gentle, forgot that Mikhail was first and foremost a gentleman, and that gentlemen never fired guns at ladies. Because all that mattered to Artur was that there was a bullet aimed at Elena's heart—*his* heart, through her body—and that was utterly intolerable. Artur grabbed Elena around the waist, picking her off the ground and spinning her so that she leaned up hard against the lobby counter. Artur surrounded her with his body—close, tight—until all he could see were her eyes, large and startled.

"I should never have let you come in here," he said, voice rough, hoarse. *"Elena."*

Elena, why? Elena, how could you? Elena, if you died it would break my heart. Elena, Elena, Elena. I am not worth it. I am not worth even the gesture of your life.

He felt Amiri and Rik close ranks around them, and he turned, grabbing Rik's arm. He pulled the shapeshifter in front of Elena. He did not have to force Amiri; the man glided into Artur's place and stepped forward to meet Mikhail, who stared at him with the most curious expression on his sagging face. The gun never wavered.

"Put that away," Artur said. "Look at me, Mikhail. I am unarmed."

"A man like you is never unarmed," Mikhail said. "A man like you is the weapon."

Artur thought he heard Elena say his name. Rik was trying to soothe her. Little chance of that—Artur knew how stubborn she was. He did not dare turn to see if she was actually struggling against the shape-shifters. He was not sure what such a sight would do to his heart. He moved even closer to Mikhail, until he stood at the foot of the stairs with that gun still aimed at his chest. Artur never looked at the weapon; his eyes remained locked on Mikhail's face.

"For God's sake," he whispered in Russian. "Shoot me if you like, but not here. Not in front of her."

Mikhail's gaze flickered past Artur. "Did you beat her?"

"Of course not," Artur snapped.

"I had to ask." Mikhail lowered the gun. "I was not going to shoot you, anyway. I just had the floors cleaned."

"Really." Tension still sang through his body. "Then I suppose the bloodstains near my feet are just a figment of my imagination?"

Mikhail shrugged. "You always were creative." He descended the stairs with slow ease.

Artur wanted to see if Elena was all right, but he did not dare turn his back on Mikhail. He no longer thought the man would shoot him, but it would be stupid, and Mikhail would respect him less for it.

Mikhail reluctantly gave up the last two stairs—he never liked being the shortest man in a room—and said, "Bastard. Why couldn't you leave me alone?"

"I need help."

"If you are back in Russia after all these years, then that is certainly the case." Mikhail walked to the front of the lobby. Artur remained at his side.

Amiri and Rik watched with apprehension. Artur did not blame them. They were putting their lives in his hands—a complete stranger—and had done so on nothing more than brief assurances of good intentions. Artur, if their positions were reversed, would never tolerate that. Not that he completely trusted the shapeshifters, either. Words were not enough. Actions—honorable actions—repeated again and again, were the only truths that mattered.

Elena, on the other hand, was already too much a part of him. No doubts, no reservations. He trusted her like he trusted himself, which was remarkable, insane. Artur had never felt that way about anyone. It had taken him years to build that same trust with his friends at the agency; with Elena, it had happened over a matter of a day.

Despite her earlier words in his head, he still remained unconvinced she felt the same about him. Unsettling to be so exposed in his heart, without any promise of reciprocation.

Although her stepping in front of you when there is a gun pointed at your chest is a good indication.

Irritation bloomed. How could he possibly spend so much energy trying to divine her feelings? Right now, with so much looming over their heads, could it make any difference in his life whether or not she liked him on some deeper level?

Yes. It did make a difference.

Elena leaned against the lobby counter. Her face was ashen, her eyes far too dark. She looked upset and angry—a bad combination.

"I think you might be in a lot of trouble," Mikhail said softly. "If you like, I can put you out of your misery."

"You would like that," Artur said.

"Yes, though I might enjoy seeing you humbled before a woman even better."

200

Artur said nothing. For Elena, he would get down on his knees and crawl.

Fortunately she did not make him do that. She did not say a word. Just gave him a hard look and then turned to face Mikhail.

"I think I hate your guts," she said to him, which surprised a giant whoop of laughter out of the short Russian. Rik made a strangled noise in his throat, while Amiri simply shook his head. Artur closed his eyes.

"Wonderful!" Mikhail crowed, still smiling. "Your accent is American, yes? What a perfect woman. I like you."

"Just so we're clear," Elena said. "I don't appreciate it when people threaten my friends."

"Elena," Artur began, but she held up her hand.

"Don't," she said. "I have had it up to here with people trying to hurt us. This is not a game. This is not fun. And you"—she looked at Mikhail—"should be ashamed of yourself."

"I am not ashamed," Mikhail said, "but I do apologize."

"Good enough," Elena said. "Artur, you have some business to conduct, don't you?"

"I do," he said, somewhat stunned.

"Then do it, and we'll get the hell out of here."

Mikhail sighed, long and gusty. "If my wife had not already branded her name upon my balls, I swear I would do all in my power to woo you. I love your fire."

"I really didn't need that imagery, but thank you for the compliment," Elena said.

Mikhail looked at the girl behind the desk and snapped his fingers. "Anna," he said in Russian. "Get Artur's friends a room they can relax in. And for the woman, some new clothes and makeup."

The girl leaped to her feet and began rummaging around the desk drawer for keys.

"If you go with Anna," Mikhail said, returning to English, "she will make you comfortable."

Elena, Rik, and Amiri stared at Artur. He nodded. "Mikhail is a man of his word. You will be safe here while he and I talk."

"If you say so," Amiri said. "But I do not like it."

"Neither do I," Elena said. Mikhail surprised Artur by holding out his gun—a spontaneous gesture, utterly out of character. Elena stared at the weapon, and then him.

"Take it," Mikhail said. "Truly. If I hurt Artur, you may use it on me."

"I don't trust you," Elena said.

"No one trusts me," Mikhail replied. "Here, take the gun."

Elena glanced at Artur. He could say nothing to her, and after a moment she took the gun, held it gingerly in her hands.

"The safety is still off," Artur warned. He did not like this at all, but even though leaving them alone while he spoke with Mikhail was not his only option, he could not bring himself to voice the other. It entailed too much risk of an entirely different nature. Elena might have accepted one part of his past, but there was more—much more—and Mikhail could not be trusted not to speak of it.

"Elena," Artur said, holding out his hands. She gave him the gun, and he clicked the safety on for her. Breathed a little easier. He gave back the firearm before she could tell him to keep it. Mikhail would never let Artur in the same room with him if he were armed. Survival instincts. Artur could still kill Mikhail in hand-to-hand combat, but a gun was too blatant. It destroyed the illusion. Still, seeing Elena hold the weapon was utterly frightening. It was not something to be handled by the inexperienced.

"We'll be all right," Elena said to him, as though she could read the conflict in his face and wished to soothe him—a far cry from only moments before, when she had been quite open with her doubts. But that was Elena: when she committed to something, she stuck with it. And right now she was committed to trusting Artur's judgment. He could see it in her eyes; she trusted him.

Dear God, he prayed. *Please do not let me do anything to abuse that trust.*

Rik and Amiri seemed far less convinced, but said nothing. Artur thought he could trust Amiri to watch out for her, if only because it was in the shapeshifter's best interests. He did not feel the same about Rik, whose spirit still seemed weak, his head planted just a little less firmly on his shoulders. Rik might not be a bad person, but he seemed more boy than man.

As Anna walked around the front desk with a key in her hands, the hotel's front door opened. A man and woman entered the lobby. Tourists, cameras hanging from their necks, fanny packs sagging down their waists. Sunglasses, tour books, brand-new clothes.

"Honey," cooed the woman, gazing up at the chipped mosaic of a naked sea goddess languidly sprawled on the ceiling. "Isn't this fantastic?"

It would have been more fantastic had they entered only two minutes previously.

"If you may follow me," Anna said, glancing nervously at the tourists. "I show you room."

"*Da*," Elena said, giving Artur a hard look. "We follow."

Artur watched Elena disappear up the stairs with Amiri and Rik close behind. He wished he could go with her. He wished he did not have to be here, calling in old debts with a man he'd thought he would never again have to see. As far as former Mafia bosses went, Mikhail Petrovich was not a bad person. But he was a reminder of harder days, which Artur could have done without.

He took off his gloves and tucked them into the back of his pants. Stretched his fingers, savoring the touch of air on his skin.

Mikhail gave him a sly look, ignoring the American couple who wandered to the other side of the lobby. "Interesting company you keep. Far more exotic than I would give you credit for."

"If you harm them—"

"I give you my word I will not. I have no interest in hurting you, Artur. Not really."

The Americans began to amble closer, talking loudly about the run-down "atmosphere" of the hotel. Mikhail frowned. "Come. We should continue this in my office."

The two men left the lobby. Shoulder-to-shoulder, of course. Mikhail was not stupid enough to expose his back either. The corridor was long and narrow. Pictures hung on the walls. Moscow in winter. Moscow in summer. Moscow at night.

Artur said, "You like to punish yourself with memories."

"It is not a punishment. Just a reminder of different days. Besides, it is not such a bad thing to remember the places you love."

"Even if you can never return to them?"

"Even so. Love hurts worse when you disparage it, when you try to drown it. If I did that to Moscow, I would be giving her no respect. I would be giving *myself* no respect. And as you know, Artur, I like myself far too much for that."

Artur almost smiled. Almost, until Mikhail said, "You do not trust the people you travel with."

Artur gave him a hard look. "Untrue."

"Really?" Mikhail gave him a knowing smile. "You could have invited them in with us. Ah, but no. You were afraid of what I might say, the things they could learn about you. Or maybe you just care what the woman thinks. I can see why. She is fine. High morals, that one."

"I could have been protecting you," Artur suggested. "Your past is far more checkered than mine."

"Ack." Mikhail held out his arms. "I am totally legitimate now. What do I have to hide? That is the secret, you know. The truth does set you free, Artur. When you tell the truth, there is no person on earth who has power over you. There is nothing that can cripple the momentum of your life when you are honest to yourself and others."

"So says Mikhail Petrovich, former Mafia. Wasn't it lies that saved your life? *My* lies?"

Mikhail scowled. He stopped in front of a narrow wooden door and held it open for Artur. "I still have not forgiven you for that."

"The dress or the doctor reports from the insane asylum?"

"Both. Plus the stickers. If I could, I would kill you for the stickers."

"They were very glittery. A nice touch. Did Ekaterina like them after you were through with their use?"

"My daughter liked them fine." Mikhail shook his head. "You are a sick bastard. You do not look it, either—which makes it worse."

"I do what I must," Artur said. "And in your case, you needed to be discredited." Insanity and cross-dressing, with a dash of childlike regression, had seemed just the thing at the time. Enough, anyway, to keep the bosses from taking seriously the accusations that had been leveled: namely, that Mikhail was stealing weapons caches from them. Which was true, but that did not make him a bad man. Nor did his family deserve to pay, as they most certainly would have. Artur had taken pity.

"You did fine." Mikhail shook his head. "I think you even enjoyed it."

His office was small, with a large window set in the wall opposite the door. A wide mahogany desk sat in front of the window, with pictures and pens and several computers gracing its surface. Bookshelves lined the walls. Artur glanced at what Mikhail was reading nowadays. Nancy Drew, for the most part.

"Do not get any ideas," Mikhail said, paying attention to what Artur looked at. He sat down behind the desk. "Ekaterina likes to read here."

"Her English must be very good."

"The U.S. consulate supports an American school. She goes there. Harvard, she says. That is what she has her mind set on."

"Smart girl." Artur sat down in a soft leather chair. He watched Mikhail open a drawer and remove two glasses and a bottle of vodka.

"She takes after her mother." Mikhail poured the drinks. "So. You are back in Russia. You are accompanied by three foreigners who are looking like punk-rock orphan outcast refugees, and you are desperate. No, no, do not give me that look. I know you are desperate, because you hate asking for favors—even those favors that are owed."

Artur took his glass—*why is he here, my shipment is late and those people with him are so odd, something not right not right and it must be because of the summit*—and sipped. "I cannot tell you anything, Mikhail. Not why or how. You are right, though. I am desperate."

Mikhail sighed. "You have always been secretive. I still remember that first time we met, down at the depot. Nikolai had just promoted you, remember?"

Artur remembered. Up until that point he had spent his days on the fringe, a, bodyguard for Nikolai's children, spoiled little brats who knew a lavish life paid for by drugs, weapons, and prostitution. Not that Artur could complain. Those same vices also paid for his food, a roof over his head—a little bit of false dignity when he walked the streets.

"Yes," Mikhail continued, eyes bright with memory. "He lifted you right up to his second hand. You know why, don't you? Because you never talked about yourself. Not one word. You kept your mouth shut and you did your job, no questions asked. Nikolai liked that. He thought it was rare."

"I hated that job," Artur said. "Every minute of it."

"Except when you got paid," Mikhail remarked. He drank his vodka. "Do not pretend to be noble with me, Artur. You liked the money, just the same as all of us. You killed for money. You beat people for money. You stole and whored for money. And now . . . now you are back again, and still, it is for money."

Artur almost tossed down his drink. He fought the urge to stand up and tell Mikhail to go to hell, then hunt down Elena and the others and take them from this place, this living memory bearing down on his pride, his soul . . .

"I am sorry," Mikhail said. "That was uncalled-for."

"What do you care?" Artur listened to Mikhail's echo in the glass he held, but heard nothing but the same concern, a low-level anxiety about some future event that had him thinking immigration, a new identity, maybe a place in Boston so Ekaterina could get a head start on her dreams—those sweet dreams.

"I care," Mikhail said quietly. "You saved my life, after all. I owe you some respect for that."

"There is something else," Artur said, still tasting memory. "When I first arrived, you thought I was here for another reason."

"You cannot blame me for being cautious. It was your companions who convinced me, though. They do not look like assassins."

"You thought I would try to kill you?"

"It is what you used to do."

Artur could not disagree. "So you think you are in danger."

"Not yet, but I expect it. There are rumors coming out of Moscow, Artur. Bad rumors."

"How bad?"

"The kind that involve unification."

Artur was confused. "I do not understand."

"All the syndicates, bound together. United."

"No."

"Under one leader," Mikhail clarified. "The bosses are coming together for a meeting in eight days—a summit, they are calling it."

"For what reason? The bosses hate one another."

"You know them. Money, power. They only hate one another out of jealousy. Stroke all their dicks at once, though, and it will keep them happy. For a short time, anyway." He took a long swallow of vodka. "Someone is stroking their dicks, Artur. Ironically enough, it seems to be an actual woman. She has presented them with an opportunity that is too good to be true."

A cold feeling twisted Artur's gut: a premonition. "A woman? Do you know her name?"

"Only that her representative is also a woman. Bentov saw her from a distance, said she looks like a skeleton." Mikhail cupped both hands over his chest. "Needs implants. Some actual hips."

Graves. Artur closed his eyes. This changed everything.

"Hey," Mikhail said sharply. "Why do you look like that? I thought you did not know anything."

"Coincidence," Artur said, and then stopped. "No, not coincidence. She knew what she was doing." He stood and began pacing. He needed to move, to hit something. This could not be happening.

Mikhail watched him. "When I look at you, I feel as though I should be reaching for my gun."

"That would be a good idea. This is bad, Mikhail. *Very bad.*"

"Tell me," he said.

"First, do you know what she has promised the bosses? Do you know what they are supposed to gain?" Because the men Artur knew would not agree to be in the same place at once unless they were assured something important—something in addition to the proposed goal of the gathering.

Mikhail stared into his drink. Quietly he said, "She is promising them all of Russia. And that is just for the meeting. If they join her, she is pledging the world."

Artur forgot how to breathe. "And they believe her?"

"They do not have to believe. She has demonstrated enough power to make them curious."

Artur sat down. Beatrix Weave could do it. If she controlled all the crime syndicates in Russia, combined them with alliances she had made elsewhere, she truly could rule the criminal underground of the world. And if she managed to infect all those bosses with her psychic worm, putting them under her control . . .

"I need to stop this," Artur said.

Mikhail laughed out loud. "You are insane. Crazy. There is no stopping this."

"I have no choice." Artur leaned forward. He placed his hands flat on the desk and saw more drinks, contracts—*oh, my God, yes, yes*—a woman's round, naked body, shuddering—

"Artur," Mikhail said, protesting.

Artur shook his head, trying to block out the memory of Mikhail having sex with his wife. "No, I know you. You think Russia is already under the control of the bosses, so what does it matter if one strange woman tells them so? You think it is impossible for a woman— a foreigner—to have so much power as to simply give the bosses *permission* to take what is already theirs. You think, What balls! What nerve. You think they will kill her for sure once they hear her preposterous message." Artur took his hands off the desk, clenching them into fists. "What you do not realize is that this woman is truly that powerful. If she wanted to, she could own every single leader of every single government in this world—and do it as simply as a touch."

Mikhail sat back. He no longer looked amused. "If she can do that, why settle for little boys with big guns?"

A good question, but even as he thought about it, the words flowed to his mouth as easily as memory, truth— Beatrix's truth, stolen from her mind during Artur's brief encounter with her consciousness.

"She feeds on the pain," he said. "Politics do nothing for her. It is too refined. There are laws that would bind her. Beatrix Weave is a woman of immediate results, absolute obedience, total power. That is what the syndicates can give her, what she is striving for."

"You know her name, even?"

Artur hesitated. "She is the reason I am in Russia. She . . . wanted something from me. From my friends, too. She has a home, a . . . facility almost one hundred miles from here. We managed to escape last night, and found our way here."

"A fantastic story," Mikhail said, studying Artur's face.

More fantastic than you will ever know. Artur remained very still, looking straight into the other man's searching gaze.

"I do not suppose you will tell me how you or your companions became involved with such a woman?"

"Only that it was against our will," he answered. "Truly, Mikhail. You must be wary of this woman. She is extremely powerful. If she controlled all the syndicates in Russia—" He stopped, shaking his head. "You know how much damage they do just on their own. But united? Do not tell me you are not a little concerned."

More than a little, if he was thinking of packing his family up to immigrate. All of Mikhail's arguments were nothing but air; he was worried, too. He would be terrified if he knew the actual truth.

Mikhail said nothing for a very long time. He sat staring at his drink, holding it so that the light streamed through the crystal just so, striking rainbows on the rich brown surface of his desk. He said, "You have changed. The Artur Loginov I used to know cared for nothing except keeping his nose clean."

"I saved *you*, did I not?"

"An aberration. I will admit, though, that I was happy when I heard you had run away. You were not suited for the life."

"Thank you," Artur said, oddly pleased.

Mikhail nodded. "You left because of a woman, did you not? The ballet dancer, Tatyana Dmitriyevna. I saw her once, onstage. Beautiful form. Pity what happened to her legs."

A shock, hearing Tatyana's name from Mikhail's mouth. Artur did not know the older man had ever been aware of his relationship with her. His surprise must have shown; Mikhail held up his hands. "Yes. Again, that was unkind. I am sorry for my running mouth. I always wondered, though, what would be the final line for you. I suppose now I know."

"Tatyana was a good woman," Artur said quietly. "She did not deserve to be hurt."

"Good women never deserve that," Mikhail agreed. He rubbed the rim of his glass. "And this new woman? The one you brought with you?"

"You have said it yourself. She is also good." Artur's voice was dull, flat, hard: a warning against any more questions.

Mikhail smiled. "I like her very much."

Artur ignored that. "I need to go to Moscow."

"To stop that meeting? Impossible, Artur. How will you do it? Call the police?"

Yes, that was laughable. The police—even the army—would not be able to touch those men. They had their fingers in everything; for the state government to cut off their hands would require a monumental effort that was, quite frankly, impossible to muster. The mob simply owned too much of Russia. For Beatrix to promise them the country—and have them listen—meant she intended to do more than simply proclaim it theirs.

If she did keep her word—doubtful, knowing what he did of her—then the gesture would have to be larger, more explosive.

"Please," Artur said. "I must at least try."

Mikhail's expression soured. "I suppose you want my blessing, yes?"

"More like your money," Artur said. "At least, enough to get me there."

"Enough for your friends too, I think."

Artur shook his head. "It is too dangerous. I will find another place for them."

"You must be blind. Or dumb. Either way, I will give you enough money for everyone. Papers, too. God. I feel like I am paying you to commit suicide."

"Or paying me to save your life again."

"I doubt that. After this we are even. Yes?"

"Yes." Artur rose and shook Mikhail's hand. He was overcome with feelings of concern, pity, affection, a—*he has come such a long way since I last saw him; what a loss; what a pity he will perish, because I think we could be friends* sense of pride. Mikhail did not let go of his hand.

"You will die if you do this," he said. "Call it gut instinct. I can feel it."

"I believe you." Artur studied Mikhail's earnest face, still grappling with the sense that here, under his nose, was a man who could have been a father to him, all those years ago. "I have no choice."

"And that," said Mikhail sadly, "is the very reason the good die young."

Chapter Eleven

Elena did not like guns. It was a personal thing, divorced from politics or philosophy. She simply did not think of them as safe, especially for someone as untrained in weaponry as she was. As soon as Anna deposited her and the others in a small suite on the third floor, Elena set the gun down on the king-size bed. The dark metal sank into the worn golden coverlet, solid and heavy and lethal. She backed away to stand by the window, rubbing her hands.

"Lady," Rik said quietly, "you are crazy."

"Just a little," Elena agreed.

"It was a good gamble." Amiri paced the edge of the room, peering behind the mirrors, checking under the lamp shades. For what, Elena did not know. Monitoring devices? Bombs? Insects? "That man was prepared to shoot us—I could see it in his eyes—but his smell was all wrong for death. He did not want to kill."

"You could smell him?" Elena found that fascinating . . . and a little disconcerting. She did not want to think of how she smelled to a person with superscenting abilities.

"I am of the shifting kind," Amiri said simply. "My nose is good, no matter what form I hold."

Elena looked at Rik. "And you?"

"My blood is in the sea. My senses on land are more limited."

"And yet you're still the same kind of people. Right?" Elena leaned against the wall, watching the men, studying their hair and golden eyes. They looked human, but she could feel that touch of the alien rubbing against her, nagging. She remembered her first encounter: light engulfing fur, forming flesh; the swift shift of dolphin to man. Magic beyond her dreams. Elena wondered at herself for taking it so well, for accepting it as she had. Perhaps the circumstances made it easier—one more crazy, impossible thing to add upon a whole host of the crazy and impossible. Or maybe *she* was crazy, and this was one giant hallucination; Elena, still back in Wisconsin, was resting on some hospital bed in a coma.

Either way, she was rolling with it. Acceptance was the only option left to her—especially now, when it felt as though the only thing she could count on in her life was the promise of complete unpredictability. Expect the unexpected. Prepare accordingly. Which meant, of course, no preparation whatsoever. Simply a life spent completely in the moment, riding the course of events like a high-stepping rodeo queen.

Artur would look good in a cowboy hat.

The image was so absurd, the thought that accompanied it so unexpected, she nearly laughed out loud. Instead she turned quickly to the window to hide her face from the shape-shifters. It was difficult to conceal her smile, and she did not want to explain what could possibly bring her joy at a time like this. Kidnapped, abused, exhausted . . . what did she have to smile about?

And yet she clung to that fleeting happiness, holding it dear and tight like a beautiful line of poetry rolling sweet wonder on her tongue: a recitation of perfect words, perfect meaning. *Artur. Artur Loginov.*

You've got a crush, she told herself. *Elena and Artur, sitting in a tree. K-I-S-S-I-N-G.*

Yeah. Whatever. She couldn't help it if Artur made her happy, if the thought of him gave her strength. Not that she was becoming needy. Oh, no. This was something different. She just didn't know quite how to describe it.

"I bet you guys will be glad to get home," she said. Rik perched on the edge of the bed at the farthest corner away from the gun. He looked very young; Elena thought he might not be older than eighteen. The realization surprised her. In the facility, out in the wilderness, he had seemed so much older.

Amiri walked to the other window, bathing in the sunlight that streamed through the dirty glass. His quiet elegance appealed to her. She found him soothing.

"I am not entirely certain I *can* return home." He pressed his fingertips against the glass; his hands were long and tapered. His skin glittered with a subtle sheen of gold. "Have you thought of that, Elena? Nothing of your previous life is safe. If you go home, the Consortium will find you again. That part of you—everything about it—is dead."

She had thought of it often, but her heart still hurt. Like a dagger, twisting. Hearing it said out loud, to her face, made it real in a way she had been trying to avoid. Home was dead. The orchard, her grandfather's legacy, were gone from her touch. Maybe, just maybe, she could find a way to pay the taxes from afar; but she would never be able to walk those green grounds again or dig her hands into the earth, harvest those heirloom fruits, those small, sugary plums and pears, those apples with their singing sweetness.

Elena swallowed hard, looking away out the window. Seagulls swarmed the skies. She felt a hand, warm, on her shoulder.

"It is not the end," Amiri said. "Just another kind of beginning."

Elena nodded. Amiri seemed to understand; his hand dropped away. He glanced over his shoulder at Rik.

"And you?"

Rik said nothing. He stared at his hands, turning them over, this way and that.

"The ocean is close," Elena said, pulled from her sad reverie by the lost expression on his face. She glanced at Amiri, who also watched the young shape-shifter with a hint of concern. "It would be easy for you to leave, I think. I don't know much about what you need when you're in your . . . other form. But the ocean is a big place, right? You could hide there—keep the Consortium from finding you again."

"How did they catch you?" Amiri asked.

Rik never got the chance to answer; Anna opened the door and walked in. She held a jumble of clothes and a small cloth bag. She gave the men hesitant looks before handing everything over to Elena.

"For you," she said. She smoothed down her skirt, smiling nervously at Rik—who paid no attention to her at all. "You others, I have nothing you wear. Maybe you ask Mikhail for man clothes. Yes?"

Rik did not respond. Amiri politely said, "Thank you for your consideration."

Anna's smile faded slightly, but she nodded. She did not look at Rik on her way out. When she was gone, Elena dumped the clothes on the bed and said, "What's wrong with you? I can't say I know you all that well, but up until now you've certainly been more talkative than this."

Rik shook his head, pressing his hands together so that his fingers formed a steeple at his chin. "Silence isn't a crime, is it?"

Amiri's mouth thinned. "I believe you are too old for petulance. I also believe you should be more considerate of the fact that none of us know one another very well at all. Words are all we have for comfort."

Elena tried not to smile. "Are you a lawyer? A psychologist?"

"A teacher. The jobs are often quite similar."

Rik did not look at them. He was so engrossed by his hands, Elena wanted to look at them herself to see what was so interesting. "I'm sorry for being rude. It's just that I haven't had time to think since I escaped. Do you know how long I was there? Three months. Three months in that tank, living in dirty water, completely restrained. The only reason I was able to break the glass was that they had started getting sloppy with my buckles. And then, when I saw Amiri—" He stopped, still staring at his hands. "I haven't had time to think, that's all. Okay? I need time."

"Sure," Elena whispered, trying to recognize what he had suffered. She knew only what she had gone through, and that was bad enough. "Is there anyone you should contact? Family?" Did his family even live on land?

Rik shook his head. "No. I . . . I don't think I could reach them. Don't see much point, if I don't even have to warn them. The Consortium didn't capture me near my home. I could return there. It's not so easy, though. Home."

"It's better than nothing," Elena said, thinking about the farm. She gathered up the clothes and makeup and went into the bathroom. The clothes were obviously Anna's things, which Elena felt reluctant to borrow. The chances of her actually being able to return them were slim to none. She just hoped Mikhail was generous about compensating his employees.

Elena looked into the mirror—scared herself.

She took a very quick shower. There was almost no hot water, but the soap felt good, as did the privacy. She dried off and dressed in tight jeans and a light-weight green turtleneck that hid the finger marks on her neck. It was a relief to know her injuries were no longer visible. The rest of Anna's makeup, a thick foundation she smeared over her bruised cheek, did the rest. She looked better, healthier. She did not look like a victim.

She left the bathroom. Amiri and Rik had not moved at all during her absence. She wondered if they had even shared words.

"You look better," Rik said, obviously trying to make up for Amiri's "petulant" comment. "I don't mean that in a rude way, but you do."

"Thanks," Elena said. She wondered how much longer Artur would be, and whether he was all right.

You could check on him, a part of her whispered. *You're still linked. Kind of.*

She tried to reach him. She tried very hard, but felt nothing. The only times she had traveled the link were during emergencies or unconsciousness, or while touching—and the driving force behind her had been instinct. No thought, just action.

Elena gave up. Irritated at herself for thinking she was capable of another kind of miracle, she pressed her forehead against the window, staring at the foot traffic, car traffic, soaking in the scents and sounds of a Russian port city.

And then she noticed someone staring back. Brown hair, green eyes.

The Quiet Man smiled.

Artur felt Elena's fear slice through his heart like the fine wire of a garrote: strangling, cutting off the breath of his soul. He jumped to his feet, knocking over the chair, spilling vodka on the desk, his pants. Mikhail cried out, shocked. Artur said nothing. He ran from the room.

The American tourists were gone. Anna sat behind the front desk, still filing her nails. Artur grabbed the girl's arm and hauled her up. Her mouth dropped open; she stared at him with the same horror reserved for death. Artur did not care.

"Where are they?" he shouted in her face, desperate. "Where did you take Elena?"

"Artur!" Mikhail roared, stumbling down the hall after him. "What is the meaning of this?"

"Elena!" Artur shouted, shaking Anna. "Tell me!"

"Artur!" Elena's voice was distant. Artur released the girl and ran to the stairs, listening to the hard pounding of footfalls. Elena appeared, followed closely by Amiri and Rik. Her eyes were huge, cheeks flushed. She held the gun in her right hand.

"He's here," she hissed, grabbing Artur's arm. She glanced over her shoulder at the hotel lobby doors. "We can't leave through the front."

Artur touched Elena's hand to take the gun and saw instantly what had frightened her so much: Charles Darling had found them. Charles Darling had looked straight up into her eyes and smiled.

"Mikhail," Artur said, staring down into Elena's eyes. "I am going to require what we discussed, and I am going to insist you give it to me now, without question."

"That bad?"

"Worse." Artur let go of Elena, taking the gun with him. He moved carefully to the front door of the hotel, peering through the glass at the street. He did not see Charles, but that meant very little. The killer might already be inside the building. Artur locked the door.

"Artur," Mikhail said, and his voice was low, hard. Artur expected questions, demands, but instead he heard, "What do you need?"

Artur moved back to the others. Amiri had already begun unbuttoning his shirt. His eyes were bright, sharp like his teeth, glimpsed behind his parted lips. Artur shook his head. Not yet. Not unless there was no other way.

"Same. Money, papers, passports. A safe place to hide."

"You ask for so little," Mikhail drawled, holding out his hand for the gun. Artur gave it to him. "Come, follow me."

Artur gestured for Anna to follow her boss. He did not bother asking if there were guests in this building. If there were, he had no time to round them up to safety—not that there was a safe place, where Charles Darling was concerned. Artur's only consolation was that Charles was here for a specific purpose. Diversions were unlikely until he got what he wanted.

Which was probably Elena.

They ran down the hall after Mikhail. Artur savored the heft of the gun. It felt good to hold a weapon again. Elena bumped against him; he grabbed her wrist, stroking skin with his thumb. He felt her fear, felt her think—*What are we going to do?*—and then he was fully inside her head, and he said, *We will fight, Elena.*

Of course, she replied, her thoughts scattering like

hummingbirds. *But there's more than just fighting. If the Quiet Man is here, there will be others.*

Maybe. Though I do not believe Charles Darling enjoys hunting with a pack. I think it is possible he came here alone.

One man for the four of us, including two shape-shifters? That would be incredibly stupid.

Unless he does not plan on returning with all of us.

"Oh, God," Elena said. "You had to say that."

"Excuse me?" Mikhail glanced over his shoulder.

"Nothing," Elena said. Mikhail gave her a hard look, but did not ask. He stopped in front of a narrow steel door locked with a digital security bolt. He punched a code into a keypad and the bolt slid back. Mikhail hauled open the door.

"In," Mikhail said.

In, forward through darkness, down a series of wide stairs, deeper and deeper, the air growing cool with a moist scent that was ocean and rock and the crusty remains of sea life. Behind them Artur heard a click; the door locking.

"There are only two ways in and out of this place," Mikhail said. "And the exit you will be using is perfectly secure. No one will hurt you down here."

"I am not just worried about us." Artur's voice, though quiet, echoed dully off the cavernous walls around them. Low-level lights, set in the stairs, kept him from falling. The technology used in this bolt-hole was impressive. "I am afraid I have put you and your family in danger, Mikhail."

"Of course. So typical."

"I will make it up to you."

"Nothing within your power could ever make up for that."

They reached the bottom of the stairs; Anna switched on the lights. The room in front of them was small, filled to bursting with equipment, gun racks, tall metal cabinets, and a long center table covered by translucent plastic bins. The walls were made out of rough-hewn rock.

"Anna, get the camera." Mikhail walked to nearest cabinet and pulled out four blue books: American passports. He tossed them on the table and pulled up a stool. Elena peered over his shoulder.

"Those look real."

"That is because they are." He waved his hand in her face. "Do not ask."

"Wouldn't dream of it," she muttered.

Anna returned holding a Polaroid camera. She gave them a tremulous smile and Artur felt guilty for frightening her. "Who first?"

They all lined up against a white screen for their passport photos. Anna set each one out to dry, and then set about cutting them with careful precision. Mikhail prepared the passports, and handed them back to the young woman.

"My niece," he said proudly. "Smart girl. Multitalented."

"You should take her with you," Artur said. "You need to get your family, Mikhail. Load them and yourself on the nearest ship to Japan. There is always one leaving from the port, yes? No waiting, no good-byes. From there, fly to America. I assume you have everything you need down here or close by? Passports, money, your bags packed for emergency?"

"One might almost think you read my mind."

Artur smiled grimly. "You are a survivor. You do what it takes and always plan ahead."

"It is that or die. Despite the fact that I already planned for the possibility, I just wish it did not have to be this way. So unexpected. We were all finally getting settled in." Mikhail reached into another cabinet and removed four small packs. He passed them out. "There is money in each bag. One thousand U.S. cash, with matching amounts in rubles. American-brand cigarettes, too. Marlboro."

"I don't smoke," Elena said.

Mikhail shook his head. "So naive. Those are bribes. Little bribes, for little men. It is amazing what one pack can get you nowadays."

Anna set aside one passport. In Russian she said, "I am doing my best, but without more time, I cannot guarantee these will stand up under close scrutiny."

"Do your best. Artur, is there anything else you need?"

"A three-band cell phone, if you have one. Something that will let me make international calls."

"Done, but I recommend waiting to make your calls until you are well out of the city. The encryption is good, but no need to risk smart eavesdroppers."

"Where are we going?" Rik asked, adjusting his pack. "They'll find us, won't they? If we go too far? They've tracked us here, after all."

"We cannot stay," Artur said.

"No, we cannot," Amiri said, "but the boy is right. We need more information. I assume you want us to keep trusting you."

"Hey," Elena said. Artur nudged her gently—ever gentle—because now required a soft touch, a quiet hand.

"What I want has very little to do with anything. I am not trying to keep you here, Amiri. If you or Rik . . . or even Elena wishes to go, you may. Just wait for the passports. You will need them." Or rather, Amiri and Elena would. Rik might just turn into a dolphin and swim away.

Amiri shook his head. "I am not threatening to leave. Only, I am not a man who walks blind. I have never given my life wholly over to any person. Do not ask me to begin now."

Do not ask me, do not force me, not when so much has already been taken from me. Leave me choice, leave me the illusion.

Artur slipped on his right glove. He extended his hand to Amiri. In the hush, the expectant quiet, the shape-shifter contemplated that gesture with a great deal of seriousness. He clasped Artur's arm.

Artur's gaze traveled slowly from Amiri to Rik, and finally to Elena. "I need to go to Moscow. Before Charles Darling appeared I would have suggested the three of you stay behind, perhaps take a ship to Japan. I no longer believe that will be safe."

"Why Moscow?" Elena asked.

Artur glanced at Mikhail, who made no effort to hide his curiosity. No doubt he wondered how this little circus fit together. "Beatrix Weave is planning to unite, under her leadership, all the crime syndicates in Russia. She will be meeting with them eight days from now. I must stop her, I am sure you all can appreciate why."

Rik shook his head. "This just gets better and better. If we go with you, we're not escaping—we're going right back to her. I won't take that risk."

"I agree. Which is why I am not suggesting you come with me. You have options the others do not."

Rik's eyes flashed gold. "Sure. Done."

"Well, I'm not," Elena said. "I'm going with you, and *not* because it's my only option. You need help."

"Tell me about it," Rik muttered.

"We will talk about this later," Artur said to Elena. He looked at Mikhail. "How are the passports?"

"Done," said Anna. "Um, but this is four-day work I

do in four minutes. Do not show to many, yes? If you do, maybe screwed."

"That's good to remember." Elena took her passport. "And . . . this is not my name."

Rik peered over her shoulder. "You sort of look like an Yvette."

"Maybe, if this birth date didn't make me fifty years old."

Mikhail gave Artur a cell phone. "So. You have everything you need, but I would say we are still not even. You may have ruined my life today."

"Fine," Artur said. "I owe you."

"If my family suffers too much from this, you will owe me quite a lot."

At the other end of the room was a narrow crevice; Mikhail led them through until they reached a door. Beyond lay darkness.

"There is another door inside that room," Mikhail said. "It opens up into a restaurant I own, down by the waterfront. Stay there. I will call you a car to take you to the train station. I recommend the Trans-Siberian for your return to Moscow."

"A train doesn't seem safe," Elena said.

"Safer than the planes. The police there will check your passports. And let us be honest: that is the first place someone will look for you, because it offers the fastest way out of here. A train is slow. A pleasure ride. No one would be that stupid, yes?"

"Charles Darling found us easily enough," she commented. "I don't think *he* tried the airport first."

Mikhail ignored her and clapped his hand on Artur's shoulder. "Take care. Maybe we will see each other again."

"You do not really believe that."

"You are right," Mikhail said. "I am such a fake."

* * *

The restaurant was a crab shack specializing in just that—fresh crabs, only minutes from the sea. Steamed, boiled, fried—as many as a person could eat for pennies on the pound. No one looked askance at Elena or the others when they exited the door into the main body of the one-room restaurant. It was as though they did not exist—or just that everyone there was familiar with Mikhail Petrovich, and did not want to cause trouble. Out of sight, out of mind. If you pretend not to see something, then it does not exist. Simple enough.

The restaurant was half-full, with the windows thrown open and the door propped with a rock. Sunlight bathed everything in a white-hot glow. It was beautiful, cheerful, homey—and all Elena could think about was Charles Darling. She was afraid of him, but not for the same reasons as before. She knew she could kill him.

And that was the problem. While she was quite certain he deserved to die, that was a choice she did not want to make. She was weak, maybe. Cowardly. But it was a hard thing, looking into the dark mirror, seeing that everything you held yourself to be was no longer true. Healer? Sure. Killer? Quite possibly. All in the same breath, no less.

Artur stood in the doorway of the restaurant. Elena joined him, but he pushed her gently back.

"You must be careful," he said.

"I think the same could be said about you." Elena felt Rik and Amiri gather close; outside, people walked and talked, enjoying the sun. Beyond lay the waterfront, the jutting piers surrounded by boats. Rik stared; he made a sound, low in his throat. The diners behind them cracking crab almost drowned it out, but Elena was close enough to hear his misery.

"We need to find a place for you to enter the ocean,"

227

Elena said. "If you're not coming with us, we have to make sure you're safe before we leave."

Artur looked at Amiri. "Will you be separating as well? If so, there are ships to Japan that leave every hour. I cannot guarantee their safety, but it would get you away from here."

"And what would I do in Japan?" Amiri shook his head. "I think I will stay with you and Elena. I will trust just a little longer."

"Even if it means your life?" Rik asked him, tearing his gaze from the ocean just long enough to look him in the eyes.

"Even so," Amiri said. "And besides, I am already dead. It is written, the time and place. Until that moment comes, I am invulnerable."

"Borges," Artur said.

"You are educated."

"No," Artur said, "but I have tried to make up for that." He glanced up and down the street. "I do not see the car, but there is a pier just across from us. Underneath, there might be a place where you can shift."

They left the crab shack. Unspoken was the decision that they all go together. Perhaps not wise—as a group, they were highly visible from a distance—but no one wanted to be left alone. Pack mentality, maybe. Or just the fear of being left behind. The embankment off the road was easy to slide down; it was littered with crab legs, fish parts, old lines and hooks. The sun felt good on her face, though Elena worried about her foundation melting off.

It was cool and dark beneath the pier, a long, narrow space of sand and rock. No people. If someone looked their way from one of the boats anchored out on the water, they might be in trouble, but Elena suspected it was the best they could do in this city.

Rick did not take off his shoes or clothes. He crouched on the border between land and water. Dipped his hand into the sea. Licked his fingers, one by one.

"Now is the time," Artur said. "Get away from here as fast as you can."

"Return home," Amiri said. "If you are able to without endangering yourself. Find your family."

"Family," Rik murmured.

He almost did it. He almost jumped in, fully clothed, fresh from the land. Elena saw the way his muscles bunched beneath his shirt, the subtle glow of his exposed skin. And then he stopped. Shook his head.

"I can wait," he said, though the crack in his voice revealed the lie. "You need all the help you can get. I still owe you."

"No," Artur said, but Rik gave him a hard look.

"I owe you," he said, in a voice brooking no argument. He glanced at Amiri, who stood quietly beside Elena. Slender and dark, like an elegant shadow. Rik's lips tightened. "And there is my brother to think of. I never imagined meeting another of my kind. I can't leave him now. Not when there's danger."

Amiri bowed his head. Softly, he said, "My decision to stay was not meant to force your hand. You are not obligated to me."

Rik snorted. "Every man chooses his own obligations, Amiri. Leave it alone."

He did. The four of them walked up from beneath the pier. Rik turned to gaze one last time upon the Pacific; his hair was tinged the same blue-gray of the horizon. Again that glow.

And then the light died. He did not look back again.

The car was there when they ascended to the street: a long black sedan with tinted windows, parked in front of the crab shack as if it were waiting on some visiting dignitary. The driver got out as soon as he saw Artur and the others. He was big, a well-dressed thug. He opened the back door and did not bat an eye at all of the strange foreigners filing past him. Artur said several quiet words to him in Russian. The only response was a solemn nod.

Elena studied the surrounding area. She did not see the Quiet Man. She did not even see the Hotel Ekvator. Mikhail's secret passage emptied out in an area completely apart from where they had entered. *God love a crook.*

It took them less than five minutes to reach the Vladivostok terminal train station, which perched on the edge of a cobblestone road congested with coughing buses and small cars. Through a choking haze of exhaust, Elena studied the ornate cream-colored building with its carved triple archway and small turrets, the fine round dormers, and the huge red sign plastered to the front of the building. More tacky than lovely, the train station nonetheless carried a certain resigned charm.

"We're still close to the water," Rik said, almost to himself.

"Zolotoy Rog Bay is just behind the terminal," Artur said. "It is not too late to turn back."

But Rik said nothing more. Their driver steered the car right up onto the sidewalk, narrowly missing several old women who hopped out of the way, flapping their arms like chickens. The driver pulled the parking brake, gave the angry women a bored look, and made a shooing motion with his hands. Insulting, patronizing— Elena thought that if any other man had done such a thing to them, there would be nothing left but a puddle of blood. Instead, the old women took one sharp look at the driver, as well as the license plates on the car, and moved on. Quickly.

No one harangued them about the flagrantly illegal placement of the car; Elena even spotted a police officer at the end of the street, who very deliberately turned around and began walking in the opposite direction. Elena was suddenly very happy that Mikhail was on their side.

Mikhail's help continued; the driver followed them into the train station, and it was clear what his purpose was. Muscle. A hired gun meant to keep them safe. Something that Artur should be familiar with. She wondered if it was strange for him, this reversal of roles. Then again, Elena suspected Artur was a man who never thought much about things like that. It would be too petty. Before, he had a job to do, so he did it. Just as the man who currently walked behind them was doing a job—nothing more, nothing less. After he got them safely aboard the train, he would no doubt return home to a girlfriend or family. One more day, working hard for the money.

Rik, eyeing the bodyguard, said, "What is it you do for a living, Artur? You seem to know a lot of . . . interesting people."

Interesting. Elena wanted to laugh.

Artur said, "I work for a private detective agency in the United States. Before that, however . . ." He hesitated, and Elena nudged him with her elbow. There did not seem much point in holding anything back from these men.

"The Mafia," he said shortly, giving her a look.

"The Mafia," Rik said. "You're kidding me."

Amiri made a humming sound, low in his throat. "I do not think he is."

231

"Oh." Rik glanced again at their bodyguard, who was doing an admirable job of pretending to ignore them. "Okay."

Artur waited, but Rik said nothing more. After a moment, Amiri said, "Shall we continue inside?"

So much for being hated and feared. Elena wanted to smile. Instead, she brushed her hand against Artur's and felt him take a deep breath. They walked into the train station.

The interior was more modern than Elena expected, though still messy with people. The crowds made her nervous. Everywhere, she expected an attack, some strange hand to emerge and snap her back into captivity. She wished Rictor were there; a mind reader would be a good friend to have right about now. She hoped he was well. She also hoped he would come back one day to explain some things to her—like why he had helped her, made that first step of resistance with her arrival.

You're better off not knowing. Yes, maybe. But unsatisfied curiosity could be a horrible thing.

The lines in front of the ticket counters were monstrous and, in fact, were not lines at all but just a giant mass of flesh, rippling in one direction. *Hours*, Elena thought. It would take hours to get through that mess, and by that time the Quiet Man would probably have her roasting on a stake.

Artur, however, did not seem concerned. He made them wait by the wall, tucked behind the first pillar of a colonnade. The driver stayed with them. Elena had no doubt he was armed to the teeth, and that was fine. Wonderful. She might not like holding the gun, but she was honest enough with herself to appreciate letting someone else do it.

From her spot next to a drooping plastic tree, Elena watched Artur struggle through the scrambled mishmash of bodies—chaos, a crowd: bent old women lugging plastic bags, swaddled in thick sweaters with brightly colored scarves covering their hair; lean men with quick eyes talking loudly on cell phones; a tour group from Asia, a tiny army of red caps and a Russian woman at the head of them, holding a flag with Chinese characters written on it. More and more—the cavernous train station felt like it housed several different nations. Artur pushed and shoved until he reached the front of the ticket line. If Elena had not watched with her own eyes, she would never have believed it possible.

"He's going to start a fight," Rik pointed out. Elena agreed.

Amiri merely smiled and said, "Look at their faces."

Elena did, and it was true: those who began to protest Artur's actions took one glance at his face and got out of his way. In fact, the longer she watched, the more it seemed to her that there was a method to the madness—a pecking order, of sorts. So much for being subtle. Elena said as much, and again Amiri smiled.

"It is the same at home. Lines are a convenience of societies that have so much to give; that its people have the patience—and confidence—to wait and go without. But when you have nothing, every little push and shove, every step above your neighbor, is a chance for you to survive, to get what you want before it runs out. It is survival."

And Artur Loginov is a master of staying alive.

Which, when Elena thought about it, was pretty damn sexy.

He certainly looked sexy when he walked away from the ticket counter, a small smile tugging on his mouth. He held four sets of paper in his hand, which he handed out to everyone.

"We are lucky," he said. "Today is an even-numbered

day, so we will be on the Rossiya to Moscow. It is the best train to travel on when you journey by rail. I bought us first-class tickets."

"How long will it take us to get there?"

"Almost a week."

"A week? Artur, a lot of bad stuff can happen in a week. And trains aren't exactly easy to hide on."

"Easy targets, yes? I know, Elena, but we cannot fly. Our passports would never hold up to the scrutiny. We cannot drive, because it would take too long. Paperwork is not checked so thoroughly on the rails, and when it is, the officials are easier to bribe. No, the train—no matter how risky—is our best bet."

"It's also cutting it close," Rik said. "What if she changes the schedule? She might, after everything that has happened."

"Unlikely," Artur said. "This meeting is too important to change at a moment's notice. Nor would the bosses like the implications of a sudden shift in timing. Altering things at the last minute means trouble— usually the kind that involves death. No. I think she will pretend everything is fine, and she will go to that meeting and begin manipulating the leaders into an alliance—with worms in their heads as insurance."

Amiri shook his head. "Her power cannot be limitless."

"How do you know?" Elena frowned. "All these things we can do . . . none of it makes sense anyway. The doctor tried to understand, but for all the people he poked and prodded, I don't think he ever came up with a satisfactory explanation." At least, not one he had been able to give her. Not that she had been given all that many opportunities to ask. Elena was still frustrated by that. Realizing she was not alone made her want more: more information, more whys and why-nots. Why could she heal while others changed shape? How could a man read the memories of others with nothing more than a touch, while another became trapped by something so seemingly harmless as a circle in the sand? Why did she share space with the soul of a person she barely knew?

"It doesn't have to make sense," Rik said. "You just have to ride the wave. Accept and ride, right up until you come to shore."

"You must be the dolphin philosopher of the deep," Elena retorted, not missing the dark circles under his eyes. "Riding that Big Kahuna to illumination."

"Totally," he said. Elena smiled, and it suddenly occurred to her that she was enjoying herself. Not the danger, not the risk . . . but the company. These three men, though she barely knew them, made the suffering easier to bear. She could be herself around them. She had never been able just to be herself around anyone—not even her grandfather, who worried constantly, who worked so hard to turn her into a good person that she had stifled herself, limited her interests and opinions so as to not offend him.

But here, now, none of that was necessary. She was free and accepted, and what a gift—what a lovely blessing, even in the midst of such jeopardy. Elena's secret was no longer hers alone to keep.

Dogged by their bodyguard, they walked through the train station, past the wide-open doors into sunlight. Elena smelled engine grease and iron, the salt of the sea; she felt the roar of a train beneath her feet, the thunder of movement coming and going, the swift approach of the future in another piece of this foreign land.

They did not go far before Artur pointed out the Rossiya. The train was long and surprisingly cheerful in appearance: a clean red-and-blue exterior with many large square windows. Most of the passengers—young men in military uniform and older women toting heavy packages—gathered around the back of the train, waiting for their turn to board. Artur walked past the locals to another carriage section that was less crowded. The people on this end dressed slightly better, and some of them spoke perfect American English. In fact, the same couple who had narrowly missed the showdown inside the Hotel Ekvator stood waiting to board the train. They smiled at Elena and the others, clearly recognizing them. Elena felt rather less enthusiastic about their presence.

She pressed close to Artur. "Are you sure this is wise? Wouldn't it make more sense for us to mix with the locals?"

Artur shrugged. "Normally I would say yes, but Rik and Amiri both have memorable faces. I would rather have them stand out in a cabin accustomed to foreigners than spend the next week in the midst of crowds who are more likely to remember an exotic face."

"I'm not sure that matters," Elena said. "Seems to me that if the Quiet Man is already here, Beatrix Weave will have her people combing this place soon enough. Someone is bound to remember us. She'll figure out where we're going. She might already know."

"Perhaps, but we must get out of this city. If we had time, luxury, I would suggest going underground. Fully changing our appearances, disappearing south into China, and from there back to the United States. Taking our time. Charles found us because we rushed, because we went to the very places that anyone who knows me well might suspect. This is my fault, Elena. It will be my fault if she recaptures us."

"Don't get all happy with the blame game yet," she told him. "I'm just saying, this feels like the worst escape plan ever."

Artur snorted. "You are always easy with your insults, yes?"

"It's not an insult when it's the truth, but believe me, I don't know that we would do any better than you do. You've gotten us this far with flying colors. This is your home territory. It's just . . . we're sitting ducks, Artur."

"Quack," Rik said, breaking into the conversation. Artur glared at him. The shape-shifter held up his hands and backed off. He pretended to hold a significant conversation about the weather with Amiri, who was studiously ignoring the discussion between Elena and Artur. Funny how privacy could be reached through nothing more than an illusion. Though considering that this discussion also affected them, she hoped the two shape-shifters were more interested in it than they acted. Artur leaned close.

"I am sorry," he said quietly. "Truly, I am. There are people who will help us, but they will never be able to reach us in time for the meeting in Moscow."

"Your, um, Dirk and Steele," Elena said.

"Yes. There is an excellent chance they are already searching for me, but until I contact them there is no way to be certain." He touched her shoulders, peering down into her face. "This has already been ugly and messy. It is only going to get worse."

"Thanks," she said, only mildly sarcastic. A small smile touched Artur's mouth; she thought he would kiss her, plant something soft on her forehead, but instead he brushed a gloved hand over her lips, and Elena suddenly knew why Amiri and Rik were giving them space, what she and Artur must look like together when they spoke. Warmth spread; her cheeks were burning.

"You could leave," he said gently. "There is still time to find another way for you, Elena." He would do it, too. She knew that much about him. He wanted on that train worse than anything, but he would step away from it to help her if she decided not to go. He would still find a way to Moscow—eventually—but he would take care of her first.

"No," she said. "I'm going." Going because she did not have a choice. Yes, she had some money and fake papers—enough, perhaps, to get her a ticket on one of the long-distance ferries to Japan that Artur had mentioned earlier. But that would mean leaving him—leaving, too, Rik and Amiri—and while sticking close meant danger, she could not bring herself to break loose and separate. She had found people who were different like her. Different in all the best possible ways. She could not abandon that. Not for anything.

And, if she were being honest with herself, the way she felt toward Artur went beyond friendship. Went far beyond anything she had ever imagined she could feel. Tenuous, thrilling—more magic than the magic she had already encountered—and the wonder of it was that she suspected he might feel the same. That was worth a little danger.

They waited in line behind the Americans and Europeans. Artur looked utterly calm, unconcerned, but every now and then Elena caught the movement of his gaze, flickering about like a Geiger counter, measuring trouble. She tried to do the same. Everything looked normal, with crowds of people hauling luggage and small children, bawling and shouting and laughing with boisterous and—to measure by some of the flasks in hand—drunk conviction. Rik hunkered down in his light jacket. He fussed with his cap. Elena wanted to tell him to leave it alone, but that would have sounded too much like a mother hen, and Rik—while younger than her—certainly did not need that. At least, she did not think he did. He seemed so very young sometimes.

Amiri, on the other hand, looked like he did not need anything or anyone. Elena knew he was with them only because he was intrigued. Perhaps he even felt a sense of duty, obligation because Artur had helped free him— but that was it. Elena respected that. She liked Amiri, and thought he liked her, too. But she knew what it was like to stand so long alone that to be with others felt odd, like clothing that might be comfortable, but with enough of an unfamiliar fit that she kept questioning, worrying at it. Much like Amiri was worrying at it; she felt his tension like the whipping of a great invisible tail. It was in his eyes, the flare of his nostrils. He was an unhappy cat.

The doors opened. Artur said a few words to their driver, who nodded his good-byes and melted backward into the crowd. Elena turned around just before she boarded the train; she did not see the Quiet Man, but she still felt the target written upon her back, could still feel that first sting between her shoulder blades. Always, for the rest of her life, she would feel that pain. Memory lingered strong in the body.

The train interior was dark and stuffy. Elena smelled cigarette smoke and fried food. The combination made her slightly nauseous. She dug her nails into the palms of her hands. No vomiting allowed. Not now.

They shuffled single-file down the narrow hall, accompanied by the sounds of slamming doors and grinding metal gears. The floor vibrated just slightly. The people ahead of them, the American couple from the hotel, stopped and walked, stopped and walked, looking for an open cabin. They finally found one, and Artur pushed ahead, quick. Elena sensed Amiri at her back, his own urgency. She, too, felt pressure to hide, to find— like a little mouse—some hole to cower in for warmth and protection. Beware the owl, beware the spider: the long reach of danger, hungry and searching with a black, swimming eye.

Each cabin contained only two beds. They took the last two rooms in the hall, right by the emergency exit—which, when Elena poked her head out to look, was merely an open-air platform that would require a potentially lethal leap from the train if there were an actual emergency. Still, it *was* an exit. Better than nothing.

When she turned around, Amiri and Rik had already disappeared into one cabin. Artur stood in the doorway of the other. He held the door open for her.

"I hope you do not mind," he said.

"No," Elena replied, though she did. It was not that she wanted to be alone in this place; simply, her feelings for Artur ran so deep and were so confusing, she did not entirely trust herself in his presence.

Their cabin was tiny, with plastic faux-wood walls and a hard metal floor. Directly across from Elena was a small window with a yellow lace curtain. Its delicate edges wavered as hot air rose from the electric heater set near the floor. Just below the window jutted a tiny plastic table. There was a bed on each side of the cabin.

"It looks comfortable," Elena said, to fill the silence.

"It is the best the Rossiya offers," Artur said. "We were lucky that Mikhail was in a generous mood."

Elena tried not to laugh. "I think the credit goes mostly to you. I've never seen a man talk so suave."

Artur shrugged. "It is a skill, like any other. You do what you must to survive."

"Then I suppose words have kept you alive for quite some time, huh?"

"More than just words," Artur said, and there was a heaviness to his voice that made the hairs on her body rise.

Rik knocked on the door and peered into the room. He studied the beds. "You don't have sheets either."

"An attendant provides those," Artur said. "Give me a moment."

He slid past Elena, touching her hand for one brief moment in passing. The feel of his leather glove on her skin—warm from *his* skin—made her stomach tighten. Oh, this was a bad idea. Sharing a room with him was *not* going to work. Or rather, it might work too well.

Elena stepped into the hall with Rik. She watched Artur walk away from them, a tall, lean figure in black. His shoulders were almost too broad for the stolen weathered shirt, the jeans almost too small.

Perfect. Elena glanced at Rik and found him watching her with a knowing smile.

"What?" she asked, blushing.

"Nothing," he said. "I just hope Amiri and I can get some sleep at night."

"Pig," she said.

"Not unless they have fins."

"They most certainly do now," Amiri said, joining them. He gave Rik a stern look. Elena smiled. At the end of the corridor Artur had stopped to speak with an old woman in an olive-green uniform. Her face resembled that of an aged bulldog, her mouth smeared red with lipstick. She looked quite stern.

And yet, mere moments after Artur began talking, her expression softened into something almost beautiful. She nodded, smiling. Artur passed her some money. Her smile widened and she walked away down the hall.

"Oh, you're good," Elena said, when he was near enough to hear.

"I am merely polite," Artur said, with a small smile that told Elena he knew exactly what he was doing. "Attendants like Ms. Gogunov are very important women on this train. It is good to be friendly with them."

Indeed, Attendant Gogunov soon returned, this time bearing a tall pile of sheets and towels, all of which were folded with military precision. She bypassed the men entirely and handed everything to Elena, who staggered under the surprising weight of so much linen.

She gave Elena a disparaging look, said several sharp words to her in Russian that could not have been polite, and then said several more words—in a much softer tone—to Artur. She smiled at him. He smiled back. She chuckled and tweaked his collar and he caught up her hand to kiss the back of it. Elena rolled her eyes.

The old woman noticed. Again, more sharp words. Elena smiled apishly and said nothing at all. Which was answer enough in any language. Attendant Gogunov grunted, whipped around on her hard-soled heels, and clipped back down the corridor. The floor vibrated with her every step.

"You know," Amiri said rather cautiously, "I do not think she liked you very much, Elena."

"The feeling was mutual," Elena said, glaring up into Artur's amused face. "Oh, yeah. Laugh it up."

He did not laugh. He pinched the corner of a creamy sheet.

"No," she said. "I'm not making your beds."

"Alas, feminism." Rik grinned and plucked away a sheet and towel before Elena could throw them at him. Amiri made a clucking sound with his tongue and did the same. They disappeared back into their cabin and shut the door behind them.

Which left only Artur. He stood very close, very warm, with his dark eyes watching her face—so kind, so gentle—and really, Elena would make the damn bed for him if only he promised to keep looking at her like that for the rest of her life.

He took a sheet and towel, and said, "We should get out of this hall."

"Oh. Oh, yeah." Elena stumbled backward into the cabin. The backs of her legs hit the bed. She sat down hard, which hurt more than it should have; her mattress looked soft, but felt like rock. Artur looked away quickly. Elena thought he might be laughing.

They made their beds in silence. The cabin was so tiny it was impossible not to brush up against each other. Every touch, no matter how innocent, made fire in her belly. She could not help herself. It was sickness, a disease, and even if she could have cured herself she would not have, because it felt too good. It was exciting, to be so near a man who was worthy of warmth. So many were not. Just illusions, parading themselves like cheap facades. Not worth keeping over the long, hard years.

Artur was no illusion. His heart was beautiful.

Their hips bumped, the tips of their elbows rubbing. A hand was placed just so at her waist as he moved past. Her own palm brushed his hip. Fire, fire, fire—she felt it as their backs met, hot, sidling sideways. Elena bent down to fix the far corner of her bed and felt him watching her, silent and powerful. She wanted him to touch her again, with purpose this time, with more, and her body ached.

Anger destroyed the moment. Somewhere outside the train a man began shouting in Russian. Artur peered from the window. Elena joined him. A lanky figure with thinning hair and a long nose stood just below, loudly berating a young blonde who held a child in her arms. She looked desperate, poor. Her face was red. The man threw up his arms and turned away. The woman made no move to follow, but screamed something at him, words that made several bystanders stop and shake their heads. The man kept walking. The woman stared, hunching in on herself, swaying.

"What happened?" Elena asked softly. She could not stop staring. The baby slept. It had a beautiful face.

"He does not want them anymore." Artur's voice sounded dull, tired. "He already has a wife in Moscow, another child. That woman down there is his mistress."

"What did she say to him?"

Artur's jaw flexed. "That she would give up the baby. That if he did not want her, she would give his daughter to the street."

"Oh," Elena breathed. "Oh, no."

Artur stepped away from the window. He sat down on the bed. Elena watched just a moment more—long enough to see the woman straighten up and walk away from the train. Elena stared at her swaying back, the tip of the baby's head. She wished them a good life. She prayed for it.

Artur stared at his gloved hands. Elena could not see his face. She sat down beside him, thigh pressed against thigh, shoulder rubbing shoulder—close, making him close with touch—and laid her hand in his. A moment later his fingers closed, holding her tight. His hand felt good—better than almost anything Elena had felt in her entire life. Holding his hand was like being anchored safely to the world, solid and strong and warm.

"This is still a poor country," he said, and his fingers gently squeezed. "In poor countries people give up their children so they can have a better life."

Elena thought of her mother. "People give up their children for all kinds of reasons. It happens in rich countries, too."

He nodded, still staring at their joined hands. "How

did you cope, Elena? What did you do when you were left behind?"

She jerked back, surprised, but Artur refused to let her go. She began to ask him how he knew, but it was simple, really. He had touched her. She had touched him. And there was the link between them to consider. A man like Artur could see everything, if you gave him the chance.

"How much do you know?" she asked. It hurt to talk about her mother.

"Only that she left you. Much like my mother left me, I think."

Elena licked her lips. Her mouth felt dry. "She tried to kill me. Or at least, that's what it looked like. There was an ax. An ax by the old shed. She picked it up. Aimed for my hands."

"Because of your gift?" His eyes were soft, dark with knowing.

"Because of my gift. She couldn't handle it. My grandfather . . . my grandfather later said that she could do things, too. That she could . . . hear people in her head, and that it always made her crazy. She hated what she was. I think she thought I would hate it once I got older. Maybe she was afraid, too, of what would happen if people found out. Like, I would get hurt. Or *she* would get hurt. Either way, my mother wanted it gone. She thought it was unnatural."

"You heal," he said. "You are a miracle."

"Maybe." Elena turned away. "But miracles hurt, Artur. Miracles make people want to lock you up or kill you." She couldn't keep the bitterness from her voice.

"Elena," he murmured. "Do not dwell in bitterness."

"Bitterness?" She forced herself to look into his eyes. It was difficult; his gaze was too far-seeing, as were his hands. "What do you expect, Artur? Yes, I do good. Yes,

I am proud of that. I wouldn't change a thing. But has my . . . my gift brought me happiness? Real happiness?" She shook her head. "No. Only . . . isolation. Loneliness. I don't call that a prize."

"You are not alone now," he said, his grip tightening around her hand.

"You can't promise that will last," she said, forcing out the words even though they hurt, even though she wanted so badly the fantasy of *yes, forever*.

"Elena," he said, but she tore her hand away and stood up. Her mother had left her, her grandfather had died, and for a long time it had been just her, an army of one.

Artur touched her again. His glove was off. He said, "No. It does not have to be that way. Some things last, Elena. Not all, but some. All you need is faith, and I know you have that. I have felt it inside you. In your feelings toward me."

"Artur," she whispered. *I am afraid*.

"Do not be afraid," he said. "Please. Do not think of past or future. Only now. Moments after moments to come, all sliding into one."

Moments. Elena sighed. She loved Artur's voice; it was becoming a weakness to her, much like his touch. She savored the strong warmth of his words, his hand, which suddenly felt like enough, sweeter and stronger than any promise.

Some things last, she thought. *Miracles happen*.

"Yes," Artur said softly, drawing her back to him. As she moved a bell rang; the train lurched and stopped. Elena staggered and Artur placed both his hands around her waist to hold her steady. She stood between his legs with her hands outstretched, careful not to touch his flesh. It was the only distance she could give herself, and even that much was difficult. She wanted to touch him so badly. She missed the warmth of his skin, though his palms felt hot through her clothing.

"Elena." Artur's lips barely moved; her name was part of his breath. His eyes were liquid with warmth, liquid like Elena's body, which she fought with all her might to control. Maybe this was wrong, a bad idea, some temporary delusion. Artur's life looked like a flash movie of pain and violence. Men like him had crippling hang-ups that never went away. Like abused dogs, always flinching at the outstretched hand. Reflex.

Elena stretched out her hand. Artur did not flinch. She touched his shoulder, fingers trailing up, up, up to his hair. She skimmed the fine dark strands. Artur closed his eyes.

"Can you sense me?" she whispered. He shook his head. Elena slipped her fingers a little deeper. "And now?"

He shook his head again. Trembling just a little, Elena buried her fingers in his hair, fingertips floating just above his scalp. She kneaded, tugged, a light massage of ethereal proportions, and Artur let out a sigh that sounded like the low last breath of a dying man. The hands at her waist tightened. Elena stepped close. She kissed the warm crown of his head, inhaling the light scent of leather and sweat. Warm, impossibly large, his palms drifted up, slow, and Elena found it so difficult not to touch his skin, to bring her lips down upon his brow, his closed eyes, his mouth.

You've touched each other before. He didn't seem to mind then.

But she was trying to be careful now. Elena had some idea of what Artur suffered when he used his gift—when he was forced to encounter something new and different. She did not want to impose that on him, refused to make him hurt simply because . . . because she wanted him.

She tried to pull away. His strength was impossible. Artur opened his eyes. Very slowly, exquisitely so, he stood. There was no room for him; Elena had been standing so close already that the only way for him to rise was to slide up against her body, inch by slow inch. His hands never lost their grip on her waist; even when Elena leaned back, he simply held her, moving forward so that their bodies still touched, rubbing against a veil of clothing.

His gaze stole her breath, and when he said her name it was another kind of touch, a whispered caress that traveled down into her stomach, twisting wet and hot. He said her name again and kissed her.

His mouth felt good. Elena shuddered, wrapping her hands in his hair, pulling his head down for a harder taste. He made a sound low in his throat. The trained lurched again. Both Artur and Elena lost their balance, hitting the bed at an awkward angle that had them sliding in a heap to the floor. Artur stretched flat, one leg propped up on the bed. Elena lay on his chest.

"Are you okay?" she asked, trying to roll off him. She touched the floor, felt something sticky, and wrinkled her nose.

Artur wrapped an arm around her: an effective trap. His gaze was hot, hungry, but a smile played on his lips. "I am fine. You?"

Elena tried to think of something clever, but being that close to his face, pressed tightly against his body, made it impossible. Artur seemed to understand. His smile died. He sat up, still holding her, almost carrying her backward in his arms until Elena straddled his lap. A good place to be. They leaned in for another kiss.

Someone knocked. The door opened and Rik peered inside the cabin. "Oh." One word, filled with great amusement. "That crashing sound makes sense now. You've already started."

Artur's jaw tightened. Rik blinked and stepped back. He shut the door.

"I think I liked him better when he was moody." Elena leaned close and nipped Artur's ear. His arms tightened.

"He is reminding me of another friend." Artur kissed her throat. "The youthful version. Which means we will have no peace."

No peace was something Elena could live with, especially if it was of this variety. But peace, she thought, was something Artur craved, and she had to ask. She had to know.

She hugged him. "Why isn't this hurting you, Artur? I know you keep yourself covered for a good reason, so this . . . this doesn't seem like it would be natural to you. Touching, I mean."

"Because I do it so well?" he asked, smiling sardonically.

Elena laughed, trying to shove him away. "No. You know what I mean."

Artur briefly closed his eyes. "You are right, Elena. This is not natural. It has been years since I allowed myself to know anyone so completely."

"Does it pain you?" she asked, afraid of his answer. "Is there anything inside me that hurts you to look at?"

"No," he breathed. "Even your shadows are sweet."

"No one is that good, Artur. I know I'm not."

"Good and bad are matters of perspective, Elena. Relative terms. You have wicked thoughts, hurtful desires, but yours are so . . . small . . . compared to the enormity of your compassion, that everything else becomes meaningless. You are lovely to touch, Elena. You are such comfort."

She would have accused him of bullshitting her, but there was so much sincerity in his eyes, she could not help but believe him. Or at least, believe that *he* believed. Elena knew herself. She had very little faith in the quality of her soul, even if she considered herself to be a "good" person.

The train began to move, a slow creep that quickly turned into the roar of wheels, the *click-clack* of the rail, stealing them from Vladivostock, the ghost of the facility; the Quiet Man, and Beatrix Weave. They were not safe—might never be safe—but Elena was okay with the illusion. For now.

"Choo-choo," she said, softly. "Up, up, and away."

Up into the unknown, wherever that might lead.

Chapter Twelve

Everyone reconvened in the dining car. There were few people there; the Americans who had the next-door cabin sat in a corner, talking between themselves. Elena watched them for a moment, envying their normality. Husband and wife, clearly still in love. No crazy people chasing after them. The only thing they had to worry about was ordering dinner in a foreign language, and praying it didn't make them sick. Elena had just seen the public toilets in their train car—not a place she wanted to spend a whole lot of time, especially when the only source of toilet paper was Attendant Gogunov. One measly sheet did not quite cut it.

"So," Artur said, when they had put in an order for beer. "We have made it this far."

"Don't jinx us," Elena said.

Amiri, who had been looking out the window at the rolling hills and birch forests, leaned forward and folded his hands against the white tablecloth. Music—some generic instrumental—played softly over the speaker system. "We must assume that if they tracked us to Vladivostok, they will discover we boarded this train. There could be agents here now, just waiting for the right opportunity to take us back."

"It is a risk," Artur admitted. "But this is a confined space. It is difficult to hide. And . . . I have already taken some precautions."

"Precautions?" Elena asked. "What, did you booby-trap our cabins?"

"Even better. I bribed Ms. Gogunov to act as our eyes and ears, and to get her colleagues on the train to do the same. She has already given me a list of all the obvious foreigners, and she has promised to tell me if she sees or hears anything even mildly suspicious."

"You trust her to do all that?" Rik looked incredulous. "This isn't some movie, you know."

"No," Artur agreed coolly. "This is real life, which I know quite a lot about. And yes, I trust her to follow through on our agreement. She is being paid well to do a job that she would do naturally on her own. Earning money to gossip is a luxury, and she knows it."

"Besides," Elena said, "she wants to bear his children. Or his grandchildren. She wants to bear something for him, either way."

"Bare or bear?" Amiri asked, amused.

"Both."

Artur coughed. "We have six days until we reach Moscow. All we need to do is lie low until then."

The beers arrived, the four bottles slammed down hard by a surly waitress. When she left to get something for the Americans, Rik said, "I'm not worried about the train ride. It's Moscow that bothers me. I mean, I agreed to come along and help, and I'll do my best, but this is crazy."

Elena agreed. It *was* crazy. But it was the kind of crazy she could catch a ride with, because she knew the alternative. She did not pretend to have Artur's understanding of what it would mean to have Beatrix Weave controlling all the disparate Mafia groups in Russia, but she had no doubt it was a very bad thing.

And maybe—just maybe—if they could keep her from doing this, they could find another way of stopping her for good. If so, Elena could go home again. Perhaps not permanently—after this, life might never be secure enough for that—but at least she could touch the soil again. Walk her little patch of earth. She would give up a lot for that.

"You have committed us to a difficult task," Amiri said. "According to you, we are faced with not just one woman, but an entire organization. Should these Mafia bosses defend her, we will also be up against every criminal group in Russia."

"Yes." Artur sipped his beer. Everyone waited for more. He said nothing.

"You know," Elena suggested slowly, "the longer you keep back your plans, the more likely it will become that we beat the crap out of you for them."

"Yes," Artur replied.

"Would you like that? Because I can start now. I think I could do a fairly good job. Pent-up anger and all that."

"Yes," Artur said again. "I'm sure."

Elena shared identical looks of dismay with Rik and Amiri. "I can't believe this. You have no idea what you're doing. You are totally flying by the seat of your pants."

"Well," he said. "Yes. It is almost impossible to assess the mechanics of the situation without having more information."

"You don't care about mechanics. You're going to bust in there balls-out with a gun and put a bullet in her head. That's what you're thinking, right? That's suicide, Artur."

"Only for me," he said. "And besides, it might not come to that. I know some of those men. I used to work for them. I cannot believe they entirely trust Beatrix. A few well-placed words might be all it takes to break up the meeting."

"That is very optimistic," Amiri said. "Where I am from, it takes more than words to sway the corrupt. Money is the better persuader, and right now Beatrix Weave has more than us."

"She also has the fear of God," Rik said. "And she's not the one doing the fearing."

"I hate to give her too much credit, but I agree." Elena fussed with her beer bottle. "I might be new to the supernatural—and no, don't you guys look at me like that—but the things she does, even the way she looks, is just not right. It's . . . too much. *Too* unnatural."

"Too much, like shape-shifters? Too unnatural, like a girl who heals?" Amiri smiled. "Can there really be limits left in your mind as to what is possible?"

"Give me a break," Elena said. "Tell me she's not freaky powerful."

"I cannot. But that does not mean she is without weakness."

"I doubt she can stop bullets," Rik said. "No one can do that."

"Some can," Artur said, with so much seriousness it was impossible to accuse him of pulling their legs. "Beatrix, however, has shown no indication she is telekinetic. Even her psychic abilities, though strong, seem to be limited to a specific kind of use. According to Rictor, and my own observations, I do not think she can read minds without first forming a link through some kind of touch."

"She'll be shaking a lot of hands, then," Elena said.

"No," Artur said, thoughtful. "She is paralyzed from

the shoulders down. She has only the smallest amount of movement in her wrists and fingers."

"Awkward," Rik said.

"Very." Artur leaned back, staring at Elena. "That is why she wanted you so badly. Besides the obvious reasons, she wanted you to cure her paralysis before her meeting in Moscow. She needs to be fully functional, or else she risks losing the opportunity to infect every mind there."

"Because not everyone is going to want to shake the hand of a quadraplegic—"

"But a beautiful young woman, who is free to move about and touch and touch and touch . . ."

"Crap," Elena said. "This sucks."

"I would think this is good news," Amiri argued.

"Unless Beatrix believes I can heal her before the meeting." Elena closed her eyes and covered her face. "In which case she'll be on me like nobody's business. Shit."

"This does not change anything." Artur touched her back. "Elena, please."

Elena ignored him, thinking fast. This was serious. This changed the equation. Because now it was not just her simple escape: it was the escape of a tool that Beatrix Weave needed—had to have—before a certain date. The stakes had just been raised. Again.

"I'm a danger to be around," she said, feeling melodramatic, but happy that for once a little melodrama was utterly appropriate. "But this could work to our advantage. You should drop me off at the next town. I'll play the wounded-deer game—'Oh, those horrible men just dumped my ass—' and they'll catch me. You know they will. Here's the thing, though: An injury like Beatrix's cannot be healed overnight. It might even be a year before she regains full use of her body. I told the doctor, but I doubt he had time to pass on the information before he, uh, died."

Amiri frowned. Artur said, "No. Letting you be recaptured is not an option."

"Stopping Beatrix is most important. If she gets me, she might not care enough to spend her energy chasing all of you. You'll have a better chance of getting to Moscow. Even *I* might get to Moscow, because if Beatrix doesn't know her paralysis can't be healed immediately, I might be able to convince her to take me along to 'continue her treatments.' Don't you see? It's perfect."

"It is idiotic," Amiri said. "We are not cubs you must lure the hunters from. We are grown men who can take care of ourselves and one another."

"I'm thinking of the greater good," Elena argued. "She won't kill me."

Although you could always kill Beatrix yourself. The thought stopped her cold. Shocking, thrilling, horrifying: it made perfect sense. She could do it with just one touch. Stop the woman's heart, burst the blood vessels in her brain.

"All this self-sacrifice is making me sick," Rik said, but Elena barely heard him. She could not breathe.

Artur leaned forward. "What is it, Elena?"

She shook her head, unable to tell him, to speak those words out loud. He peeled off a glove and touched her hand. His expression darkened.

"No," he said again. "No, you cannot. Leave it to others, Elena. Let me do it."

"Do what?" Rik asked, but Amiri laid a hand on his shoulder, quieting him. Elena did not think Amiri was a mind reader, but he looked at her with such a knowing gaze, she suspected he had a very good idea of what Elena was considering.

"It would be perfect," she said, struggling to keep her voice steady. "It would save lives."

Artur wrapped his fingers around her hand, squeezing gently. "You have dedicated your entire life to healing others. Do not stop now, Elena. Not like this."

"You don't like killing people," Elena said. "I don't think anyone at this table does. But you're willing to do it if it means stopping a tragedy from occurring. I feel the same, Artur. I could do this."

"I know you could," Artur said. "But I do not want you to."

Elena yanked her hand away. "It's my choice."

"Whoa." Rik stared at her. "Am I imagining things? Are you seriously saying you would and could off this woman?"

"Rik." Amiri tried to quiet the young man, but Rik shook him off.

"No," he said, "I want to know how."

"I can heal," Elena said, growing cold inside her heart. "I recently discovered I can also kill with that same gift."

"So if she captured you, got you ready to heal her—"

"I could do it."

"Stop this." Artur sounded angry. "You already fought off Charles Darling. What makes you think he did not tell Beatrix what you did to him? What makes you think she did not feel it for herself through their link? And what of the worm? She could infect you, control you, and you would never be yourself again. You would never have the chance to carry out this foolish plan, and your sacrifice would be for nothing."

Elena looked away, out the window. Mountains touched the sky, blue sky so bright it hurt her eyes, hurt her heart. She stood up and grabbed her beer. "I'll talk to you guys later."

"Elena." Artur stood with her.

"Don't," she said. "Just . . . leave me alone."

She thought she heard his voice in her mind, whispering, *I do not want to leave you,* but she pushed it away, trying not to feel the ache in her heart that was not entirely her own. She left the dining car and, though she wanted to, did not look back.

Her solitude, of course, did not last. Less than fifteen minutes after returning to the cabin—dodging Attendant Gogunov, who looked at Elena as if she counted as one of Artur's "suspicious people"—Artur himself knocked on the door and peered inside.

"May I come in?" he asked, and Elena could not bring herself to say no. She was, in fact, rather pleased to see him. It mattered to her that he cared enough to come and talk, that he gave her time to be alone, but not enough to wallow in self-pity. He was showing himself to be a good friend that way.

She lay on the bed, staring at the rough ceiling. Artur sat across from her, elbows braced on his knees. His gloves were on. They did not talk for a very long time. Elena relaxed, listening to him breathe. She tilted her head to look at Artur. He sat, watching her.

"I don't *want* to kill her," she said quietly. "I just don't want anyone else to get hurt because of a missed opportunity to end this fast."

"I will not repeat my argument as to why I think your plan will fail. I believe very strongly in what I said, but even if I did not, I would still refuse to let you do this."

"Because it's dangerous?"

"Yes," he said, "and because innocence lost can never be regained."

"I'm not that innocent."

"You are, Elena. And that is not a bad thing. Tell me:

If you did this, would you ever trust yourself again to heal someone? Would you ever put the same faith in your gift, knowing you had used it in a premeditated murder?"

"It would be self-defense," she argued.

"Charles Darling was self-defense. Beatrix Weave would be . . . an offensive strike."

Elena rolled over on her side to look at him. "You're getting technical on me, Artur. All I want to do is help."

"You are helping," he said.

"In what way? Out of all of us, you're the only person who knows how to do anything here. Even Rik and Amiri are feeling useless. I can see it in their eyes."

"Elena—" he began, but she cut him off.

"I'm a fighter, Artur. Just not *that* kind of fighter. No matter how much I want to be, I'm no warrior princess. That doesn't mean I'm helpless, though. I can still watch your back. I can still . . . contribute."

Artur moved across their small cabin to join her on the bed. He gazed down at her, and the look in his eyes was so kind, so exasperated, she wanted to throw her hands up and weep. Lost, a goner—Artur might not realize it, but that look on his face had just ended the argument.

"This has nothing to do with contribution," he said. "And there is nothing shameful about being unfamiliar with this part of the world."

"Maybe not, but I feel as though you're shouldering it all. Every little bit of hardship."

"It is, as they say, all in a day's work."

"Ha."

"Yes, I know. But it is true. Since I was twelve years old, I have spent almost every day doing something that brings me close to death. I have never been able to escape it. I am not sure I would know how. I am a survivor, Elena. That is what I do. What I am paid to do, only now it is for the benefit of others."

"You help people," she said. "With your detective agency. I think you would do that work for free."

"It brings me joy," he agreed.

"Purpose," she said.

"Family," he finished. "Friends, whom I do not need to hide from."

"Sounds nice," she said wistfully.

Uncertainty passed over Artur's face. It was strange, out of character for a man who was always so quietly confident.

"You could come back with me," he said finally, soft, slow. "When this is over. I am sure there would be a place for you at the agency."

"Fighting crime?"

"Or doing what you love best. Healing people. The agency has resources. You would have the opportunity to use your gift and be among people who appreciate it. Dirk and Steele is not the Consortium. No exploitation. No fear. Just acceptance."

It sounded wonderful. Too good to be true. But here was Artur, and he had lived that dream—he and others. Was it possible to do such a thing? To actually live the life she had dreamed of for so long?

"Amiri said I can never go home again. The Consortium would look for me there."

"That is true."

"But the Consortium kidnapped you, too. What about your home? It can't possibly be safe for you, either."

"No. I will also have to leave. The difference is that I will not be alone. Neither will you. We protect our own, Elena. *I* will protect you."

"Even if I don't join your agency?"

"Even so." A simple promise, sweet and lovely.

Elena curled around Artur's body. She touched his hand. He took off his gloves and tossed them on the bed. Pressed his fingertips, light as butterflies, on her face. He closed his eyes, and then Elena was with him in his head—easy as breathing—and she saw what he saw: the vastness of the past and present, streaming together as jeweled windows of memory—her memories, bright—and then his mouth touched her mouth, *hot*, and his hands moved, sliding warm and strong against her face into her hair until she stopped looking at herself and moved deeper into him, deep like his tongue, searching . . . searching soft and delicious, making her high on his taste, which was sweet as the slide of his skin beneath her hands, sweet as the memories she saw of a little kitchen filled with two women, older and young, white ducks scattered on aprons, wielding spoons and singing songs, dancing, *dancing* around a little boy with a thumb in his mouth, sucking—sucking on her lower lip—pressing her down upon the bed as he lay beside her, wrapping his leg around her hip to draw her near, close, tight—tight as his mother's grip on his hand, tight as her grief—

"No," he murmured, breaking their kiss. "No, please. Not that one."

"I'm sorry," she whispered. It was hard to keep her eyes open; her body felt heavy. She nuzzled his cheek, running her lips against his skin, drinking in his close strength, the sense of oneness that filled her heart every time she touched him. "But I'm only sorry because it upsets you. There's nothing to be ashamed of, Artur. You can show me anything."

"If I did not want you so badly, I would never risk sharing my memories. I would never risk seeing yours."

She pulled back just far enough to look into his

eyes—his old-soul eyes—soft with desire, hunger. She breathed, "Say it again."

"I want you," he whispered. "That first time we met I wanted you. I wanted to know you inside and out."

She kissed him, smiling against his mouth. "You move fast. I think you accomplished the inside part within five minutes of our first encounter."

"Oh, no." He drew her even closer, running his hand down her side, cupping her, tracing the crease of her buttocks through her jeans. She shuddered. "You are more complex than five minutes. I think I will need a lifetime to know you."

"Cocky man," she said, breathless. "You think I'll give you a lifetime?"

Artur thrust hard against her body, pushing just so. The sensation made her gasp. She sank her fingers into his shoulders and he kissed her, burying himself against her body as though their clothes would disappear by will alone, by desire, and it felt so good to have him on top of her, heavy with want, strong against her mouth. She reached down; there was not enough room between their bodies to touch him, and he said, "Not yet."

"You have got to be kidding."

He laughed, low, and she felt the sound move through her body like pleasure. He touched her face, tracing the fine lines with a reverence that stole her breath away.

"It has been a long time for me," he murmured.

"Is that a warning or a promise?"

He laughed again, which was her intent. "You are so wicked, Elena."

"Dangerous, too. Fiery."

"Lovely," he added.

Elena cradled his face in her hands, wondering just how much he could see, still afraid he would find something that disturbed him. Hypocritical, perhaps: she wanted Artur to feel comfortable sharing himself with her, and yet she was afraid of doing the same.

But I am here, she thought. *I am here, touching him.*

"Yes," Artur whispered. "We are both here."

"How deep does it go?" Elena asked him. "When we touch, when we don't touch, how deep does this connection run?"

"It runs down to our souls," Artur said. "We did something to each other when you healed me. We left holes, and then we filled them up."

"With pieces of ourselves," Elena said. "So is this real? What we—" She stopped, realizing the presumption of what she was about to say. Artur stroked her mouth with his thumb.

"Say it," he said, so gentle.

"What we feel for each other," she whispered. Not she or he, but both of them. A unity of emotion.

He smiled. "When you first saw me, you refused to look into my face. Why was that?"

"Oh." Elena's cheeks warmed even more. "Can't you read my mind?"

"I am not a mind reader," he said. "But when I touch you, I do sometimes hear your immediate thoughts."

"I don't hear yours," she said.

"My gift," he explained. "But do not change the subject."

"I wouldn't dream of it," Elena said. Then, softer, she admitted, "It was like looking at the sun."

"Excuse me?"

"The reason I couldn't look at you. You were the sun. Stare at it too long and you get burned. Too bright, too hot, too much of everything." She took a deep breath. She suddenly could not look him in the eyes; it was that first moment all over again.

Artur touched her chin. He peered down into her face, silent for such a long time that she became nervous.

"I think the only thing you need to fear about the two of us is that I am not as good with words as you are." He pressed their hands together, palm-to-palm, lacing their fingers tight. "We are real, Elena. I have always doubted my ability to remain sane—there is always so much unwanted in my head—but you . . . you I want there. I have never been able to say that about anyone."

A lie. She remembered her first vision inside his head. His body curled around another, whispering, *I love you.* Artur must have heard her thoughts; a line formed between his eyes, which grew pained, sad.

"Her name is Tatyana," he said. "We were together for a year. She was my . . . first love. In more ways than one."

"Oh," Elena said. And then, a moment later, *"Oh."*

"Yes." He looked embarrassed. "You must understand, Elena . . . what you and I have should be impossible for me. I have never been able to stand the prolonged touch of anyone. Even with Tatyana it was difficult, but I loved her, and so I bore the discomfort."

"What happened?" Elena wanted to know. Asking questions about Artur's former girlfriend did not hurt her as she thought it would. Perhaps because he had his heart in his eyes—so fragile, those eyes—and his hand was warm and strong. Because now they had history, the two of them, the shared test of trials past and still to come, the promise of more—more danger, more harm—and still, still they were together, and Elena could not imagine anyplace else she wanted to be. She had always been a stable person. Despite the way she had been abandoned by her mother, her grandfather's love and compassion had made the difference. She did not have hang-ups about people leaving her.

"I happened," he said, when enough time had passed

that she thought he would not answer. This time it was Artur who looked away, and Elena pushed close, seeking his eyes. He did not fight her.

"Artur," she whispered.

"Elena." He stopped, pained. "Elena, when I worked for the mob, I had to do many distasteful things. I did them because it was better than the street. To be without money or a home is a hard thing, but it is worse in Moscow. There are no safety nets, no helping hands. Everything you have must be fought for, to the disgrace of your dignity and pride. When Moscow is done with you, Elena, you have no pride. But I worked my way up. I got a job running errands for rich men, and later for their bosses, who were even wealthier. And then I stopped running errands, and I started carrying a gun."

He paused, and Elena said, "You used that gun."

"Yes. I used it many times. Sometimes to defend myself, sometimes not. My gift helped me avoid some trouble before it reached violence. Not always, though. Not enough. And then there came a day when the next bullet was suddenly too much, when I could no longer look in the mirror and *not* think that perhaps I should die as well. I decided to stop. My boss did not like that. I suppose he thought I would turn to the police or some nonsense. I would never have been so stupid. I just wanted out. I would have worked in the steel mills or the coal mines—anything but what I was doing. I was so stupid." He blew out his breath. Closed his eyes. "They took mallets to Tatyana's legs. Crushed the bone. She was a ballerina, Elena. The rising star of the Kirov. She loved to dance more than anything in the world, and they took that from her. *I* took that from her."

"Oh," she breathed, horrified. "Oh, Artur. You couldn't have known—"

"Yes, I could have." He looked at his hand. "All it

would have taken is one touch. But I had stopped doing that. I was so tired of feeling the darkness in my head. Just a little break, I thought. No more testing the waters. And you see what happened, yes? I should never have gotten involved with her. My job, my circumstances . . . they were not safe."

"The heart wants what the heart wants," Elena said softly.

"That is no excuse for endangering another. I promised myself I would never fall in love with another woman, would never take that same risk, and now here, look at me. I cannot help myself. I am such a fool."

Elena did not take offense. "Did you just say you love me?"

The pain in his eyes did not ease. "What if I did?"

"Nothing," she said, but with a faint smile that stole the bite from that word. His mouth twitched.

"Just nothing?"

"Well, maybe a little something. Just a little."

"I can live with that," he said. He kissed her, and his mouth was sweet; it soothed, lulled. Elena had never been kissed so long or with such gentle passion: the concentrated focus of a man who wanted nothing more than to touch her with his mouth, again and again and again. His touch relaxed her to the point of insensibility, until she could not move; she simply clung to his shoulders, soaking in the pleasure. He eventually pulled away, and Elena sighed.

"You are tired," he said.

"I haven't slept much since waking up in the facility," she confessed, wondering if that was a subtle hint that she had not been doing enough to please him.

"It was not," he said wryly. "Trust me, Elena. I have not felt this good in a very long time."

"Yeah?" She moved her hips against him. Artur briefly closed his eyes. He swallowed hard.

"You should rest," he whispered hoarsely. "You need to be strong, at your best."

"At my best for what?" she asked archly. "Maybe you should get some sleep, too."

"Do not worry, Elena. I am used to going without."

"In more ways than one," she teased. He groaned, burying his face in her neck.

"You are awful," he said, and then, "Really. I have not slept in true safety since I was twelve years old."

Elena frowned, all of her mirth fading away. That was a hell of a long time not to get a decent nap. She wondered how he could be so calm about it. "But you've been at Dirk and Steele. You've been safe there."

He hesitated. "I have nightmares."

He said it simply, like a child, except Elena suspected Artur's nightmares were far more vivid than any child's visions of the deep dark. She touched his face, tracing bone, smoothing back hair.

"Close your eyes," she said. "Rest a little. I'll keep the bad dreams away."

"Elena," he said, but she covered his mouth with her fingers. His lips moved against them, soft: a kiss to build a dream on.

"For me," she whispered. "Let me do this for you, Artur."

"I cannot," he said, but his eyes were already drifting shut. She could see now what she had missed before, that she had mistaken his quiet coolness, his stoicism as something natural. And maybe it was, but right now it seemed like nothing more than a soul-deep weariness—years old—rocking down upon his shoulders like the nightmares he feared. Artur, whom she'd thought feared nothing.

"I fear losing you," he said, and then: "That makes you uncomfortable to hear."

"Because I know you mean it. And no one except my grandfather has ever felt that way about me."

"I suspect you're wrong about that."

"No. People can't fear losing what they don't know. And I've . . . kept to myself. You know why."

Artur sighed. "It is difficult to have secrets. They are so much like breathing—like heartbeats, because everyone has them. Inescapable, yes? Some are less harmful than others, but for each individual it is the same: he or she believes their secrets will destroy them. For some that is true. Usually, though, the fear is an illusion. One more waste of time."

"Not for us."

"No. Nor can we hide from what we do."

Elena buried her head under Artur's chin. "Rictor gave me the statistics. There may be a lot of us out there, keeping our kinds of secrets."

"But there is one less now." Artur kissed her. "And your secrets are safe with me."

"And yours?" she asked. "Are you ever going to trust me to see the things you're scared of?"

He hesitated. "I have not always been a good man. Even now I am not good, but I was worse before. I am afraid of how you will feel toward me when you see the things I have done."

"You sound resigned to rejection."

"How can I not? It is always a possibility."

"Then you don't know me as well as you think." Elena closed her eyes. "Get some sleep, Artur."

She felt his silence weigh upon her, but she refused to look at him. She was not angry—she was not even hurt—but she did feel stubborn. Stubborn to prove him wrong. Determined to face down her own prejudices and see this man for who he was. She knew the gentle side. She needed to see the violence, too. Not to judge, but to understand.

Artur's arms tightened around her body, but he remained silent. After a time his breathing deepened. His body relaxed. Elena, comforted by his warmth, joined him in sleep.

Chapter Thirteen

She awakened alone. The bed felt cold. Artur stood by the window. The sky outside was dark, but he had the curtains pushed back. His shirt was off. He held the cell phone in one hand.

"You don't look happy," she said.

"The phone Mikhail gave me does not work. No service. I will have to wait until we reach a town before I can try again."

"Were you trying to call your friends?"

"Yes. They need to know that the agency has been compromised. They can also help us when we reach Moscow."

"Must be nice having friends like that. How did all of you meet?"

Artur placed the cell phone on the small table beneath the window and crawled back into bed with her. Elena ran her hands over his smooth, hard chest. Touching him felt so good.

"Dirk and Steele is currently run by two individuals, Roland Dirk and Yancy Steele. They are distantly related to the original founders, who are also powerful psychics. Over the years both of them have cultivated a vast network of contacts around the world, people who are paid to tell them when they hear rumors of anything . . . unusual. Individuals who can do remarkable things. It is not easy finding people this way—luck, more than anything—but it does pay off. And sometimes the precogs in the organization, the men and women who catch glimpses of the future, also see those we are meant to find. As they did with me."

"They had a vision?"

"Nancy Dirk, the founder of the agency, knew where to find me and how. It was not easy. Tatyana was in the hospital and I was living on the streets again. Roland Dirk found me sleeping in an alley in the middle of a Moscow winter. He did not know quite what to make of me."

"I bet you didn't take much convincing."

"You would be surprised. I thought it was a trick. Roland, however, is almost as stubborn as you. He refused to give up. It took a week of discussion, with me still living in that alley, before he convinced me of his honesty. That, and I finally became too desperate and hungry to care. Lucky, yes? He brought me to America, found me a home, paid me well—and all to do the kind of work I never dreamed was a possibility."

Images and sensations flashed in her head as he told his story: a biting cold, the smell of cardboard and trash, piss; a pair of sharp brown eyes, peering down, and a voice saying, *"Fuck."* Then, warmth, a hospital room with a familiar face looking up at him with hatred, disgust, and oh, that breaking heart, that grief, that *You are such a freak, Artur.* A freak, a monster, running away to another country, another world, and . . . and . . .

Safety, fulfillment. Such a shock. Years spent thinking

it was all a mistake, an illusion, that he would be betrayed by Roland and the others. Until one day trust became natural. He knew there was no illusion. It was all truth.

"Yes," he said. "As incredible as it may seem, there is no ulterior motive. The agency is what it is."

"And you really like them? The people there?"

"I do."

"Then yes."

"Yes, what?"

"Yes, I'll go back with you. I'll join that agency of yours, if they'll have me." It was another start, and better than nothing.

His arms tightened around her. "You still have doubts. Your old home."

"My farm. My grandfather's farm. *His* father's farm. It's in my blood, Artur. I love that patch of earth. It's my paradise."

"We will find a way," he promised. "We will find a way for you to have both."

"I don't know how."

"We have come this far. I think we can manage some more miracles. You know all about that, do you not?"

Elena smiled, sad. Artur kissed her. It was more awkward than before. She could not relax enough to enjoy his fingers on her shoulders, his lips at her throat. Artur stopped kissing her.

"I am sorry," he said. "You are not comfortable."

"No, I'm not," she said. "But that's not your fault."

She was afraid he would disagree, that he would beat his chest and bemoan his lack of manly skills—either that or bemoan hers—but instead he nodded and turned her around, pulled her tight against his chest so that she spooned between his legs, cocooned in warmth and the scent of skin and smoke and iron. Artur had very strong arms, a hard chest. Long legs that wrapped around her legs, folding her up like some small, dainty thing. Which was nice, because Elena did not think of herself as especially small or dainty. He tucked his chin in the crook of her neck, rasping her with stubble, rubbing her with warmth that spread, delicious and sweet. Her heart ached.

"I like this," she whispered, unable to speak louder. Her voice felt weak. She was still uncomfortable, but now for an entirely different reason.

Artur said nothing. His arms, which crisscrossed her stomach, tightened. His fingers softly outlined the shape of her ribs. Elena's breathing quickened.

"You like this better," he murmured. "Slow."

"Slow," she breathed, leaning back against him, tilting her head so that he had better access to her neck. He pressed his lips behind her jaw. His fingers stroked upward to the sides of her breasts. Elena shivered, pushing against him. She heard, through their thin walls, a bed creak, the hard click of dice. Bottles clinking. Amiri and Rik, still awake. Farther away doors rattled, and she heard the hard plod of thick boots that could only belong to Attendant Gogunov. The walls were thin.

Artur's fingers grazed the tips of her breasts. Elena sighed, forgetting all about the other inhabitants of the train. What did she have to be ashamed of? It was not possible that she was the only woman enjoying a man's caress on this long trip. Let everyone listen. Let them watch, if they wanted. She was through being afraid, of living a life ruled by caution and fear and concealment. All that mattered was Artur, that space in her heart where he lived—the space in his heart where she wanted to be.

Elena arched upward, twining her fingers around him as he touched her clothed body. Exquisite torture. He traced a path around her breasts, down her stomach to the hard band of her jeans. A breathless pause, and then he turned them so she lay on top of his body, her back still against his chest, and his hands traveled up her clothed thighs, resting inside the heat between her legs. Elena sucked in her breath, and then, fast, he unbuckled her, pushing down, down, until her lower body lay exposed in the cool air, the jeans nothing but a pile on the floor.

Her legs were dry and coarse from mistreatment. Artur did not seem to mind. His touch was reverent. His touch was slow and sure and gentle. His touch made Elena writhe in silent despair as his fingers deepened and curled into her body: stroking, stroking, stroking.

She gasped, unable to swallow all her cries, and held one of his hands as it traveled up her body underneath her sweater. He touched her breasts.

"I have condoms," he said. "They were in the bag Mikhail gave me."

"Okay," she breathed, and it was okay. It was more than okay. She wanted him badly.

They both sat up and undressed. It was surreal, knowing what was going to happen. Ready for it, and scared, too. It had been many years, and not very memorable, but this . . . this was going to be different. She *knew* this man on a profound level, and to be with him, to have him inside her—

"Slow," he said, and she realized that he was nervous, too. Elena planted a quick kiss on his cheek. He looked at her, startled, and then smiled. Cupped her face in one hand. Elena could only imagine what he saw when he looked at her, and he said, "Home."

Which was about all the foreplay she needed. Artur pressed her down on the bed, touching her, kissing her body, and when she was more than ready, he put on the condom and lay between her thighs, shaking with the effort as he nudged himself inside her body, inch by inch. It had been a long time for both of them; Elena thought she had the better part of the bargain. Her control was close to fraying, tearing, ripping away, and that was all right—okay—because Artur wanted it that way, was trying so hard to be the one with control so that she could make love to him without any.

Elena grabbed his backside and pulled him tight against her, thrusting upward. They both cried out—sharp, hard—as hard as the struggle to keep him deep within her as she ground against his hips.

"I'm tired of slow," she told him through gritted teeth. "Artur—"

He cut her off with a kiss, thrusting hard, again and again. Less than a minute later his body jerked, shuddering against her.

"Oh," he gasped, even as he continued to move, unable to stop. "Oh, I am sorry."

"Don't be," Elena said breathlessly, meaning it. Even that short time had been better than anything else she had ever had.

"No," he said, holding her tight. "No, give me some time."

And she did, and when he was ready—which was sooner than Elena thought possible—they began again. Slow. Learning each other. They somehow ended up on the floor, with blankets and pillows spread beneath them, experimenting with different positions, trying—*oh, that's nice*—and—*bozhe moy, kakoy ty vkusniy*—and—*oh, God, oh*—and—*voz'mi v rote*, Elena—and she did, and he liked it, and—wow—and—yes—and—*stan' na koleni*. She braced herself against the cot as Artur grabbed her hips and thrust hard from behind.

Braced on one knee with a foot planted hard on the

ground, he moved against her, swiveling his hips. Elena cried out, biting down on her pillow to keep from screaming. Artur grunted, louder, louder, reaching under her body to touch her breast—reaching with his other hand for her head, burying his hand in her hair, pushing and pulling until it felt like he was trying to climb into her body, right through her skin, and this time he lasted; this time she felt herself rising, rising with that subtle ache that made her buck and twist and writhe, fighting for the culmination of terrible pleasure, fighting—

She thought she would die from the pleasure as it broke her body, cresting again and again because Artur did not stop, did not slow his frantic pace in the slightest, and Elena felt his sweat drip on her back as he leaned even closer, riding her hard like an animal until at the very last he buried himself right up to the hilt, releasing it all up to the last seed, the last drop, jerking against her with enough strength to make her come one more time.

Artur gathered Elena against his stomach, holding her tight in the aftershocks of their pleasure. Sound slowly trickled past the roaring in her ears: the train, once again coming to life. He said, "Better?" and all Elena could do was nod weakly, gasping for breath.

They collapsed together on the floor. Elena could not move. If a gun had been pointed at her head, all she would have managed was a "meep," and then a snore. Making love to Artur was like running the race of a lifetime, wonderfully exhausting.

"*Ya tebya lyublyu*, Elena," Artur whispered. "I am sorry. I forgot all my English."

"The Russian is a turn-on," she said. "What did you just say to me?"

"I love you," he said, and then, before she could respond, he added, "I think I broke my kneecap."

Elena began laughing.

Because they were being pursued by very powerful and highly psychotic individuals, Elena found it difficult to enjoy what could have been—by any standards—the journey of a lifetime on the Trans-Siberian railroad. In just one night they crossed vast swathes of taiga, steppe, and desert, mountains rising like knives to cut the sky, bleeding clouds across the high horizon. It was beautiful and sharp—much like the man who stood behind her, naked, his strong arms wrapped her body as they watched the world speed by.

"You love your country," she said.

"Sometimes," he agreed. "But I love America more. I think perhaps my memories there are better."

"You had a good childhood," she said. "At least, what little of it I've seen looked good. And yes, the white ducks were from you."

"I remember now. My mother and grandmother had them on their aprons. Those were good times."

"Have you ever thought about trying to find them again?"

Artur sighed. "My grandmother is dead. I lost her when I was ten. As far as my mother . . . I do not know what I would say to her. I do not even know if she is still alive. And if she is, what if she had another family? What if she abandoned me, only to go out and have more children? Children she raised herself? I am not sure I could take that, knowing she gave others what she could not give to me."

Elena did not have much of an answer to that. She thought about her own mother, and how it would feel to discover she had moved on, made a new family. Twenty years was a long time.

"Yes," Artur whispered. "It is."

They got dressed and went to meet Amiri and Rik for a breakfast of hard bread and strong coffee. Not one of them said a word to Artur and Elena about the previous night's activities. Elena was certain they knew. Amiri's hearing was supposedly as good as that of the animal he transformed into, but he was a gentleman through and through, and gave no sly glance, no smile. Elena appreciated that. It had been interesting enough waking up beside Artur. Wonderful and weird.

Elena opened the window above their table. The wind smelled clean and sharp. Its scent reminded her of Rictor's prison when she'd cut the circle: full of life, eternal in its beauty. She wondered where he was, although her curiosity at *what* he was burned far brighter.

"What do you think?" she asked the men, after telling them what was on her mind.

"I do not know Rictor as well as both of you, but after what little I have seen and heard, I do not believe he is human." Amiri sipped his coffee. The bread on his plate remained untouched.

"Well, okay." Elena frowned. "If he's not human, and he's not a shape-shifter, then what is he?"

"Does it matter?" Rik asked. He had pulled his blue-streaked hair into a tight ponytail. Elena reminded herself to ask him where he was from; he looked very Hawaiian this morning. "In case you've forgotten, he was a member of the Consortium. You know, participated in kidnapping and experimentation? I'm not sure I buy this whole magic-mind-control thing."

"Cynic," Elena said.

"Realist," he argued. "Face it, he may have helped us escape, but that still doesn't make him good. I remember him coming down to watch me. Just staring with those eyes of his. He didn't lift a finger. Not once."

"I'm not saying he wasn't a bastard, but that's not the point of this conversation. I want to know what he is. I mean, what else is out there besides shape-shifters and humans? What kind of world are we living in?"

"A strange one," Artur said. His leg brushed up against hers and stayed there.

"That doesn't help," she said, twining her ankle around his. "Does magic exist? I mean, *real* magic? Because that's the only way I can explain the circle binding Rictor—and the fact that he vanished right before my eyes."

Rik laughed. Artur and Amiri did not.

"Oh, God," Elena said, watching their faces. Rik's mirth died. "What do you know that I don't?"

"Not enough," Artur said. "Only that there are people born with the power to . . . twist reality. I have seen it done, but only once before. That was more than enough, I can assure you."

"I have also seen the gift," Amiri said, "but those who wield it remind me more of Beatrix Weave than Rictor. She visited me only once, and that was enough. But Rictor? I still say he is something else."

Elena frowned, momentarily distracted. "Beatrix came to you?" She looked from Amiri to Rik. The young man nodded.

"I remember her. She visited me several times."

Elena sat back. How could she have been so stupid? "You were there for three months. How did you and Amiri avoid succumbing to her control?"

"She touched me," Amiri said. "But I felt nothing. And she . . . she was clearly unhappy about that."

"Maybe your physiology makes you immune," Artur said.

Rik closed his eyes. "I'm going to pretend I'm not hearing this. What I went through was enough. I don't want to think about mind control or magic or disappearing non-human bad guys. As far as I'm concerned, they don't exist."

"You're a shape-shifter," Elena said. "Shouldn't you be open to all the possibilities?"

"Hey." He held up his hands. "Don't hold my heritage against me. Just because I change shape doesn't mean I have to believe in all this hokum."

"Wow," Elena said. "And here I thought dolphins were supposed to be all cheerful. Where do you get Prozac when you live in the ocean?"

"Fuck you. Oh, wait. I forgot. You *already* got nail—"

Amiri clamped a hard hand on the back of Rik's neck. His expression was cold, unforgiving. Rik shut his mouth.

"You will remember your manners," Amiri said quietly. "And if you do not, I will teach you to remember."

"As will I," Artur said in a hard voice. His hands pressed flat against the white tablecloth.

A whistle blew; the train began to slow.

"Khabarovsk!" called the waitress.

"Saved by the bell," Elena said. "But don't worry, Rik. I wouldn't have let them hurt you."

"Oh, wow. Comforting." Sweat covered his forehead. Amiri still held the back of his neck.

"You'd better believe it," Elena said. A brief smile flickered over Amiri's face. Rik did not see it. She almost felt sorry for the young man.

The train stopped in front of a small station surrounded by rolling green hills and small, plain homes. Makeshift shops leaned against a low wall, with cheap trinkets and clothing for sale. Nearer the train stood a large group of women who displayed—with a quite a bit of pride and bluster—large shopping carts that over-flowed with food. Elena smelled hot grease. Her stomach rumbled. She had not eaten much of the bread.

"Are you hungry?" Artur asked. He held her hand. His gloves were on. His gaze did not linger on her face, but swept across the small crowd. *Danger, Will Robinson. Danger.*

It was difficult getting close enough to the women to see what they were selling. It seemed that everyone on the train wanted a taste of their food, which Elena thought was a good sign. Artur, though, was a master at getting to the head of the line, and managed to push and prod them right up to one of the carts.

"Here," he said, after a moment spent talking to the small woman hawking her wares. "Have some piroshki. It is very good."

"What's in it?"

"Cottage cheese, meat, and vegetables."

Artur paid for two large, steaming cakes wrapped in thick wax paper and handed one to Elena. She took a bite. It was indeed very good. As she ate, she watched Amiri and Rik wander through the station platform. Several old women made a special effort to talk to them in broken English, and the two men obliged with quiet responses—although Rik was the more hesitant of the two. He still seemed rattled by Amiri's anger. Elena thought it was good that there was someone around whom he respected, a strong personality who could keep him in line. She liked Rik. She thought he was a good kid. And yes, being in that facility had damaged him. She could give him some leeway on that. But she sensed that more had happened to him even before the Consortium, and that his occasional outbursts—that hardness—were continuing symptoms of something more than just his captivity.

"I'm worried about Rik," Elena said. Artur followed her gaze. "There are times when he just seems . . ."

"Broken."

"Or bent. He's hurting."

"Everyone hurts." His tone surprised her; it was devoid of emotion, almost cool. "Some have been hurt far more than Rik. I think, however, that he was taken from an easy life, and that his experience was more painful because of that."

"Start out young with the pain and you toughen up? This isn't Sparta, Artur."

"No? Tell that to the children I grew up with. Tell that, even, to yourself. You have not had an easy life either, Elena."

"Do I deserve a medal for that? I don't think so. Life is what it is, and some people are better equipped than others to handle it. The ones who fall behind shouldn't be punished."

"Sometimes they should," he said grimly. "After enough time, that's all they understand."

Elena raised an eyebrow. "Why do I get the feeling you're talking about something more than Rik's lapse in verbal judgment?"

Artur shrugged. He ate his piroshki. Elena wanted to kick him. She was getting tired of the silent treatment from the men around her. She did not want Artur to get any bad habits.

"Artur," she said. She gave him ten seconds to respond to the warning in her voice. If he did not, she was never sleeping with him again. Elena touched his cheek with her fingertips.

You got that?

"I do not like bullies," he said immediately, scowling. "And no, I do not mean you. Although threatening to deny me your body almost makes you cruel enough to qualify."

"Desperate times," she said. "So you think Rik is a bully?"

"I see the potential. He is young and angry, and sometimes has poor restraint. Lashing out as he did at you can become a habit."

"I did goad him," Elena said. "He's actually very sweet sometimes."

"If he is so sweet, he should have chosen a different way to respond."

"You're just mad because he insulted me."

"Yes."

"All right," she said. "Just don't let it turn *you* into a bully."

"And you?"

"I have carte blanche to act any way I want," Elena said. "For I am both lovely and cruel, and you like me just the way I am."

He tried not to smile.

They went to gather up Amiri and Rik. According to Artur, the train stayed at each station for only ten or twenty minutes at a time, and the conductor would give no warning before leaving. Love 'em and lose 'em, that was the way the Rossiya ran. Elena saw Attendant Gogunov peeking out one of the windows, giving her the dirty eye. Elena waved cheerfully.

There was a line to get back on their section of the train. The American couple from Vladivostok stood in front of Elena. The woman turned to look at her. She was small and nondescript: unremarkable brown hair on an unremarkable face. Nice enough, though—at least from Elena's limited observations.

"I've seen you around," said the woman. Her voice

was smooth, soft. She seemed less bubbly than before.
"Is this your first trip to Russia? You must be having a
wonderful time."

"Um, yes," Elena said, well aware of her male companions watching with some amusement. *First time to
Russia, thank you very much. Oh, how did you get here? I
was kidnapped by a major criminal organization and forced
to undergo human experimentation under the threat of torture and lifelong imprisonment. How about you? Gee,
United Airlines? How horrible!*

"This is my third time," said the woman. "Fred and I
never get tired of the scenery."

"Oh," Elena said. "That's nice."

"Yes," agreed the woman without a hint of arrogance.
The people in front of her shuffled forward. The man
at her side—Fred, presumably—tugged on her sleeve.
He barely touched her, but that brief contact might as
well have been a baseball bat. She tripped and collided
hard against Elena. Both women went down to the
ground just as something small and fast rasped the air
where Elena had been standing.

It was not her imagination; out of the corner of her
eye Elena saw a small iron dart bloom from the duffel
bag of a soldier in uniform, one of many who had disembarked from the cheaper cabin of the Rossiya. If the
young man felt the impact, he did not show it. He kept
moving, doggedly trying to get back to the train.

Artur grabbed Elena under her arms, hauling her off
the ground. The American woman, who was being
helped up by her husband, kept apologizing for her
clumsiness. Elena did not hear a word of it. She was too
busy looking through the crowd at the Quiet Man.

Whatever it was with which he had shot at her was
now tucked away, out of sight. He stood less than thirty
feet away, one man among a hundred, his gaze sharp and

keen upon Elena's face. Elena, in a burst of madness, held up her hand, palm out, and wiggled her fingers.

Remember this? she mouthed, counting on him to read her lips. He smiled and placed his hand over his heart, like a benediction. Apparently he had gotten over his near-death experience. Elena was willing to go another round, to put him back in his place. Or underground, if she could go that far. No fear. She was an army of one. Her own heart pounded—loud, a thunderous drum—and she thought, *I can do this. I can finish it. Just give me a chance.*

Ugly thoughts, murderous. But this was survival, and the one thing she had learned since being taken from that hospital room was that sometimes if you wanted to survive, a little ugliness was needed. A little craziness. That she could heal the sickness from a person's body was a beautiful thing—and if she wanted to keep doing it, if she wanted to stay free and alive long enough to reclaim a life where she could once again help others, she would have to fight, and fight to win.

Don't be ruthless, a part of her whispered, still staring into that face of death. *Don't be so hard or cold. What's the price of that, Elena?*

She did not know, only that right now she was willing to pay it.

"Get on the train," Artur said. "Elena, right now."

"Not without you or the others," she said.

"Elena." Amiri wrapped his hand around her wrist. Rik looked torn between running and fighting. The American couple was gone, presumably already on board.

The Quiet Man walked toward them.

Charles Darling, she corrected herself. *You give him too much power when you call him the Quiet Man.*

Artur began to step in front of Elena, but she

grabbed his arm and held him still. She felt as though they were back inside the facility, in that first moment of their meeting, except now Elena knew what she was capable of and that made all the difference.

"Hello again," said Charles, stopping less than five feet away from Elena and the others. "It is good to see your face, Elena."

"I can't say the same for you," she said.

He smiled, and it was eerie the way he never looked at the others. It was as though they did not exist—as if the only person in the world who mattered was her. His focus still terrified her, but Elena swallowed down the fear with the memory of his heart, so fragile beneath her will. She wondered if she could kill him without even a touch. She did not try. She was not that far gone yet. But soon, maybe.

"Are you alone?" Elena asked.

"I had companions," he said. "They lasted until Vladivostok, and then I got an itch." He finally looked at Artur. "You remember what that's like for me, don't you?"

"I hope you made it quick," he said.

"Quick was all I had time for. You're good, Mr. Loginov. Surprisingly so. It's rare for people to give me the slip."

"You should not have let yourself be seen."

"I couldn't help myself." His smile widened. "Elena is a wonderful temptation. She makes a man want to shine."

Rik made a strangled sound low in his throat. Elena wished he would get back on the train. Down the line she heard the engine rumble to life. The station platform had almost cleared of the disembarked passengers; the few remaining scrambled to board. Elena heard some woman yell from an open window. Attendant Gogunov, shouting at Artur.

"You'd better go," Charles said to the men. "You all wouldn't want to miss your train."

Elena glimpsed a golden glow from the corner of her eyes; Amiri's hands, rippling light into spotted fur. Claws sprouted through his nails. Charles saw, too.

"Oh, meow," he said.

Amiri attacked. He was fast—faster than anyone Elena had ever seen in her life—a cheetah moving as a man, all wiry, lean strength running through his muscles like sunlight. And yet, despite his speed, he got in only one good blow. Amiri's hands raked a trail of bloody lines across Charles's chest. Charles ducked the next strike, lashing out with an underhand strike into Amiri's side. The shape-shifter grunted, but did not stop.

"Run!" he shouted at them. "Get back on the train!"

No one listened. Rik launched himself off the steps. Charles clipped him hard in the face, sending him down to the ground. Artur moved—and got slammed in the gut for his efforts.

Charles Darling turned back to face Amiri. Elena darted forward, slapping her hand against his neck. She shot her power into his body, punching through his barriers, searching for his heart. She did not find it. Instead she faced a worm.

He is mine, Elena heard inside her head. *Just like you will be.*

No. And then she was ripped away from Charles—from his mind and his body—as Artur picked her up and threw her on the train. Attendant Gogunov still shouted. She sounded frantic. Rik was barely on his feet; Artur grabbed the back of his shirt and pants, also throwing him up the train steps. The Rossiya began to move. Amiri still fought Charles Darling, who now had steel glittering in his hand. Elena saw blood running down the shape-shifter's face.

"Amiri!" Artur shouted. He threw himself at Charles Darling, who lashed out with one long arm. Elena heard clothing rip, flesh tear. Artur grabbed his belly, dropping down to one knee. Elena cried out, trying to jump from the train. Rik stopped her and she fought him. Fought . . .

Men in police uniforms began running from the station. The train picked up speed.

"Elena!" Charles shouted, holding up the knife. The blade was red.

Amiri took the opportunity to grab Artur. He slung the bigger man over his shoulder and ran—ran so fast Elena would have known he was not human even if she had never seen him shift his shape. Humans did not run themselves into blurs, into streaks of pumping muscle and swinging limbs. They did not race the wind.

At the last possible moment Amiri grabbed the handlebar on the edge of the train door and swung himself and Artur up the stairs into the Rossiya. Artur fell off the shape-shifter's shoulder and collapsed on top of Elena. His face was too pale; cold sweat covered his forehead. His hands were bloody.

Amiri did not waste time. Light covered his hands, fur retreating into flesh. He slung one of Artur's arms over his narrow shoulders and dragged him down the hall toward their cabin. Attendant Gogunov met them, babbling in Russian.

"Get me some towels," Elena snapped at her. "Towels, water. Please."

The old woman apparently understood some English after all. She ran to get what Elena needed. Amiri lay Artur down on the bed. He ripped open his shirt, buttons scattering. Elena elbowed him aside, crouching to lay her hands on Artur's stomach. The injury was very bad. Charles Darling knew how to cut a man to kill. Artur did not speak. His eyes were closed.

Elena poured herself into his body, laying the groundwork for his healing, binding her strength into his. She was not kind. She was not gentle. She slammed his wound with power, her skin burning with a charge, burning so hot she felt the men back away from her. She had never used her gift in such a way; it had been always gentle, always coaxing—not this rape of another, raping to heal, overwhelming the body's own natural abilities to force it faster, faster, faster. Yes, with Rik she had done something similar, but she'd had help then. Nor were his injuries as severe. Artur was dying. Again, dying.

I am sorry, she heard inside his fading mind.

Shut up, she said. *Save your strength.*

Elena.

No. She refused to hear any more. She refused to waste his precious life on words, on meaningless words, when all that mattered was that he breathe and stop bleeding. Breathe and stop bleeding.

She gave herself up to him.

Chapter Fourteen

Artur dreamed. In his dream he sat beneath a tree, its branches sagging beneath the weight of plums. The grass was green, the sky blue, and he felt good. Safe. Warm.

"It's because of Elena, you know."

He looked up. Rictor sat beside him. His eyes glowed.

"What are you doing here?" Artur did not like seeing Rictor in his dreams. He would much prefer Elena's presence.

"She's busy now," Rictor said. "Saving your life."

Artur remembered: Charles Darling, the knife slicing deep into his gut, Elena inside of him, Elena healing him—

He stood up, afraid. Rictor said, "That's right. You should be afraid. She's killing herself for you."

"So why are you here?" Artur asked him, angry. "Why are you not helping her?"

"Because the only thing I can give Elena is power, and she doesn't need that. She's got enough all on her own. What she really requires is for you wake the fuck up. She's running so high she doesn't know you're out of the woods. You need to stop her, Artur. *You need to make her stop.*"

"If she stops touching me—"

"Amiri already pulled her off your body. This runs deeper than that."

Artur tried to will himself back into consciousness. He fought against himself, scrabbling for some way out of the dream.

"You are keeping me here," he accused Rictor.

"No," the man argued. "You build your own prisons, Artur. This is just another symptom of that."

"I do not understand."

"You're not waking up because a part of you knows what will happen if you do. She's so deep inside you that this is the only place left where you can hide. You break these walls and she'll see everything. *Everything.*"

"Rictor—"

"Fuck you, Artur. I know what you're going to say, and it's shit. You need to give as much of yourself to Elena as she's giving to you. You need to stop holding back, or else you'll never be able to handle what's going to happen next."

"I hold nothing back," Artur protested.

"Then why won't you let her see it all?" Rictor leaned forward. "You take and take and take. You take the memories of others, but you won't share your own. What are you afraid of? What's worth more to you— your pride, or saving Elena?" He backed off, his body fading like mist, a fine shadow. "Fuck your fears, Artur. Jump, like she's jumping."

"I am not afraid," Artur said, but Rictor was gone and his words sounded hollow. He was afraid. He had said as much to Elena. He was scared to death to show her everything of his life, terrified she would reject him for all he had done in the name of survival. Artur was not even sure she needed to see any of that; it certainly had not affected their coming together.

But if they remained close—longer than a day or a week, longer than a year—what then? What of being honest with the one he loved? And how did that have anything to do with keeping Elena alive?

Instead he heard Rictor's voice once again saying, *What's worth more to you—your pride, or saving Elena?*

"Elena," he said, and for the first time in his life, he took that leap of faith. He said yes—yes to it all, to the truth, to letting her see all of his darkest secrets—and the dream shattered around him, the prison walls disappearing; the core of him, hidden and safe from Elena's eyes, now exposed.

He woke up. His stomach felt tender, but he touched the spot where the wound had been and found nothing. His skin tingled. He looked, and found Elena curled up on her own bed, eyes open, staring blindly. Inside him—she was still working inside him. He could feel her presence.

"Artur," Amiri said, but Artur held up his hand to silence him. As he had done before, Artur wrapped his spirit around Elena, holding her tight, this time soothing and whispering, trying to stave off the immense energy pouring from her. *I am well. You have done it; you can stop now.*

At first he did not know if she would respond, but he watched her eyes—saw the flicker of her lashes, the deeper stir of her chest—and the power ebbed to a trickle. He still held her spirit, though. It was difficult for him to let go. His fear of losing her was overwhelming, made him weak. Or strong. Both, perhaps. Like a man from a fairy tale: Artur thought no quest would be too large or too dangerous if it meant her safety.

"No," she murmured from the other bed, finally closing her eyes. At first Artur thought she was disagreeing with him, but then he reached out with one long arm to touch her hand and felt the surge of memory pouring through her. *His* memories, filling her up. He had opened up everything, too fast. He saw—*the first night in the orphanage, lost without protection, without his family, sleeping in a cold corner smelling of piss and then waking to find his clothes being stolen, stolen, beaten for his pants and shirt*—or—*that first night on the street after running away, the nights that followed, desperate and hungry, being shown a wad of cash and hearing, "If you touch a man just so, it can be yours, yours,"*— and—*oh, God, oh no*—

"No," he gasped, but it was too late. He could not stop her from seeing—he had taken Rictor's advice and broken the walls, left his prison to save her—but if this lost her, if she turned away from him . . .

He watched with her, reliving his life, and felt her shock, her fear, her horror, spinning her down into the nightmare; and just when Artur thought that he had done it again, that once more he had harmed the one he loved, he felt the stir of her compassion, and he was done. Done with the world, because all he needed was her, and she still wanted him.

I love you, she said. *You never needed to hide all this from me.*

I did not know, he said.

Now you do, she replied, and her spirit retreated all the way back into her body.

Artur tried to sit up. Hands touched him, holding him down: Attendant Gogunov, her eyes large as river stones, round and soft with wonder. Amiri checked Elena, feeling her neck.

"Her heart is strong," he said. "But we were worried. Even after your wound was healed, it seemed she would not stop."

"I had to wake up," Artur said quietly, still watching her. And he had, in more ways than one.

Attendant Gogunov picked up some towels from the end of the bed and pushed them at Artur. In Russian, she said, "You were dying."

"Yes," he said.

"She saved you. I saw it."

"Yes." He did not bother denying it. "Will you tell?"

She shook her head, marking herself with the sign of the cross. "It is a miracle. She performs miracles."

"You have no idea," Artur said, and lay back down to watch Elena sleep.

Elena slept for a very long time. During her sleep she was invaded by memories not her own, but even unconscious she realized she was seeing the past. Artur's past. She let it flow through her, taking what good she could and letting the bad die where it should: in shadow, an insubstantial state of harmlessness. Artur, she knew, feared her reaction. And he had good reason to, but not because Elena saw anything worthy of rejection. Merely, it hurt to see him hurt. It hurt a great deal, because Artur's life—while laced with good moments, even in the orphanage and on the streets, or with the mob—had been tragically difficult. If not for his strength, the inborn compassion and character cultivated before he turned twelve, Elena thought the man she loved might have turned into a gentler version of Charles Darling: out for blood, ruthless and powerful and cold.

When she finally opened her eyes, she did not see Artur. Rik sat on the bed across from her, staring out the window. His golden eyes spun light, his blue hair matching shades of the sky. He looked very young.

"Hey," Elena croaked. Her throat hurt. "You have water over there?"

He did, and fetched it quickly, stumbling over himself. Elena drank clumsily, water dribbling down the side of her mouth into her pillow. She wiped it away, not caring how she looked.

"How do you feel?" Rik asked.

"Lousy. What happened? Where are the others?"

"You've been out for almost four days," Rik said. Elena closed her eyes. Four days? How was that possible?

You gave too much. You almost gave away your life. Not her voice, speaking inside her head. Artur. She did not know how it was possible, but she was grateful to hear him.

Are you better? she asked him, shaky with relief. The door to their cabin opened and Artur entered, tall and strong, as healthy as any man had a right to be. It was a beautiful sight.

Rik left, silent. Artur sat down on the bed beside Elena.

"If you ever do that again . . ." he said, and there was no laughter, not a trace of humor in his voice. *If you ever do that again, Elena, I think you will just kill me instead of save me.*

"You're not touching me," Elena said. "Why can I hear your voice?"

"Something happened," Artur said. "I think we are closer now. Again."

Elena reached out for Artur, skimming across the link in her heart, and for the first time there was no barrier. It was like flying—right into his skin, into his soul. She felt his weariness, his lonely aching fear, and she said, "I'm not gone yet."

"It was close," Artur said. "Or maybe that is an exaggeration."

"No," Elena said, testing the way her body felt. "No, I think that's right."

She caught the flicker of a green memory and said, "Rictor."

Artur hesitated, but it was no use. Not that Elena thought he would lie to her, but hedging the truth was impossible now; they were both open books. "He saved your life. He forced me to wake up so I could save you."

"That was nice of him," Elena said, sounding far more sarcastic than she intended. "I don't suppose he gave any indication as to where he is, or why his great diversion didn't work?"

"Of course not."

Elena smiled, burying her face in the pillow. "Any other news? Serial killers on board the train? Evil psychics ready to control my mind?"

"No," he said, and Elena felt the image of a cell phone tickle her, along with a deep voice saying, *Artie, you lucky fuck, what the hell happened?*

"Roland," Artur answered for her. "My boss. I finally was able to reach him."

Elena frowned. "This mind-reading thing is going to take some getting used to." She noted the pained look that passed over his face, and added, "It's only fair, you know. You've always been able to see what goes on in my mind."

"So I've been reminded." He did not sound happy.

"Hypocrite," she said affectionately.

"Martyr," he replied. He kissed her. Elena wondered what her breath tasted like. She knew it couldn't be good. It wasn't. She saw that in Artur's head, much to her own personal horror. Artur kept kissing her, though.

I have tasted worse, he said, laughing inside her mind. Elena pushed him away.

"How are the others?"

"We have been taking turns watching over you. The rest of the time we spend patrolling this particular section of the train. We have made several other stops since you fell asleep, but Charles was not at any of them. Not that we could see, anyway.

"That doesn't make sense," Elena said. "He wouldn't give up so easily. Especially not if Beatrix is ordering him to find me."

"Then we can only hope he got caught up somewhere or that the police in Khabarovsk were able to detain him."

"Maybe shoot him?" she asked hopefully.

"Even better."

Someone knocked on the door. Artur stood quickly, but it was only Attendant Gogunov. She bore a plate of fruit and bread, along with several bottles of water. Her eyes widened when she saw Elena awake, and it was quite odd, seeing reverence where before there had only been contempt.

She thinks you are a saint from God, Artur told her. *She saw you heal me.*

Elena felt a moment of consternation, but as the woman crouched before her, pale and shaking, she realized she had nothing to fear. Attendant Gogunov was not going to tell anyone, and if she did, it would not be to relate the story of a monster, but only of a woman who had helped another.

She said something in Russian, and through Artur, Elena understood her words.

"I'm feeling better, thank you," Elena said, and Artur translated.

"Good," said the old woman in English, setting down

the plate. "I have been worried about you." She rubbed her hands on her thighs, clearly nervous. Clearly with a question in her.

Elena said, "What do you want to ask me?"

The old woman looked at her as though she thought Elena had read her mind instead of just her body language. That was how legends were created, she realized. Do just one crazy thing, and then everything else got blown up to magical proportions.

Well, you are a mind reader now, Artur said, sounding amused. *Only it is just my mind.*

Trust me, yours is enough.

The old woman said, "I am sick. It is in my breasts." She spoke in Russian, but through Artur, Elena understood every word.

"Sit down," she said.

"Elena," Artur warned, not bothering to hide the sharpness in his voice. Attendant Gogunov gave him a fearful look, but Elena reached out to touch her hand. The woman flinched, but did not pull away.

It was an easy thing to do, despite her weakness. Cancer needed just a whisper, a nudge in the right direction. The lump was large and malignant; Elena pushed, hard, and finally felt that subtle twist, the assent. The path to healing. The old woman also had heart disease, but Elena could do only so much, feeling as she did. This, at least, would keep her going for a while longer, and with a decent quality of life right up until the end. That was all anyone could ask for. It was what her grandfather had gotten. Walking as strong as a man in his twenties, and then boom! Dropped dead beneath a tree while Elena was out buying groceries.

There was nothing you could have done, Artur said, sensing her lingering pain over the loss.

I know. Elena did, truly. He was too old, and had always refused Elena's help.

No natural extensions of his existence, he had said. Let a man go when it's time. Let a man go into that place he sees coming. Let a man rest.

It was just that she had never gotten the chance to say good-bye, to tell him how much he had shaped her life for the better. To say, "I love you, Grandpa. I love you, I love you, I love you." To have him hear those words, instead of speaking them to the air above his grave. He was buried on the farm in the family plot, next to his father and mother and brothers. Elena expected she would be buried there one day, too.

But not for a while yet, Artur said. *And when it is time, I will be there beside you.*

Her breath caught, and he smiled. The old woman saw, and thought it was for something else. She looked at Elena—so hopeful it made the eyes ache—and Elena said, "Your cancer will be gone in a week. I can't guarantee that another tumor won't appear somewhere else, but for now you're safe." *Until your heart gives out, until your time runs from the glass.*

As Artur translated, Attendant Gogunov began to cry. She pressed her palms to her face, knuckling her eyes, rocking back and forth like a small child. "Oh," she gasped. "Oh, I was so afraid. Thank you, thank you."

She got down on her knees and began kissing Elena's hand, so reverent, so in awe that it turned Elena's stomach. She did not deserve such gratitude. She never would.

Let the woman have her miracle, Artur told her quietly. *Let her feel that presence of the God that she holds so dear. Give her that much.*

Elena felt shame—just a little. *I should be more gracious, huh?*

You are always gracious, Elena. The word I was looking for was patient.

Patience, appreciation. Taking heart in the miracles she could give others, all the Olivias and Gogunovs and John Burkleses.

And the Arturs of the world, he thought.

I swear, you're getting hurt on purpose.

I am a man of danger, Elena. There was some humor in his voice. *I expect you will always be healing my wounds.*

"God," Elena groaned. Attendant Gogunov stopped kissing her hand and gave her an odd look. Artur assured her that Elena was fine, just simply in a mood to pray.

The old woman smiled. "May I tell others of your gift?"

"No," Elena said. "There is only one of me and too many of you. It would kill me."

She nodded. "Thank you, then. For choosing me. I hope there are others who feel the gift of your touch."

"I also hope so," Elena said. Her head was beginning to hurt. She wanted to sleep again. Her eyes drifted shut, and she heard the woman say something to Artur, something quiet, and his response: "Yes, she is mine and I love her."

Love you back, she said to him, and then promptly fell asleep.

Chapter Fifteen

Home.

The old home, the first home, with those endless gray skies that in summer made Artur feel cold—where winter dragged on like a coma, settling thickly into his bones until even his dreams felt numb, and flesh refused to part with sensation, where sensation was reserved for normal little boys, not the ones locked in rooms without beds, alone and alone and alone, where bodies were taught not to feel or think, where the lost were tolerated only in a fit of brazen government-funded pity.

Moscow. Artur hated it.

Mikhail would probably call that a symptom of Artur's continuing inability to cope with his childhood, and he would be right—Artur had hang-ups and he was not afraid to admit it. Nor would he deny that there had been good times. His life until puberty had been good. His life with Tatyana had been enjoyable as well. Everything else he could have done without.

Time always helped. Time living another life, with

better people than he deserved. It gave him perspective. Just not enough ever to compel him to come back and live. Moscow was, as some said, the most beautiful mistress a man could ever want, but never cross her: like any good woman, she might just cut off your balls for the hell of it.

"This is a beautiful place," Elena said. It had just rained and the pavement was slick, silver with shine. The air smelled clean and there was a hint of rainbow in the sky. He had to admit it was a good day to see the city for the first time. It looked the same, except for a few more high-rises cutting the sky.

Elena wore a fresh set of clothes that Attendant Gogunov had scrounged and laundered for her. She still looked far too pale and weak, and though her bruises were beginning to fade, the ghost of injuries lingered on her face. The doctor's mark and Charles Darling's fingers haunted the flesh.

Despite that—though not because of it—she fit in perfectly with every other woman on the street, all of whom looked as though the hard life had begun aging them from six years old. There were glimpses of girls who still carried youth in their step, but life was hard in Russia. It wore down the heels of your soul as fast as you could breathe, and the burden rarely eased.

Even now, just outside the train station, Artur caught sight of a pack of young boys, ragged and tough, leaning against a distant wall. Pickpockets, scammers, whores; Artur had been one of them once. He felt compassion, but not enough to do anything foolish, like actually try to help. He knew the game, and so did they. If he walked up to them, all they would see was a threat and an opportunity. They would never trust him enough to take the help he could offer. Not that he was in any great position to help the helpless. They probably had a better chance of living to the end of the week than he did.

Amiri and Rik stood out, but that could not be helped. They also had new clothes, courtesy of Attendant Gogunov, who had made it her special mission to take what she could from the old lost-and-found bins to make them comfortable. Artur had left her a far more generous wad of money than he originally intended. He appreciated kindness.

No one asked where they were going. The plan had been discussed again and again, and while Artur had tried to argue with the others, deterring them from participating was impossible. Elena refused to leave his side, and for whatever reason Amiri and Rik did, too. Curiosity, perhaps—honor, even. Rik certainly seemed to have matured. Or maybe it was just that they had nowhere else to go, and some camaraderie, companionship—even in the face of danger—was better than none at all. Artur understood that all too well.

Which was why, when he saw a crow swoop down to land on the cobblestones before him, golden eyes winking, he was not entirely surprised by the surge of happiness that swept through him. Elena gave him an amused look. Amiri and Rik both crouched, staring with intense concentration at Koni's much smaller form.

"Greetings," they both said, and the crow bowed his head, fluttering black wings.

When Koni again took to the air, the group followed his meandering path, walking the gray city streets with a lazy air that belied the urgency they felt.

It was Elena who saw Koni enter an open window on the third floor of a ramshackle apartment building. Artur, who had been surreptitiously trying to see if they were being followed, led them up the wide staircase lined by cracked walls stained with graffiti and pornographic drawings—something Dean no doubt admired, or had participated in creating. Artur smelled urine, alcohol, the lingering miasma of unwashed bodies, and then above him a door creaked open, and a familiar face peered over the stair railings. Teeth flashed, as did the dark steel of a gun.

"Yo," Dean said. "When I said you needed a vacation, I wasn't talking about an all-expense-paid kidnapping to the mother country."

"Did you miss me?" Artur asked.

"Nah. Your place is nicer than mine. I moved in after you disappeared. My hands have been all over your underwear drawer." Which was probably less of a joke than Dean made it sound. Artur could very well see Dean living in his home, attuning himself until he could track Artur's every movement. He was only surprised it had taken his friend so long to find him. He said as much.

Dean shrugged, holstering his weapon. "For some reason, I could never pinpoint your exact location, though I knew you were in Russia. And then there was that message your old girlfriend left. We went to visit her to see if she could tell us anything about those people who paid her off. She, uh, wasn't very helpful."

"Tatyana?" Elena asked Artur. "She sold you out? Bitch."

"Yeah." Dean smiled and shook Elena's hand. "That's just what I said."

Suddenly Artur remembered Dean's preference for short, dark-haired women, and he watched, frowning, as his friend held on to Elena's hand far too long. Artur knew he should expect nothing less; Dean was the only sex addict he knew who never actually got any. It impaired his judgment, sometimes.

Elena's smile widened, and Artur knew it was for his

benefit. Dean, of course, thought it was for him. He edged closer.

Artur said, "Do not think about it, Dean. She is mine."

Dean froze. Everyone stared at Artur. He stared back, shameless.

Elena's lips twitched. In his head, she teased, *Me big man. Me have woman. Me kill man who touch woman. Grrr.*

Dean said, "Fuck. You've only been gone a week and you already got a girlfriend? You were kidnapped, man! How does this shit happen?"

"Sheer talent," Elena said. "He's a sex machine."

Dean made a choking sound. Rik complained, "How come everyone else can talk trash without getting threatened?"

"Because," Amiri said, and left it at that.

Dean, once he recovered, led them into a small apartment just off the staircase. Artur watched the halls; no nosy neighbors peered from their homes to watch and gossip. He wondered if Dirk & Steele owned the entire building, or at least this floor.

There was very little furniture inside: a wide table covered in maps and other loose paper, several chairs, and a tall metal cabinet that Artur suspected was filled with illegal weapons. Several computers were set into a hidden alcove off the main room. Blue, the agency's resident electrokinetic, rolled away from them and stood up. Koni came out of the back bedroom, buttoning his jeans. The tattoos on his arms and chest rippled against his lean muscles.

"Good to see you," Blue said, looking immaculate and pressed, and ready to get down to business. His dark hair was slicked back into a tight ponytail. "I would hug you, but you smell."

"Oh, my heart," Artur said dryly. He turned and gestured for his companions to move closer. "You got my message to Roland, yes? This is Amiri and Rik. They are shape-shifters whom the Consortium kidnapped. And this"—he tugged Elena close, well aware that his friends watched his bare hand on her hand—"is Elena Baxter. She is also like us."

"Hey," she said. "I, uh, heal things."

"Cool. I see shit. Sometimes literally. Maybe we should go around in a circle, like in an AA meeting, and introduce ourselves," Dean said. "I think that might be fun. A little more bonding before we start shooting people."

"Maybe later," Blue said. "After we shoot the people. And then when it's just you and the mirror."

Elena struggled not to smile, but Artur could hear her laughter in his head.

I think I like them, she said.

I hoped you would. They are good friends.

Koni had already pulled aside Amiri and Rik. The three shape-shifters huddled together by the window, not speaking, just staring at one another. Elena thought it was eerie. Artur was not as surprised, having seen Koni react to Hari before.

"You guys aren't going to start kissing, are you?" Dean called out. "'Cause, you know, we got rooms for that."

Koni gave him the finger, as did Rik. Amiri simply rolled his eyes.

"Dean," Blue warned, but he was trying hard not to laugh. He gestured for Artur to join him at the computer and tapped the screen. "Okay, I took all the information you gave Roland and cross-referenced it with what we've got on the crime syndicates here in this country. There are twenty major groups, all of whom are deeply embedded in drugs, prostitution, and weapons sales. If what you're saying is correct, and this Beatrix Weave can really control their minds, then the world is in a shitload of trouble."

"She has to touch them to control them," Artur said.

"Which is where I come in," Elena remarked, coming up behind him. "Beatrix is paralyzed from the shoulders down. Which doesn't mean that someone won't shake her hand, but she presumably wants me to heal her before that meeting."

"Which is tomorrow, right?" Blue shook his head. "We need more intel, man. Roland's got our sources running ragged, but this one is going to need some footwork. You know anyone who would talk to you?"

"Yes," Artur said. "If he does not shoot me first."

"You willing to take that risk?"

"Hell, no." Elena stared at them both. "Or are you forgetting that spot in your gut I just had to heal? Now you want me to tackle bullets? Man of danger, my ass."

"He may not try to kill me," Artur said mildly, trying to ignore the fact that all of his friends were watching their exchange with the intense interest of greedy old women starved for gossip.

"Oh, he'll try," Elena said. "*I'm* ready to try."

Artur wondered if she knew who he was thinking of seeing, and she said, *Of course. You can't hide anything from me now.*

I am beginning to regret that.

Keep talking.

He was smart enough not to, except only to say, "I need to do this."

"How about a vest?" Blue asked. "Backup?"

Artur shook his head. "They will search me and see I am wearing it. That would be considered . . . weak.

They would probably shoot me in the head as a matter of principle. They will also not trust anyone who comes with me."

"*I'm* coming with you," Elena said.

"Dean." Artur took the gun Blue handed him and checked the ammunition. "Keep Elena here."

"Sure," he said, but he looked unhappy.

Elena shook her head. Artur glanced at Amiri and Rik; the two men silently positioned themselves behind her. Elena turned. "No. I know what he wants you to do. Don't."

"I'm sorry," Rik said. "But I'm way more scared of him than I am of you."

Artur reached out with one long arm and kissed Elena hard on the mouth. She kissed him back fiercely, and then bit his lower lip. Artur tasted blood.

"I assume that is because you love me," he said, running his tongue over the sting from her teeth.

"You know how I feel," she said, and he did. He could feel her love running through him like a river, strong like her anger and fear. She was terrified he would die, and that she would not be able to save him. It scared her to death.

He could not take that kind of emotion. He could not look into her eyes and not beg for forgiveness. So he left. Fast. As he did, instinct overcame him and he threw up a barrier, a shield against his mind. He did not know he could still do that. His soul felt lessened without Elena there inside of him.

He tried not to think of what would happen to her if he died.

Nikolai Petronova kept his offices in Chistye Prudy, but only because he had a view of the Kremlin from his northeast window. The area had once been known for its butchers and its ponds—the latter of which, centuries ago, had run filthy with the blood of slaughtered animals. The waters were clean now. Relatively so. Artur saw bits of trash floating alongside the paddleboats, which were being rowed by sweaty young men trying to impress their bored girlfriends.

The area also boasted the first Moscow post office, which was little more than a house with only a sign to make it official. Behind that old building was the white spire of Menshikov Tower. Trouble had always plagued its owners—lightning strikes, exile, death—but it was, first and foremost, a church, and Artur knew that, every evening before going home, Nikolai liked to pray before the altar of the archangel Gabriel.

Artur passed through the large double doors, following the church's main aisle as it led left, toward the rear antechambers. Nikolai, after his initial benedictions, always retreated into the private prayer rooms so as to better contemplate his somewhat dubious existence. It was not difficult to find his location; Artur simply watched for his bodyguards, whom he found without any trouble at all.

Artur approached slowly, gloves off, hands extended at his sides. Two men in black leather stood before a wooden door, arms folded across their chests. Very menacing they were, although such postures would make it difficult to reach the guns presumably holstered in the shoulder rigs beneath their jackets. Nikolai, however, cared about appearances more than practicality. He had probably told those men to stand that way, uncaring that in a firefight they would likely be shot before they could touch their guns. Artur, on such matters, had never listened to Nikolai; common sense had always ruled the day.

He did not recognize the men, which was unsurprising. In this business, hired muscle was promoted quickly, or died just as fast. They smelled strongly of cheap cologne, which drowned out the scent of candle smoke. He heard the murmur of voices, the tread of heavy shoes. Not a good place for a shoot-out—not that such considerations had ever stopped any bullets before.

"I am here to see Nikolai," Artur said. The men stared at him, silent and expressionless. Typical. Artur had done the same once upon a time. Such treatment was a good way to intimidate someone who did not really mean business.

Unfortunately for these men, Artur was quite serious about wanting to see their boss. He began to walk between them. They placed hands on his chest and Artur touched their shoulders—*just one more job and I can afford to pay for that dress Katya wants, that vacation to the Black Sea—and—fuck, I do not like the looks of this man; I think he is armed, I think he is dangerous*—and he looked into their eyes, one man to the other, and said, "If you love your Katya, you will find another way to pay for that dress, and to you, yes, I am a very dangerous man. Unless you want to discover just how dangerous, you will open this door right now."

Their hands flew off his body. He saw the fear in their eyes and savored it as just one more moment of life. The man on his right knocked on the door. Artur heard a familiar voice from within. He did not wait for anyone to give permission. He brushed past the guards, opened the ornate wooden door, and entered the small prayer room.

Nikolai was alone, kneeling before a smaller version of the altar of the archangel. The air was dark, smoky—much like the man himself, who had had spent far too many days in his youth on the fishing boats his father ran. He was tough like a leather strap, his eyes like pinholes, and when he saw Artur he straightened slowly, bones cracking in his knees and back.

"So, you return." His voice was low, rough from years of cigarettes. "I thought I would see you again, though much sooner. I expected you to come crawling back to me from the street. I am oddly pleased that did not happen." He looked at the men behind Artur and said, "Search him."

They took his gun and jacket, leaving him with nothing that might hold a weapon. Nikolai said, "You must have scared my men for them to let you in here armed. You must have scared them more than *I* scare them. How did you do that, Artur?"

"You always did praise my talent."

"Yes, I did. Have you seen Tatyana lately?"

Artur barely managed to restrain himself. Nikolai sighed. "I must admit I feel some guilt over what I did to the poor girl. I check on her every now and then. From a distance, of course. Trust me, I have no more interest in hurting her. In case you are interested, she is still living with her parents in their lovely flat. Her new boyfriend is quite attentive. Not as exciting as you were, I am sure, but he does not mind that she is in a wheelchair. She's put on some weight, but that's to be expected. Our Russian women are always easy to hold. Keeping them for the long term, however, is another matter entirely." He peered into Artur's face. "And what of you? I looked, you know. I never discovered what happened, except that I was sure you were not dead. Men like you do not die."

"I found other work," Artur said coldly. As he looked at Nikolai, all he could hear was Tatyana screaming. "And now I am here on business. Your business. I know about your meeting tomorrow. The gathered syndicates. The promise made by Beatrix Weave."

Nikolai's smile was cold, mirthless. "My, you do get around. And still, you are the most unsubtle man I have ever met. Are you here for a cut of the action?"

"I am here to warn you," Artur said. "No, do not get the wrong idea. I still hate you, but I hate the woman you are about to do business with even more. She will ruin you, Nikolai. She will take your mind and twist it."

"All women do that. You remember my ex-wives, yes?" He shook his head. "This one is nothing. Just a poor paralyzed whore with money and power."

"If she was nothing, you would not be going to see her. You would not be risking yourself in the presence of the other bosses. You would not be opening yourself to the possibility of ruin."

"Ruin? What heavy words you use, Artur. Curious. Of all the men in the world I would expect to hear a warning from, you are at the bottom of the list." Nikolai seated himself on a narrow altar bench. His finely tailored suit bunched uncomfortably around his heavy-set body. "If you must know, we have been hearing rumors of this woman's organization for some time. It promises to rival our own, even as a collective. Most of us view this meeting as a means of studying the enemy."

"She cannot be studied," Artur said. "She must be killed first, and *then* studied, if you still like. That is the only safe way to handle Beatrix Weave."

Nikolai leaned back against the wall, folding his hands over his round stomach. Candlelight softened his face until he looked almost grandfatherly. A patient man. A hushed man.

"What are your motivations in this?" Nikolai asked. "Why do you care what happens to the person who destroyed your life?"

"Because the others respect you. Because if you tell them not to go to the meeting, they will listen."

"It is just a meeting, Artur. We are not marrying the woman."

"You might as well. Can you imagine all the syndicates in Russia under one hand? *Her* hand? I can, Nikolai. It scares me."

"Little boy lost," Nikolai murmured. "We are grown men now. We cannot be controlled. We cannot be talked into giving up our power to one woman, no matter what she has promised us. Which is quite a lot, I must tell you."

Artur shook his head. "This is useless. You do not believe me."

"I believe this is important enough that you have risked your life to speak with me, but will I listen to you and not my own eyes and ears? Especially when you give me so little to go on? No, Artur. That . . . you ask too much."

Artur did not know what else to say that would not endanger himself or his friends. He held out his hand. "I will go, then. Thank you for seeing me."

Nikolai hesitated. "God only knows I owe you that much."

An odd thing to hear out of Nikolai's mouth, something he would *never* say. But it was too late: Nikolai touched Artur's hand and Artur felt the man's thoughts, slippery and dangerous, like a black worm, writhing—

He could not free himself. Nikolai's grip felt like iron, implacable, and he heard a voice inside his head, whispering, *I knew you would return, Artur. I knew I would find you here.*

"Mr. Loginov." Artur glanced over his shoulder. A familiar figure stood outlined in the open doorway: a walking skeleton, pale and tall. Ms. Graves. Nikolai's bodyguards stared at both her and their boss with pitiful indecision. Clearly, they were just as shocked as Artur. Unfortunately, they were also expendable.

Graves was a fast draw. The silencer on her pistol puffed twice and both men collapsed, dead.

"Uncontrollable witnesses are such a pain," she said, sauntering into the room. With her gun still pointed at Artur, she reached out and patted Nikolai on the head. "Good boy. What a fine pet you've made."

Anger flashed on Nikolai's face, but he retained his grip on Artur's hand. He had no choice. Beneath the presence of the worm Artur saw a story: a private meeting, a great deal of extravagance, seduction, first with money, and then with the promise of taking pleasure in a fragile body that was utterly helpless. Beatrix Weave, *l'araignée*, had sprung her trap with that first kiss. Wrapped Nikolai Petrovona tight in her black cocoon, spinning a thread down into his brain. He was trapped now, like a zombie. Nikolai did not know what Beatrix Weave was, but he wanted her dead—called any man who felt the same his brother, his son, his friend.

Nikolai was the only reason the meeting between the syndicates was taking place. It was Nikolai, caught in the web, who had convinced the others that Beatrix could be trusted, that Beatrix had something to offer. The truth was that she had nothing. All she had promised—preying on dreams of avarice—was a lie. Beatrix would steal away the minds of the bosses just as she had stolen Nikolai, and turn them into nothing more than pets. She'd make them bay at the moon or wear diapers and play with rattlesnakes. She could do it. She would, for her amusement.

Artur pushed deeper into himself, searching for Elena. They were two sides of the same coin now; touching her was the same as thought, breathing. He ripped down the barrier.

Artur, Elena said, and he felt her anger turn to fear as she sensed the darkness hovering on the very edge of Nikolai's grip. *Artur what is going on?*

Beatrix Weave has found me. You need to tell the others. You need to prepare an alternative plan. The meeting—he concentrated, searching—*the meeting is taking place at the Taganka Theatre tomorrow at eight P.M. You must stop it.*

We'll stop it together. I'm coming for you.

No! Elena—

I'm coming.

She cut him off. Complete, startling. He'd been unaware she knew how to do such things, unless she had somehow learned from his own mind, instinctively taken the skills and knowledge, much as he did with others. He wondered what else she might learn—and what he could learn from her.

"You may release him now," Graves said to Nikolai. Artur did not know if Beatrix could hear her, or whether Graves was also allowed some control over the thread. Either way, Nikolai did as he was told. Sweat pouring down his face, shaking with rage, the Mafia boss retreated backward on the bench, clutching his hand. Artur did not feel terribly sorry for him.

"Well, now." Graves looked Artur up and down. "Aren't you a sight for sore eyes? I knew I would see you again, though really not quite this soon. I thought you had more brains than to get involved in something like this."

"Intelligence," Artur said. "Or have you forgotten?"

"No," Graves said softly. "No, I wouldn't forget that. What a pity, Mr. Loginov. Seeing you again makes me realize that killing you will be so unsatisfactory. And yet I do believe that it is what I will be forced to do before this night is through. You have almost outlived your usefulness. Truly, this time. No bluff."

"I think I will believe that only when I finally eat the bullet."

"Always the optimist. I like that about you. But see"—and here she leaned forward, smiling softly, so cruel—"Ms. Weave no longer cares about the secrets in your head. She'll find her answers another way."

"She dislikes failure," Artur said. "So do you. That you have never been able to break me must burn, yes? Better to kill me than to live with that defeat—or suffer it again with another failed attempt at control." He noticed Nikolai watching him, intense, and wondered if it was simply the man—or the woman, too, learning and judging.

"You must have learned English watching soap operas," Graves said. "You're always so melodramatic. Yes, she hates failure, Mr. Loginov. But she hates *you* even more."

"And yet I still live."

"Right. Don't pat yourself on the back too much for that." Graves snapped her fingers. Two large men appeared in the doorway of the prayer room; they looked at the woman for direction. "Take him home. Keep him from touching you, if at all possible."

"More secrets?" Artur asked.

"No. You're just dangerous."

"Finally, a real compliment."

"I thought you deserved one. Every man should have something nice done for him on his last night of life."

"Now who is the optimist?"

Graves smiled. The men took him away, out of the church to a waiting car. One of them jabbed something sharp into his hand.

Darkness.

Chapter Sixteen

Elena liked to think of herself as a straightforward person. No real problems, good sense of humor, sometimes brave. Despite her need for privacy and loner tendencies, she knew very well how to interact with people, and enjoyed doing so on certain occasions.

This was not one of them. As soon as Artur left, she retreated to the kitchen with Amiri. The shape-shifter wanted to fix something to eat, and Elena desired some familiar company. She was stuck here, and that made her angry. If she had to look for one more minute at the people who were doing the actual sticking-of-her-feet to this place, she was going to hurt someone.

Elena thought she might eventually appreciate the company of Artur's friends, but she did not know them. There was a history that she was not part of, and she did not yet feel comfortable mingling or asking questions. To be honest, the three men acted far too busy to be bothered. They were Very Important People with Very Important Jobs, and she . . . she was just the wannabe. A poor organic farmer from Wisconsin who could perform the occasional miracle.

Which made her lonely, in addition to being angry. That was not her way. She did not get lonely. She said as much to Amiri, as his strong, dark hands mixed together eggs and flour and green onion. Oil spit and crackled in a cast-iron pan.

"What is it John Donne says? 'No man is an island, entire of itself'?"

"I always thought that saying was crap."

"Oh, Elena. Arguing with the great thinkers . . ."

"You know what I mean."

"And I know what I used to tell my students. I would say, 'No man is an island, but oh, if only.'"

Elena snorted, leaning against the cracked plastic tabletop. Its surface felt sticky beneath her elbows. Amiri poured the batter into the pan, and the air smelled good and hot with grease.

Then, suddenly, Artur was inside her head. She had wondered at his silence, at the absence of his warm presence, and to feel him again came as a shock.

But to hear his words, to hear that name . . . Oh, oh, *oh!*

"Elena," Amiri said, as she began to leave the kitchen. He turned off the stove and ran after her, catching her arm just as she entered the living room.

"It's Artur," she said, and everyone stopped what they were doing to look at her. "Beatrix has him."

"What?" Dean shot to his feet. He had been analyzing maps with Koni, while Rik hung back, just watching.

Blue appeared from the alcove. "How do you know this?"

"We have a . . . a link. I can hear his thoughts."

"Can you hear him now? Where is he?"

Elena tried to reach for him, but slammed up hard

against a barrier. Like being brain-dead—or maybe just a normal human. She could not reach him, and the horrible part was, she had put the block there herself. She had not been able to bear his protests, his denials. Of course she was coming for him. Of course she would find some way to save him.

And, of course, knowing where he was would be a great big help with that.

"I can't reach him. I . . . I don't know." Elena fought hard to remember. She had felt the impression of darkness—a dark heart, a dark room, with a hand on her hand, and beyond that the statue of a man with wings. She felt bits and pieces of Artur's memory seep slowly into her consciousness. It was so frustrating, not being able to recall more. "He was in a church, I think. A . . . a *tower*. The name of it starts with an M."

"I think I know where you're talking about," Koni said, unbuttoning his pants. "I roosted there once."

"He said to tell you that the meeting between the syndicates is being held tomorrow at eight P.M. in the Tanganka Theatre."

Dean blew out his breath. "All right, Koni and I will head over to that church. Blue, can you handle the recon on the theater?"

"I'll help," Rik said. Amiri said nothing. He watched Elena. She knew what he wanted to do. She felt the same.

"I'm going with you," she said to Dean. He was a short man, not much taller than herself, but at that moment he had the authority in the room, and that made him big. She hated that. Dean shook his head.

"Artur will kill me if anything happens to you."

"Wuss," she said.

"Hey."

"Don't make me hurt you."

He gave her a look that clearly said he did not think

she could hurt a fly. Which was true, but Dean wasn't a fly.

"We don't have time for this." Blue walked between them both, his gaze hard. He tried to stare Elena down, but he was no Charles Darling. Elena didn't bat an eyelash. Maybe that hard-nosed stubbornness gave her some credibility—or maybe Blue was smarter than Dean, and knew better than to underestimate her. Either way, he backed off, but with the same message as his friends. "You can't go, Elena. Dean's right. Besides, if you get hurt, we lose our only potential link to Artur. You need to stay here with me and keep trying to contact him. That's the best use of your energy."

Spoken like a politician. Elena did not bother disagreeing with him. She would bet the farm—quite literally—that there was nothing she could say to change this man's mind. All he saw was an unknown, a woman who had yet to prove herself. Fine. She knew how to play games, too. She was becoming a master at them.

Poor little innocent farm girl, my ass.

"Okay," she said, and glanced at Amiri. He did not trust her acquiescence—she could see it in his eyes—but he respected her enough not to challenge her motives.

"Perhaps I may go with you," he said to Dean. "I know Artur's scent."

"Yeah." Dean shrugged on a shoulder rig, arming himself. Over that he put on a lightweight jacket. Koni moved into the bedroom. Elena glimpsed his naked backside as he pushed down his jeans. Light enveloped his body. Elena heard the flapping of wings.

"You need anything?" Dean asked Amiri.

The shape-shifter shook his head and held up one hand. Light shimmered, muscles ripping into fur, the fine lines of claws. And then, quickly, he was all human again.

"God, that still skeeves me." Dean ran out the door. Amiri gave Elena one last lingering look—of reassurance, maybe, or just compassion—and followed him. Elena turned around. Blue was already tucked away in the alcove, pulling up computer files on the theater. Rik joined him, moving right behind his shoulder to peer at the screen. A little dolphin pup, eager to please.

Don't be unkind. You understand how he feels.

And she did—she knew what it was like to be adrift, alone, desperate to find some place, some kind of responsibility. A definition of her identity and personhood. But she was past that now. Elena knew who she was. She knew what she had to do.

She walked to the window, reaching deep within her heart for Artur. Again she hit that barrier. Again and again, she was denied. Elena stared out at the street below her, soaking in the masterful architecture of the inner city, the fine curves and lines of buildings made to last. Stonework that would remain in this world much longer than her.

Elena listened to Blue and Rik. They were wholly absorbed in a discussion of surveillance and electronics. She remembered what Rik had said about his hearing, that it was not anything special outside the water. She thought about Blue, and had to gamble that he faced similar restrictions. Only human, up to a point.

She was quiet. She was lucky. They underestimated her. Elena left the apartment and they never noticed.

She walked down the sidewalk and started moving, just to get away, far away in case they came looking. She limbered up her mind, chanting Artur's name in her head like a prayer, unable to understand why she could not reach him, why it was so easy sometimes, and then when it mattered: nothing. She tried to watch where she was going, following the ebb and flow of the crowd, but it did not matter that she became hopelessly lost. Elena was free, away, and coming for him. Somehow coming for him. Standing still felt too much like letting him die. Letting him lose his mind to the worm, to pain.

Elena had the first inkling of trouble when a small body ran hard into her legs. A cherubic face peered up at her. Elena glanced around. She had walked herself into a quiet side street, walked herself right past a group of boys idling against a wall. They looked rough, hungry. Elena remembered feeling that kind of hungry desperation, except it was not hers—it was Artur's—and looking at these boys was like seeing what he once had been. It hurt. It hurt badly.

They began moving when they saw her looking at them. Kicked off the wall in slow motion, like a pack, turning circles in the street with noises in their throats. They said words to her in Russian. Elena did not run. She wanted to—knew it made sense, like all the books said to do—but she could not bring herself to flee from children, no matter how lethal they might be.

The oldest could not have been more than fifteen. He was gaunt, sharp like the knife that flashed in his hands. Dirty skin, dirty hair. Elena did not take her gaze from his face. He said something and looked at her bag, the one Mikhail had given her. Elena slowly pulled it over her head and tossed it to him. She had some money tucked in her pockets, but her papers were in there, however useful they really were. She hated to give them up, but only because she was sentimental.

The boy did not look inside the bag. He kept staring at her face. His gaze dropped to her breasts. Elena did not like the way his expression changed, that hunger changing to a desperate curiosity.

This is how it begins, she thought. *Things you never think will happen*. She wondered at this boy, living so wild on the street, maybe hungry for some love, a taste of what others had, wondering if it was good, if it was something that would make him a man, wondering if yes, this would add a little sweetness to an otherwise nightmarish life. Never knowing or imagining that to do such a thing would start yet another nightmare.

He steadied the knife and looked into her eyes. The other boys, the older ones, were smiling. The young ones just looked confused. Elena got ready to fight.

And then something small and wicked sprouted from her young mugger's upper arm, and the boy howled, dropping her bag. Blood stained his clothes, spreading down, down, a fast drip that hit the ground in a rainfall of red spatter. Everyone turned to see who had thrown the knife.

Brown hair, green eyes. That familiar cold smile, like chewing ice. Charles held up another knife, twirling it through his fingers in a complicated dance that was both hypnotic and terrifying. The boys, despite their numbers, knew when to cut their losses. They ran. Elena did not.

She stooped to pick up her bag and slung it over her head. Charles Darling ambled close. The knife was gone, though Elena did not know where he kept it hidden. She wondered if it was the same one that had nearly killed Artur. She felt very calm.

"I enjoy how we keep meeting like this," he said. "I would have caught up with you earlier, while you were still on the train, but I was unavoidably detained."

"You're good at finding me," she said. "One might think you've got a sixth sense."

"One might." He smiled. "And very good on healing Mr. Loginov. That was a lethal cut I gave him. A bad way to die."

"You know where he is?"

"Oh, yes. *L'araignée* has him. I'm supposed to bring you to her."

"I could always refuse to heal her."

"That is why she has Mr. Loginov." He rubbed his chin; his tongue darted out, moistening his lips. "I feel a little jealous."

"You already belong to her."

"No," he said. "I feel jealous because you belong to *him*, and vice versa. This time, Elena, she did not take Mr. Loginov to possess him. She took him to possess you. She knows what he means to you."

Elena wanted to close her eyes and die. "Don't you ever get tired of it? Being owned by her?"

"There are benefits." He held out his hand. "Come with me, Elena. You know you can trust me not to kill you. Yet."

"But if you get the chance?"

"Oh," he said. "What a lovely dream."

Elena took his hand. It was the most difficult thing she had ever done in her life. His skin was cold, like death. Charles Darling looked down at their connection of flesh. Palms rubbed.

"I have never met a woman who can kill me," he whispered. "I like that about you, Elena. It makes me hot."

She almost stopped his heart, but then he looked at her—really stared—and she could tell he meant it. Those were not words calculated to make her afraid. He was sincere.

Which meant she was almost as fucked-up as he was.

"Take me to Artur," she said. "Do it now."

He did.

They took a cab and drove past beauty: St. Basil's Cathedral, a chaos of color and shape; bold statues of dead men, defiant and immortal in memory; high spiral towers, wooden needles striking the gray sky; even the wide boulevards—classic in line and design. Elena could appreciate none of it. All she could think of was Artur, and with him, the strange circumstances of fate that had seen her kidnapped and then psychically linked to one man, even as she held hands with a serial killer. She thought snowballs must be freezing in hell. Which might just explain the frigidity of Charles Darling's skin.

"I've read that severe trauma at a young age creates people like me." He looked at her, a smile haunting his lips. "I prefer to think I was born this way, ready-made."

"I suppose it only makes sense," Elena said. "If I could be born with the power to heal, then the world is certainly capable of producing the opposite."

"Which always attract," he said. "I think that is what disturbed Rictor so very much. He could see inside my head and look at the truth. He knew that you and I were perfect pieces of the same puzzle. Symmetry. Poetry."

"You and Rictor had an interesting relationship," she said carefully.

"He hated me. He hated what I did, and that I could flaunt it at him. He was powerless to stop me."

"Not so powerless."

"He could not kill me. Death is the only thing I respect, Elena. If you cannot give me that, then there is nothing. You are not worth life."

"Survival of the fittest?"

"They are the only people who will inherit the world."

"And because you were not allowed to kill Rictor or me, what does that make you?"

His eyes narrowed. Elena clarified. "I'm just saying. Are there really all that many benefits to wearing a leash?"

He never answered her. The cab stopped. They got out.

The building was old, with remnants of charm that was the same charm permeating every other piece of the long stone row running the length of the boulevard. Nothing deviated or stood out. Simple lines and a stark silhouette against the dull sky.

Inside, the decorations were tastelessly ornate. The front door opened into a dark narrow hall that had been assaulted by the color red—red and gold—in a variety of flower patterns that bore no relation to anything found in nature. Gilt everywhere. Mirrors covered the walls. Candles burned in sconces. The polished walnut floor reflected light.

Charles led Elena down the hall. They passed two large men sitting in chairs, looking like they were waiting to hurt someone. She almost expected them to be wearing white, and wondered if perhaps they had, not so long ago. A thug was a thug was thug, no matter what he put on.

Charles opened a door. Inside, Artur lay on a long couch. She tried to go to him, but Charles held her back.

"He's not dead," Charles said. "Though I doubt his life will last much longer."

"I still have mixed feelings about that," said a new voice. Elena turned just as a woman appeared in the doorway behind them. She was very tall and very skinny, with the kind of frame that would probably look nice on television, but in real life was just awful. Her eyes were as cold as Charles's grip, her smile just as cruel. Elena recognized her from Artur's memories.

"So," said the woman, "the infamous Elena Baxter. I meant to visit you during your stay at the facility, but I never got the chance."

"This is Ms. Graves," Charles said. "The fly to the spider."

"Your insect jokes got old a long time ago," Graves said. "I understand the metaphor, but really."

On the couch, Artur stirred. Elena still could not breach the barrier between them. She had been inside his dreams before, but that was a natural sleep. She wondered if their separation was due to the obvious sedative keeping him under. She needed to touch him and make sure there was nothing else in his head. Nothing like a worm.

"I like your fear for him," Graves said softly. She closed her eyes. "It tastes very good. Very . . . pure."

"What are you?" Elena asked, disturbed by the expression on her face.

"An empath," Charles said, when Graves remained silent. "She feeds on emotions like I drink pain. Her cousin is much the same. Isn't that true, Graves? The spider doesn't like blood as much as she likes the hurt that goes with it."

Graves frowned. "I will never understand why she humors you, Charles. You talk too much."

"She likes men who can talk." He smiled, sly. "She likes me, too, for the other things I do for her."

Which was disturbing on many different levels. Again Artur stirred, signs of restlessness, and Elena said his name out loud. Graves gave her a sharp look. She reminded Elena of the dead doctor, and Elena wondered: If Beatrix Weave and Graves were cousins, had he also been a relation? How odd to think of the Consortium in such a way. A family business.

Wow. Dysfunction.

Elena heard the whir of a small motor, the slippery tread of wheels. Charles tightened his grip on her hand. Graves threw back her shoulders, a small triumphant smile softening her face.

Beatrix Weave rolled into the room, a small blond woman, fragile, even. Her body was not entirely shriveled, but it was obvious she had been without its use for some time. Her eyes were completely black. No whites, no definition of color. Just darkness through and through. Elena had never seen eyes like that on a real human being. She was so terrible, so utterly disturbing, the emotions Beatrix stirred in Elena's heart went beyond simple fear. All Elena could muster was a sort of numb awe, a sense of looking into the abyss, and all that stared back was emptiness: endless and undying.

And yet, this woman was not all-powerful. She had limits. She needed help. All the damage she had done could not have been possible without the people around her, without money. That part, anyway, was still human.

"I never dreamed you would cause so much trouble," Beatrix said.

"Thank you," Elena replied.

"I suppose that was a compliment." Beatrix looked at Graves, who reached out and grabbed Elena's other arm. Her grip hurt. She and Charles forced Elena to her knees. On the couch, Artur's eyelids fluttered. Beatrix said, "He is insurance. I've run out of time for anything else."

Graves reached out and picked up Beatrix's hand. Elena struggled, but it was like fighting bands of steel. Graves tugged her cousin close and laid her palm upon Elena's head.

It was as though all the darkness of night coalesced inside her mind, coating her thoughts with a sheer, tight web, binding down the heart of her soul. Elena struggled, fighting with all her might, and she felt something tickle the back of her brain. Like a mouth, seeking.

Elena could not send her own power into Beatrix. Even as she fought, her resistance continued to slip, and that mouth, that horrible mouth inside her head, got closer and tighter, until she felt the scrape of teeth.

The barrier between herself and Artur trembled, and she screamed his name with both her voice and his mind. His eyes opened. The barrier shattered. Strength poured into her—strength enough to match her own—and Elena flung away the worm, piercing the shadow in her mind, scratching and clawing with nails of light. Beatrix shouted; her hand dropped away as Graves scrambled to the couch, the butt of her gun raised over her head. Elena heard a meaty thud and then Artur dropped away from her mind. The barrier was still gone, but she sensed only an ambient quiet; stillness, pierced by vibration, a low hum along their link.

It was enough, though. Beatrix leaned her head against the wheelchair's neck support. She looked very pale.

"Remarkable," she breathed. "Too bad the shape-shifter killed the doctor. I would like to have learned more about this phenomenon."

"You could just ask," Elena said.

"And have you say no?" Beatrix smiled. "I prefer hearing yes, always. I like my perfect guarantees."

"You're spoiled."

"Yes, very." Beatrix pushed a switch on her wheel-chair and rolled backward. To Graves, she said, "Go and prepare my things. Greta has already been transferred, correct? Good. Charles will handle this."

Graves hesitated. "I don't think you should be left alone with her. You know what she's capable of."

"We'll be fine," she murmured, looking at Charles. He let go of Elena's hand and walked to Artur. A knife appeared, twirling between his fingers. He stood above the unconscious Russian and looked back at Beatrix, waiting. Elena's heart pounded.

"Go," Beatrix said again, and this time Graves did not

argue. She shut the door behind her. Silence fell heavily, punctuated by breath, the faint tick of an antique clock.

"You know why you're here," Beatrix said.

"Yes," Elena replied.

"And you know what will happen if you do not obey, or if you try to kill me. No, do not bother denying your feelings for him. I could sense it in his heart that one time I touched him. Even then he loved you. You must love him. Love makes beautiful leverage."

"I suppose it does," Elena said, looking from Artur to Charles. He now watched her instead of Beatrix. Elena wondered if his mistress noticed his attention, could feel her pet's thoughts, but all she said was, "Charles will cut Mr. Loginov's throat if you hurt me. And then I will let him begin cutting you."

"Really." Elena stared at Charles. "Just cuts? How sad for him that you won't let him do more."

Beatrix frowned. Elena sensed her uncertainty, but still she did not suspect, and still she said, "Sometimes you must control your pets. Charles can become overly enthusiastic without his leash."

Elena smiled. "I like enthusiasm. I like the thrill. Charles knows that about me. I think he likes it, too."

Beatrix's frown deepened. She looked between Elena and Charles, and whatever she saw—the thoughts she now heard from her pet—cast her face in confusion . . . and then jealousy. "You seem like an ill-matched pair." Her voice was hard, cold.

"Oh, no," Charles said softly. "We are perfect."

"Perfect," Elena echoed. "Let me ask you, Ms. Weave. What would happen to your link with Charles if I killed you? Would it set him immediately free?"

"It would," Charles said, before his mistress had a chance to answer. He smiled, flexing his wrist just so, light sliding along his knife like a long kiss. "Oh, yes. It would."

"Good," Elena said, and she took one long step and slammed her hand down on top of Beatrix's head, ramming power into her brain. Beatrix tried to fight back, to push, but Elena had momentum and surprise on her side and she knew the human body well. Beatrix's eyes flickered in Charles's direction; Elena felt him move and knew she had only seconds before he was forced to kill her. She dug her mental fingers into Beatrix's head, into the root of the cortex, and—*The power was always with me, all I needed was a teacher, and I looked for him, I looked for my great-grandfather, the immortal, and I could not find him but I found another, another, and*—

"I am just one," Beatrix hissed, blood bubbling past her lips. Charles took another step, but he seemed to be fighting the control now—able to fight, taking advantage of it to shrug off the worm. "But I am just the beginning. I opened the gates. I woke them up."

Her teeth flashed and they were sharp. Incisors, wicked to a point. Elena stared into those black eyes and that yawning hole of a cutting mouth, and she cried out in fear, disgust, and struck the final blow. Elena felt all the blood vessels in Beatrix's brain explode—felt her heart stop—and the woman sagged forward in her wheelchair, dead.

Charles knelt before Beatrix. He smelled her hair and caressed her face. When he stood, he continued staring at the dead woman. He rubbed his neck with the flat of his knife. "Startling. I did not think she could be killed so easily. I like her better this way."

"I thought you would," Elena said, and grabbed his hand. He looked at her, startled, but even Charles could not move as fast as thought. Elena squeezed his heart, closed his lungs. He tried to cut her, but he staggered, falling to the ground. The knife slipped from his fingers.

Elena crouched beside him, still holding his hand, still killing him slowly, with a soft touch. He stared at her in wonderment.

"You surprised me again." Charles wheezed. "How . . . lovely. Thank you for the chase."

"You're welcome," Elena said. "Now, please. Go to hell."

"Of course," he said. He closed his eyes and died.

Chapter Seventeen

Elena could not move Artur by herself; he was too heavy. She resorted to slapping him around and then sending herself into his head to jump-start his consciousness. It worked better than she thought it would. Artur opened his eyes, and there was nothing fuzzy or confused about his gaze. He turned his head and stared at the bodies of Beatrix Weave and Charles Darling. He touched her hand.

"You have been busy," he said, and she was grateful— more thankful than she imagined she could be—that she felt no recrimination, no disappointment in his heart.

"How could you ever imagine I would be disappointed in you?" He sat up, swaying slightly.

"I know you didn't want me to use my gift to kill." But kill she had, and right now she did not feel an ounce of guilt. Elena did not know if that was good or bad— or whether, in the future, if the memory of this day would haunt her with a fury. She suspected it might.

Artur grabbed her face and held it tight between his

hands. He looked haggard, worn out, but there was a song in his heart that sounded like pride. Warm, fierce, loving pride. He still loved her, no matter what, and he was desperately relieved that she was still alive.

"I should not have to say the words," he said. "You know what I am feeling."

"Yes," she whispered, drawing in a shaky breath. "And I doubt you could express yourself any better."

He kissed her. The door to the room slammed open. Graves entered, accompanied by the two thugs from the hall. She stared at the bodies on the floor and a low, horrified cry emerged from her throat, hoarse and strangled.

"No!" she screamed, beating her fist against the back of her head. "No, no!" Her entire body shook with each awkward punch; sweat rolled down her face, which contorted into something lost and wild. It reminded Elena of the one time she'd witnessed a drug addict at the hospital suffer a psychotic episode during withdrawal.

She pulled out a gun from within her jacket and aimed it at them. Her hand shook. Artur shoved Elena behind him.

"Why?" she screamed, spittle flying from her mouth. The men behind her looked terrified. "Why did you do it?"

Because they both deserved it, Elena thought, and she felt Artur's acquiescence. Despite his earlier reservations, when it was time to act he was practical to a fault. She felt his love pour over her like light, warming the inside of her soul, until it seemed to her that Graves could send out that bullet and nothing would touch them, nothing ever, because together they were just too strong.

Guns fired. Elena and Artur flinched, but felt no impact. The men behind Graves fell down, and a mo-

ment later Graves joined them; screaming, still crazy
with grief. And then silence. The gun slipped from her
fingers.

A man and woman appeared in the doorway before
Artur could pick up the gun. Elena recognized them,
but she thought so much violence must be warping her
brain. This had to be her imagination.

"You," she said, stunned. "The American couple. You
were both on the train."

The American couple no longer looked so sweet or
bubbly. They both held guns, handling them with the
ease of long-term use. Their clothes were simple, loose,
and dark.

"What is going on here?" Artur stood poised above
the gun, and the man—Fred, if that was really his
name—gestured for him to pick it up. Artur did, and
Elena felt his relief, his comfort at having a weapon in
his hands. His confusion, too, at being allowed to do so.

"We're not here to hurt you," said the woman. She
slowly lowered her weapon. Fred did the same. "If you
are both all right, we'll be going. Everyone else in the
house has been neutralized. You should be safe."

Elena did not trust herself to speak. Artur felt simi-
larly. Their thoughts mingled, flashing questions, possibilities, interlinking theories, and still, nothing. Just
bafflement. It was too much to handle. How many people were involved in their lives, anyway?

"Not so many," said Fred. "I believe it is more a question of how many lives *you* are involved in."

"Oh, no." Elena closed her eyes. "Not another mind
reader."

The woman gave Fred a sharp look and he shrugged.
A short conversation seemed to pass between them,
probably in much the same manner as the one dancing
between Artur and Elena, which consisted mainly of

wonderment that once again they were being slapped in the face with the fact that far more of "their kind" existed than either one of them—especially Elena—had ever believed possible.

"Why are you doing this?" Artur asked. "Who sent you?"

Fred, who looked like he had just gotten a severe talk-down, deferred to the woman. She gave him another hard look and said, "We were asked to investigate your disappearances and, when we found you, to shadow and protect your lives. Little angels, ever since we found you in Vladivostok. We used our resources to distract Charles Darling and keep him from catching up to you again after the incident in Khabarovsk. Once we reached Moscow, however, it became more difficult to track your movements. We both split up. Fred followed you, Mr. Loginov, while I was responsible for Elena."

Elena thought of the alley and her mugging by the street gang, and knew Artur shared the memory. He said, "You did not do a very good job at keeping her safe."

"We had other considerations," she said. "But I would have intervened had it become necessary."

Artur shook his head. "You do not work for Dirk and Steele and, I would guess, not for the Consortium, either. Who else would go to so much trouble for us?"

The woman said nothing. Fred shrugged, clearly uncomfortable answering that question. He looked at Elena. "We were given an apology to pass on to you. The Consortium found you only because *our* organization located you first. There was an . . . unfortunate leak of information. The Consortium knew we were going to approach you, and took measures to take you away before that could happen. I can assure you we would have handled *our* first meeting with you much differently. Um, you could still come with us even, if you're interested. Which . . . I can tell you're not."

Elena barely heard him. All she could think about was the impossibility of . . . of . . .

"*Another* organization?" Elena stared at them. "*Another?* I must be high. This has to be some kind of drug-induced dream, because I have reached the limits of my belief. There is no fucking way so many of us are out there, organized like psychic scout troops. I'm sorry. It's just not possible."

"I agree," Artur said. "Which is highly ironic."

"The world is a big place," said the woman. "And there are many players, all of whom are living and working in secrecy. Some of them have been around for a long time. You think they're going to hold some parade or juggle their balls in public? You know better than that."

"But why hide from one another?" Artur asked. "Why hold secrets when we are all the same?"

"Because we're not all the same," she said. "Not in the slightest."

She and Fred backed out of the room. Elena could not move to follow them; she felt numb, dumb. Every time she thought she had her life figured out, something new destroyed all her carefully constructed truths. How could she live like this?

Together, one step at a time, Artur said, and then: "Wait."

The woman said, "Not a chance. But I'll tell you this much. The stage is set for something big. If you want to know why, you should ask one of the directors. I think you know who she is. I think she's the reason *you* were kidnapped. She is, as they say, the dagger in the steel."

And with that cryptic remark, she and Fred disappeared down the hall. Artur ran after them, Elena close on his heels. She saw the couple slip out through the front door, but by the time she ran outside, they had vanished. Not a trace remained.

Artur made a phone call. Elena listened to his conversation in her head, and it was brief, to the point. Yes, he was fine. Yes, he knew Elena was gone because she was here with him. No, she was the one who had saved the day—and listen, in case you did not know, there was yet *another* group of psychics running amok in the world.

Ha. Ha. Ha.

Artur hung up the phone and looked at Elena. "They'll be here in five minutes."

"Can we get out of here that fast?" It was a joke—albeit a halfhearted one—but Artur grabbed her hand and pulled her down the hall. They left through the front door, hit the sidewalk, took a left, and just kept moving. Elena could not hide her surprise. She thought his priorities would be different.

"My priorities have changed since I met you," he said.

"Oh," she replied, liking the sound of that, but not wanting him to get into trouble. The air felt good on her face. Everything felt good, after what she had just endured.

"There will be no trouble."

"They might need to talk with you. What happened back there was significant, and not just for us. All of your friends are going to be affected."

"They can wait," he said firmly. "Besides, with our luck, we might have only hours before the next catastrophe strikes." His arm snaked around her waist, holding her close against his side as they strolled down the wide boulevard. She felt his desire, his fierce need to protect her, and it was breathtaking to be loved by such a man—this strong, streetwise, gentle man.

"What if they get worried?" She had trouble speaking.

"Let them worry," he said, and his voice was just as husky. His fingers curled against her sweater, stroking her ribs. "We are alive, Elena. Somehow, we are alive. Nothing is more important than that. Let us enjoy the moment for just a little bit."

Because moments of happiness are so fleeting, he continued silently. *And I am tired of being surrounded by death.*

"So am I," she said, leaning against him, stealing his warmth into herself. She felt his concern, his question, and she said, *I just killed two people. I don't know how I feel about that. Strange, maybe frightened. But yes, I think I'll be all right.*

I have killed more than two, he said. *And for far less than you. If you ever need to talk—*

You are here, she said, and her throat was thick with love. *Will you always be here, Artur?*

He stopped walking. Elena thought he would kiss her—his hands curled so warm and fine against her face—but then he looked past her, and she turned. Behind them was a church. It seemed to Elena that everywhere in Moscow there was a church, but this one was small and plain, and there was a man in robes brushing the front steps with a broom.

She knew what he was thinking. She said yes.

It was surprisingly easy. They did not want anything special. The church interior was small, the walls dark with centuries of candle smoke. Artur, his hands gentle upon her own, spoke his vows before the priest. He said them in Russian, and then once more in English. In his heart he gave her a ring.

Elena repeated after him.

And then they were married.

Epilogue

Three days after returning from Moscow, Artur went to visit Nancy Dirk. He wore his gloves. William, her husband, met him at the door. Well into his eighties, his spine was still straight, his blue eyes sharp, clear. He did not look happy to see Artur, which was fine, because Artur did not want to be there.

"She's expecting you," William said, and led him through the foyer, through the open-air courtyard in the middle of their Spanish-style ranch, right up to an open door that revealed a large, comfortable room, decorated with the light touch of a woman who had been around the world.

Nancy Dirk stood at the window of her office, a slender figure, pale and shining with power. William said not a word. He left, closing the door behind him. Nancy did not speak either.

"You know why I am here," Artur said quietly. "It is simple, really. I want to know why Beatrix Weave targeted me to get to you."

Nancy did not look at him. She continued to stare at her garden, the green labyrinth of bramble and rose.

"Mrs. Dirk," he said, and she raised her hand.

"You touched this once," she said, waving her fingers at him. "What did you see?"

"Power," Artur said immediately. "So much power you blinded me." More power than a simple precog should have. More power than anyone he had ever encountered.

"And you never said a word?"

"Never."

Nancy finally turned to look at him. "You are a good man, Artur Loginov. I knew that all those years ago when I saw you in my head. I knew you were the man for us. I just had no idea how truly loyal you would remain. So, thank you. Thank you from the bottom of my heart."

"It is nothing," he said, taken aback by her sincerity.

"No," she disagreed. "And I am so terribly sorry you had to endure this fiasco, all because of my poor planning. I had a vision, you see. Those murdered women. I knew the culprit would have a direct connection to this agency. I just did not realize quite how direct." She shook her head. "I cannot believe all of this pain was brought about by a spoiled little girl who could not live with her family's secrets."

"I do not understand. Are you referring to Beatrix Weave?" When Nancy made no reply, Artur said, "She could hardly be called a spoiled child. Her power—"

"Was tremendous. Yes, I know. But she was still spoiled, and compared to her elders, very much a child." Nancy's lips tightened. "She was my great-niece, Artur. She was blood."

It was good that there was a chair nearby. Artur's knees buckled. He sat down hard. He tried to talk, but his voice would not work. Nancy crouched before him. Her silver gaze searched his face, her far-seeing eyes delving into his secrets.

"You cannot tell anyone," she finally said. "Not a soul. Except for your wife, of course. The two of you are so much a part of each other, it would be foolish to exclude her. Isn't that right, Elena?"

Elena, who had been eavesdropping in his head, mentally flinched.

"You knew," Artur said hoarsely. "You knew about the Consortium."

"No," Nancy said. "But I foresaw the possibility of its existence. I just did not anticipate the players within it."

Artur swallowed hard. "If Beatrix Weave was your great-niece, then you must have siblings. It was always my impression—everyone's impression—that you were an only child."

"Impressions are not truth, Artur. Impressions are illusion."

"Why, then? Why allow everyone to believe you have no family?"

"Because mine is not the kind of family who should be known. Nothing good would ever come from it. As you saw for yourself."

Artur sat back. He closed his eyes, trying to make sense of everything he knew, everything Elena showed him, again. Graves, also family. Beatrix's cousin. Calling themselves a corporation, businesspeople running experiments, playing with unnatural forces—trying to control the world through criminal power. The American couple, who had been told to investigate, who represented yet another player, and who had pointed the finger directly at Nancy Dirk.

"The man and woman who shadowed us from Vladivostok claimed they worked for an organization that had originally been interested in recruiting Elena. And yet they investigated *both* our kidnappings. I find that very curious. How did they know I had been taken? Why would they even be interested? Unless someone from *our* agency contacted *them*. But why do that? Why go behind everyone's backs ... unless there was something to hide? Something that could not be investigated so carefully by our own without jeopardizing secrets. Your secrets. So let me ask you, Ms. Dirk. Where are your siblings? Where are they and what do they do? And why, again, is it so important that no one from Dirk and Steele know they exist?"

Nancy went very still. "You are asking me if I have betrayed this agency."

"Perhaps," he said, and felt Elena wrap herself around his soul to comfort him as he said such a terrible thing.

There was another chair beside him. Nancy sat down. "Can I tell you a story, Artur? Can I tell you one part of the truth? You and Elena must never speak of it. Never."

"I promise," Artur said, hearing Elena echo the same.

Nancy smiled grimly. "I am afraid to tell you. The truth can be an ugly thing. It can turn hearts."

"I know," Artur said. "I have been told that a leap of faith is often required in such situations."

"Faith," she whispered, and then: "Many years ago my sisters and I fell apart from one another. I had certain ... visions ... of a world that could be, and it was not a good place. I wanted to change that future. I thought I knew how. My sisters did not agree. They wanted to focus their energies on other things. Power. Wealth. I wanted those same things, but for a different reason. And so we went our separate ways. I promised never to interfere in their business—no matter how much I disagreed with it—and they promised never to interfere in mine. And we kept that promise to each other, up until the day Beatrix Weave kidnapped you from your home."

"How did you know it was her?"

"I didn't. But I had a feeling your disappearance was linked to my family. I contacted my sisters. They assured me they had no knowledge of any wrongdoing, but they promised to look into it. What they discovered was quite startling. Members of the family had taken it upon themselves to . . . branch off. My sisters, despite their motivations, are in their own way quite moral. They refused to dabble in certain criminal activities that would have been lucrative. Their children, however, had no such compunctions."

"Beatrix Weave did not kidnap me for money. That might have been the story she and Graves originally told, but what she wanted was you. She wanted me because I had shaken your hand, skin-to-skin, and somewhere deep inside me, she thought I had your secrets."

"You probably do," Nancy said. "And if it had not been for Roland's safeguards, your stubbornness, and Elena's power, she might very well have drilled deep enough into your unconscious to discover all that I left behind in our one brief handshake."

Artur frowned, somewhat disturbed that deep within him he knew exactly what Nancy Dirk was trying so desperately to hide. "Beatrix gave up in the end, but only because she grew tired of failure. She still wanted the knowledge."

"Spoiled. No patience. Better she never got it." Nancy sighed. "Better that she died than have it."

Artur shook his head, sharing his disbelief with Elena. Everything he knew about this agency and its founder was unraveling at the seams. "What are you hiding that is so terrible?"

"Tell me," Nancy said, and her voice was hard, unforgiving. "Was Beatrix human when you found her?"

He hesitated, recalling those black eyes, her impossibly sharp teeth. "No. She was not human. I believe, though, that she was experimenting with things of a . . . magical nature. In her last moments, she told Elena that she had . . . opened a gate. That she had awakened someone, or something." And then there was Rictor to consider. A man who was so much more than human, and who had been trapped by nothing more than a ring of light. The unknown was becoming a frightening thing.

Nancy leaned back, her gaze distant. She covered her mouth with one hand. "Yes. It is very good she died."

"What happened to her? How is this all connected?"

Nancy did not answer right away. She seemed to be in a trance, one that she finally shook herself from with a blink and a shrug. "Beatrix finally found her teacher. She found what she was looking for."

"No," Artur said. "If she had found that, she would not have gone searching for your secrets. Whatever she found was not enough. It might have changed her, but it was not enough." Anger stirred within him; he was growing tired of these games, which bordered on betrayal. He could not stand that, to be betrayed by this organization that had become so much like family. He could not take it, and yet he had to know. He had to know what he almost given up his life to protect.

"Mrs. Dirk," he said. "Nancy."

"You will not be satisfied with anything less. Yes, I know. All right, then. I will give you one more truth, which is only one part, and not even the most startling part, if you knew the entire story. Beatrix was looking for her great-grandfather. My father. The only man who could have possibly taught her how to use her legacy."

"Which was magic," Artur said. "She was not just a psychic."

"Sometimes the two are not so far apart, but yes, that is the simple answer."

"Who was your father, then? Surely she could not have expected him to still be alive."

Nancy shook her head. "Who do you know, Artur? Who do you know, however indirectly in your lifetime, who managed to achieve immortality, who had the power to alter reality?"

Artur stared into her face, searching, searching, and for a moment felt sure he would lose his mind to her impossible secret. It was too much, more than he could bear, and Elena held him tight, soothing him with her voice. He could not be soothed, though. Elena did not fully understand the ramifications, the absolute *insanity* of this one small truth. The wickedness of it was horrifying and simple.

"The Magi," he said. "Your father was the Magi."

A man who had lived for two thousand years, made immortal by the curse he had placed on another. A man whose evil had led him to spend millennia bearing daughters in the hopes that one of them, one day, would be the key to freeing him.

"Fate is a funny thing, isn't it?" Nancy said. "My granddaughter marrying the one man whose curse gave me life. My father would never have existed to have my siblings and I had it not been for Hari. Who then promptly took him away."

"He was a monster," Artur said.

"Yes," Nancy agreed. "But I would have liked to have

erest

met him again. Just once. Just to look into his eyes and see if he recognized me."

"He did not recognize his great-granddaughter," Artur said coldly. "He tried to murder her. He might have raped her, given the chance."

"And for that alone, I would have killed him myself." Nancy stood, pacing the room, ending up once again behind her desk to stare out the window. "I hardly knew my father. Most of what I learned has been through Dela and Hari, and I have rarely enjoyed what I heard. So you see, Artur, why I keep my secrets close to my heart. You know the damage they would do."

"And you say that is not the most startling part?" His voice was weak. "What are you doing here? What is Dirk and Steele *really* for?"

Nancy gave him a cold look. He felt power shiver through his body, and he thought, *Yes, she very well could be the daughter of that man.* She said, "The agency was created to help those who need it. It was formed so that *we*—our kind, with power—would not waste it on the trivial and mundane. This world is headed toward dark times, Artur. It needs every helping hand it can get. My job is to cultivate those hands. To build them fast. Do you understand, Artur? Beatrix was just the beginning. She was small potatoes."

A terrifying notion, to think of Beatrix Weave and all she represented as somehow insignificant. He could not imagine what would be worse, but Elena reminded him again of those dark eyes and that gaping maw of sharp teeth, her darkness and fury and control. Perhaps that was a glimpse, a taste, and it filled him with fear.

Artur could not take any more. He was afraid of what Nancy would tell him next. He stood. She said, "Are you leaving us?"

Us. The agency. Artur thought about it for a moment and shook his head. "Not yet. I will be watching, though. I will be . . . more careful."

"As will I," Nancy said. "The covenant between myself and my sisters has been broken. I don't know what will happen next."

Artur had no response to that. He began to leave, but stopped in the doorway. "Dela and Hari deserve to know the truth about the Magi."

"Eventually," Nancy said. "Preferably after I'm dead and gone, and can't hear their complaints."

"That could be a while," Artur said.

"Maybe," Nancy agreed, impossibly grim. Artur did not like the look on her face. It was the expression of a woman who had already seen her death, and had no taste for it.

Artur left. He did not see William on his way out. He walked down the long, curving driveway to where he had parked his car, a small black convertible with the top down and a beautiful woman sitting in the front seat with her sunglasses on. Elena tilted her chin to peer at him over the lenses.

"Your agency is screwed up," she said. "I'm not so sure I want to join this circus."

"You may have a point," Artur said, equally disturbed. He removed his gloves and gathered up Elena's hands. He buried his face in her palms, inhaling the clean scent of soap and water. Oh, he loved this woman. If he lost everything else, at least he had her.

"Let's go," Elena said, pulling one hand away to trail teasingly up his thigh. "And put the top up. There's something I want to show you."

He did, and she did, and it was very good.

* * *

It was strange for Elena, thinking of herself as a married woman. She did not feel married. She felt the same, except now there was a weight to her relationship with Artur. A good weight, another kind of link, and it felt right. Crazy, too—she had never imagined herself capable of such fast and immediate commitment—but here she was, living in his home, with a heart so full she thought it might burst. How strange. So much could change in such a short time. Life, plodding along, and then *boom, boom*. Yee-haw. A happy ending.

Kind of.

They had dinner that night with Amiri and Rik. The two shape-shifters, who had been staying at one of the guest apartments Roland owned just for out-of-towners, came to Artur's home bearing gifts of dessert and flowers. Elena knew Artur was reluctant to let them in—they would infect his floors and walls and God only knew what—but it was easier than meeting in a restaurant, especially with what they had to talk about.

"So it's safe for us to go home." Rik did not look terribly happy about that. He leaned on the table, fiddling with his napkin. "And if we don't want to?"

"Why not?" Elena asked. "Even though you stuck with us this long, I can't imagine staying on land is your first choice. What about your family?"

Rik's jaw flexed. Elena saw an emptiness in his eyes, and she realized that despite his bouts of strength and good humor, she had felt that missing piece of him from the start; as though he were a vessel waiting to be filled. Elena did not believe Rik was broken, but his captivity had certainly stripped him down to the very basics. Or maybe it was not just his time at the facility; she knew almost nothing about the young man or the life he had come from.

"I don't have family," he finally said, confirming her

fears. He challenged them all with a hard stare. "Not any that wants me, anyway."

Silence around the table, broken only when Amiri sighed. "I cannot imagine that. Why did you not speak of this before?"

Rik gave him a look, and then tore his gaze away to stare unblinking at Artur. "Will Dirk and Steele hire me? I don't want charity or special treatment because of what I am. I can learn things."

Elena felt Artur's indecision. After eavesdropping on his conversation with Nancy Dirk, she knew why. God. She felt like a full-fledged inhabitant of the Twilight Zone, except this was worse. How did a person deal with craziness, and then go on pretending life was normal? How did she go back to being a regular girl—albeit a regular girl who could perform miracles?

"No favors," Artur said quietly. "But I am sure Roland would offer you a job, though it would be a trial position at first."

"Good enough." Rik studied his hands and hesitated. "What about you, Amiri?"

Amiri also gazed at his hands. "Even with Beatrix gone, home might not be safe for me. I do not know where those photographs ended up. So, I will stay. I have already spoken to Roland. He is preparing my paperwork."

"Nice." Elena sipped her beer, noting the relief that passed, fleetingly, over Rik's face. "The old gang is hanging around. We can reminisce about being lab experiments when life gets too boring."

"I've got you all beat on that one," Rik said. "I bet none of you were probed."

Elena held up her hands. "Do not say another word. Please."

"When are you leaving for Wisconsin?" Amiri asked, politely cutting his steak into portions. The golden highlights in his hair seemed especially bright tonight, the undertones of his dark skin shimmering smooth and warm.

"At the end of the week. I'm going to teach Artur how to be a farmer."

For a little while, anyway. Long enough to work the harvest. Long enough to visit the hospital and check on the children. Elena did not tell them that after Wisconsin they would be returning to Russia. They had unfinished business there. Or rather, Artur did. It was time, he had told her, to go back to the orphanage. Time to find his mother. Time to walk those old streets and come to terms with his nightmares—nightmares he did not want to burden Elena with.

It was funny: she did not know what was going to happen to them, knew it would not be easy, either way, but she looked forward to the adventure of living and loving Artur Loginov. He was her best friend, and she was his. They were each other's heroes. It could not get much better than that.

The doorbell rang. Artur frowned.

"Are we expecting anyone?" Elena asked. She knew the answer before she asked, but the question was for Amiri's and Rik's benefit. Everyone stood, and it was as though they were back in the facility or in the woods or on the train: ready for fight, for flight. Maybe they would always be like that, for the rest of their lives. Primed for the worst, hoping for the best.

They followed Artur to the foyer like children, crowding at his back. He opened the door.

"Hey," said Rictor, holding a potted fern. "You guys miss me?"

Artur almost shut the door in his face. Elena grabbed his arm.

"Yes," she said, giving her husband a stern look. "We did."

"*I* didn't miss you," Rik said, picking his teeth with a fingernail.

"That's okay," Rictor said. "I really didn't come to see you."

Elena made a place for him at the table. Rictor handed her the fern. She put it down in the center of the table, alongside a vase of white tulips, a gift from Mikhail, who had just recently arrived in Boston with his family.

Rictor sat down. There was a long moment of silence. Elena was glad for the quiet. It gave her time to adjust. It was bizarre, seeing Rictor, remembering him cutting her hair, dragging her through halls . . . and his body wracked with sobs.

He looked at her, and it was impossible to say what he was thinking. Only that he had heard her thoughts. Only that he had come back.

"So," Artur said. "How is it they say? Long time, no help?"

"I helped," Rictor said, tearing his gaze away from Elena. "If you remember."

"I do," Artur admitted. "And I am very grateful. I just thought we would see you again before the actual fighting was done."

"I couldn't get involved," Rictor said, which invited derision from the other men at the table.

"That does sound pretty weak," Elena said. "Especially coming from you."

"I did what I could," he said, quieter, and Elena was again reminded of the facility, that cold, hard man who had turned into a friend. She could give him the benefit of the doubt. Rictor was as Rictor did, and it was nothing more nor less than that.

"All right," she said. "I believe you."

"Elena," Artur said, but she gave him a look and he shut his mouth.

"She's training you," Rictor said. "Be afraid."

Artur said nothing. Elena knew very well he did not mind her "training" in the slightest. Rictor quirked his lips, but fortunately, said nothing.

The five of them sat at the table and talked until the night grew long and the dawn was near enough to taste. It was nice sitting with these men, whom she had known only under extreme circumstances, and discovering that she still liked their company, that she still trusted them to be near and dear.

In the end, as they were readying themselves to leave, Elena went to each man for a hug. She was not the hugging type, but it was a gesture she wanted to make. She saved Artur for last, but he—unlike the others—did not let go. She turned in his arms with her back pressed against his chest, his strong arms loose around her waist, and savored his comfort—his first true comfort in years: he was not alone, he could touch without pain, and it was good.

"I haven't had a single friend since my grandfather died," Elena told them all. Her throat felt tight. "Not a friend I could truly be myself around. And now . . . now I have four. Thank you, guys. Thank you so much."

"We are the family you make," Artur said. "And that is a tie stronger than blood."

"Because it involves choice," Rictor said. "Beautiful, sweet choice." He picked up Elena's hand and kissed the back of it. "I still owe both of you. I'll be around."

"Rictor," Elena called, before he could walk out the door. "What the hell are you?"

He stayed silent, just looking at her. Elena shook her head. Typical.

He smiled, a devil in his eyes, and left the normal way, without vanishing into thin air. Amiri and Rik followed on his heels, saying their good nights and good mornings. Artur closed the door behind them. He turned around and leaned against the hard wood, his arms folded over his chest. His gaze was hungry, hot, and she felt the fine thread of his amusement as he studied her body and imagined all the different ways he could take her clothes off.

"It's so late," she said. "I'm tired."

"I do not care," he said.

"I know," she said, backing slowly away. "You're a bad man."

"Yes," he said, following her. "I used to be a thief. A gun for hire. I am very dangerous."

"So am I," Elena said. "Or so I've been told by dangerous men."

"Ah, but you know how I feel about dangerous women."

She moistened her lips, loving how his gaze moved to her mouth and stayed there. She kept retreating. He continued to follow. Elena backed right up against the dining room table. Artur picked her up and set her down, pushing between her legs until he stood tight against her body, hot and ready.

"You know how I feel about you, right?" Elena peered up into his old-soul eyes. She knew, now, what gave a man those eyes, and it was a hard and beautiful knowledge, sacred between both of them.

"I know," he said. "Just like you know."

And then he kissed her, gently, and she felt herself wrap tight around his spirit, spin slowly into his soul, and he said, "You and I, Elena. We will keep each other whole and safe until the end of our days."

"Sure," she murmured. "But you're asking for trouble."

"Always," he said, and then laughed as she gave him some.

CRIMSON CITY

Don't miss any of this fabulous series!

Tiger Eye

Marjorie M. Liu

He looks completely out of place in Dela Reese's Beijing hotel room—like the tragic hero of some epic tale, exotic and poignant. He is like nothing from her world, neither his variegated hair nor his feline yellow eyes. Yet Dela has danced through the echo of his soul, and she knows this warrior would obey.

Hari has been used and abused for millennia; he is jaded, dull, tired. But upon his release from the riddle box, Hari sees his new mistress is different. In Dela's eyes he sees a hidden power. This woman is the key. If only he dares protect, where before he has savaged; love, where before he's known hate. For Dela, he will dare all.

Dream of Me
Lisa Cach

Theron, undying creature of the Night World, knows everything about making love. But though he's an incubus, a bringer of carnal dreams to sleeping maids, he has grander ambition. He plots to step into the mortal world and rule as king.

The beautiful Lucia is imprisoned in a fortress atop a mountain. Her betrothed, Prince Vlad of Wallachia, wants her purity intact; but when the prince breaks his vow, nothing can keep her safe. In the name of vengeance, Lucia will be subjected to Theron's seduction; she will learn all his lips might teach.

A demon of lust and a sheltered princess: each dreams of what they've never had. They're about to get everything they wish…and more.

CHRISTINE FEEHAN
DARK DESTINY

Her childhood had been a nightmare of violence and pain until she heard his voice calling out to her. Golden and seductive. The voice of an angel.

He has shown her how to survive, taught her to use her unique gifts, trained her in the ancient art of hunting the vampire. Yet he cannot bend her to his will. He cannot summon her to him, no matter how great his power.

As she battles centuries-old evil in a glittering labyrinth of caverns and crystals, he whispers in her mind, forging an unbreakable bond of trust and need. Only with him can she find the courage to embrace the seductive promise of her . . . *Dark Destiny*.

CHRISTINE FEEHAN
DARK MELODY

Lead guitarist of the Dark Troubadours, Dayan is renowned for his mesmerizing performances. His melodies still crowds, beckon seduce, tempt. And always, he calls to *her*. His lover. His lifemate. He calls to her to complete him. To give him the emotions that have faded from his existence, leaving him an empty shell of growing darkness. *Save me. Come to me.*

Corinne Wentworth stands at the vortex of a gathering storm. Pursued by the same fanatics who'd murdered her husband, she risks her life by keeping more than one secret. Fragile, delicate, vulnerable, she has an indomitable faith that makes her fiery surrender to Dayan all the more powerful.

ATTENTION
BOOK LOVERS!

Can't get enough of your favorite **ROMANCE**?

Call **1-800-481-9191** to:

＊ order books,

＊ receive a **FREE** catalog,

＊ join our book clubs to **SAVE 30%!**

Open Mon.-Fri. 10 AM-9 PM EST

Visit **www.dorchesterpub.com**
for special offers and inside
information on the authors you love.

We accept Visa, MasterCard or Discover®.
LEISURE BOOKS ❤ LOVE SPELL